Dark Place
Where Two Worlds Meet

His head bore antlers, and he stood up like a man; but he was like no man or beast, only himself. Matt saw the long, narrow head, the fine curve of the nostrils, the shoulders of a man and the cloven hoofs of a goat. Slowly the sight and the smell of Cernunnos slid deep into him. He could not move before the huge horned shape.

Anna stepped forward. Neither Matt nor Kate could stop her.

Then, beside him, the light burst. It shot outward from a core brighter than the entire sky. Before Matt's eyes a shape reared out of the light. It was a chariot, and standing in the chariot was pure light in the shape of a man.

It was Manannan.

Matt saw Cernunnos' towering antlers turn, but his eyes were on those pointed fingers. They closed quietly round Anna's wrist.

Matt's heart shuddered and he waited for Manannan's light to fade before the great dark bulk of the Horned One.

And then Manannan's other hand came out, shining, and grasped Anna's shoulder.

She hung between the two, the dark and the light.

ALISON RUSH

THE LAST OF DANU'S CHILDREN

A TOM DOHERTY ASSOCIATE BOOK

Copyright© 1982 by George Allen & Unwin (Publishers) Ltd.

A Tor Book

Published by Tom Doherty Associates, 8-10 W. 36th St., New York, New York 10018. Reprinted by arrangement with Houghton Mifflin Company

First printing, January 1984

ISBN: 0-812-55250-4
CAN. ED.: 0-812-55251-2

Printed in the United States of America

Distributed by Pinnacle Books, 1430 Broadway, New York, N.Y. 10018

Part One

THE SCRYERS

I

HE MUST HAVE HEARD THE PELICAN FALL

"Well, hullo, Anna. Nice surprise," said the man, appearing out of nowhere at the side of the road.

Matt gasped as he skidded to a halt on his bicycle, just missing Kate Marchant's front wheel. The green expanse of fields around them, called the Moss, lay level for miles; no one could hide their approach, and yet he was sure he hadn't seen the man coming. He heard Kate's sharp intake of breath, and glanced in confusion at her sister, Anna.

"Ned!" A glowing smile burst out over Anna's face as she jumped off her bicycle. She caught the man's hand as he held it out to her. "Oh, Ned, how—" she broke off with a laugh, as if too happy to speak.

"Quite easily," said the man, with a curious smile. "Come and have a drink at my house, Anna. It's just across the fields." He glanced at the other two, a queer glint in his eyes. "You must be Kate—and Matt Cooper, yes? Come with us. Thirsty work, cycling in this heat."

A shiver went down Matt's back. Those eyes, resting on him, were large and magnetic, oddly compelling. A rook flew overhead with a harsh caw, and the day seemed to change indefinably, as if a black shadow had passed across the sun and drained away some color from the landscape.

"Who are you?" Kate shot out rather rudely, tossing her yellow hair back.

"Edward Kelly," said the man blandly. "Haven't you heard of me, Kate? Why, I've known your sister for—a long time." His thumb stroked Anna's hand.

"You can't have done," said Kate bluntly. "We've only been here a week. We're on holiday—staying with Matt's aunt."

"A long time, for all that," Kelly smiled, watching Anna's brilliant face. "Come along, now." He took Anna's bicycle and pushed it over a flat turf bridge that led across the roadside ditch into the field. Anna followed.

"Where to?" Kate demanded. "I can't see any house!"

Matt swallowed, feeling uneasy. The only building in sight was a small isolated radar station, scanner sleepily revolving about a mile away. Kelly couldn't have come from there.

"Ah." Kelly paused and looked back, smiling. "See those trees, Kate? My house is behind them."

Across two fields, a long bank of elms—Kite Wood—broke the skyline. The trees grew closely, dark and thick, and Matt couldn't see through them. Kelly and Anna went on hand in hand, along the side of the barleyfield where the air rustled softly.

Who was the man, Matt wondered. What did he want? He looked more than thirty, too old to hold Anna's hand like that. "We don't have to go if you don't want to, Kate," he said tentatively.

Kate shrugged impatiently. 'Oh, come on!" She pushed her bike across the bridge, and Matt followed.

There were no hedges or fences dividing the fields on the Moss, only deep drainage ditches, with plenty of water in them despite the fine weather. Glancing down into the one beside them as they crossed the field, Matt thought how difficult it would be to climb out, if you fell in. The sides were steep, like the sides of a pit.

"Where did he come from, Kate?" he said in a low voice, catching her up. "Did you see?"

"One minute he wasn't there, the next he was," Kate scowled, blue eyes glinting. "I don't *like* him."

"How did Anna get to know him?"

"I don't know what Anna does any more! She's been so moony and faraway ever since—you know . . ."

Matt knew. Ever since their parents, out in Africa to report on a guerrilla war for their newspaper, had disappeared. It was ten days since anything had been heard of them. Were they alive, were they dead? No one could tell. And, though he'd known Kate all his life, he still couldn't think what to say to her about it.

His own father was out there too, reporting on the war for television. If there was any news about the Marchants, he would be the one to give it; and for the first time Matt found himself dreading to see his father on television.

Across another field, they rounded Kite Wood and saw a little stone cottage, alone on the other side of a ditch. With its thatched roof and tiny windows, it looked as old as the wood, as old as the Moss itself. Matt crossed over another of the turf bridges after Kate, and propped his bike against the cottage wall, beside the other two.

"By the way, don't worry if you hear peculiar noises," Kelly said with the flicker of a smile, opening the door. "It's only rats in the thatch."

Kate gave a grimace, and followed Anna in. Matt went after her, with a twinge of reluctance.

There were two steps down into the room, and with only one small window it was suddenly dark. But Matt's eyes opened wide at the sight before him. The walls were bare stone, and along one side ran a massive brick furnace, full of shelves and doors and compartments, with an assortment of chimneys disappearing into the roof. A clutter of retorts, alembics, mortars and other vessels crowded randomly along shelves, into corners, and over a booklittered

9

table. Along another wall stood a long cabinet with at least a hundred small drawers, each one marked with a glinting symbol rather like a sign of the zodiac. Colored charts bearing similar signs hung on the walls.

It was more like a picture from an old book than a real room, and Matt and Anna began to wander round, peering curiously at one thing after another. But Kate went at once to the window, turning her back on the room and blotting out most of the remaining light. Kelly, seemingly quite content for them to do as they pleased, seated himself on an odd stool; his eyes followed Anna, with a queer look of satisfaction.

The other walls bore shelves, mostly stacked with more bowls and jars, but above a desk in a corner Matt noticed some calf-bound books. The lettering on the spines was worn and difficult to read. A thick black book was nearest to him, and with some effort he read "The Key of Solomon" on the spine. It meant nothing to him.

"This is lovely," Anna said from the cabinet, lifting something up.

Matt went to look. It was a disc of yellow metal, and she held it in both hands as if it was heavy. It was engraved with a strange bearded face, and more of those zodiac-like signs. Something in Latin was written round the rim. Matt made out "Ecce faciem et figuram eius" and "omnes oboediunt creaturae" at the top. The words in between ran upside down round the lower half and he couldn't read them. He wasn't sure what it meant.

"Let me see," said Kelly, holding out his hand. Anna gave it to him, and a smile came to his lips as he looked at it.

"What is it?" asked Anna.

"A votive object . . . belonging to an Oriental sect," Kelly said, quietly. "I engrave these things for them, in precious metals."

"Is that gold?" asked Matt.

Kelly nodded, gave it carelessly back to Anna and rose. "Well, let me get you something to drink. Carry on looking round. This place is quite interesting; it used to be an old alchemist's laboratory many years ago, and I like to keep it as it was."

He went out, and at once Kate turned from the window, scowling.

"What a rubbish tip!" she said, kicking at some pots that stood on the floor. They toppled over with a clatter. "Laboratory!" said Kate, with scorn.

"Stop it, Kate," Matt said patiently, stooping to pick up the pots. One, a double-bellied sort of vase with two handles, was chipped on the lip from its fall. "He'll hear you." Matt warned, placing the pots on an empty shelf of the furnace.

Anna spoke, from the gloom by the cabinet. "Don't, Kate," she said. "He's kind. He wants to be our friend."

Suddenly, the inner door creaked. They started round, thinking of rats, and at once Kate gasped.

Full in the doorway stood a man in a loose brown robe. He had a long beard as white as milk, and he was looking them over in a curious, rather chilling way, as if they were specimens in glass cases.

Matt stared back as the dispassionate blue eyes passed over him, and he had the sense of being examined and classified all in a moment; then the man had closed the door and disappeared before any of them could gather enough wits to speak.

"I'm *going!*" Kate said, her voice shaking, and made for the door.

The inner one creaked again. "Ah," said Kelly's voice, and Kate stopped as if she had been pulled. Matt's eyes widened as he saw her turn and look at Kelly, then go back to the window, shoulders hunched.

"The drinks are as cold as possible," Kelly said pleasantly. He came into the room, carrying a tray with four

11

tankards on it. He paused by Anna, and she took one. "Here you are, Kate—and Matt." His eyes came round to them.

Kate took hers. "What is it?" she said, peering suspiciously down at the contents.

Matt raised his cautiously to his lips, aware of an ironical look for Kelly. The taste made him shiver slightly, it was so full and strong.

"It's beer," he said. "Is it home-brewed?"

"It's local," said Kelly, with a glint in his smile. He set down the tray, not bothering to pick up the fourth tankard, and his gaze traveled past Matt to the strangely shaped pots that he had placed on the furnace shelf. "Do you find these things interesting, Kate?" he asked.

Kate stared back at him with open hostility. "Not really."

Matt said, "We knocked them over. I'm sorry."

"It doesn't matter. It doesn't matter at all," Kelly said, moving over to the furnace. He touched the chipped place on the vase-like pot with one casual finger. "I only keep them as curiosities," he said, smiling at Matt. "Do you know what they call this sort of receptacle?"

"No," said Matt.

"Who was that man," Kate demanded, her voice loud and a little higher than usual, "who came in and had a look at us and then went away without saying anything?"

Matt bit his lip, wishing he could get Kate away. He wanted to go himself. The room was beginning to oppress him; the dimness, and the vague clutter in the darkest corners, had taken on a feel of menace. Perhaps the sudden appearance of the bearded man had jolted him more than he realized.

"They call it a pelican," said Kelly, looking blandly at Kate and softly tapping the tall pot.

Matt felt Kate coming to a boil, and wished Kelly would stop being so imperturbable. Did he get some complicated kind of fun from hearing that shake in her voice?

Anna came forward, the tankard in her hand. "Was that Doctor Dee, Ned?" she asked, and her voice smoothed away some of the tension between Kate and Kelly. "He scared us a bit."

Kelly glanced at her. "Ah," he said. "He needn't have done, Anna. Yes, that was John Dee, the man who shares the house with me. He's rather a shy chap. I didn't expect him to come down." Quietly his finger tapped the chipped pot. "He must have heard the pelican fall."

Kate put her tankard down on the top of the furnace, hastily. "I'm going!" she said, her voice trembling, and turned to the door.

"No!" Kelly's voice shot out, his hand as well, and Kate stopped dead. Matt saw Kelly's fingers just touching her arm; then they moved down and lightly took hold of her hand. "Don't go, Kate," Kelly said softly, almost cajolingly. "You haven't finished your drink."

Kate looked up at him and her eyes dulled over in a cowed way. Slowly she reached out her free hand for the tankard, lifted it to her lips and took a swallow. Matt saw her mouth quiver at the taste.

"May I look at the books?" she said, expressionlessly.

"By all means," Kelly said. He let her hand go. "Can you reach them?"

"I think so—thanks." Kate walked over to the shelf above the desk and lifted down the black-bound book with the title Matt had read; Kelly watched her, that odd look of satisfaction in his eyes again.

Matt saw Kate's hand tremble slightly as she turned over the pages of the book, and knew that she felt Kelly watching her.

"What do the signs mean on this chart?" he asked.

"Which one?" Kelly turned his head.

Matt felt an inward shudder as he met the large clear eyes. Suddenly he knew he *didn't like* Kelly; he didn't like

13

the way his lips turned up at the corners in not quite a smile, nor the hair that grew down over his ears, and least of all those eyes of his. They seemed to leave a stain on whatever they looked at.

He pointed, at random. "That one."

Kelly moved over to the one he indicated, turning his back to Kate, and Matt saw her relax at once. Poor Kate. However tough she tried to act, she was all on edge, ready to be scared by the least little thing. It wasn't *fair* of Anna to have brought them here.

"These are the signs of power," Kelly said, very softly, but the words came so clear through the gloom that Matt was half startled. He looked around at the chart he had pointed to.

It was just a meaningless jumble of lines and dots and curves, in different colored inks.

"Power?" he said. He stepped nearer to the chart, narrowing his eyes to make out the signs.

"If these signs are drawn in the correct way, at the correct time, and in conjuction with the correct rites," Kelly went on, in that soft, distinct tone, "marvelous deeds can be done." He looked at Matt again, and smiled; his eyes seemed to flicker, as if with promises. "Would you like to try, Matt?" he murmured.

Matt stared at the dancing signs, and a haze grew up in his brain, making it hard to think . . . then there was a quick sound of feet behind him, and the haze vanished. He glanced around to see Kate pulling open the front door and darting outside.

He thought he heard Kelly shout as the landscape seen through the doorway tore apart. Earth and sky crumpled like paper, and blackness shot across like trickling ink— and Kate's body arched through the chaos, her mouth wide open as if she was screaming. But in an instant it all smoothed back into place, and Matt wondered what his eyes had been playing at.

14

Then he saw Kate lying face down on the ground.

"Kate!" he shouted, starting forward.

No.

Matt stopped, all movement drained out of him, and shock collided with fear. He couldn't move. He couldn't move an inch. His limbs were as helpless as a marionette's —someone else's will was all that held him upright. Slowly, he shifted his gaze around to Kelly.

Kelly was looking at him with eyes about as human as stones from the seashore. *It's him,* Matt thought in horror, *he's doing this.* He tried to open his mouth, but even as he did so he knew it would be useless; Kelly wasn't a person now, just a pure will dominating him. He wouldn't hear anything said to him.

His legs pulled at him, and his feet carried him over to the window as if he were sleep-walking.

"Is she all right?" said Kelly's voice.

Matt gripped the windowsill, his knuckles whitening. Outside, Kate was grabbing her bicycle, jumping on it and cycling recklessly away over the rough ground, within inches of the ditches. Dizzy partly from shock and partly from relief, Matt felt as if he were watching a film silently unreeling as Kate's bike whipped away and the rocks wheeled above her in the sky, turbulently.

"Yes," he said huskily. "She's riding off."

After a moment, he found he could move properly again, and he turned around to look at Kelly. The stoniness had gone from his face. He had his arm around Anna and she was leaning against him with her eyes half closed. For the first time, Kelly looked discountenanced; Kate's hostility and Matt's awkwardness had seemed to suit him down to the ground, as if wrong things were the right things for him, but now Kate had actually run away there was a new calculating frown in his eyes.

"I'm sorry," said Matt. The sheer force of Kelly's personality made him apologize. "Kate's upset—I suppose it's because of her parents," he fumbled, then hated himself for exposing that wound to Kelly. He said stiffly, "I think we ought to go after her, Anna."

Anna looked up at him, and Kelly's arm tightened around her. "You go, Matt," she said coaxingly, as if asking him not to be angry with her. "I want to stay a bit longer."

Dismay jarred Matt. Couldn't she tear herself away even now? "Anna!" he exclaimed desperately. "It's *Kate!*"

Anna gave Kelly a look of entreaty and Matt felt as if a door had been shut in his face. Didn't she care what happened to anyone, so long as she could be with Kelly?

"Yes," said Kelly deliberately, after a long pause. "Perhaps you had better go after her, Matt." He held out his hand, and Matt took it, reluctantly. "Remember," Kelly said, "I'm your friend, Matt. If you need help, you must come and see me. Any time."

I'll never come here again, Matt swore to himself, never! But all he could say to Kelly was "Thank you." And then "Goodbye."

Kelly let go of his hand, and Matt saw the clear, contented look come back to his eyes. "Goodbye for now, Matt."

He turned and went towards the open door. The brightness of the sun outside was overpowering as he reached the threshold; he seemed to feel the rays slowly crinkle through him, as if it took a long, long time to make that step out on to the boggy ground outside. He paused, feeling like an escaped prisoner. It must be the beer, he thought.

His head cleared, and he went to get his bicycle, pushing it away over the fields without looking back at the house.

Kate was sitting on the grass at the edge of the road, her back to the fields and her bicycle on the ground beside her. Matt could see that she'd been crying, but the tears had stopped now, and she sat still and tense, staring out over the opposite fields.

He leant on his handlebars. "You all right?" he said cautiously. Kate didn't answer, and after a moment Matt said, "How did you manage to trip like that?"

"I didn't trip," Kate said definitely.

Matt's brow wrinkled. It hadn't looked as if she'd tripped but . . . he waited.

"I'm sorry I was horrible to you." Kate looked up, appealingly, with one of those swings of mood that made it impossible to be angry with her, and Matt saw a raw graze on her cheek.

"Look at your face!" he exclaimed.

Kate put her fingers up to her cheek, gingerly. "It was when—all that awful stuff happened," she said, and Matt could hear the fright in her voice. She looked up at him again, screwing her eyes up against the sun. "It's a spooky house, Matt, and you needn't pretend to laugh, it *is*," she said earnestly. "When I tried to get out, everything seemed to go round and round and in and out of itself, as if it was all breaking up—it was like an explosion." She frowned a little at Matt. "I didn't trip, whatever it looked like. Something *happened*."

Matt said slowly, "It didn't look as if you tripped. I thought something had happened, too, then it seemed to go all right again. But when I was leaving I felt peculiar, as if it was a terrifically long way to go. I thought it was the beer."

"That's another thing," Kate said eagerly. "I drank all that foul stuff while I was pretending to look at his rotten books—I didn't want to, but I kind of had to. I'll bet there was a pint there, and I reckon a pint of beer that strong would normally get me a bit high, but I don't feel any different. In fact, I feel just as thirsty as before."

"You might have been drunk, and imagined all that business of things going round and round," Matt

17

pointed out. "You might not feel drunk now because of the shock—a real shock can sober you up immediately."

"What about what you saw?" Kate countered instantly. "And don't say it was because you were drunk. We couldn't both have imagined the same thing."

"I suppose not." Matt remembered the chilling way in which Kelly's mind had imprisoned his limbs. He pushed it away, not wanting to think about it. "Well . . . so what?" he said. "What does it mean, just that we both felt peculiar when we left? Going in was quite normal."

"Yes—but *he* was there then," Kate said. "Don't you remember, he opened the door for us and stood there, with one foot on the doorstep and one on the ground outside, and we had to squeeze past him? I bet that made the difference."

Matt looked pensively across at the trees that hid the house. He remembered. Kate had shrunk past Kelly as if she couldn't bear to touch him. He hadn't liked it himself.

"Yes, okay . . . but I still can't see how it could really mean anything," he said. "It's just queer. That's all you can say."

"There's more," said Kate insistently. "I was looking out of the window the whole time, and the wind was blowing those trees about and the birds were flying around, but you couldn't hear them. You couldn't hear a thing inside, except what was going on in there." She looked at him, triumphantly.

Matt's eyes widened. He remembered looking out the window to see if Kate was all right. A silent film . . . but Kate couldn't have been silent; her feet should have thudded along the ground, her bike should have rattled as it went over the bumps, the rooks should have cawed as they circled above her. Why hadn't he heard?

"All right," he said. "It was spooky. All that stuff in the room was pretty queer too, what with Oriental sects

18

and signs of power.'' His brows knit. "Kate, what was in that book?''

"It was all in Latin," said Kate. "I couldn't understand it. It had lots of those creepy symbols and diagrams in, though.'' She gave him a look, and her quick blue eyes read his mind, in that sometimes irritating way of hers. "You mean you think he's some kind of magician?'' she said, scathingly. "Because of all that rubbish there?''

"Oh, all right, never mind," Matt said.

But Kate took no notice, her mind leaping on ahead. "Matt, perhaps he is," she exclaimed, eyes brightening. "Perhaps he's a member of one of those witch covens! I read about them in the papers I was delivering last summer.'' She grinned. "What a laugh! I bet he does all kinds of funny rites out here with the others after dark.''

Matt stared at her, aghast. "It's not funny!" he said. "We've left Anna with him!''

Kate screwed her nose up at him, crossly, then rose and pulled up her bicycle. "Don't be stupid," she said. "They can't *do* anything. They just mess about. There aren't any real witches nowadays—that paper said so.''

"He doesn't have to be a witch to be able to hurt her!" Matt exclaimed. A line of worry creased his brow. "Anyway, he can do things. After you'd gone, he hypnotized me, or something. I saw you on the ground outside, and I was going to dash out to you, but I couldn't move an inch. I could feel him stopping me.''

Kate shrugged impatiently, as if she didn't want to listen. "We can't make her leave if she doesn't want to!" she said. She put her foot on the pedal, and glanced up with that sudden appealing look. "Don't go back to that house, Matt. Come on home.''

Matt gave in at once, knowing he couldn't leave her when she asked him not to. After all, she was no older than him, despite the way she talked . Whereas Anna was sixteen, a year older than both of them, and probably knew exactly what she was doing . . . though he wished she could have told him.

"All right," he said, and his unease lifted a little as Kate smiled at him. "Let's go, then."

They mounted their bikes and rode back down the road on which they'd come.

2

HE MIGHT CALL IT MAGIC

I

When war suddenly broke out in that African state, Matt
had been pretty sure his father would go to it. Jeff Cooper
found reporting on politics at Westminster unexciting
after assignments in Vietnam and the Middle East. The
Marchants, their closest friends, had gone, and there was
nothing to keep Jeff Cooper in England; he had been
divorced from his wife three years ago, and if Kate and Anna were old enough to be left on their own for the summer
so was Matt. He applied to go, and the TV company he
worked for agreed. Other friends promised to keep an eye
on Matt, Kate and Anna. So Jeff Cooper followed the Marchants, and arrived just in time to have to report their disappearance in a mountainous area to the north where the
guerrillas were believed to be based.

A few days after this news came through, Matt got a let-
ter from Aunt Phyllis, his father's sister. "Your father
telegraphed me about the Marchants' daughters," she
wrote. "He thinks they shouldn't be left alone in London
at a time like this, and I agree with him. Come up here
and bring them with you. Your father'll let us know the
moment there's any news."

So here he was in Lancashire with Kate and Anna, at
Aunt Phyllis's small house. Matt's mother had written him

as well, from the Cornwall town where she lived now, just telling him not to worry. She would remember the Marchants, but she probably only knew about their disappearance from the television reports, and the papers.

It was ten o'clock now, and at last getting dark outside, enough to draw the curtains and switch on a lamp. Alone in his aunt's sitting room, Matt sat down to watch the ten o'clock news on the television, with the sound turned down low.

Pictures followed one another across the little screen; a terrorist bombing here, a resignation there, a conference somewhere else—already the African war was low on the headlines. But there was a short report by Matt's father, filming a group of Africans on their way south out of the hill country where guerrillas and government forces were currently clashing. Matt's fingers knit tight together, as his father's voice came impersonally from the television; then he found himself searching the screen for two other European faces, as if the camera, being in Africa, must sooner or later hit on the Marchants.

Kate came into the room, and involuntarily Matt moved to get up and switch off the television. He stopped himself and stayed in his seat; she would only be angry if she caught him treating her like a child.

The picture changed to what had once been a village on the side of a hill, and went steadily along one narrow street, showing heaps of earth and rubble where shells had landed. Here and there a white wall was left standing, the house around it in ruins; and there was no sign of life anywhere. Matt's father's voice told them that the village had been shelled two days ago, by the guerrillas—probably because some of the men had been persuaded to join the government forces.

Kate said gruffly, "I don't see the point of showing us this. It doesn't tell us any more about what's actually happening, who's winning, or anything."

The plodding refugees appeared again, with their bundles and silent, gaunt-looking children who stared listlessly back at the camera. Matt's father's voice said that it was such places the refugees were leaving; few of them actually knew if there was anywhere to go; but it was certain that between the guns of the guerrillas and the guns of the government there was no place for them. Then the announcer in London returned to the screen and began to give the cricket results.

Kate said, "I wonder where Anna is."

Matt, still staring at the television, felt a pang of apprehension. Anna hadn't come home, and he didn't want to think what might have happened to her. Perhaps she was all right—ten o'clock wasn't late, especially in the holidays—but what if Kelly was keeping her against her will?

The door opened and Aunt Phyllis came in. Quietly, she sat down and watched as a man told them what the weather would be like tomorrow. She looked tired, as usual; she drove to Manchester every day to her work with an advertising firm, which made her day very long.

A commercial about soap powder began, in an excited gabble.

"Do you want this, Auntie?" Matt asked.

"No, dear. You can put it off."

Matt rose and switched off the set. Kate yawned wearily.

"Sleepy?" said Aunt Phyllis.

"A bit," Kate said.

There was a moment's pause. Then Aunt Phyllis said, rather carefully, "Do either of you know where Anna is?"

Matt hesitated. Kate said dispassionately, "I expect she's still with her boyfriend. We met him while we were on the Moss, and he invited us into his house."

Aunt Phyllis looked up, off guard, and Matt saw the thought in her eyes—Boyfriend? *Now?* "I didn't know Anna had a boyfriend here," she said, with reserve. She didn't ask who he was, or where Anna had met him; she

23

made a point of not asking such questions, as if she understood it would be unbearable for her to behave like a parent to them.

Matt said unhappily, "I think she's only just met him. He lives in that house on the Moss . . . I don't suppose you know him, do you, Auntie?" If Aunt Phyllis knew Kelly, perhaps she could reassure them.

But his aunt gave him a puzzled look. "On the Moss? I don't think so, Matt."

"It's an old house, behind a clump of trees," Matt said. "You can't see it from the road. You have to cross two fields and go round the trees to get to it."

Aunt Phyllis's face changed, oddly. "I know the house you mean," she said after a moment. "We used to play there when we were children. At least, it's the only house I know of on the Moss." Matt saw constraint on her face. "It doesn't matter, dear, it's none of my business; Anna's sixteen, she's absolutely free to do as she wants. It's just . . . well, I do know that house. It's a ruin, isn't it? It has been for as long as I can remember."

Matt stared, thunderstruck.

Aunt Phyllis looked away, as if embarrassed at catching him out in a lie. "You know I don't want to pry," she said. "Only perhaps you could say to Anna it would be—*better*, really, if she did stay here. For the time being." She rose. "Let's get the couch made up for you, Matt."

Dumbly, Matt helped her spread his sleeping-bag on the couch, with a sheet inside. Kate had a camp-bed upstairs in the main bedroom, with Anna; Aunt Phyllis had moved into the spare room for them. There was nowhere else for Matt to sleep except down here on the couch.

"There." Aunt Phyllis adjusted the sheet. "Well, good night," she said and smiled at them, looking tired.

"Good night, Miss Cooper," said Kate.

"Good night." Matt cleared his throat.

Aunt Phyllis went out, and Kate looked round at Matt.

The blue eyes were desperate. "I *told* you it was a spooky house!" she said, in a low voice.

"But it wasn't a ruin," Matt said helplessly.

"Your aunt ought to know," Kate pointed out. "She's lived here all her life. The house we saw can't have been the real one."

Matt rubbed a hand over his forehead, feeling as if he were going mad. "What are you talking about?" he protested.

Angrily, Kate jabbed him in the chest with her fist. "Don't be so stupid! He made us *think* it was a real house —just like he made me drink all that beer, and made you so you couldn't move! Don't you *see?*"

"It isn't possible," Matt exclaimed wearily.

"Oh, all right, go on thinking what you want!" Kate snapped. She turned her shoulder on him and her voice began to falter. "A lot you care! He's already taken Mum and Dad away, and now he's got Anna too—he'll take you next, I suppose, because you're so stupid, and then there won't be anybody!"

He? Who was he? Kelly? But Matt could tell she was crying again. "Kate, stop it," he said awkwardly. "We'll go to the house tomorrow, if you like, and look at it again. But Anna'll be home any minute now, you'll see."

Kate sniffed. "Bet she won't," she said, more steadily. "Anyway, I'm not going near that house again." She looked back at Matt, the tears still bright in her eyes; but he saw she was too tired to go on crying. "I'm going to bed. 'Night," she said dully, moving away towards the door.

Matt sighed as the door closed behind her, and rubbed his face with his hands. He might as well go to bed too. It would be inconsiderate to put the television on again when Aunt Phyllis needed her sleep, and he didn't feel like reading.

Lying on the couch, which was too short for him, he

wondered again who Kate had meant by "*he*". Kelly? But what had Kelly got to do with the disappearance of her parents? It was often difficult to follow Kate; she was so quick, grasping things apparently by intuition and leaving him to work them out painfully, step by step.

He couldn't understand it, any more than he could understand about the house; and he wished it hadn't seemed to Aunt Phyllis that he was lying.

Where *was* Anna? Why can't things stop happening to us, Matt thought, miserably; it's bad enough for Kate to lose her parents, without having to lose her sister as well. For heaven's sake, Anna, *come home.*

Much later, he fell asleep, without having heard anyone open the front door and come in.

2

The Moss was just as deserted as the day before, and by the clump of trees, which broke the wind, it was so hot that even the rooks seemed languid.

"Well," said Kate, jerkily. "Now what?"

Across the ditch, the house lay like a piece of rubbish. Long ago the thatch had fallen from the roof, and the roof itself had caved in at one corner. The windows were boarded up, and lichen grew undisturbed on the crumbling old walls.

There was a kind of horror in the place, making Matt wish they hadn't come. Yesterday Anna had been with them in a real house; now both she and that house were gone. How? Where? It frightened him more than Kate, for she'd obviously expected it.

"I don't understand," he said.

Unmoving, Kate stood beside him, staring at the ruin. Now that he'd at last got her here, she was more subdued than she had been for a long time. She'd refused to come at first, and it had taken him almost an hour to persuade her that they had no choice, they must find Anna. Perhaps

26

she'd known, with that intuition of hers, that they wouldn't find her here.

"What do you think happened?" Matt said tentatively.

"I told you last night," Kate said, without looking at him. "He made us think it was a real house."

Matt tried not to reject the idea. "You mean he really is a witch?" he asked, wondering at his own words.

"I'm not talking about magic," said Kate, with a touch of scorn. "You can hypnotize people to believe anything. *He* might call it magic, I suppose."

Matt tried to make sense of this. "What do you mean?" he said at last.

Kate looked at him, and he saw at once that, after all, she was really scared. "Well—he must be something peculiar," she said after a moment, her voice low. "Look at all that stuff he had in the room. Maybe he calls himself a witch and says he can do magic . . . but it's not fairytale stuff, with wishes and wands and all that—it's real. He really can do things."

Matt wrinkled his brow. Kate's face was pale; she had stopped jeering, she believed and was afraid. To her, *magic* was a silly word fit only for children's story books; whereas Kelly, and what he had done, were terrible facts.

"So he hypnotized us, and Anna too," he said slowly. "But what's he done with Anna?"

"How should I know?" said Kate. "Taken her away somewhere, I suppose."

Taken her away—where, and for what purpose? Matt felt himself shiver. He turned his head away from the house and looked into the grove of trees instead. It was dark and untidy in there, with ragged grass, and trees too close together; it makes the countryside round London look like a park, Matt thought. Then his eyes sharpened.

"Look at that, Kate," he said, pointing.

Kate turned and looked.

The tree nearest to them was scraped as if something big and clumsy had blundered past it, and gone on into the grove. The grass was flattened into a straight, obvious trail, and bark had been ripped off the trees beside it so that stretches of bare wood showed.

"I wonder what did that," Kate said, and swallowed.

"I'll look," said Matt. He stepped into the grove, making his way along the trail. Fresh ruts in the ground made him slip, and it was dim under the trees. There was a sense of danger, as if an enemy nearby were just awakening. Matt knew it wasn't unusual to have such feelings in a wood, and tried to ignore it. Trees were peculiar things.

In front of him, something lay on the ground at the foot of a dented tree-trunk. The bark had been smashed away by a direct blow, and Matt stooped to see what had come crashing there with such force.

A mass of twisted steel bars, and two buckled wheels.

Matt found himself holding Anna's plastic saddlebag.

It was torn and scratched, and some of it missing as if it had actually been melted away. The bicycle was a write-off, so squashed it was hardly recognizable.

Matt dropped the saddlebag and turned, getting out of the grove as fast as he could. Ridiculously, the trees seemed about to move and block his way—then he was out, white and panting.

"What is it?" Kate said.

"Anna's bike," Matt said, getting his breath. "It's been wrecked. It looks as if it's been sent crashing through the trees—at some speed, too."

Kate looked into the grove, then back at the ruined house. The trail of destruction through the trees led directly away from it. *"He* must have done it," she said.

"Kate," Matt said hesitantly, "last night, when you said he'd taken your parents, and now Anna, did you mean him? Kelly?"

Kate looked at the house, frowning in a troubled way.

"Sort of," she said. "Someone's out to get us."

"Who?" asked Matt.

Kate shrugged. "Him." She never spoke Kelly's name. "Maybe not just him, but he's in it."

Puzzled, Matt wondered how she could sound so sure. But then, Kate was rarely unsure about anything.

"Where can he have taken Anna?" he said. "What did he want her for?"

"I don't know." Kate turned her back resolutely on the ruined house, closing her lips tightly. Brow creased, Matt looked at the house; and then the idea came into his mind.

"Suppose he's still got her in there!" he whispered, his heart jolting at the thought that Kelly might have been listening to them all this time. Kate looked up, and Matt saw that she'd had that fear from the first. So that was why she'd been so quiet.

"We can't do anything, Matt!" she said, in a low frightened voice. "He's too dangerous! It ought to be grown-ups looking for him, not just us."

Matt's heart thudded a little. "There aren't any, though," he said, trying not to sound as if he was thinking of her parents. "There's only us."

"What about your aunt?" Kate said. "What about the police?"

"The police'd never believe us," Matt said. A line came on his brow. "And I can't see Aunt Phyllis believing us, either. You heard her last night."

"Of course she'll believe us, if we tell her properly," Kate said, her voice growing more sure. "She doesn't just disbelieve things."

That was probably true, Matt reflected, and the thought was comforting. It would be a relief to unload at least some of their troubles, and straighten out that business of the house being a ruin.

"But we won't see her till tonight," he said, anxiety

29

returning. "Anything could happen to Anna before then. Let's just *look*, Kate. If there's nothing there—well, we can't do any more."

"And if there is?" Kate demanded.

Matt thought of looking between the chinks in the boards, and meetings Kelly's clear, frightening gaze. "You stay here," he said, "and I'll look. If anything happens, ride away like mad—and phone Aunt Phyllis and tell her."

Kate looked away. "All right," she said. "Be careful."

"Yes," said Matt, and walked across the turf bridge to the ruin.

There was no way to hide his approach. If Kelly was there and saw him, there was nothing he could do about it. He made his feet walk steadily over to the nearest window.

Close up, he could see the boards were old and rotten, and there were plenty of cracks to look through; but there was nothing in the room but a collapsed beam from the ceiling and rubble scattered around it.

He went past the boarded door to the other window. This one was the room where Kelly's laboratory had been the day before. Close to his face, the boards smelt damp and rotten, and at first he couldn't see anything inside. His stomach knotted as the gloom made itself into shapes in front of his eyes, before settling down and letting him see what really was there.

After all, there was nothing much; in fact it was as bare as if someone had recently cleared it out and swept it. There was only one thing—a chalk pattern on the floor. Three concentric circles in the middle and round them a double-lined square. Each corner of the square was the center for a smaller double-ringed circle.

What a queer thing to do, Matt thought. Relief at not finding Kelly there mingled with a sense of unease—who should want to draw patterns on the floor of a ruined house? But there was nothing else there, and after a moment he went on, looking through each window on the ground floor. Old tyres, a rusty pram, bits of brick, old shoes, broken bottles and all the junk that always found its way into places no one cared about any more—the house was deserted. That much was obvious.

Coming round to the front again, Matt saw Kate standing halfway across the turf bridge. As she saw him, she pushed her hands into her pockets and came forward.

"There's nothing there," Matt said at once, knowing she was still afraid.

Kate came right up to him, and whispered, "What about upstairs?"

Matt looked up to the higher windows. They too were boarded up, but above them the roof beams were mostly rotted, and parts of the wall were crumbling. He shook his head. "Surely not. Those beams could fall in any minute, or the floors . . ." He found himself whispering too, and his brow began to crease. "We'd better look," he said at last.

"How can we?" Kate whispered, nervously.

Matt looked at the cottage, beginning to hate it, with its blind windows and loathsome mould on its walls . . . but suppose Anna really was in there, hearing their voices and praying they would find her.

"We'll have to break in and climb the stairs," he whispered. If the stairs were still there. He hesitated. "Are you coming?"

"All right," said Kate, almost defiantly.

I'm as scared as she is, thought Matt. "Come on, then," he muttered, and went to the window where the boards had seemed most rotten.

They pulled apart quite easily, snapping with dull thuds. Matt brushed the slimy crumbs from his fingers and pulled himself up on the window sill.

It was the room with the pattern chalked on the floor.

31

Matt jumped down, and the broken flags of stone struck chill under his feet. Kate came behind him at once, as if she couldn't risk hesitation, and immediately grabbed at his arm. "What's that?" she gasped.

"I don't know," Matt said, glancing around at her. Her face was white and her eyes sharp with fear. Matt looked back at the chalk pattern.

It was different. Matt felt his heart begin to race, and involuntarily he pressed himself against the wall. Somebody must be in the house, for in between the double lines of the square and the outer circles, and all around the three inner ones, fresh chalk marks glared triumphantly up at him. Symbols. Symbols, like signs of the zodiac, which he'd seen before, on charts that hung on the wall . . .

"*Matt!*" Kate screamed, and her fingers slipped from his arm.

Matt made a reflex grab for her, missed, and in a second she was out of his reach. The double chalk lines opened and something like a giant invisible hand hauled Kate screaming into the inmost circle. As Matt opened his mouth to gasp, he felt the hand leave her and come grasping at him.

"No!" he exclaimed, and flung himself at the window, catching hold of the one board at the top which he'd left intact. He fought off the pull of the hand with all his will.

"Matt!" Kate cried again.

Matt looked at her. His hands were locked on the board, but suddenly all he could see were the blue, terrified eyes. His will faltered—then the board split under his hands with a tearing sound, showering him with acrid dust, and the hand had him. He went staggering into the center circle, and the chalk lines closed behind him.

He took hold of Kate, and she clutched at him; but now, try as they would, they could no more step over those chalk lines than over walls a hundred feet high.

3

THE FACE OF SHADDAI

"Welcome back."

Matt, grasping Kate tightly to him, realized his eyes were closed. He didn't want to open them. Perhaps the danger would go away if he just didn't look . . . but the sound of the voice, which he recognized, was enough to tell him it wouldn't. He half opened them.

Daylight had gone; the laboratory was back, lit with the wavering light of candles. The window was curtained. Matt knew the shelf of books, the charts, the alembics and retorts, and the pelican which stood on the furnace. Inwardly flinching, he looked up at the clear eyes watching him.

Kelly smiled at him. "Well done, Matt," he said.

Matt stared at him. He was different, too, standing there in a long black robe trimmed with fur. What's happened, Matt thought with dread, how did he fetch us here —*what is he?*

Kate's head lifted. She looked round, eyes huge with fear; then a sob burst from her and she buried her face in her hands. Matt's arms tightened around her, but she shrugged him roughly off and looked up at Kelly with a set face.

"Where's Anna?" She took one step toward Kelly.

"Where is she? Give her back to us and let us go—we won't do anything, we've never harmed you!"

Kelly looked past her at Matt. "You can come out of the circle now, if you like, Matt," he invited pleasantly.

Numbly, Matt stepped over the chalk lines, and at once they faded, leaving the stone floor blank again. Kate saw it happen, and her eyes dilated.

"How did you do that?" she whispered.

"It's a trick, Kate," Kelly said, looking down at her with his smiling eyes. "Unnecessary, of course—I could have brought you here without any fuss, but I thought you might enjoy the circle. I used it a great deal at one time. Didn't you recognize it? It comes straight from that book of mine you were reading . . . yes, like most things in this place. Those metal discs do, as well. Odd that your sister should have chosen to pick up the one bearing the sign of the Face of Shaddai—the sign that gives me power over all created things, body and soul."

"What did you mean," Matt said huskily, "well done?"

"Ah." The serene eyes returned to Matt, causing him the same inward shudder. "I wanted Kate, Matt—as well as Anna," Kelly said softly, standing there with his hands clasped in front of his dark gown and looking like a monk except for the hair that crept down over his ears. "She took me unawares, dashing out like that—you could have killed yourself, Kate, if I hadn't been quick. You can't just crash straight through the polylabyrinths of time and space. Can you?"

"How should I know?" Kate said roughly. "You made us think it was just an ordinary house."

"Another trick," Kelly said, gentle-toned. "But you noticed, didn't you—that you couldn't hear the rooks? An oversight. I'm out of practice. But I had no intention of letting you die yesterday, Kate, which was fortunate for you. I see you were slightly hurt—" he raised a finger

34

toward the graze he could see on her cheek—"my apologies."

Kate was silent.

"I don't understand," Matt said hoarsely. "This house is still in the Moss, even if it's really a ruin and you've made it look different—isn't it?"

Kelly shook his head. "It stood on the Moss once, Matt, when another Elizabeth ruled England," he said, and smiled in the flickering light. "Then it was stone and mortar. It has since been rebuilt many times, and the ruins of the last rebuilding are still there. But this house isn't real any more. It's a picture I paint inside your mind, and it exists outside everything you think is real. When Kate ran, she tried to cross the infinite boundary between my universe and another. You saw what happened, Matt, and yet you would have done the same if I hadn't stopped you. Strange. Did you want death so much?"

Matt shuddered under the clear-eyed gaze. "No," he said thickly.

"That's strange too—if you know so well what you want," Kelly said. The quiet, riddling words were beginning to daze Matt and he rubbed a hand across his eyes. Kelly watched him serenely. "I had to let Kate go, but I still wanted her, Matt," he said softly, "so I had to let you go too—to bring her back."

Kate swept the pelican off the furnace so that it went smashing down on the stone floor. "Stop it!" she shrieked. "He's trying to hypnotize us again, Matt! Don't listen to him!"

Kelly laughed, without a sound. "That was what I meant, Matt," he said, "when I said 'Well done'."

Matt stared from his untroubled face to Kate's wild blue eyes and the fragments of the pelican on the floor. So Kate in her fear had been right, and he, trying to be brave, had just proved himself a fool—he had dragged her into Kelly's trap, as Kelly had known he would.

"Oh, Kate—" he said.

"Don't listen!" Kate said, furiously. "Don't let him hypnotize you, Matt!"

"Hypnotize," murmured Kelly. "It's as silly a word as 'magic,' isn't it, Kate? Not but what you were the easier one to master—Matt fought like a bull. Did you think you would win, Matt? You understood you never could, Kate; with such a knowledge it's not easy to fight."

"Stop it!" Kate cried, this time in pain. Matt took her hand, and she didn't shake him off.

"Tell us where Anna is," he said doggedly, raising his voice. "Tell us why you brought us—"

He stopped, as the inner door clicked open behind them and Kelly's gaze sharpened above their heads.

"Ned, Ned!" A low beautiful voice throbbed with horror. *"What are you about?"*

Matt and Kate whirled around, Matt's heart leaping to his mouth at the thought of someone else being there, someone who might help them.

It was that tall bearded man again. From the doorway he stared down at them with eyes no longer impassive, but wide with consternation. He came into the room, long gown swishing, and held his arm out in their direction. "I saw them before, but I thought they were spirits!" His voice was deep and musical like an actor's, but there was anguish in it. "How long have you been calling up human creatures and turning them to your will?"

Matt stared, his hand tightening over Kate's. Spirits? Was *that* the reason for the emotionless scrutiny the day before? Were apparitions more common here than human beings? But the man cared enough now; grief, misery and dread jostled across his countenance, and Matt's heart reached out to him after Kelly's loathsome serenity.

"It was necessary," Kelly said abruptly. Looking back at him, Matt saw the frowning, calculating look; Kelly was taken aback at this interruption.

36

"Necessary!" the other echoed. "What was necessary?"

It was only a moment before the clear, tranquil look returned. "Ah," said Kelly, looking back at Matt and Kate as if remembering them. "Kate, Matt—this is my friend, Doctor Dee. I believe you've met?"

"Where's Anna?" Matt said, hoarsely.

"Of course." Kelly moved toward the desk, smiling. He picked up something in a round, flat case. "Come and look, John," he said, to the man, "if you've given up your scorn. There still may be something worth seeing in the scrying glass."

He opened the case and slid out a round black mirror with a small handle. It seemed dull and dead in the candlelight.

"I never scorned scrying!" Dee said tensely. "But not all is seen in the glass! Will you not tell me in plain words, Ned?"

Kelly smiled again, dangling the mirror, and looking back at Matt and Kate. "Maybe you'll look, Matt—or Kate?' he said softly.

Matt looked for help to Dee. The man stood there with trouble in his face, and that made Matt feel he was somehow on their side. He looked at them, full of uncertainty, and Matt noticed his eyes were as blue as Kate's; at last he seemed to make up his mind, but he did it as if he had no option.

"Come then," he said to them, quietly. "We will look together."

They followed him to the desk, where the candles flickered on the black mirror. Taking it by the handle, he held it up in front of them. "Look into it," his deep voice said, softly, "and presently the curtain will be drawn aside."

Matt looked at the blank surface. There was nothing there, just a piece of obsidian, gleaming a little . . . he stared and stared, torn between fear and longing to see, until the mirror seemed the only thing in the room. Then at last, he realized he was seeing something. Small and clear, as if seen through the wrong end of a telescope, there was a golden curtain, partly drawn aside; and as soon as he saw it, he was seeing something else.

A girl, a lovely girl with long dark hair, shining brown eyes and a gentle mouth. She turned her head and smiled, and Matt knew the smile. It was Anna. What was she smiling at?

Then he saw Kelly, and the sense of sickness came back. Anna was smiling at him, holding her hands out to him, as if nothing and no one else was of any account. They stood in a nothingness, Kelly with his hands folded in front of him, Anna slender and fragile before him. She seemed so small; and then she was even smaller, Kelly looming massively over her as if she were nothing and he all. Matt saw she was on her knees.

Then Kelly stooped and lifted her up in his arms. He straightened, holding her close to him, and stood motionless, looking down at her. Anna lay there lightly, as if she were made of air, and Kelly's face seemed to wonder at her for a moment; then he looked up with eyes like stones and cast her from him.

Anna fell away through a mass of splintering light. The sight hurt Matt's eyes, and he could no longer see her properly; she seemed to become light herself, parting, flickering, diffusing. After some time she was lying in complete darkness; but Matt was not sure that what lay there was still Anna. After a moment, parts of the darkness thickened and became vague, shadowy forms of men; they picked up the motionless figure and carried it away, deep into the darkness until they were buried from sight. Briefly, Matt saw a shape like two branching horns fill the mirror.

A sigh came uncontrollably from the man beside him. Matt stirred, blinking; the black mirror was dull and opaque again, and his head ached hotly.

"Come," said Dee, his voice full of pain. Laying down the mirror and taking their hands, he drew them to a stool and sat down, his shoulders stiff and tense. "I am weary," he whispered, "and young eyes see clearest. Tell me what you saw, Kate."

Kate looked slantwise at him, and Matt saw her hand trying stealthily to slip out of his. Clearly, she trusted him no more than Kelly.

Dee felt it, and looked up. Kate froze at once, not meeting his eye. Dee opened his hand, and Kate let hers lie loosely where it was, as if it had nothing to do with her.

"The young have always feared me," Dee said quietly, almost as if to himself. He clasped Kate's hand again, gently. "My library, my astrolabe, my crystal, the furnace glowing red at night—they saw these, and ran from me in the street. But, truly, Kate, now there is nothing to fear. I could never harm you now."

"Tell him, Kate," Matt urged, at once. Surely Kate must see that Dee was good . . . Yes, good. That was the word. In the threatening clutter of the laboratory with the witch Kelly there in the shadows, Dee was the one wholesome object.

"All right," said Kate, after a moment. Her throat sounded dry. "But my head aches, and I feel funny."

"The scrying has drained you," Dee said. "It will pass —I promise. But tell me, Kate, quickly, before the sight fades."

"Go on, Kate. It's okay!" Matt said, as she looked at him.

"All right," she said again, unsteadily. "I saw Anna. She was just—standing there."

"Go on," said Dee gently.

Kate swallowed. "Then *he* came."

Dee nodded, not asking who she meant.

"He went up and put his arms around her," Kate said, "and then Anna was just—gone!"

"Bravely told," Dee said softly, and pressed her hand. Kate choked almost silently on a sob, then pressed her lips together with determination.

"But I didn't see anything like that!" Matt exclaimed urgently.

Dee turned his head. "No scryer sees all that's in the glass," he said sombrely. "No two people can stand in the same place, and look with the same eyes. Tell me what you saw, Matt, as well as you can remember it."

Matt hesitated, then began to recount what he'd seen, haltingly; it was hard to put into words. After the first few sentences, Dee's eyes fixed on him intently. That searching stare made Matt stumble once or twice, but Dee's eyes didn't move from him, so he hurried through as best he could to the end. Dee looked at him in silence for a few moments, then shook his head as if unbelieving.

"It is strange!" he said, low. "I would find your vision hard to interpret if I did not know the truth; but indeed it is strange that you should see so much!"

"Oh," came Kelly's voice ironically from the shadows. "Matt has a deal of talent."

Matt said huskily, trying to ignore Kelly, "What did you see, Doctor?"

Dee let go of their hands and rose, looking through the gloom at Kelly as if his eyes carried their own light.

"You know what I saw, Ned!"

"Yes," said Kelly, in soft-toned satisfaction.

Dee stepped towards him, swiftly, and for a moment Kelly looked as if he might flinch back. But his face didn't change, and he held his ground.

"How could you do it, Ned?" Dee's voice came unexpectedly low and desperate. "The wickedness of this is past measure!"

"Wickedness," Kelly countered, with scorn in his voice but not in those clear eyes. "The word's never off your lips, Doctor Dee. You know nothing of what I've done—

why, she begged me to do it, the dear lass. She loved me."
And he smiled.

Kate's head jerked up, tears forgotten. "Loved you!"
she whispered. "Loved *you?*"

Both Dee and Kelly looked around at her, and saw the
disgust and disbelief that fought in her face.

Still smiling, Kelly said softly, "Don't you think I'm
handsome then, Kate?"

Matt saw that the man's gaze scared her, making her
shudder inwardly as he did himself whenever it rested on
him. But at last Kate squared her shoulders. "No," she
said bluntly. "Some people might think you were good-
looking, but only at first. After a bit there's something
wrong with your face—like a squint."

Kelly's eyes flickered momentarily and nastily, and in
that instant Matt saw what she meant. Those eyes were not
right. And then the calm serenity returned, as Kelly laughed, noiselessly—but Matt knew the eyes were still not
right.

"That's not what Anna thought, Kate. Through the
centuries she called to me. She was only a voice until I
came, and gave her shape."

"Oh, Madinia!" Dee whispered, his voice like a mourn-
ful harp.

"Stop moaning," said Kelly, in an undertone. "She
would have come to you, but you decided you knew better
—what was she to do?"

Desperately, Matt stepped forward and caught the long
trailing sleeve of Dee's gown. "Doctor—what does he
mean? Where is Anna?"

"Who's Madinia?" Kate demanded.

Dee sighed as he looked at their faces. "Ned," he said,
his voice low with entreaty, "do you feel no pity?"

Kelly smiled. "Tell 'em yourself, John," he said softly.

Kate said fiercely, "You've *got* to tell us, Doctor! Tell
us so we can understand!"

41

Dee sighed again as he sat down on the stool and drew Matt and Kate to him. "It is no easy story to tell," he said, heavily. "But it cannot be kept from you any longer. Listen, then, and try not to disbelieve me." He looked up at them, and the candlelight etched lines across his face.

"It is a strange story. When Anna heard the news of your parents, Kate, she felt all you felt, but there was something else besides. It was as if the news struck her so hard that for a moment she fell unconscious—and, awaking, was somehow terribly changed. It is hard for you to understand, I know—she seemed to have become a shadow, adrift from her real self, and there was no *I* inside her, no real person.

"Her very self had left her, shaken loose by that shattering blow, and gone wandering it knew not where in the universe. Anna had to find it again—and all the time while she seemed to be there in front of you, she seemed to herself to be walking through a kind of darkness, through all the bleak, empty ends of space and time, searching and searching for her lost self."

Dee closed his eyes, unconsciously gripping their hands a little tighter; and Matt stared, heart thumping, hardly knowing whether the man was talking sense or not.

"It is unknown, uncharted place, that darkness. It is outside time. To you, the change in Anna seems to have lasted only a few days; to Anna, it is already eternity. To Ned and me, three hundred years have passed since we first saw her face. It was when the first Elizabeth sat on England's throne that we found a window to look into that darkness; it was I who wished to, for it was said all lost things were there, and I believed much could be learned from it. But I had little skill in scrying. So, for long hours every day and night, Ned gazed into that mirror—our window— and tried to see what was there in the darkness. At first he saw little. But then, one night, he saw that poor lost self of Anna's. He called me to him, and I saw it too—

floating there like a face about to drown. At first we hardly knew what it was, but we pitied it, and tried to calm it."

His eyes opened, with a blind look fixed on the floor.

"It was like her. Pale, afraid, and only half awake, but even then it had her look. We soon saw that she would die if she were not brought back to it—it was growing fainter every moment. So we called, using all the art we had . . . and Anna heard us. She came like a bird to us, flying, arrow-straight through all that darkness—back to herself. We saw the poor pale face suddenly grow, and brighten— the eyes woke up, like stars rising—and she looked out at us, alive, more than ever herself again. I saw the unbelieving joy in her, the great moved thankfulness, and I knew she would never wish to leave us."

He paused, looking up through the shadows as if he saw more than the candles revealed. Then he rose, stepping over to the desk, and touched the dead mirror with both hands. "She came to us," he said, his voice low. "Night after night, day after day, she looked out of this glass and spoke to us. Sweet Madinia! So we named her, for she could say only that she was a maiden, and at first her speech was unclear to us. But she was our guardian, letting no evil spirit appear to deceive us . . ."

"Tell them!" Kelly said rougly.

Kate cried, "Do you mean Anna's a —*spirit? A ghost?*"

Dee turned slowly, leaning the mirror on the desk, and looked back at them. "We are all spirits," he said.

"But Anna's real! She's my sister!" Kate protested obstinately.

"Are spirits not real?" asked Dee. "You saw Ned in the glass—is he nothing?"

Kate was silent.

"Tell them," said Kelly again, softly.

Dee sighed. "Yes—I deserted Madinia. I ceased to believe that wisdom could be found in the scrying glass, and no longer came to speak with the spirits. So Ned held

Madinia in the palm of his hand; and when he called, she came. It is true, Kate. Anna loved him. He gave her herself."

Matt said hoarsely, "What's he done with her?"

"Be brave," Dee said numbly. "What I have told you was the tale of perhaps a little foolishness; now I must speak of evil. He has sent her to Cernunnos."

There was a short silence. Then Kate said, her throat dry, "Is that a place—or a person?"

"He is a being," said Dee sombrely, "and he holds Ned's soul and mine in fee. Ned sent Anna to him as payment, to free himself."

Matt and Kate stared at each other; unconsciously Kate's hand came grasping at Matt's arm. *"Who* is he?" Matt demanded.

"He has many names," Dee said, almost stonily. "He is called the Horned Man, Herne the Hunter, Pan, Robin Goodfellow—and also the Devil."

Kate gasped. Matt felt dizzy; a blackness seemed to creep through the air to him, weakening his limbs.

"That isn't right," Kelly said, rather quickly. "Devil is a name given to all old gods, whom foolish people wish to forget."

"But he *can't*—he *can't* have her!" Kate cried, wildly.

"She wanted to go, Kate—out of love for me," Kelly said, and smiled.

Dee turned to him. "Stop your torment of these two!" His voice rolled like a drum. "Can you not be satisfied with having done the rankest evil ever known to man, that you must play cat and mouse with two children as well?"

Kelly looked back, for once not answering.

"Ned!" Dee's voice softened, and he stepped nearer, putting his hands on Kelly's shoulders. "It's not too late, Ned," he whispered imploringly. "He has not claimed her yet. Fetch her back—let me teach you safety—Ned, if you ever loved me, let us fetch her back."

"We can't," Kelly said, lightly. The clear eyes regarded Dee without much regret. "She is out of our sight," Kelly said. "She is in Otherworld. The Fomors have hidden her in the Mound."

"What are you talking about?" Matt cried. Every word from these two men was beginning to make his head reel; they talked like no human beings Matt had ever heard.

Kelly turned and looked at him, as Dee's hands fell from his shoulders. "Doesn't speak very clearly, does he, Matt?" he said, and smiled. "Well, I'll tell you. Don't listen to all that talk of devils. Cernunnos is one of the Old Ones, with powers more ancient than any. Only people who are afraid of him call him a devil. He gives his powers to others, as he has done to John and me—that's why we haven't died—but he wants a price for it. If I didn't send him a maiden, like Anna, he'd destroy me—and I don't want that, do I?"

"You've sold your soul to the Devil!" Kate shouted at him. "And you're giving him Anna's soul instead!"

There was a silence in the room. The long shadows jumped and fell from the candle flames, and Matt stared at Kelly's tall, black figure. The sense of evil poured from him like a stench. Yes, his eyes were wrong, the man himself was wrong; as fish could breathe in water and drown in the air, so Kelly had his natural home in a frightful darkness where no human being could live.

"Well," said Kelly, after a moment, "not just I." He turned his head towards Dee. "You're in mortal danger, too, John," he said, softly. "You can't do anything about Madinia now; so why not save yourself? Give him this one —the boy as well, if you like. Three should satisfy him."

Dee looked up. Matt, catching hold of Kate, felt as if a strong hand were choking all breath and voice out of him.

"Did you fetch them here for that?" Dee whispered.

"Of course."

Dee turned his back on Kelly, his face waxen in the

45

pallid light. "You have walked further towards the abyss than I dare follow you," he said, his voice dull with exhaustion. "There is no saving you now, Ned—not even Madinia could truly save you now." Then he straightened his shoulders, "But you shan't harm these two! You'll let them go free, back to what's left of their lives—and I can force you, Kelly, you know that!"

"Yes, I know," said Kelly, casually. "I don't mind. It's up to you. One's enough for me." He looked at Matt and Kate, with that upward turn of the lips which was not quite a smile. "You can stop being afraid now, Kate. You too, Matt. My friend here doesn't want me to help him. So you can go home."

Matt let go of Kate, numbly. He longed to be out of the room, with its darkness and sense of half-alive evil in every object. Even the air seemed tainted in here.

"We can't," he said. "We've got to go to where Anna is, and fetch her back."

Kelly's gaze jumped out at him, like a light suddenly switched on.

"Matt!" he said softly. "And you say you're not anxious to die?"

Matt looked back at him, hating him. "We've got to get Anna back," he said.

"You've a low opinion of Cernunnos, then," Kelly said, "if you think you can wrest his due from him without even giving him anything in return." His gaze held Matt, glinting a little. "Unless you're thinking of offering him an exchange . . ." he said, and his eyes slid smiling towards Kate.

Kate grabbed Matt's hand. "Shut up!" she cried savagely. "You make me sick!"

"You don't have to come, Kate," Matt said, feeling sick himself at Kelly's words. He wrenched his eyes away from the man, and looked down at Kate. "You go home, Kate," he said. "One of us had better stay."

46

"No!" said Kate, with decision. Her hand tightened on Matt's and there was a look of appeal on her face. "I'm not going to be afraid any more, Matt," she said resolutely. "We mustn't split up again."

"You will be afraid, you know." Kelly came forward, watching Kate with lurking delight. "Some people go mad with horror, even before they see him."

Matt wouldn't look at him. "Doctor," he said.

Dee turned his head, his eyes sombre with foreboding.

"Will you help us?" Matt asked.

Pain flickered across the man's face like a flame, and his eyes flinched away from Matt with a look of desperation. Matt stared, not understanding.

"Doctor!" Kate cried, incredulously.

Kelly smiled. "He dares not," he said, with measured relish. "Why, Kate, Cernunnos owns his soul too. He'll go no closer to him than I would."

Dee's face, turned away, was hidden in shadow. "It is true," his voice said, on a low cadence of grief. "My life is in fee to the Horned One. I know enough to be able to contain him without offering him another's life like you, brave Kelly; but Matt, Kate—I dare not approach him."

"Oh!" Kate couldn't repress a bitter murmur of despair. "We'll never do it on our own, Matt!"

"We've got to," Matt said. All the darkness in the room seemed to have gathered in a load on his shoulders. "You don't have to come, Kate. I can go by myself."

"Oh, stop saying that!" Kate snapped. "I've said I'm coming!"

"It's foolishness, Matt!" Kelly said gently. "What could you do? You'll only die, both of you, and no good'll come of it." He paused, but Matt refused to look at him. "You're a strange lad," Kelly mused softly, "so set on death."

"Enough!" Dee turned, heavily. "Who are you to preach failure, Kelly? These two are not steeped in self;

they do not look for unholy gains, out of ambition; they seek only what was theirs.'' Dee stared at Kelly, the blue eyes looking older and stained. ''Send them,'' he said, shortly. ''There lies the only hope left for you.''

''Well,'' Kelly shrugged, lightly. ''You always did preach better than me. Come on, then, you two—I've got another drink for you, and no phantom this time.''

Matt and Kate stood silent as Kelly moved towards the great cabinet. They watched as he opened two of the drawers and took from each a small dark phial. He set out two metal cups and poured in a drop from each phial, then mixed in water from a glass jar.

Dee picked up one of the cups and lifted it to sniff at the contents. ''What's this?'' he said, in a low voice. They could see disgust on his face. ''Aconite and belladonna?''

Kate stiffened. ''That's poison!'' she whispered.

Kelly smiled. ''Courage, Kate—it's the least you've got to face.'' He looked round at Dee, the smile glinting. ''They mustn't struggle,'' he murmured, ''or Cernunnos alone knows what'd happen.''

Without a word, Dee set the cup down again. Kelly picked it up, and held them out, one in each hand.

''Take one sip,'' he said. ''It may be enough. It's not strong enough to do much harm.'' He smiled again, as both Matt and Kate hesitated. ''Come on—two minutes ago you were eager enough to die!'' he said, softly. ''I'll wish you a good journey to the Castle of Bones if it'll make any difference.''

Matt came forward and took one of the cups, Kate following suit. He had no feelings left as he lifted the cup to his lips and smelt the odd, medicine-like smell; he was conscious only of Dee standing there silent, and of a resentful little grudge against him for refusing to help. He sipped the stuff, and it vanished in his mouth, leaving a foul taste. Over the lip of the cup, he felt Dee's eyes on him.

All weight slipped from his body and it swooped upwards in the air. There were faces around him and laughter in his ears, as if he had been caught up to fly with a great company through the sky.

4

DID THE LORD OF LIGHT SEND YOU, OR HIS SHADOW?

His head seemed to be spinning meaninglessly, like a dropped coin, and all he was aware of at first were the violently intense smells of earth, live wood and rotting leaf-mould. A greenish twilight swayed about him, and under him it was soft and slimy. Suddenly, he was very sick. When that was over he stayed still, shivering, until at last he could look up and see where he was.

Giant trees marched away into dimness, their roots buried in drifts of dead leaves. The summer foliage was so thick that there was hardly any light, and the girths of the trees were immense; the oak nearest him, fantastically gnarled, could have hidden three men behind its trunk.

He listened, hard. There was nothing, apart from the clamour of birds high above—songbirds, magpies, crows, doves—and in his nostrils there were only the forest smells. No hum of distant cars or drone of aeroplanes, no tang of hot tarmac roads. He had never felt so lost, so disoriented.

He got up, unsteadily. Layer upon layer of soft dead leaves covered the forest floor, studded here and there with bright orange fungi. Twigs and broken branches were scattered about, but there was next to no undergrowth, too little sunlight penetrated that roof of living leaves.

He turned towards what looked like a glimmer of sky between the trees. The humus sank under his feet and he felt weak and giddy, but a few steps brought him out on to the edge of a clearing. The ground, bright green with grass, dipped down to a pond, and there were yellow flowers growing.

Still he didn't know where he was. Somewhere, beyond these gigantic oaks, there might be houses and people. He looked for a way to climb one of the trees. Nearby a young sapling was half unrooted as if the earth had moved under it, and in falling it had tangled itself in the branches of a massive oak. It hung slanting there like a ladder. Gingerly, he approached it and began scrambling up. Normally he enjoyed climbing, but now he felt giddy and sore, and he was afraid of falling.

He reached the majestic branches of the oak, and the craggy greyish bark felt reassuring under his hands. It was easy to climb, the branches going up like a staircase; soon the forest spread out beneath him and, astride a high limb, he could feel the wind on his face and the leaves moving round him. But his heart was sinking.

There was nothing to see—nothing but the ancient forest, endless, furrowed with wind, rising and dipping until far away it met the horizon. Here and there were bright flashes of green grass in between the trees, and brown water threaded and pooled everywhere, cutting the forest up into a confusing mass of islands. Above him grey and umber clouds chased across the sky. But there was no trace of humanity—only flocks of birds, flinging themselves vociferously over the trees, and, below, the stealthy scuffles of little animals and the abrupt crashing sounds of bigger ones.

He began to descend, feeling sorer and weaker and not knowing what on earth he was to do. The smell of the humus met him as he climbed down from the sapling, and it seemed like the smell of fear and defeat. But there was something he had to do. He glanced back into the gloom of the forest.

"Kate!" he shouted.

His voice cracked, raw and unrecognizable. He cleared his throat and tried again.

"Kate!"

There was no answer. A crow began jeering. He turned back into the forest, dizzy and sick, and began looking for Kate.

He had no idea where to look; inside him, his mind lay shocked and motionless like something wounded. He only knew that amongst the trees there should be someone called Kate, but as he repeated the word to himself, no corresponding picture rose in his mind. Kate. What was Kate? He tried to move quietly, remembering those crashing sounds, and in the dimness a squirrel bolted away from him, red tail flying.

Suddenly, it went dark. It was as if all the trees had clenched their branches together in a solid roof; and the birds fell silent.

He blinked through the dark, trying to see. Was this night? There were places where night fell at once, without any dusk—but no, looking back towards the clearing he saw light still shining on it, yellow and baleful.

He felt sweat running down his body, and the air was thick and stuffy. He must get out, into the open air. The trees were choking him. He stumbled back towards the clearing, and lost his balance as he lurched out on to the green ground; it was spongy, giving under him like a mattress.

He got to his feet again, panting. The air was no better, wrapping around him like a smothering blanket. Above, a single black cloud covered the entire sky, with only one or two breaks; light poured through these, making the darkness seem worse. But the grass glowed green and fresh, and he started down towards the cool brown water.

He sank at once to his waist in the earth.

He heard himself cry out, an inarticulate yell of shock, and a crowd of rooks shot headlong across the sky, as if fleeing for shelter. The mud beneath that fresh green carpet sucked at him deliberately, and he could feel himself being drawn down. His mouth opened, gasping for air. Fool! Idiot! Anyone with a grain of sense could have seen that water and the bright green meant swamp!

He dared not struggle, knowing instinctively that the mud would suck him under the quicker. Slowly, carefully, he arched his head back, trying to stretch away from the mud; slowly he drew in a deep breath, then opened his mouth and yelled as hard as he could.

"Help!"

Even that drove him deeper. He was up to his chest, spreading his arms out in a vain attempt to float. It was no good. There were no people to hear him, only birds to chatter at him from the trees. He gasped for breath, heart hammering; he was done for.

Suddenly the darkness split with a blaze of lightning. Thunder crashed about his ears, and rain came down in solid sheets. The forest vanished behind it as he sank deeper and deeper, the mud climbing up to his throat. Then at last the shock brought his mind out of its paralysis —he knew again that he was Matt Cooper; pictures of the laboratory, of Dee and Kelly, flickered before him; he knew he had been sent to a place called Otherworld, where Anna was held prisoner, and Kate was his friend, lost here too and needing him. With a last effort, he shouted again.

"Help!"

Only his head and his hands still stuck out of the mud; something light and rough hit his left hand. He grabbed it at once. A rope! Gasping for precious breath, he lunged through the swamp to get hold of it with his right hand too, and for an instant thought the mud would close over his head. But the rope was pulled and, his grip locked on it, he came up out of the morass; he felt the beating rain on his shoulders, and another great flash of lightning showed a figure crouching beneath one of the towering oaks, the other end of the rope in its hands. The flash dazzled him, but he felt the next strong pull and even through the thunder heard the hiccuping sound of the mud loosing its hold on him. His knees met more solid ground, and ridged bark scraped his arms; at last he found himself lying safe between two massive roots of the oak tree.

He felt too limp to move, and lay still as the rain dropped in splashes from the branches above, washing some of the mud away. He seemed to lie there a long time, but at last he became aware of light before his eyes, and the returning sound of the birds.

Weakly, he pushed himself up into a sitting position. What a mess he was in! The storm had ended as abruptly as it had begun, leaving a shining sky above the forest. Behind him, the green carpet had closed over the top of the swamp again, and with its yellow marsh flowers was looking as innocent and lovely as a springtime glade at home. The pool had swollen to twice its size.

He looked round, eagerly, for the man who had pulled him out; then he stared, for he could see nobody. The trees loomed, cutting out the light, and in the dimness there was nothing alive but himself.

"Hey!" he called, not believing the man could have gone far.

There was no answer, except for the jabber of birds.

Incredulously, Matt looked down at the rope which he still held in his hand. Underneath the coating of mud, he could see it was made of twisted plant fibres. He pulled it towards him, beginning to coil it, to see how long it was. At once it went taut. Six feet away a mouldering tree-stump held on to it; it turned its head, and Matt looked into eyes such as no man ever had.

The thing was the colour of mud. It had long, skinny arms, with hands like spiders, and legs like sticks; the hair was as brown and slimy as dead river-weed, the nose flat, the mouth lipless and full of pointed yellow teeth. There was no visible white to the eyes; they were the colour of dull amber, and the pupils were oval, like a cat's.

Matt choked back a yell as the creature rose, tall, and padded over to him. A knife of flaked stone was thrust towards his throat, and he pressed himself back against the tree, the rope slipping from his fingers. For the second time he thought he was about to die; but the knife came no nearer than an inch or so. After a heart-stopping pause, he began to breathe more slowly, and at last ventured to look up at the botched face. The amber eyes regarded him steadily. As if from far away, a voice came.

"Did the Lord of Light send you, or his Shadow?"

It was not human speech; it was a wild, brown sort of voice, as if an owl had spoken, and the words were a different shape. But to his amazement Matt could understand it, though he didn't know what its words meant.

"What?" he said hoarsely.

The eyes flickered, dangerously. "Did the Shadow send you?" it said, and the stone blade moved a fraction closer.

"I don't know who the Shadow is," Matt said hastily. "Or the—the Lord of Light. I've come to find someone. Her sister came with me, but she's lost too."

"Sister? That other?"

Matt's eyes widened. "Other? D'you mean you know where she is? Where?"

The dull amber eyes were steady, unblinking. The pupils narrowed a little. "The Lord of Light sent her," said the creature. "She is lily-white."

Matt stared, and nausea rose in him. Had Kate been captured by *this*? Then, as he struggled to make his face impassive, he smelt it.

He would have expected a filthy stink from that muddy

55

hide, but he was wrong. The smell was like a wood after rain—clear, and faintly fresh.

He looked at it again. The horror lay in its being so man-like, yet so unlike any man. It was taller than him, and skinny; but, if it had pulled him out of the swamp, it wasn't lacking in strength.

It had, after all, saved his life.

"Please," he said huskily, "will you take me to her?"

"Yes," said the brown voice, "it will please her when she wakes. She will thank me. Get up, and be silent. If you are of the Shadow, I will kill you later. Come."

It watched him as he got carefully to his feet, and coiled up the rope in its hands. Then it turned, without a sound, and Matt followed it as best he could into the forest.

It was hard to follow, for its mud-coloured skin blended almost invisibly into the shadowy gloom of the forest. Twice Matt nearly mistook it again for a tree-stump. He tried not to make such a noise through the leaves, for the creature moved quite silently; it seemed to be picking definite paths, tortuously winding and indistinguishable to Matt. Tree after tree loomed up and was left behind, all seeming the same. Then Matt dislodged a mouldering branch from under his feet; it rolled only six inches to his left, splashed and sank, leaving a dark gap in the single layer of leaves that had hidden thick swamp water. Matt felt the sweat start out of his brow, and as he went on he strained his eyes after the creature, to see where it was putting its feet. So that was why their course was such a meander; there could be hardly any safe ground in the forest.

At last they came out upon one of the brown rivulets. The creature stooped and dragged out from beneath some overhanging rushes what looked like a canoe. It had a wicker frame covered with a sort of leather—animal hides, Matt supposed.

"Get in," said the creature.

Matt obeyed, stepping in gingerly. The flimsy thing would have capsized with his weight, but the creature's wiry arms held it still as he squatted down. Then, easily, it stepped in without so much as disturbing the balance, knelt down in the prow and began to ply a wooden paddle.

The marshland slipped past swiftly as the canoe threaded through its waters. It was a strange country, neither land nor sea; one moment they would be nosing their way down a channel hidden under a roof of trees, rushes brushing the canoe either side, and the next speeding down a broad sparkling waterway, moorhens rising with alarmed cries to flap away and hide in the surrounding marsh grass. The sky was the same, brilliant and stormy with confounding alternation. Matt, afraid to move in case the canoe overturned, wondered about Kate and Anna. Was Kate safe? And how would they ever find Anna, without being swallowed up in the marsh first?

The canoe glided to a halt beneath dark trees whose roots went down into the water. The creature climbed deftly out on to one of the massive roots, toes gripping like a monkey's. Matt followed, cautiously, hardly able to see in the gloom; above, thunder was rumbling again. The rope snaked up from the creature's hand and wrapped itself round a shadowy branch.

"Climb," it said, "and to not fall, or between two heartbeats you will sink."

Steadying himself against the great trunk, Matt felt his mouth go dry. He could hardly see the ground, but it lay under him like an enemy, willing him to fall.

"You live in a tree—over this?" he said hoarsely, more to give his nerve time than for any other reason.

"Do you think I live in a hole, like a Fomor?" the creature said, and Matt saw its teeth in the gloom. "Follow," it said, and went up the side of the trunk like mist.

Matt gripped the rope and pulled himself up, scrabbling for footholds on the side of the tree. He had lost both shoes in the swamp, and the bark hurt his feet, but, just before his toes slipped and left him dangling by his hands from the rope, the creature's fingers closed around his arm and heaved him up on to the broad branch.

He got his breath again, feeling himself safe at least for the moment. There in the crook of three great branches a light shelter was built on a platform, quite solid and steady. The creature lifted a leather door-flap and Matt crawled inside after it.

It was dark inside, but after a few moments Matt began to make out the shapes. The shelter was a kind of wicker-work, like the canoe, but the sticks were woven tightly together and mud plastered over to make solid walls and roof. The dim forest light filtered through chinks here and there.

Close to him, the creature sat motionless. On the other side of the hut, Matt began to see a paleness. He realised it was fair hair.

"Kate!" he whispered, crawling over to her.

She was unconscious, still, and so cold that Matt thought she was dead. Kneeling by her side with one muddy hand touching her arm, he began to despair. Probably Anna was dead too, by now, and what good was it to be the only one left?

Then the creature leaned past him and laid a leaf on Kate's lips. Matt stared, wondering why—then almost imperceptibly the leaf stirred.

She was breathing. She was alive.

"She has come on the road that is not to be trodden," said the creature, as if to itself. "But she lives."

It turned and crawled outside. The leaf fluttered again on Kate's lips, and Matt began to chafe one of her hands, hard, trying to bring the warmth back.

Presently, he smelt wood-smoke, and realised from the

crackling sound that the creature had lit a fire out there on the platform. He wished it could have lit it in here, to warm Kate; then, as he went on rubbing her hands, another fresher smell drifted in. At last the creature came crawling back inside, carrying a rough wooden bowl from which the fragrance steamed. The spidery hand went behind Kate's head and lifted her, and put the bowl to her lips.

The smell alone was heartening. Matt, still aching in every limb, wet from the swamp and sore footed, seemed to feel better and less tired. It was like breathing in life. After a moment, he saw Kate swallow.

She swallowed again and, feebly, her eyes opened. Matt was in front of her, and he was glad she couldn't see the mud-coloured thing crouching behind her head.

"Are you all right, Katie? Do you feel better?" he whispered.

She didn't answer, as the creature still pressed the bowl to her lips. She drank some more, and then it let her lie back again on the rush pillow, and gave the bowl to Matt.

"Finish it," said its voice.

Kate started back against the wall, eyes, huge with fright, on that unmanlike face. Her hand went to her mouth to stop a scream.

"It's all right, Kate!" Matt seized her other hand. "It's saved both our lives. It's not going to hurt you."

Sitting there, the creature looked with its steady amber eyes at the two pale faces. Slowly, it shifted, and Matt saw it go on to its knees; then it bent forward until its forehead touched the floor.

"Do not fear me, white flower," said its voice. "I serve you. I have served the Lord of Light himself, and run from the Shadow."

Kate looked at Matt. "Where are we?" she whispered, her voice no more than a breath.

"I don't know," Matt whispered back. "It's a kind of

marshland. There aren't any people. It pulled me out of a swamp—I'd have drowned otherwise—and brought me here. It'd already got you."

There was a moment's pause, then Kate said "Oh!" and Matt saw memory snap back in her eyes. "Oh, the house, and those two, and the drink—Matt, wasn't it horrible?"

"Do you feel all right now?"

"Yes," Kate said cautiously. She pointed to the bowl. "That stuff's good, actually."

Matt lifted the bowl to his mouth and drank what was left. The taste was fresh and astringent, and after only a moment he felt the pain and weariness begin to ebb.

Kate looked at the crouching creature, on the other side of the hut. The thought of its face made her shudder; but it had called her "white flower" and bowed to her, and seemed to mean no harm. "Who are you?" she said, bracing herself.

"I am the Dulachan," the voice said.

"What?" Kate frowned, unable to make out the word.

"The Dulachan," said the creature. It was less of a word than a soft faraway sound. "Once there were many of us, white flower, as white and innocent as you; we dived in the streams and ate only weeds and grass. But the world changed; others came; and now I am the only one left. The land became swamp and stained my skin brown, and these others hunt me and hate me, and call me monster. And truly I am a monster, for I have lived too long; my wits wander in this world of bright swords and anger. I am like a stone axe, which breaks under the blow of bronze."

"Dulachan," Kate repeated uncertainly. The rest made little sense to her. "Is that your name?"

"No." The creature straightened, slowly, and its amber gaze looked at Kate. "I have no name. Once I had, but too long ago. I have forgotten it."

"You can't forget your own name!"

60

"There have been none to use it. I am the only Dula-chan. There are no others."

Matt said, "What about the Fomors?"

In the dark, they felt the creature stiffen. Then it turned its head and the amber eyes fastened on Matt with a dangerous rolling flash. *"What do you know of them?"* its voice hissed.

"Nothing," said Matt, hastily. "Only Kelly—someone said they'd hidden Kate's sister "in the Mound." And then you said something about them, before we climbed up here—about them living in holes."

"So they do." The Dulachan's voice grew quieter, but the grim eyes stayed unchanging on Matt. "There is a fair land beyond the western sky. The Fomors lived there long ago, but the Children of Danu came also, and the Fomors would not live in peace. So Danu's Children drove them into the Mounds, to live out of their sight."

Matt swallowed; the words were harmless enough, but the hunch of the creature's shoulders and the glare of its eyes seemed to be saying different, deadlier words to him. He tried to take no notice. You couldn't expect this ancient thing to act like a human being. "Are they here too?" he asked. "The Fomors, I mean?"

"They are everywhere. Some say that they came first from the sea, and that they still graze their cattle on seaweed beneath the waves. Many a night I have heard the lowing of beasts without seeing a single one on the land." The amber eyes glowed faintly.

"You couldn't keep cattle in a swamp," Kate said.

"There are islands in the swamp, white flower." The Dulachan's gaze never moved from Matt. "They rise like hump-backed beasts from the mud. There are doors in those Mounds, it is said, which lead to the Fomors' world."

Matt swallowed again. "We have to go there," he said, "and fetch Anna."

The beast-like eyes went on looking at him, fixing him in a dark ray of silence.

"Yes, and quick, before the—the Devil gets her," Kate said huskily. "Will you show us the Mound, Dulachan?"

"Hush, white flower." Still its eyes never shifted. "You should not be listening to this one. The Shadow sent him —I knew it from the first—to make you mad like the night, like the moon which steals away men's wits. I should have let him drown in the swamp."

"No!" cried Kate, and saw the stone knife in its hands. She flung herself forward and gripped the skinny wrists with all her strength; the Dulachan froze instantly, and at last its eyes left Matt and looked down at her.

Kate's mouth grew dry. The mud-coloured skin wasn't slimy and loathsome, as she'd expected; but she felt dreadfully close to those pointed teeth. "Listen!" she said, speaking out over the crack in her voice. "You mustn't hurt Matt. He's my friend, he's on my side. He didn't *make* me come here. He didn't even want me to, but he couldn't stop me! We're both here to find my sister, Anna; she's in the—the Fomors' Mound, and we've got to go and get her!" She stared desperately at the brown face, willing it to understand.

Fists clenched, Matt did the same. He dared not move, but he was afraid to see Kate so close to the great, brown, shadowy creature; in front of it she looked like a cut jewel.

The Dulachan's mouth was moving, as if in pain or illness. After a moment, Kate let go of it and sat back on her heels.

"We've got to go to the Mound, Dulachan," she said determinedly.

"It is death, white flower."

"We've got to!" Kate insisted. "It's what we came for."

"The Fomors are not such as you, white flower; they deal in darkness and evil dreams. Each one has a cap and while he wears it he fears nothing, for its power has no bounds. Their blood is as cold as fishes'. They have no mercy. They will kill you with their faces turned away and throw you into the swamp for the Horned One to take.'' The Dulachan's voice sank low; it turned its own head away, dully, as if already it saw Kate dead in the mud.

Kate looked round at Matt, biting her lip.

''I don't see what else we can do,'' Matt said, in a low voice. ''We came to find Anna. We can't give up now we've got this far.''

''Suppose we do find her,'' Kate whispered, ''how do we get back?''

Matt was silent. That question had been nagging at him ever since the Dulachan had saved him from the swamp. He could see no answer to it. Kelly wouldn't have sent them unless he was sure they could die here.

''There must be a way,'' he said at length. ''Doctor Dee wouldn't have let Kelly send us if he didn't think we could get back safe.''

''He sold his soul too,'' Kate said in a hard little voice. ''Suppose he just sent us for Cernunnos to have, as well—''

''Do not speak that name, white flower!''

The Dulachan's voice rushed like wind round their ears. Matt saw the huge appalled eyes; its hands came up to hide them, the stone knife rattling to the floor. ''What are you!'' it moaned, hunching up. ''You, who talk fearlessly of the Fomors, and now speak that name aloud, without care or trembling! He does not sleep here. This is his own country; he holds all beings in fear, and draws the Fomors forth from their Mound. Do not speak his name, white flower. Do not call him!''

Kate was silent, aghast. Matt folded his arms round his chest to contain his battering heart.

''Who is he, Dulachan?'' he whispered. ''They told us he was the Devil.''

"I do not understand all your words," it said, the owl-voice thin and faint from behind its hands. "Be silent! The Horned One is not his names. He does not live as a man lives; he is, and he goes to and fro across the earth like the tides, or a star across the sky. He does not speak, he does not hear; he does not know there is such a thing as himself; but, if you open your heart to him, he will come in his might. Do not think of him, white flower! Let your mind edge round him with unclear names that never touch him!"

Kate was shuddering.

Matt said huskily. "I'll go to the Mound, Kate. You stay here with the Dulachan.

"No!" said Kate, turning to look at him. Matt opened his mouth to insist, then saw the trembling glitter of her eyes and looked past her at the dreadful hunched shape. Yes. Even if the alternative meant facing Cernunnos, she couldn't stay alone with this thing. She was right. They mustn't split up.

"All right," he said instead. "We'd better go, then."

"Come on, Dulachan," Kate said, more quietly. "You've got to show us the way."

The hands fell and the amber eyes looked mutely at Kate.

"Do not go, white flower."

"We've got to!" Kate said forcefully. "We've made up our minds. Now come on, we can't find the Mound without you." She took its arm briefly, giving it a pull; and, casting its gaze downward, the Dulachan crawled outside. Kate followed, and after her went Matt.

The Dulachan let down the rope and vanished into the dimness below. Kate looked over her shoulder at Matt.

"I'm not going to be afraid, Matt," she said. "There's no point. If we get scared and start making mistakes we're going to get killed."

Matt wished he could take decisions in the same definite

way. Kate had a strength he could never understand. "I can't help being afraid," he said. "But I couldn't just—*leave* Anna. Or you."

Kate's fingers sought his and gave them a quick sisterly squeeze. Surprised, Matt followed her down the rope to where the Dulachan waited silently with the canoe.

They climbed in, gingerly, and as soon as they had knelt down the Dulachan began to paddle the boat swiftly away through the marsh. Kate shivered as they came out of the gloomy trees on to a windy marsh, where grass and brilliant flowers grew on a thin carpet over black swamp water. Above them, birds called desolately; she looked up, and saw they were seagulls.

"We must be near the sea, Matt!" she said.

Matt nodded. The cry of the gulls was just the same above Aunt Phyllis's house, back in their own, safe world.

"Kate," he said in a low voice, "do you think we've travelled back in time?"

"Back to ancient Britain, you mean?" Kate considered the idea, frowning. At length she shook her head. "I don't know. *He* said something about a place called Otherworld. I suppose it could just be another time . . . maybe it's the same thing, really. But"—she nodded towards the Dulachan's turned back—"what I don't see is how we and that thing can understand each other," she said lowering her voice.

Matt knew what she meant. The Dulachan's queer brown voice was so different from theirs that it seemed to be speaking another language.

"Kelly must have given us the power to," he said.

"Maybe," said Kate. "Or maybe if you travel back through time you sort of travel back through language as well. I don't know." She shrugged, and looked back at the wheeling gulls.

Matt was silent too, aware that there was really no way to explain what had happened to them. But, wherever they were, it made nonsense to call this place the past; it was real, it was here and now.

"Look, Matt, there's the sea," said Kate.

Matt followed her gaze, hearing it now, and smelling the salty freshness. The sun was low in the sky, and there to the west, through a gap in the trees, he could see the glittering silver coming up to the flat marsh. On a high tide, he thought, the whole marsh would be flooded, for there was nothing to stop the sea.

Only in that one place was the horizon open; and, as the Dulachan paddled on, the great tree closed the gap. To the south, the forest was around them again, with only one landmark.

A round hill stood up, bare of trees except for a clump of seven on the top. It looked strange in the flat marsh; and, although the sun was an hour off sinking, a darkness hung round it as if every side was in shadow. The Dulachan paused, trailing the paddle in the water.

"On that hill you could not escape from Fomors," it whispered, as if afraid even at that distance. "It stands where Belisama's river joins the sea, and looks towards the western land which the Fomors lost." It looked over its shoulder, the amber eyes sick and heavy. "Only the Children of Danu, with their iron swords which the Fomors fear, could enter such a place and live."

Kate said, in a low voice, "Matt, if this is a different time, could we be killed in it?"

"I don't suppose so," said Matt, remembering the Dulachan's knife at his throat and thinking otherwise.

"May the Lord of Light protect you," said the Dulachan, the brown voice dry and far off. "The boat cannot go closer. The ground is safe from here."

Matt climbed from the frail boat on to land that was soft, but firm under his feet. Kate got out after him, and turned to look down into the great pleading amber eyes.

"Goodbye, Dulachan," she said.

"I will listen," said the Dulachan, "and if you leave the Mound alive, I will know. White flower . . ."

The forest seemed very quiet.

"May the Lord of Light protect you," the wild voice whispered again. The paddle dipped, and the canoe slid away along the brown water, soon hidden by the trees and the trailing clumps of marsh grass.

"Come on," said Kate, and they turned towards the round hill.

There seemed to be a kind of path, as if the whole forest radiated from it like a force field. They could feel it grow quieter with every step they took, and Matt noticed how no bird ever flew to any of those seven young pines which stood like a crown on the hilltop. Almost before they were aware, they were standing at the base. It was more of a mound than a true hill, rising round and regular just above the crests of the forest trees, and as quiet and cold as the moon.

"How do we get in?" Kate whispered.

"I don't know." Matt could see no opening in the smooth turf. "Maybe at the top." He began to scramble up the steep side of the Mound, Kate following.

It blew chill at the top, and the trees were withered from the salt wind. The sun, low in the west, shone clear and lovely from the other side of the sea, and Matt thought of the fair land the Dulachan had spoken of. Here the desolate mud, looking treacherous, spread from the trees out to the waves, and, looking a short way to the south, Matt saw the line of a river opening out to a broad estuary, fringed by the same bare mud. The gulls flew above, but never landed on it.

Kate said, "I wish we could see just one house!"

Matt nodded, knowing what she meant. It was hard to be so remote from all humankind, deep in this savage forest. But nothing human belonged here; if they had come back in time, perhaps it was to a time before men, or to a place too desolate for them to penetrate.

They began to look for a way to get into the hills. After a while Matt was convinced it was useless; how could anything, human or not, live underneath a hill? The green turf was smooth, like grass anywhere, without even a rabbit hole. The pines seemed to be whispering with amusement at his search.

"Matt!" Kate whispered urgently.

Matt turned to see her crouching on the ground, near the mound's base. He scrambled down to her, and looked at what she had found.

It was a crack in the hillside. A wicker frame covered over with pieces of turf, indistinguishable from the hill, was set in there like a door. His heart pounding, Matt put his eye to the crack.

He could see nothing, only feel, at once, a great quietness. It was totally black—but no; was that a faint light? It was his imagination, surely. No, there definitely was a patch of paleness there, far away, like the memory of a star; yes—there was light. It was glowing softly, upon a white face, with closed eyes and a sort of waxen stillness so much more still than sleep. And it was Anna's face.

Then he was seized by the shoulders and thrown before he had time to cry out. He fell through the door into the dark, Kate's scream ringing in his ears as he crashed to the ground at the feet of a man.

But it was no common man, it was more like a pygmy. He stood less than five feet high, wrapped in a cloak and on his head was a leather cap. His face was completely in shadow.

Two more of them came, thrusting Kate to the ground with her arms pinned behind her. "Stop it!" she cried. "Matt . . ."

Matt tried to rise, but the Fomor set a foot in his chest, and at once total weakness invaded his limbs. Small as the Fomors was, his foot pinned Matt to the ground. The three pygmies stood in silence for a full minute, a silence so dense and heavy that not a single word would come to Matt's lips. Then another came out of the dimness, carrying a coil of rope. Their cold, strong hands forced Matt's arms behind his back and though he tried to struggle his wrists were quickly lashed together, then his ankles, so that he lay helpless. Kate lay beside him, similarly trussed; and, still without a word, the four Fomors turned and walked away into the gloom.

Beside Kate, Anna lay. Her arms and legs were free, but she lay unconscious, unable to help them. Kate's eyes, huge and frightened, sought Matt's and they both listened helplessly to the great silence underneath the hill.

They lay on straw, spread over a floor of sand. Matt could just see the glimmer of the crack in the hillside, far above them. The faint light seemed concentrated round him, Kate and Anna, so that he could see their faces, but nothing else, not even the walls of their prison.

"Listen," whispered Kate.

Matt could hear nothing. But, like Kate, he knew there were people there. They moved in the darkness, invisibly and silently, but with a presence that could be felt as surely as if they were seen. So they were the prisoners of this people; and out in the swamp the Horned One waited for them.

5

None Ever Wish to Leave Lochlann

"Wake Anna up," Matt whispered desperately.

Kate wriggled closer to Anna's unconscious form and jogged her, clumsily. "Anna! Anna, *wake up!*" she hissed. She prodded her with her feet.

It was no good. Anna's eyes remained closed, and not a muscle of her face stirred.

"Is she alive?" Matt whispered, not knowing whether to hope or not.

"Dunno. Wait a minute," Laboriously, Kate inched over on to her knees, pulling herself up until she was kneeling upright. She edged closer to Anna and, just managing to keep her balance, bent to put her ear to Anna's chest. Matt watched her wide, listening eyes.

"Yes," she breathed, at length. "I can hear her heart." She looked back at Matt, beginning to straighten again. "She's in some sort of trance—oh!" She lost her balance, toppling down on to her back. "Ouch!" Her face twisted with pain.

"What's the matter?" Matt managed to sit up.

"It's all right. It's that stupid old knife. The handle dug right into my back." Kate sat up, grimacing, and Matt saw, attached to her belt, the sheath knife that his father had given him, years ago, one summer when he went camping with the Scouts. It was like being hit in the face.

He remembered Kate appropriating it after he'd left the Scouts.

"Will it still cut?" he whispered, hardly believing their luck.

"Oh! Oh, *yes!*" Kate's eyes opened wide, and she reached for the haft with her bound hands. Her right hand closed around it and, bending forward, she managed to pull it out.

The blade was dull and spotted here and there with rust, but it looked still to have an edge. Kate and Matt wriggled round back to back and Kate, twisting her head round to see what she was doing, began to saw at Matt's bonds. One strand parted, then another. The blade wasn't sharp, but these grass ropes had no chance against it. Slowly the tension of the bounds relaxed. Matt pulled against them, and suddenly his wrists were free.

He quickly grabbed the knife to cut the ropes round his ankles; then, without knowing why, he froze. Gripping the knife behind his back, he looked up.

A Fomor was sitting there, watching. The mysterious light hung in a globe round him, and Matt could see his face; he had never seen anything so grotesque. Dead white, the forehead a great dome, the nose a beak—the bones looked paper thin, the skin stretched gauntly over them. Matt jogged Kate, urgently.

She looked round and gave a gasp. About ten feet away the Fomor sat motionless, cloak falling back to show a smock-like shirt and belted trousers. On his head was a small green cap. He was looking at them, but his eyes were like holes in paper, quite empty; yet there was something menacing in their gaze.

"Who are you?" Matt said, but his voice seemed to lose itself in the silence. His hand closed tighter and tighter on the knife behind his back. The Fomor never moved. It might have been a statue watching them.

Matt dragged his gaze away and looked round at Kate.

Her eyes were wide and listening. She sat quite still, unaware of Matt's gaze; perplexed, he strained his ears, but there was only the silence.

"Kate," he whispered, and jogged her again.

She looked round at him, remotely, busy with what she was hearing. "Listen," she whispered impatiently.

"What to?"

"Listen *inside your head.*" Her eyes turned away from him again.

What was she talking about? Tension knotted tighter in Matt; he looked back at the Fomor, the white face glowering like a starved hawk's. He looked hard into those empty eyes, and all at once his mind seemed to lose its footing and teeter against something, something that broke through—then he knew what Kate meant. Shapes grew and moved inside his head, without colour or words; it was a terrifying language.

"*. . . no escape from the Mound. You may think your-selves brother and sister of the sun, sky-treaders, wind-walkers; but once inside the Mound you will never again be free.*"

Matt's chest heaved, gasping, as the echo died turbulently away inside his head. For a moment, he couldn't think. He didn't understand.

"What do you mean?" he said at last, barely conscious of his own voice as the silence pressed down on him.

The empty eyes looked at him, and now there seemed to be something bitter and taunting in their emptiness.

"*I forgot. The Children of Light have always need of explanations. None of you can be silent in the face of the dark. Ask what you will, son of sky. I will answer if it pleases me.*"

Matt took a hold on himself, getting his breath. This was the worst yet, down here in the dark in front of those malignant eyes; it was bewildering, senseless, like a nightmare that wouldn't stop. But even dreams must have some

72

rules; if he could find out what they were, perhaps he would be able to stop it.

"What do you want with us?" he said, as steadily as he could.

"We want nothing with you. You are for Cernunnos."

"Why?"

"Because you are from the sky, and we of the dark hate you. We will choke the bright air from you with a noose, and lay you under the swamp; and, unsleeping, you will know that darkness is more powerful. Cernunnos will take you."

Matt heard Kate choke back a gasp beside him. "But we're nothing to do with him!" she broke out. "He wants —*him*, and Doctor Dee. They're the ones who sold their souls to him, not us!"

A sour sort of gladness seemed to flicker from the Fomor's mind to Matt's. *"They are fools. Is Cernunnos a pedlar, to buy and sell? Whatever tricks they play, he will have them: and we will give him you three as well. In return he will strengthen the power that lies under our caps, until even Danu's Children cannot withstand us. In the end, we will conquer. Then there will be only one vast Mound . . . and great grave."*

The hate was growing stronger, trampling over Matt's mind so that it became harder and harder to think. Beside him, Kate was trembling. He said, thickly, "Who are Danu's Children?"

The empty gaze seemed to narrow, the thin lips to curl slightly. *"It is like the arrogance of the sky-folk. I know my father's name and my father's father's back to the dawn of time. You do not care who you are; you think to be yourselves is enough. It is like you!"*

Matt could feel the sweat beading on his forehead; I can't keep this up much longer, he thought. Blunderingly, he said, "We do care. Tell us."

"I will tell you." The shapes inside Matt's head grew

73

more pointed, with an angry flicker like flames. *"They came from the sky, and took the earth away from us. We had done them no harm. We were the kin of the earth; we climbed out of the sea like otters and gave it our love; it nourished us and in death we returned to it. But the battle of Moytura ended all that. Danu's Children, who never die, with their cold iron swords . . ."*

The shapes faltered, suddenly lost their shape, and Matt shuddered with a great writhe of pain and fear inside his head. He shut his eyes and gradually the agony ebbed, and the hard, bitter shapes crept back.

"In their pride, they claimed the earth for themselves. They bred a new race of men to tread it alongside them— you, the Sky Children. You possess the earth now, while we, its dearest brothers, must hide in the Mounds. Do you wonder that we hate you?"

Matt shifted, leaning his aching head against his knee for a moment. The darkness and hate seethed like a brew round him, and he knew he couldn't stand much more: he, Kate and Anna couldn't survive for long in the Fomor's world. He knew he was afraid, terribly afraid.

But so was the Fomor: *"Danu's Children, with their cold iron swords."* This was one rule he could break. He gripped the knife behind his back; it was Sheffield steel, and steel was made from iron, only a hundred times stronger and sharper. He could feel the Fomor's fear throbbing. Then he whipped the knife out from behind his back and, openly, cut the ropes round his ankles.

"Stop." A black wave of hate and horror filled his head. *"Stop."*

"Oh, Matt, be careful!" Kate gasped.

"We've got to get out of here!" Matt shouted as, struggling to his feet, the silence knotted round him like a stranglehold. The Fomor's *"stop—stop"* raged inside his head, so that he could hardly see where he was going.

74

Blindly, without thinking, he hurled himself at the globe of light.

He crashed into something, there was a flash of light and a twisted, screaming face; and he was slammed on to his back, every muscle wrung with pain as if from an electric shock.

"Matt!" Kate's desperate voice penetrated to him as if from far away; his mind struggled up to it, dazed. "Matt! Get his cap!"

Blindly Matt forced himself up, staggering back towards the patch of light—and saw the Fomor lying still at his feet. The globe of light was fading, rapidly, and there was a livid scar down the side of his face. Matt's right hand, holding the undamaged knife, felt sore and burnt.

He went down to one knee on the ground, stupidly. There was something so limp and useless about that small body; the scar stood out hugely, everything else drained away. Something twisted inside Matt.

"Matt!" Kate's voice came again, trembling with urgency.

Numbly, Matt reached out and snatched away the green leather cap. There was no sense in taking risks. He got up and went back through the dark to Kate. His hand shook as, kneeling down, he cut her free.

"Thank goodness!" she breathed, rubbing her wrists. She gave Matt a look, then said with a hint of sternness, "Are you all right?"

Matt swallowed. He had won. What was the matter with him? "Yes," he said, roughly.

"Good," said Kate, and left it at that. "Now, how do we wake Anna?"

Matt got up, glancing round to where Anna still lay pale and motionless. Whatever triumph there had been ebbed, and he began to feel cold again. "I don't know," he said. He had disarmed only one Fomor—and in this blackness

75

how could they find their way out of the Mound?

Kate knelt down by Anna's side and shook her hard. "Anna! Anna, come on! Wake up!"

It was no good. Matt glanced over his shoulder at the Fomor, but he had vanished, swallowed up in the black. There was only the silence, and that sensation of people crowding invisibly around them. Now he could feel their hate bearing down on him. *No escape from the Mound. . . .*

"She won't wake up, Matt!"

Matt tightened his lips. The second round had been his. He *would not* lose again. But even now the light round Kate was thinning, soon she, and Anna too, would be lost in the black.

There was only one thing left to do. Fingering the soft leather cap, he remembered the Dulachan's whispering words—"its power has no bounds." Slowly, he lifted the cap and placed it on his head.

The noise nearly split his skull. He staggered, clasping hands to his ears and screwing up his eyes against lancing light.

"Lay aside your sword, Iron Man! Aah!"

"Mercy! Mercy!"

"Give back the cap!"

Slowly, he straightened, forcing himself to bear it. There seemed to be a glare of gold all round him; gradually, he resolved it into roof, pillars, walls, all of gold; he stood on a floor of white marble tiles. Darkness had fled with a vengeance. He was in a high hall of gold, the pillars, walls and roof wrought fantastically into flowers, fruit, beasts and queer peering faces, all apparently of solid gold. But it was cold, and there were no windows.

Slowly, he looked down at the Fomors.

He could see them now. A green milling crowd, each one pressing forward to stare at him, then whipping back as if terrified, only to dart forward again; they were like a field of long grass in a storm. On every side, Matt saw grotesque, dead-white faces with carvernously empty eyes. Their garments, flickering as they moved, looked soft and rich, and were finely embroidered, but all were green, a peculiar tone of green that made Matt think of snakes and poison. Their lips were closed, but the turmoil inside his head was more real than sound. His hand reached out to Kate; but it met nothing, and he turned his head, panic-stricken.

He saw her kneeling by Anna on the marble floor; but he could see through them, like ghosts. Kate looked up at him, and consternation grew on the faint shape of her face; her lips moved, but he could hear nothing. Could she see him?

"Kate!" he shouted at the pitch of his lungs. She stared at him like a figure from a dream, and he saw though her face to the curling ivy embroidered on a Fomor's dress behind her.

The clamour dulled to a mumur, and the swirling movement slowed. Matt looked up, his throat thick with dismay. A path parted in the crowd down the whole length of the hall, revealing a dais on which was set a massive golden throne. A Fomor sat there, looking like a doll amidst all that wrought splendour; and the clamour inside Matt's head stilled to a hush.

The eyes that met Matt's were just as empty as all the rest. After a moment the Fomor rose with a proud erectness, stepped down from the throne and came walking through the ranks of the other Fomors towards Matt. He stopped in front of him, small and straight, and Matt looked again into one of those gaunt, unreadable faces. He noticed a thin circlet of gold round the green leather cap.

The silent voice came silver and listless, like a salmon sliding through deep water.

"I am Elatha, Prince of Lochlann. Forgive us, Iron Man. We did not know you were so mighty."

Matt stared, gripping the knife hard, not sure he'd understood. Mighty? In that remote, mechanical tone? And with all those Fomors round him? Involuntarily he lifted the knife, and the crowd rippled away from him with an agonising clench of fear inside his head.

"*Yes, mighty.*" Elatha's mouth twisted with pain, and the shapes of his speech seemed to cringe, sullenly. "*As mighty as any of the Fianna, Iron Man, as mighty as Coohoolan himself; but the strong should show mercy!*"

Matt could feel hate inside the cowering shapes, but he brushed it aside, unable to care for anything except Kate, Kate and Anna. "What's happened to my friends? What have you done to them? I can't see them!" he said desperately, looking away from Elatha and straining his eyes at the two faint forms.

Out of the corner of his eye he saw Elatha's thin white hand lift, pause, and turn indifferently upwards. "*They are left behind in the darkness. They have not your strength, Iron Man. By your might you have won a magic cap, and it has brought you into Tethra's kingdom, which we call Lochlann; look, and see my golden halls.*" The white hand stretched up towards the roof.

Matt's hands tightened to fists. He had broken the rules of one nightmare, but had come into another, worse one. He turned back to Elatha, pointing the blade of the knife at him. "Never mind the golden halls!" he said hoarsely. "I want to go back to my friends!"

Elatha's eyes looked up, the void in them so massive that silence seemed to take Matt by the throat.

"*None ever wish to leave Elatha's halls. A thousand years they have stood here amidst the orchards of Lochlann. Come, Iron Man; let Ethlinn, Balor's daughter, show you the fruit-trees.*"

The narrow white hand stretched out again, and moving to Elatha's side came a Fomor woman.

Matt's first thought was that he couldn't bear it if she touched him. Her brilliant green dress and her black hair, hanging stiffly down her back, made her face cruelly white. She had the same swelling forehead as the first Fomor, but her nose was a narrow spike, and her eyes seemed even emptier, like the bits of sky in between the stars.

He could feel the change when her thoughts entered his head instead of Elatha's. There was less shape to them; they came like a cold, heavy scent.

"Come, Iron Man; come and look on the apple-blossom of Lochlann."

"No!" said Matt. "I want my friends back!"

Like Elatha's her white palm turned slowly upwards. *"They are left behind; they are to be forgotten. Let us be amongst the apple-trees, whence the birds of Rhiannon flew."*

Matt looked up, hands clenching again. The floor under his feet changed from cold smoothness to a dry, fibrous grittiness; and all around him, blotting out the Fomors and the golden halls, grew great white flowers on twisted branches. Matt found himself looking down a row of old, dark trees whose branches, bunched with flowers, hid the sky completely. It was grass under his feet, but it felt coarse and dead. If it was supposed to be apple-blossom on the trees, the flowers were stiff and waxen, and gave off only the graveside scent of yew. He couldn't see Kate and Anna any more.

"In Lochlann you have only to wish, and what you wish for will appear. Such is the power of the cap you wear, Iron Man. In Lochlann there is no regret, no sadness. Every longing is fulfilled."

Matt looked down at the girl. Suddenly the thought entered his mind that if he had lived a thousand years in the dark, till he'd forgotten what a human face looked like, he might think her beautiful. His whole frame shuddered.

"No!" he said hoarsely. "I'm going back home, with

my friends.''

The white hand came out again and her thoughts drifted in his head.

"There is no need to go, Iron Man. If they are so precious, wish for them. They will appear, and bear you company for as long as you will. None ever wish to leave Lochlann.''

Matt felt as if he were choking, and fear spun dizzily in his head. ''I do!'' he shouted, and wildly slashed at the apple-blossom with his knife. ''It's not real,'' he shouted. ''You've just made it up! It *couldn't* be real!''

Abruptly, the white flowers with their bitter scent were gone, and darkness pressed down almost tangibly. Matt could see nothing; then, in front and a little above, Elatha stood.

"Your sight is clear, Iron Man.'' The Fomor's face gleamed clammily white like a fish's belly, and the emptiness of his eyes glared from it.

Matt tried to get his breath, his sore hand throbbing as he gripped the knife harder and harder. ''It's not real,'' he said. The soft leather cap on his head seemed to be growing hard and tight. They had made it up, with these magic caps, constructed the golden hall and the orchard out of wishes; it had no more existence than a dream. They had tried to fool him, as Kelly had fooled him and Kate with the house that wasn't really there. ''It doesn't even look real,'' he said.

"It is a thousand thousand years since the Fomors last walked the earth.'' Hate pulsed in the shapes. *"After such a time your memory may falter too, Iron Man; when you try to call up the scenes you once knew they may come to you deformed and awry; and the beauty of your friends will be the beauty of Ethlinn, Balor's daughter!''*

''No!'' Matt shouted. ''I'm not staying here!''

"You will not escape. Your people drove us into the Mound; shall we let you leave it?''

80

Matt stared at him, both hands knotting round the knife. Horror fought with fear. The unreal hall, the unreal orchard; and now darkness again. To live so long in the dark that so much was forgotten, and so much hate remembered. . . .

Huskily, he said, "I can't stay here! Leave the Mound yourselves, there's nothing stopping you. There's nothing outside, no human beings anyway, no Children of Danu— only the Dulachan."

Elatha's mouth girned like an animal's in pain. *"Fool! Do you know nothing of your fathers? Do you know nothing of what Danu's Children have done to the world?"*

Matt's head was throbbing. He looked away from Elatha's face and set his gaze on the small spotted blade of the knife that glimmered faintly between them. "I don't know what you mean," he said, huskily.

"No; you Sky People forget everything you cannot touch and feel." Elatha came a step nearer, mouth twisting as Matt's grip tightened again on the knife. *"Listen, then! Know your own nature! When we walked the earth, in the morning of the world, the sunlight was gentle and kind, and if it grew too bright for our eyes there was shade in the forest. But the coming of Danu's Children changed all that. They were born of the sky; the light that shines from them is terrible; and the touch of their iron swords is impossible to endure. . . ."*

The tumbling shapes wavered and dissolved into a black tumult of fear, and Matt clutched at his forehead, feeling as if his head was going to burst. Elatha flinched from the little knife as it shook in Matt's hand, and, girning grotesquely, backed away. The shapes gradually returned, bitter and edged.

"Once I stepped outside the Mound, and stood under the sky for the space of seven heartbeats. It almost killed me. Danu's Children have walked across the upper world

81

since they overcame us at the battle of Moytura; and wherever their feet have touched is death to the Fomors. Only on the blackest nights dare we venture out for long; then their power is less and ours is greater. But do not speak such foolish words, Man of Iron! We could not bear to live in the world your people have made!

Matt, one hand pressed to his brow, could hardly think; the burning hatred left no room in his mind. Eventually, he said, stumblingly, "But Kate and Anna and me—we've never done anything to harm you! And killing us won't make anything better for you! Why can't you just let us go?"

"Do you dare to say you have never harmed us?" The white hand shot out, a thin finger pointing at him, and the empty eyes glared sickingly. *"You, who stabbed one of my people with that iron knife"*—the shapes shook, writhed and recovered—*"you, who stole his cap?"*

Matt's throat tightened, and for a moment it was difficult to breathe. Again he saw the limp, doll-like body on the ground, and the livid scar standing out; again something twisted inside him. "I never meant to hurt him," he said hoarsely.

"The Children of the Sky never mean to do anything!" A cold, creeping light came from Elatha's hand, like the underside of darkness. *"Look, despiser of dreams; look, and see the world of Ruadan, whose cap you stole!"*

The cold visibility grew. Matt saw he was standing on filthy straw now, with things moving in it. His teeth went into his lip as he saw the sharp snouts of rats. A foul smell crept into his nostrils. He heard a rustling, then a sound of stertorous breathing, and as his knuckles whitened on the knife and the light spread he saw limbs on the floor; then he saw it all. It was an underground hole, crowded with unconscious bodies.

The stench was almost choking. Most of them lay in a stupor on the ground, but a few sat against the earthen wall, legs drawn up and heads resting on their knees. Matt could see lice on the ones nearest to him. What was left of their clothes hardly covered them, but as he looked along the starved unconscious faces he saw that each one wore a cap over the tangle of matted hair. Suddenly, he recognised one of them—the broad forehead, the narrow little nose, the long black hair. The skin was brown with dirt, her features small and unremarkable, her face lined and dragged down with weariness; it was Ethlinn. He felt sick as he saw a rat creeping over her leg.

Behind him, someone moved.

Matt whirled round, knife at the ready, and rats scuffled away at the sudden movement. Matt stared, feeling sicker than before; for crouching in the straw there was a Fomor who was awake, without a cap. His eyes were no longer empty, but full of crazed agony. He was rocking himself to and fro, moaning, and he kept covering his face with his hands, then reaching round to fend off the rats. The moaning was a real sound, audible, inarticulate, animal-like. Matt saw a long, bloody slash down the side of his face, just missing the eye.

"Have mercy, Iron Man! Give him back his cap!"

The shape inside his head was etched with despair. Matt looked round and saw Elatha here too; standing amongst the straw, his white hands so tightly knit together that they looked like a single spike of bone.

Slowly, the empty eyes turned from Ruadan down to the verminous Fomor at Elatha's feet.

Matt looked, and saw it was Elatha himself lying there—starved, filthy, sunk so deep in a dream that he could believe himself to be standing upright at his own side. Matt's mind reeled, refusing to believe. Then Elatha's hollow gaze turned to him, and Matt saw it burnt.

"Wide is my princedom, truly. Look on the Fomors' real world, Iron Man; this is real; this is the inside of the Mound. Do you tell us to bear it? Do you tell us to build

*no rich Lochlann inside our minds? Having stolen all else,
will you steal from Ruadan even his dreams?"*

Matt couldn't speak.

*"Valiant was my grandson Ruadan at Moytura. A young
lad, he went forth at the head of the army and cast his
spear at dread Govannon. He drew first blood. Then did
Govannon seize him and hurl him down into the dark;
and Ruadan first of us all lay in this place."* Elatha's fury
exploded like a star. *"Give back his cap, thief! Give back
that last of your spoils!"*

Matt's hand moved towards the leather cap. With an effort of pure will he stopped himself and looked at those
empty holes in Elatha's face. It seemed that hate had
burnt all the life out of them; certainly there was nothing
left there to trust.

Painfully, he forced his dazed mind to think for itself.
"If I do," he said stumblingly, "will you let us go?"

Elatha's white hands shot upwards, two trembling spires
of pain. *"The cap is nothing to you, Iron Man—what do
you care for Lochlann? Give it back, have pity; yes, you
and your friends will go, as free as the air outside this
dreadful Mound!"*

Matt's teeth went into his lip. He couldn't close his ears
to Ruadan's ceaseless moaning, nor forget the sight of the
crusted blood on his cheek and those wild eyes. He'd
thought he'd killed him; and surely that would have been
better; yet he couldn't trust Elatha. The Prince had dis-
missed the fake halls and orchard of Lochlann for him, ad-
mitted they were fake, and shown him the truth of the
Mound; but Matt felt in his heart that, for Elatha, the
truth was only one more trick.

"I don't believe you," he said hoarsely. "As soon as I
take it off, you'll fool me into dropping the knife, and
then—" He wrenched his mind away from Elatha's grasping shapes, dragged his eyes away from the bone-white

84

stare, faced around towards darkness. "Where are my friends?" he said, breathlessly.

At his words a dim form seemed to trace itself in the darkness, and suddenly Matt understood the rule that would save him from the nightmare. Ruadan's cap could call up reality as well, not just dreams—its power had no bounds. He clenched his hands, trying to forget Elatha, Ruadan, Ethlinn, the whole frightful place. *"Kate!"* He yelled.

The darkness danced before his eyes, half-seen colours glinting. *"Kate,"* Matt gasped, throat aching; and at last there she was. The soft light bloomed around her as she started up from Anna's side, blue gaze coming at him as if from another world.

"Matt! *Matt,* what's going on?"

The clear sound of her voice after all that silence was like life again. Matt almost choked.

"It's all right, Kate. We're going to get out."

The blue eyes examined him, tensely. A sudden fear twisted in him.

"Kate—it is you, isn't it?"

"It's me all right," her voice came, Kate's voice, unmistakably—but oddly distant, as if there were a glass screen dividing them. "What about you?" she said bluntly.

"Yes, it's me." Matt looked at her, beginning to feel cold again. How could you tell? The filthy hole with the bodies had been the real inside of the Mound; this darkness, with only Kate and Anna visible, must be just another dream. But Kate and Anna were real, at least they had been before, in this same darkness—he didn't know any more. Perhaps everything was just dreams.

His right hand, which had felt burnt, was feeling numb now, and a cold pain started in it. He winced, opening his fingers, and saw Kate stoop swiftly to pick up the knife as it fell. He felt better now she was holding it, but fear nudged him again. Was he becoming afraid of iron, like a Fomor? Was that what the cap did to you?

"We've got to get out," he said, and wasn't sure whether Kate heard him or not. He stepped past her, and bent down to Anna. "Come on, Anna," he said huskily. "Wake up!"

Her eyes opened at once, and looked straight up at him. Matt took her hand, and she rose to her feet without a word, like a good child; he looked into the deep brown eyes, knowing it should have been good to see them again; but he could feel nothing. He turned away, avoiding Kate's eyes as well.

"Where's the door?" he said, his voice rough. Above him, he saw the roof of the Mound appear, and the turfed-over door with a wooden ladder leading up to it. He led Anna over to it, and Kate followed, mouth grim and knife at the ready.

Matt paused, finding himself fighting for breath. He felt weak and stretched out, as if the darkness was getting inside him. "Kate," he whispered, "can you see the ladder?"

"No." Her eyes went past him, seeking. "I can only just see you." She paused, and Matt stared at her, struggling to make her real. "Can I touch you?" Kate said, with a blunt challenge in her voice.

Matt swallowed, "Try."

Her hand took hold of his arm, so cold it sent ice to his very heart. He flinched away, grabbing a rung to keep himself upright. "I'll send Anna up first," he whispered. "And you—get hold of my ankle as I go up, and *don't let go.* Try to climb by feel."

Kate gave him a measuring look. "*Is* there a ladder there?" she said. A dull pain radiated at him from the point of the knife, as she lifted it slightly.

"Yes. . . ." Matt's voice cracked desperately. He began

86

to shake as the Fomor's hate suddenly shouldered in on him. *"Stop—Iron Man—no escape from the Mound."*

"Get up it, then! Quick!" Kate half turned away, the knife raised against the darkness.

"Climb, Anna!" Matt pushed her towards the ladder, and she went swiftly and lightly up the rungs. He followed, dragging himself up; then Kate's icy hand closed round his ankle. It took all the movement out of him. He cried out, and his cry, thin and bodiless, seemed to hang in the air, bringing time itself to a stop. He wanted to kick her away.

"Go *on!*" Kate's voice shouted, and only the impatience in it cracked that frozen feeling. It forced him up the last few rungs and out into the evening forest. Kate came out beside him.

"Run," she said, seizing Anna's hand.

Matt stood there, unable to move. The great bare sweep of sky, still stained from the sunset, struck an indescribable horror into him. Kate caught at his arm, and he flinched away from her freezing touch, crying out again; but this time he knew his cry had no sound.

"Listen!" Kate's voice broke in on him, desperately. "Listen, if you are Matt, run! They'll be out on us in two seconds!"

His mind wouldn't work. All he wanted to do was hide from that awful endless space above.

"Anna, get hold of his hand," Kate said imperatively. He felt the touch of warmer, more gentle fingers; but the horror of the sky, of its boundless light, was growing. *No Fomor would come out under the sky,* he thought, and didn't know whether he'd spoken or not. He let Anna pull him along after Kate, but every touch of the earth sent a freezing shock of despair through him. Stars were coming out, and they peered down at him like pitiless eyes. As the awful helpless horror built up in him, he knew that if he couldn't get out of this world he was going to die.

87

He heard himself splash through water, and then something dark, with a pale snarl of pointed teeth, came up and crashed against his chest. He fell back to the ground, and the sky stared straight down at him, so infintely vast that he felt himself melting away, appalled, into nothing. He heard Kate's voice ring out, distant, no longer anything to do with him.

"Stop! Stop it! You *mustn't* kill him!" She shouldered the creature back as it knelt astride Matt, grabbing huge hands that brought a stone knife down at his throat.

The hands stopped in mid-air. Then a rustling voice came softly through the quiet night.

"He is death, white flower. He wears the cap. Though the Shadow did not send him, he is of the Shadow now." Amber eyes looked up at her. "He will kill you, white flower. It will be kinder to kill him first," the Dulachan whispered, hands knotting on the stone knife.

Kate ripped the scout knife back out of the sheath, and set its point against the scrawning throat. "If you kill him, I'll kill you!" she said, her voice uneven but ringing like steel.

The Dulachan flinched back sharply, then became motionless. The starlight was dim, and the moon had not yet risen; an owl called faintly, and some creature hushed through the grass. Kate didn't take her eyes off the botched, unhuman face.

"To kill me would not harm you, white flower; but to let him live might," the Dulachan whispered at last, the lipless mouth hardly moving.

Kate took the knife-point from its throat and turned her head away. Matt lay motionless amongst the reeds, head back with starlight mirrored in his open eyes; he seemed faint, hardly there. "Dulachan," Kate said huskily, "he got us out of the Mound—me, and my sister. We'd still be in there but for Matt. I didn't think it was really him, I thought it was an illusion the Fomors had made to trick up; but it is him. We've got to help him.'' She looked back at the brown face. *"Please,"* she said, and the word shook.

Its eyes dulled over hopelessly; then the Dulachan slid the stone knife back into its belt. "I must take the cap from him," it said, as if from far away. "Take your sister and get into the boat, white flower."

Kate said tightly, "You won't—"

It shrank a little, amber eyes patient. "I will save him, white flower," it whispered. "I would harm none of yours. Truly I serve you."

Kate rose. "Come on, Anna," she said, reaching out and taking her hand again. Anna came with her unresistingly, and stepped into the canoe that lay wedged amongst rushes at the waterside. Kate stepped in after her, and both crouched down. Kate looked across at the shadowy shape of the Dulachan, then back at her sister.

"Anna," she said.

Anna turned her head a fraction and looked at Kate, but still she said nothing, and in the dim light Kate couldn't tell what, if anything, was going on behind that silent gaze. Something came up in her throat, and she swallowed it fiercely. It felt almost as if Matt and Anna had deliberately deserted her.

She looked back at the Dulachan. Matt, lying in the long reeds, was hidden form her. She saw it slowly reach down into the reeds, its shoulders rigid.

She thrust her hands against her ears as a terrible scream soared through her head. It went on and on, full of despair and pain—she shook her head to get rid of it, but it wouldn't stop—then suddenly it cut out.

She looked up to see the Dulachan lurch back, long-legged, teeth bared in dismay. She thought she glimpsed something in its head—then Matt springing to his feet like a bow, face white as bone and twisted more than Kate thought possible. His hands pressed against his temples as if trying to crush his own head. An echo of that first dreadful scream came, and without knowing it Kate's fingers dragged the knife from its sheath again. Then Matt swayed, and the Dulachan's long arms shot out to catch him as he sank towards the ground.

The Dulachan lifted him up as if he weighed nothing. It stood motionless for a moment, head bowed as if totally exhausted; a low whispering moan came to Kate across the marsh grass, but it might have been only the wind. At last the creature turned and came through the reeds, looming up beside the canoe like a great shadowy scarecrow.

"He is safe, white flower," it whispered, and knelt down on the bank by Kate, still holding Matt. He lay limp and still in the Dulachan's arms, staring up at the sky. His head was bare.

The Dulachan looked from him to Kate; there was something fixed and aghast about the amber eyes. "Let you hold him, white flower," the brown whisper came. "He has gone far from this world; and you are life."

"No," said Kate huskily. "It hurts him when I touch him. Put him next to Anna."

Slowly, it rose again, and its mouth seemed to be moving with that look of pain or sickness as it stooped to lay Matt gently in the canoe by Anna. He lay without moving, hunched up in the small space, and the Dulachan climbed in at the prow and lifted up the paddle.

"Let's go—quickly," Kate said jerkily. "They'll be here any minute."

Matt's voice came from low down in the boat, like the shadow of a voice. "No Fomor would come out under the sky. . . ." His head turned a little so that his eyes stared upwards again.

"Rest," whispered the Dulachan.

"What does he mean?" said Kate urgently. "Are we—safe?"

"No, white flower." The Dulachan's voice grew fainter

with fear as it pushed against the bank with the paddle. The canoe floated off, low in the water; the four of them filled it completely, Kate at one end and the Dulachan in front at the other. "Once we were safe in the forest, away from the Mound," the owl-voice whispered. "But the Fomors have grown in strength, serving the Horned One; and on such a night, with clouds and little moon, he can draw them forth. The sun is set now."

The wooden paddle dug the water and the canoe moved sluggishly forward, away from the round black hill that crouched in front of the stars. Looking back, Kate's mouth went dry, and she lifted the knife with her knuckles white on the haft.

"Here they come," she said.

6

LADY OF THE SILVER WHEEL

They were coming from the Mound like a single shadow slipping towards them over the earth. The Dulachan's bent back knotted as it flailed at the water with the paddle, using all its strength to get the sluggish canoe away.

"Come on!" Kate said through gritted teeth, kneeling up in the back. They were hard to see, though their faces were as blue-white as stars, for they were coming like smoke or a smell or a feeling of fear, and it was a shock that they were visible at all."

The canoe gathered speed, lurching along low in the water. Matt, lying in the bottom, could feel inside his head the shapes of murderous hatred coming closer, then a painful clench and jerk back as Kate's hand shot out, holding the knife. He lifted his head a little and looked past Anna at her; he could just see her profile, set and grim, with the pale hair tossing back.

The canoe shot away, speeding along at last, and the feel of the following Fomors died like an echo. Matt lost sight of Kate's face, and, looking up, saw that trees had taken over the sky. In front of him, he could hear the Dulachan's breath tearing its lungs. The splash of the paddle had stopped. The canoe drifted into pitch darkness, and along the hide Matt could feel the creature shaking.

"We've lost them," Kate whispered.

The Dulachan's raw whisper came from low down, as if its head had sunk on to its knees. "We—cannot lose them! The Horned One leads their hunt!"

There was a pause. "We've got to," Kate's voice came, low and forceful. "They can't get us now! Look what's happened to us—and we're still alive, even Anna. Come on, Dulachan! Keep going!"

The harsh breath seemed as if it couldn't ease.

"I cannot." Its voice was scarcely audible between the laboured gasps. "My strength is water—I cannot, white flower."

"What?" Kate whispered incredulously. "You've only been paddling for five minutes."

"Nay, for years, white flower." Its voice was no louder than dry grass rustling. "Year after year I have sailed these streams, long before the Fomors came. I should have died long since. But I waited for the Lord of Light . . ."

"We haven't time for that now! Give me the paddle!"

Matt felt the creature shaking with its heaving breath. He put out a hand and touched its back. The skin felt different, dry and harsh like a sick dog's. Again its voice whispered, as if from far away.

"White flower—is the name the Dulachans had for the morning star, the light-bringer. You are the one who will bring him back, and I would have followed you even into the Mound, had you asked. Instead, I haunted the streams, waiting for you, while seven times the leaves fell from the trees and grew again, for I could not believe you would die."

There was a pause, broken only by the forest sounds, and as the words sank into Matt's mind time extended itself in a great unnatural gap. While seven times the leaves fell from the trees and grew again. . . .

"Seven years!" came Kate's whisper, awed. "What are you talking about? It couldn't have been more than an hour in there!''

"It is said that time flows differently in Lochlann, white flower." Its whisper was dry and exhausted. "It is said that those who leave the Mound after a day or an hour inside will find the outer world changed, and their friends aged or dying. I do not know. Never before have I known one strong enough to escape from that place." Its voice quivered, going to shreds. "Why did you not return sooner, white flower? I was old before, but I had more strength then."

There was silence as, under his hand, Matt felt the creature's helpless tembling. Words drifted through his head. *"My wits wander in this world of bright swords and anger. . . ."* Seven years in this place, with its thunderstorms and slashing rain, seven cruel winters. And the Dulachan wasn't immortal; not like Danu's Children, he found himself thinking, without knowing why. Or the Lord of Light.

"Dulachan," he said. His voice sounded husky and attenuated to himself. "Dulachan, who is the Lord of Light?"

Its breath rasped hard. "He is lost. The Shadow has taken him," the Dulachan whispered abruptly, and the heavy head seemed to turn away from him. "All things have their shadow," its whisper came again, bitter in the black. "The white flower is a star, but you have led her into deep darkness."

"Matt," Kate's voice cut in, low and imperative. "If you're okay now, you'd better use the paddle. Or give it to me."

Matt felt the paddle, and knelt up carefully. His limbs seemed to be obeying him normally again, after the depth of darkness, shouting and pain that he didn't clearly remember, and didn't want to. But his mind felt different, dazed, emptied out like a husk. Those last words of the Dulachan's had struck home. He had brought Kate here,

94

it had been his idea, and every moment in this place was a vying with death.

"I can't see," he said. "Which way are we going?"

"Tell him, Dulachan," Kate said.

"Follow this channel," the brown voice said, hardly more than a breath. "But it is of no avail—they will hunt us down, white flower."

There was no room to use the paddle. Matt laid it back in the canoe and reached out, feeling for the bank. He grasped a clump of reeds on each side and pulled the boat along in that way, easing it blindly through the narrows until it began to drift more freely. Then he picked up the paddle again and dipped it in the unseen water.

He hardly realised they were moving until, muscles aching, he began to see the Dulachan's hunched back in front of him. The trees had opened out on the bare marsh; he looked up, saw the prick of stars, and at once felt as if Elatha's hand had been laid on his neck.

"Kate—they're back!" he whispered desperately, not stopping to think.

"Who? I can't see anything." Kate raised the knife.

But he could feel them, like a malignant whisper growing. There was no doubt about it. "They're coming, anyway—which way, Dulachan? Dulachan!"

"Forward, forward," the creature whispered dully. It huddled down and Matt's arms felt treacherously weak as he tried to paddle faster. Kate helped, scooping the water vigorously with her free hand, and somehow the canoe gathered a little speed along the mazy channel of water, but the mutter of the Fomors grew and grew inside Matt's head.

"I can see them now," Kate whispered.

Matt looked over his shoulder. About fifty yards away, they were running in a long weaving file. The safe paths in the swamp meandered as much as the streams but, dim and hardly to be seen but for the white glare of their faces, they were coming steadily closer.

There was a groan from the Dulachan, and great shaking hands seized the paddle from Matt. "The hunt is up! Row with your hands, and close your eyes lest the Horned One takes shape!" The paddle crashed into the water, and Matt and Kate oared desperately with both hands. In moments, the canoe was flying along like a clumsy bird; and eyes half shut, Matt could feel the vengeful mutter dying a little—but not leaving him.

"Faster!" Kate panted. "Anna, for God's sake help!"

"They come, they come," moaned the Dulachan. Ahead of them, Matt saw the river suddenly spread out, smooth and black.

"Get out—into the river," he gasped.

"They can follow us to the bottom of the sea!" the Dulachan's voice cried, rough and broken with despair. "Down! The touch of their bolts is death!"

Hardly daring to, Matt looked over his shoulder again. He saw there was a path built in the marsh, half-buried logs leading down across the bare mud to where their channel joined the river. And he saw the Fomors come streaming along it. "Get out into the river!" he shouted again, scooping hard at the water. He had seen little bows in the Fomors' hands. If they could beat them in the race down to the river and get out into the middle of it, they might be safe. . . .

"Row then! But do not think Belisama and her fuaths are more merciful than these," the Dulachan's voice sobbed. "There is no safe place—down, down!" It turned round, hands darting out to press Kate down into the bottom of the boat, pushing Matt and Anna down in the process. A whirring sound filled the air.

Matt heard terrible little noises coming from the Dulachan's throat as, using strength it no longer had, it sent the canoe flying out into the smooth black emptiness of

96

the river. The current tugged. Things whizzed overhead, scraped the side of the canoe and splashed in the water, and he dared not lift his head; all he could see was the Dulachan's belt, and the soft green Fomor's cap pushed through it. His fingers almost reached out for it, but then he heard the Dulachan scream.

It reeled in the canoe, almost capsizing them, and Matt heard Kate shout out. He grabbed the Dulachan to hold it still. They were out in the middle of the river, drifting fast downstream, and the night was suddenly quiet again.

Slowly, Matt sat up. The Dulachan lay still in his arms, and the river seemed to cast back some of the starlight so that he could see its face. For the first time, white showed round the amber irises. A bolt with a short feathered shaft was in its side.

"White flower—" is voice was high and faint like the wind.

"It's all right," Matt said huskily. "You've been hit, but it's only just in you, it's not deep. . . ." Very carefully, he took hold of the shaft and eased the arrow out. It was like a toy, barely seven inches long with a tiny flint head, and had made a cut about half an inch deep.

The blood oozed blackly. The Dulachan shuddered, and its great hands seized at the wound, tearing violently. "Don't!" Matt gasped, trying to pull it away. "What's the matter? Leave it alone!"

"You son of dark," the Dulachan groaned, kneading the wound hard so that blood spurted. Then its hands slackened, and slid powerlessly away. Its head fell back in Matt's lap.

"You're not hurt," Matt said, urgently. "Not much, anyway."

He heard the rattle of its breathing. "Did I not say their bolts are death?" it whispered, slowly, and its eyes opened a little, looking upwards at the cloud that hid some of the stars. "They are dipped in hemlock. I shall not see the

Lord of Light return in this world's age.''

"Kate," Matt said. His voice cracked, and he had to stop to steady it. With a shudder, he dropped the evil little arrow into the river. "Kate," he said again, forcing himself, "the Dulachan's—dying.''

"Oh, no!" Kate breathed, in dismay.

"White flower, I would have served you—''

It was a wisp of a voice she couldn't possibly have heard. Matt held on to the stringy body in his arms desperately; would it really die? Hemlock was poison, yes, but there could have been so little on that tiny flint arrowhead, surely not enough to kill a human being, anyway . . . then, unbelievingly, he saw the amber eyes go dull and fixed, and the body became suddenly heavy in his arms.

He opened his mouth, but couldn't speak. This would never have happened to it but for us, he thought, and once again something twisted inside him.

"Kate," he said at last, huskily, "it's dead.''

"Now what are we going to do?" Kate said, in despair.

"I don't know," said Matt. He couldn't think; the darkness felt very thick.

"Matt"—Kate's voice was urgent—"we've got to think of something! How do we get out of here?''

Matt shook his head. "I just don't know, Kate." The river was widening out to the estuary, and he thought he could make out the black hump of the Mound, far over to the right.

"Can't you wake Anna up properly?''

Matt looked over his shoulders to where Anna knelt, head bowed with the long dark hair trailing forward. "Anna," he said, and awkwardly reached a hand back to touch her arm. The canoe rocked a little, but Anna never moved. "I don't think she can hear me when I haven't got the cap on," Matt said.

"Don't put it on again, for God's sake!" Kate exclaimed, sounding scared. Matt saw her face, pale in the night. "Matt," her voice said desperately, "we've just got to find some way to get back out of here!"

Matt could hear that fear was beginning to get the upper hand in her, now that the Dulachan was dead. If only his mind would work, if only he could stop feeling so empty and exhausted.

"Yes, I know," he said wearily. "Give me a minute to think then."

"All right." Kate's voice trembled, and with a quick movement she leaned her head forward into her hands, covering her eyes. Matt closed his eyes too, feeling the Dulachan heavy on his knees. They were both tired, and probably hungry too, if they could only take time to think about it. . . .

Then something moved inside his head, a little menacing whisper.

Matt's hands slowly clenched. Oh no. Here they came again; they hadn't been shaken off; here was that white hand again, touching the back of his neck—and he felt tired, so tired. His lips parted to warn Kate, but hesitated, not wanting to scare her any more; he knelt there, feeling suddenly quite helpless, not knowing what to do as those clutching shapes grew imperceptibly inside his mind. The river bore the boat on quietly, and it was so hard to think.

There was a soft splash, close too. Matt didn't move, but Kate jerked around, rocking the craft, and gave a cry. She ripped the knife from its sheath and thrust it out.

There was a flurry across the water, and Matt winced with that old wrench of horror inside his head. He hadn't realised that they'd come so close. They were here in the water, following them down the current, like a school of killer fish.

"Get us away, Matt!" Kate cried, and he could tell from her voice that she couldn't bear much more. Wearily, he let go of the Dulachan and picked up the paddle. As he looked up, beginning to use it, he saw the water was full of pale glaring faces. They came swimming in a long swathe from the right-hand shore, the closest ones trying to come right up to the boat, but flinching back, unable to bear Kate's knife. Their hate hung weights on Matt's arms. *"Iron Man—no escape—never will we leave you."* He ducked his head to avoid those empty hating eyes.

"Faster!" Kate said, her voice cracking. Matt's arms were aching again, and the canoe began to toss as waves, rolling in from the sea, lifted it up and down. The pale faces, with their cold watching eyes, swam along with them almost without effort; the Fomors were back in their dream-bodies and able to do anything they wished, or at least so it seemed to Matt. Looking out, he saw three close together, two Fomors supporting the one in the middle, whose face was death-like with a long livid scar and whose head was bare. Shuddering, he looked away, and tried to paddle faster, but it was no good; they couldn't out-distance the Fomors. Many-fingered, their hate grasped out towards the boat.

"Matt!" Kate called, over the crack in her voice. "Matt, throw the Dulachan over the side!"

The paddle almost slipped from his hands. Gripping it tight, he stayed quite still; it made sense, the heavy body was only one more weight to push along. Almost as if to make it harder, the clouds were parting to let more star-light through, and never had the quiet beast's face looked so like a man's.

"Do it, Matt!" Kate cried savagely. "Quick!"

Numbly, Matt laid down the paddle and took hold of the dead shoulders. The body was heavy, and terribly awk-ward. He heaved it half over the side, Kate leaning over the other way to compensate, and its hair floated out in the water, its face calm up to the stars; then he lifted its legs and it slid away from him. He hunched round quickly in the rocking boat, so as not to see what the Fomors did with it. He seized the paddle, the canoe leapt forward; and

100

under one of his knees was tucked the green leather cap.

He felt the Fomors' baulked anger as the canoe edged away from them. They might be able to do anything, but he had a cap as well now; the lightened craft shot bird-like between the rough waves, just that bit faster than they could swim. They sent their last weapon, hate that filled Matt's head and cramped his arms till he could barely move them; but, unable to think, he fought the pain, and Kate, sheathing the knife, paddled with both hands. The white faces were falling behind.

"They're going," Kate whispered.

Cradling his aching arms, Matt looked back over his shoulder. The dim trail of white had turned back for the shore, leaving them. The pain in his arms eased, and his head began to clear.

"Why didn't they shoot at us?" Kate whispered, huskily.

"They want to sacrifice us," Matt said. "We're no good to them dead."

They let the canoe drift, watching the Fomors.

"Now what?" whispered Kate.

Matt rubbed a hand over his eyes, exhausted. Their position wasn't much better. True, they'd escaped the Fomors, but here they were floating in a frail craft almost out at sea; if another storm came, it would be the end of them. At last, he faced the fact that they might never get back home.

"Kate," he said, "where do you think we are—really?"

"We could be anywhere! How should I know? We could even be in a parallel universe, if you know what that is."

"We'll be all right," Matt said, hearing the suppressed tremor in her voice. "We have been so far."

"We had the Dulachan then," Kate said, and, looking round at her, he saw her bite her lip. Yes; he too had trusted the Dulachan to get them out of everything.

101

"We'd better make for the other shore," he said.

"What good will that do?" Kate demanded. "There are probably Fomors there too."

"Well, we can't stay out here, can we?" Matt said. "Look, Kate, sooner or later we'll have to find somewhere warm, to rest. And something to eat. We haven't eaten since we got here, and God knows when that was."

"I hate this place," Kate said desperately. "These swamps are dangerous, anyway. . . ."

"What else can we do?" Matt asked after a moment.

Kate looked up at him. "Keep going out to sea," she whispered. "The Dulachan talked about a land to the west. The Children of Danu are there—and I think they'd help us. Let's go there, Matt."

"In this thing?" Matt exclaimed. "The Dulachan didn't say how far this land is—it might be hundreds of miles!"

Kate looked away. She looked over her shoulder, back at the right-hand shore.

Matt looked too, and stiffened.

It wasn't easy to see anything in the dim starlight; but over there on the shore there was something, felt if not seen. His eyes could only make out a pale blotch. Some other sense told him there was a vast silence there, a grim sort of power.

"It's them!" Kate whispered. "Just standing there!"

So that was it—a great crowd of Fomors. Matt seized the paddle. As he thrust it into the water, turning them towards the other shore, a cry came.

He couldn't tell whether he heard it or whether it was inside his head as before; but whichever, he heard it not only with his ears but with his whole body, and the waters and the earth heard it too and moved in response. Envy, hate, vengefulness—all were in that cry, and yet it was of such despair that it turned his heart over. He stopped paddling, and looked back.

Silence returned, deeper and tenser than before. He and Kate looked at each other over Anna's bent head, not wanting to speak; he noticed that Anna was trembling.

Something began to grow in the silence, far away. Matt listened, hard; it was a dim roaring. The stars above sickened, and the roar grew nearer, savage.

"Matt, get us out of here!" Kate flailed the water with both hands.

Matt thought how far away the other shore was. Something in that cry made him feel the bitter cold of the sea wind, the soreness of his feet, the ache and fatigue going all through him. He put his hand on the paddle. They've giving us up, he thought with sudden certainty, passed us on to something else, something huge enough to answer that cry. I can't do any more, he thought then; I'm finished, we're all finished. His hands wandered, and he found himself touching the soft leather cap under his knee.

"It's no good, Kate," he heard himself say, "we can't get away." He felt vaguely surprised at his own words, but still didn't try to use the paddle.

"Matt!" Kate cried, terror-stricken. She lunged across Anna, rocking the boat crazily, and grabbed the paddle. "Come on, Matt, help me!"

The canoe began to pitch roughly over the waves as Kate made frantically for the other shore. Holding on to the sides, Matt looked upstream as the roar became louder, closer, a great throat howling for them.

The water was coming down in a wall towards them. Matt saw trees tossing in it, and time stopped for him. His fingers closed round the cap and, without his will, lifted it up and put it on his head.

It was Belisama. The cap on his head, the dark world became clear and he could see everything. Slowly the mass of water turned above him, and Belisama rode it like a steed, her green hair flying over all the sky, her eyes looking unseeingly down at the tiny boat. Matt knew her for a goddess. Her hand came up, lifting a vast trident too bright for him to look at; but he only wanted to look at that wild ivory face, for he had never seen anything so beautiful in all the worlds. Around her river-wraiths swarmed, webbed and foul; and on the shore Elatha stood with Ruadan in his arms, eyes fixed on Matt with bitter gladness; all those things Matt saw as he looked up into the great cool eyes of the goddess as she rode the foaming water curled above him.

Then all the clouds tore apart and out soared a blazing moon. Matt screamed at the light, covering his eyes, but it seemed to burn through his hands, through his eyes, into his brain. Around him a great echo rose of his scream, and the Fomors writhed like fish on the shore.

There was a splashing leap of the water beside them, and suddenly a man was with them in the boat, tall, shining, with hair as bright as the moon, and the sea running off him.

"Come, Lady of the Silver Wheel!" he called, his voice free, ringing, and terrible to Matt's ears. The full moon cast its light on to the water in a broad bright round of silver. "Up!" called the man, and before Kate knew it he had caught her by the hands and swung her up out of the boat. She opened her mouth to scream, then gasped as she found herself standing up on a solid disc of light. Anna followed, then Matt flung himself away in horror as the man's hands reached out to him.

"Peace!" he said, stooping, a laugh in his voice. Matt felt a deft hand pluck away the cap, but even as he flinched he realised he felt no pain. He looked up, and saw the cap thrown in a long, high, spinning arc over the water, away and down, down into the cupped, distant hands of Ruadan. A pair of sea-green eyes glinted at him, awesomely clear, from the face that was more than a man's, then he was seized and tossed. He found himself next to

Kate on that spinning circle of light, and the stars went wheeling past.

Far beneath them Belisama, green and white and bronze, rode the seething wave on down to the sea, going over the tiny canoe as if it was nothing. Behind her, for an instant, they saw that bright-haired being rise like a fish in the water, one hand raised towards them. "Say Eil Ton sends greetings!" Matt thought he heard laughing; and then the earth passed away from beneath them.

7

WAVES IN THE ETHER

Under their feet the silver wheel thrummed softly, but otherwise it was completely dark.

"Matt!" Kate whispered urgently. "Help me hold Anna. She's falling."

Matt reached out unseeingly and touched Anna. She was swaying, about to fall, and he put an arm round her.

"Can't you wake her up?" Kate's voice said. "You could before—in the Mound!"

Matt looked into the darkness towards her voice. He could see the silver disc and their feet against it, but nothing else. And yet it wasn't a frightening darkness.

"I haven't got the cap now," he said.

"Where are we?" Kate whispered. "Are we moving?"

Her arm was round Anna as well, and it touched his. Matt began to feel curiously peaceful in this darkness; for the first time he had no sense of danger. Kate's voice sounded as if they were in a great empty space, with nothing else there to threaten them.

"I don't know," he said.

"Well, are we still in that swamp place, or not?" Kate demanded impatiently. But he could tell from the sound of her voice that she wasn't really afraid either.

"I don't know," he said again. "I don't think so. I saw

it go when we went up on the wheel. Perhaps that—that fish-man's got us out.''

"Maybe he's one of the Children of Danu!" Kate exclaimed. "Matt, maybe it's going to be all right!"

And at that, strangely, Matt did feel a touch of fear. Danu's Children, great bright merciless beings with iron swords—that was how Elatha had seen them, and his thoughts had come with that shape into Matt's mind. He tried to expel the fear, roughly. Just wearing a cap didn't make you a Fomor. Anyway, Kate seemed to have the idea that Danu's Children were on their side, and her intuition was worth trusting.

" 'Course it's going to be all right," he said.

"I wish Anna would wake up," said Kate.

She felt limp between them, her whole weight hanging on their arms. She's got to be all right, Matt thought; after everything we've come through she can't die now. . . . But he wasn't afraid for her either. Perhaps all these weird adventures had finally exhausted his capacity for fear.

"Matt."

"Yes?"

Kate's voice sounded forbidding, as if warning him not to try being sympathetic. "Did it hurt—the Dulachan?"

Self-reproach stabbed Matt. Yes, she had cared about the Dulachan, really. He should have seen that and got rid of the body quickly and quietly, instead of making her shout at him.

"No," he lied. "I don't think so. It only took a few minutes."

Kate was silent, and he wished he could see her face. He could imagine her blue eyes, with the slight, unaccustomed frown of pain that had often come since her parents were lost.

Kate stirred, shaking off the wicked memories. "Anna," she said urgently, and Matt felt her shake her.

107

"Oh, come on, wake up," Kate whispered, on a pleading note. 'Matt, what if she—dies?"

"She can't," Matt said stubbornly. She was still breathing lightly, he could feel it. He looked up, trying to see through the darkness. He knew they couldn't stay for ever in this peaceful silence. "Let's shout, Kate. Someone might hear."

He heard her take in a breath to shout on; but in that instant a sound came, and he thought he saw a flick of light far above. Both of them held their breath. The silence seemed to throb.

"What was that?" Kate whispered.

"I don't know." Matt's muscles were tight again; perhaps they'd only imagined it.

The sound came again, almost too high to hear, but closer, clearer. Matt's eyes ached with staring; it was as if the whole darkness had begun to flicker with light from beyond the end of the spectrum, existing but invisible to them. "Hey!" he shouted, unable to bear the return of tension.

"Matt!" Kate's arm tightened against his. "Did you hear it again?"

"Yes—"

"It sounds . . ." her voice was queer, unbelieving. "It sounds like someone trying to *talk*, Matt."

"What?" Matt said, incredulously.

"Listen."

It came again, directly over their heads, a loud crackling chime like thin glass rods falling together, abruptly cut off. And there was a shape in it, like words struggling to be formed. Matt gasped.

"Who are you?" he shouted, voice raw.

"Do not fear me—" The words broke through, unhuman and full of echoes, as another crackling chime raced round their ears. "Wait—I will take shape—"

From nowhere light shot all round them, moving and

108

scintillating in a brilliant cloud that blotted out the silver wheel. With a little cry, Kate pressed a hand over dazzled eyes, and Matt screwed his up, more blind than in the darkness.

"Stop it!" he cried.

"I will not hurt you," came the high, alien jangle. "Look up. Do not fear me!"

"Matt . . ." Kate's hand reached round, gripping his wrist. "Matt, it's the light talking!" she cried, and he heard the fear slip away from her voice in a throb of pure excitement. He forced himself to look up, heart hammering—light that came out of unfathomable darkness, and spoke? How could Kate not fear it?

The cloud of light sparkled softly around him, mostly white, but here and there blue or violet or silver. It ran over him like water, and he could almost touch it.

"Peace," came the crackling chime, from high up in the cloud. The sparks throbbed with it, and the words fell down to them like breaking crystals. "I am Arianrod, Danu's daughter. I have not come to harm you, only to guide and care for you. Raise Madinia's head, that my light may heal her!"

Matt knew then that after all he'd been full of fear; for the release of tension came like a great breaking snap. Safe, at last safe—it was impossible to doubt those edged, brilliant words. His knees felt like water, and he had to pull his wrist away from Kate to press a shaking hand over his eyes.

"Matt!" he heard Kate whisper after a moment, awed. "Matt, it's all right!"

At first he couldn't speak. Eventually he said "Yes, I know", in a queer shaken voice. He took his hand away from his eyes, looking up into the heights of the turning cloud. It was all over now. What was wrong with him?

Light bathed his face. "Have you found peacefulness, mortal?" came the chimes.

109

"Yes," said Matt.

The light moved over his face, lingeringly. "No." The chimes seemed to trail off into a register beyond human ears, with an inaudible ring of grief. "I cannot heal your fear, though I know it. You have worn a Fomor's cap; you have set foot in Lochlann, which is the land of death. Mortal, that was a dangerous thing to do!"

"I had to," Matt said.

"We'd have been killed otherwise," Kate whispered, and her arm pressed Matt's behind Anna, comfortingly. He looked at her and saw her searching the light, a look of anxiety stealing into the blue eyes. "Please," she said, after a moment, "can you wake Anna?"

"Yes. That is why I came." The cloud sparked with the echoing words. "Let her look up into my light."

"Lift her head up, Matt," Kate whispered hastily. He saw her gaze fasten on to Anna's face as, awkwardly, he tilted her chin up with a still unsteady hand. Anna's eyelids were closed, the lashes laid down in dark crescents, and she looked as white and unbreathing as marble.

The light smoked about her, sparking, and some shadow of sound seemed to pass across his ears, like unheard music. Suddenly Anna's lips parted, and her ribs heaved with a deep, gasping breath, as if she were breathing in the light; then her weight left his arm and the brown eyes jerked open again, staring up into the cloud.

"Oh!" Anna gasped, and her hand clutched at Matt. "Oh! Thank goodness the light's here!" she cried, and her voice ached with fear.

"Anna!" Kate's voice cracked. "Oh, Anna, you're back!"

Matt let go of her. She turned to Kate and her eyes, heavy with panic, slowly quietened. She took Kate's hand, as if to convince herself she was there. "What are you doing here, Kate?" she murmured sadly. "And—Matt, too?"

The light quivered. "Peace, Madinia," said the chimes from above. "This is not the place where you were lost—this is a different darkness."

Anna looked up, and her eyes grew silver with reflected light. She gazed through the many folds of light, to whatever lay outside. "Yes," she said after a moment, huskily. "I can see it is. It's just dark, and empty—not haunted. Please—I don't know who you are—" Her eyes turned back into the cloud.

"I am Arianrod." The words came glinting down.

Anna gave an uncertain shake of the head. "I still don't know . . . are you—*made* of light?"

"There will be a time for my story, if you wish to hear it." The chimes softened, sounding more like fragments of human voices. "Now tell your own, Madinia, for here there are no evil listeners."

Unconsciously, Anna let go of Kate's hand, and her own slowly clenched. "I don't know—I can't," she said despairingly. "It's so hard to remember!"

"You must." Again that ring of grief, too high really to hear. "These two mortals must know what to defend you against, Madinia."

The silver light smoked on round them, and Matt watched Anna, unconsciously willing her to open her lips and speak. He could see her struggling to; and Kate looked up, her eyes darkening with a hurt she didn't understand.

"Does she have to?" she said. "It's all over—it's finished—isn't it? Aren't we safe now?"

"Would I could believe that!" came the splintered voices, and the light shivered. "Perhaps, maiden; the fears of Danu's Children should remain their own, not to be passed on to mortal minds. But let Madinia speak; remember that first darkness, Madinia, and speak it out of yourself. Come! Remember!"

"Yes," Anna whispered, and her eyes closed for a mo-

111

ment. "Yes, I do remember. It was when we first heard about Mum and Dad, with the sun setting. . . . ."

"Remember!"

The light was racing. "Yes!" Anna cried, eyes wrinkling up against it. "I do remember! I didn't believe it—I didn't have a chance to—everything screwed round in a whirlpool, and I was sucked away. . . . I was sucked away. I wasn't there any more." She stopped, pressing her fist to her lips. "I'm back now," she whispered, behind the knuckles. "I'm really back."

"Go on!" The light glittered inexorably.

"It's all right, Anna!" Resolutely, Kate tightened her arm round her sister. "Go on," she said, mouth determined.

"All right," Anna whispered. Slowly, her eyes opened and gazed outward, gradually seeing less and less. "It was dark," she said quietly. "Even in the daytime, I was only a ghost, and I was really far away, lost in the dark. At night I used to dream I was walking through it, and there were things there, but I couldn't see them and I wasn't real enough to be afraid, anyway. But it was so cold. . . ." The brown eyes winced and turned pleadingly to Kate. "I really did feel like that, Kate. I wasn't putting on an act," Anna whispered.

Kate's mouth tightened. "Yes, I know," she said roughly. "Go on."

Anna drew a deep sigh, looking up into the cloud. "Don't you know what happened?" she said pleadingly.

The light moved slowly on, with a piercing silence.

"Go on, Anna," Matt said. He watched her, remembering the laboratory and the black mirror, and all those words tossing between Kelly and Doctor Dee; she's been in Otherworld as well, he thought, a different part, maybe more frightening. He knew that somehow he needed to know about it. He said, as gently as he could, "Tell us how you met—Kelly."

Kate didn't move, but he felt a kind of flinch in her.

"Oh," said Anna with a sob, "I know it was Ned, I really know, but—" She stopped, swallowing hard, and Matt dared not speak any more. At last she set her mouth resolutely, like Kate. "He called me," she said, "and I went, and he looked up and saw me. I think he was—surprised. He was sitting at the desk in the laboratory, with candles, and I think someone else was there—I remember a shape, near him. He looked up; and as soon as his eyes came on to me, I was back—I was myself. It was like waking up out of a dreadful dream and seeing the person you loved most, everything safe and real and right again. . . ." Her lips twisted and she stopped again, fighting herself. This time Matt almost wished she would be silent; but after a moment she went on again, in a thin voice as if she was crying.

"Being out of the dark—being warm and really, really alive again—I could only ever be those things with him. When he wasn't there, I was just a ghost in the dark, along with other ghosts. He used to call me—I don't know how, or how I got to him—but I always did. And then I could be real again, for a while."

"Anna!" Kate's voice came anguished and harsh, unlike her. "Why didn't you tell someone?"

Anna shook her head. "There was no one to tell," she whispered. "And I wasn't there, anyway. . . ."

Wanting it to be over, Matt said, "Go on, Anna. Finish it."

Her lips twisted again. "He needed me," she said with difficulty. "He had to know things—I can't remember what—but I could always tell him. Perhaps it was about the dark, and the cold, and the ghosts. And I kept him safe—kept the other ghosts away from him, in case he couldn't make them real like me, and they hurt him. And then . . ."

Kate couldn't repress a shudder. Her lips framed a word

113

—"Don't" or "No"—but made no sound.

"I thought he was going to let me be with him for good," Anna said, in a thread of a voice. "I thought he was going to make me real for always; but he sent me into the Mound for him. He said he would die if I didn't; and I couldn't bear that, so I went. It was only for a little while, he said, and then I could sleep, and it wouldn't matter any more about being real. It was so dark in there, much darker than before. I could hear and feel, but I couldn't move, couldn't speak—I was just lying there, and I was sure I was dead; until Matt touched me, and then I could move. After the brown beast took the cap away, it got harder and harder, as if I was fading away into air . . . and after the fish-man threw it back to the Mound-folk, I couldn't do anything at all. . . ." Her voice ended, seeming to trail off like Arianrod's into silent weeping.

Matt's heart twisted; it was worse when you could only half understand what someone had been through. He put a hand on her arm. "It's all right! It's over!" he said vehemently. "You're back again, and you're real!" His voice faltered as she turned her head and looked at him, her eyes oddly fixed and blind with grief. *"Anna,"* he said.

"I know." Her voice was low, as if she was afraid it would break.

"But if it's over"—it shook "if it's over, I'll never see him again, Matt."

Matt's breath caught in his throat.

"Anna!" Kate gasped, horrified. "Look at what he *did* to you!"

Anna didn't look at her. "He made me live," she whispered carefully. "He explained it to me. He said he was like a radio set, and his black mirror was the aerial; and until he tuned into me and received me I was nothing but waves in the ether. I'd always been like that, I think, though I didn't realise it. I'd never been anything but waves in the ether; I never remember being so real as when he was calling me, or looking at me. It was like having a shape for the first time.''

Kate was silent, but her face looked pinched and cold. Matt felt cold too, and shaken; he'd never dreamt things could be like this.

''It is time to be at peace.'' The cloud quivered as the high, silver voices fell down to them. ''Ease your heart, Madinia; all things pass.''

Anna looked up, and the light sparked softly over their faces. Without his own will, Matt felt strength returning as he breathed it in; and he saw that look slowly fade from Anna's eyes.

''Thank you,'' she whispered. A tear flashed, and she lifted a hand to brush it away. ''Go on talking, Arianrod. It helps me to bear it,'' she said huskily. ''What—what happens to us now?''

''You are being returned to your own time,'' came the voice, gently. ''We did not wish to interfere; we hoped you would slip simply back, of your own nature; but when Belisama rose we could hesitate no longer. It was my son, Eil Ton, who called my silver wheel.''

Her son? Matt looked up at the inhuman light, wishing the voices would go on. Kate and Anna stood silent, arms round each other, and he sensed that they too didn't want to talk any more, only to listen. After a moment, he said, ''But he was a man, wasn't he?''

The light shimmered softly, ''And I have borne a woman's form, mortal.'' The voices shifted like a kaleidoscope, and a strangely human wistfulness gleamed out. ''I too was once made real—received a shape which did not melt away like fleeting light. Once all of Danu's Children walked amongst mortals, different only in the glow that still hung about them; and the blood of the sky now runs

115

in human veins.''

''You've lived on earth?'' said Matt, half unbelievingly. ''You?''

''Yes; and still live there, all of us, though we have withdrawn to make room for mortals. We are unseen and do not trouble you. But Manannan still rules the northern seas and guards his castle there; Oengus dwells yet by the River Boyne; and my son, Eil Ton, still sports in your bright oceans.''

It was hard to imagine, this bodiless light inhabiting his world. ''What are you doing there?'' Matt asked, bewildered.

''It will not be for ever, mortal.'' Sadness slipped off the end of the high crackle. ''We are sky-travellers. Long ago, on our journey through the universes, we passed near your sun—we were weary, longing for rest, and before us rose your earth, green and blue and most beautiful of all the planets. Danu led us. We fell down through the new air like shooting stars, and touched the fresh ground.''

The chimes quivered, like singing. Matt looked at Anna, but she was listening, her own grief strangely overborne. The voices rose, piercing them almost unbearably.

''Never shall I forget how Danu's Children descended out of the void between the stars and stood on tingling grass and heard the whine of wind and echoing water . . . I am bound to your world, mortals. I was the youngest; the last of Danu's Children. And they gave me a moon for a plaything, a silver wheel to roll across the sky each night.''

Matt narrowed his eyes against the light. It seemed scarcely to be talking to them any more, caught up in its own shining memories; but another, darker, memory was stirring in his mind. He said, ''What about the Fomors?''

Pain shivered high up in the voices. ''We did not mean to harm them! We went to greet them; Govannon bore in his hands new knives and hunting spears of iron, better and stronger than their weapons of bronze—but they fled

116

from us. So it was again, when we went to Moytura; they were so afraid, we could not come near to comfort them. One flung his spear at Govannon, then ran in terror and hid beneath the earth from him. They all followed.''

Matt was silent. That story was very different from the one Elatha and Raudan had told him, and he had a feeling of hopelessness as he tried to reconcile the two. Perhaps it was hopeless; perhaps the Fomors and this cloud of light could never see anything in the same way; perhaps pure light and pure darkness would always blind each other. But he heard in Arianrod's words the echo of Elatha's bitter bafflement—*"The Children of the Sky never mean to do anything."* When the light and the dark had met at Moytura, it was the dark alone that had been hurt.

"Can't you get them out of that Mound?" he said hoarsely.

"We would dazzle them if we tried to approach." Again that unheard ring of grief. "We should have been gentler. Forgive us; we are wiser than mortals, for we do not die as you do. But still we are not very wise.''

"They'll stay there for ever, then," said Matt, rather hardly.

"What is for ever?" came the crackling chimes, after a long moment. "I am immortal, but I know only length of time, not eternity. Only the Lord of Light himself could tell. . . .'' The voices trailed into a shrill of inaudible grieving that made the hair rise on Matt's neck.

He saw Kate give a slight start, and look searchingly up into the cloud. "The Dulachan talked about him," she said, rather tensely. "Arianrod—who is the Lord of Light?"

The light smoked on around them, endlessly, with a silence deeper than the pitch-blackness around it. At last the glinting words fell down to them, as if from an immeasurable distance.

"I do not know. He is not a sky-traveller. He used to

117

care for your world, and once he saved your island from darkness, bringing you a king to keep your fires alight. He is the Lord of Light; but light throws a shadow, and long ago his shadow grew so great that it overcame him. He is hidden from view. All hope he will soon cast off his darkness and begin to care for your world again.''

"He must," Matt heard Anna whisper, very low, as if to herself. "He must. . . ."

"Peace, Madinia." The ring of grief died away and the silver light touched Anna's forehead gently. "Danu's Children will not desert you. I will send Manannan, the son of Lir, to watch over you; his island faces your shores, and he above all of us can outguess the wiles of these dark things Kelly has roused. Though immortal, he has mastered death, and his craft is subtle and manifold; he will be your best champion."

"Isn't it over, then?" Matt said, with a feeling of cold returning.

"I do not know." A blackness glimpsed out as the kaleidoscope of voices turned again. "I fear for you. It was a great wrong to tear you thus from your own time; a turmoil arose in the universe which all beings could sense, and came hurrying to heal. I do not know if it can be healed. What if Cernunnos and the Old Ones should follow you forward into your own time? You have lost the skill to quieten them and keep them safe; they would devastate your world."

The light beat troubled about them, as if a wind had touched it. Matt looked into the wild heights, feeling helpless.

"What can we do?" he said.

Slowly the whirling calmed, and the light sparked softly again like clear water; but as the many streams of it flowed round him Matt felt a bitter keening, hidden from him in the topmost register of sound.

"I should not have spoken my fears to you." The words

118

fell slowly, more than ever like edged, splintered crystals. "It is your world. You mortals have your own wisdom, and strengths unknown to us, who must some day rise and travel on again through the empty reaches of space." The light smoked on whiter than before. "Do not heed my fears. Forgive me! Manannan will watch over you, and if you are careful perhaps Cernunnos will sleep again."

They were silent. There was a kind of loneliness in the echoing words that made it hard for them to talk.

"Come." The light quickened a little. "It is almost time to return. Kelly sent you weak and unconscious through the cunning barriers of time, but I have borne you back on the straight way unknown to him. Your journey will end in your own time and place, and only a few hours will seem to have passed. Join hands, be ready for it."

They did so, Kate and Anna on either side of Matt. It was Anna who looked longingly up into the pure, rippling cloud. "Arianrod—will we see you again?" she whispered.

"Pray not to, Madinia." A desolation slipped unbearably upwards out of hearing. "I had forgotten the warmth and sweetness of mortal company. We are mere patches of light, we cannot touch one another. Once I lived as a woman in your world, loved mortal men and bore them sons who lived as heroes; but those I loved all grew grey and old, and died while I lived on unchanged." The light shivered softly, its piercing pain bright about them. "Perhaps you are descended from those sons. Did not the Fomors call you Sky Folk? But the time is over when Danu's Children could walk and talk freely with mortals; we could not come to you now save in some terrible danger. Pray not to see us again! Danu's Children have brought great ill to your world!"

The voices seemed to be fleeing, higher and much further off, and the silver wheel was glowing again under their feet. Matt looked up, straining his eyes, and suddenly the light disappeared, as if behind a door in the dark. But the darkness was not complete.

Far above them a shape flickered out, thin and hard to see properly. But Matt made it out: a dark-haired woman with light falling from the hands she held out, looking after them with eyes as bright as stars in water—then it was like swooning, all weight leaving him and his head spinning dizzily. Through it all he seemed to hear the high, flying voices—''Remember me!''

The sun was on his bare arms, earth hard under his feet. A streak of silver vanished back into the blue summer air as he looked up from his aunt's garden and heard two doves cooing in the chestnut tree opposite.

PART TWO

THE HAUNTED HOUSE

8

MOMENTS WITH MADINIA

"Are you still here?" Frowning, Kate came into the sitting room.

"Um—yes." Matt pushed himself up and looked across at her from where he lay on the couch. His eyes seemed to have trouble in focusing.

Kate surveyed him irritably. "Got sleeping-sickness or something? You're never off that couch!"

Matt sat up clumsily and rubbed a hand over his face. "Sorry," he said, muzzily.

"Oh, don't mind me!" Kate flashed, going over to the window. "It's really lively around here, with Anna mooning about like an idiot and you permanently asleep!" She stared out at the trees of the park opposite, one foot unconsciously scuffing the carpet.

Matt screwed his eyes up hard, then looked up. "Where is Anna?" he asked. His voice sounded slurred.

"God knows." Kate glanced back over her shoulder, still frowning, "Her O level results came this morning."

"What?"

"Oh, for God's sake! O levels—exams you take at school, remember?" Irritably, Kate pulled a postcard out of her pocket and flicked it across the room to him.

It fell at his feet, a white rectangle on the blue carpet. Matt picked it up, fumblingly, and put his head on his hand to stare at the writing. Anna Marchant, Upper Five A—then a list of subjects, in Kate's firm writing, and a grade noted by each one, in a different hand. Grade A, Grade B, Grade A again—eight subjects, all grade A, B, or C.

"Where did it come from?" he asked.

"From the school," Kate said, in tones of exaggerated patience. "If you can't go in yourself to find out your results when they post them up, you write out a postcard like that and they fill in the grades and send it to you. Complicated, isn't it?"

Matt closed his eyes wearily. "Oh, all right. She's got amazing grades, anyway." He looked up. "How come you wrote it out?"

Kate gave a shrug. "Well, you know what she was like, just before we came up here. I knew she wouldn't." She looked frowningly at Matt, then abruptly came from the window to sit down on the couch at his side. "What is the matter with you, Matt?" she said appealingly. "You never used to just lie around like this!"

Matt looked at the unhappy blue eyes, and felt miserable. "I dunno," he said hazily, and rubbed his face again. "I—don't feel too good, actually."

"What—ill, you mean?"

"No—I don't know."

"Well, what, then, Matt?"

Matt shook his head. "It's weird," he said huskily. "I can't stop dreaming. I just have to close my eyes, and the first thing I think of starts a dream off—like a film inside my head. It was nice at first, because I can dream whatever I like. I can make anything happen that I want to. But all I want to do now is sleep, and I can't—the dreams keep waking me up."

"Waking you up?" Kate said uncomprehendingly. "How?"

"I dunno." Matt searched for words. "They're not like

ordinary dreams, more like—visions, I mean, I'm not really asleep while I'm dreaming them. They fill my mind up too much. I just doze for, I dunno, a few minutes, I suppose—then one starts and wakes me up again. I've hardly slept for three nights now.''

Thinking about it, he felt afraid. It had been like having a wish come true at first, to dream of doing the things he'd always wanted to; but now he couldn't stop, it was too like being back in Lochlann. *There is no escape from the Mound,* he thought, with an inward shudder, and wished he could stop thinking and go to sleep.

''You mean,'' Kate said rather tautly, ''they started after we—got back?''

Matt stared across the room, through the window at the sunlit trees outside. Yes; this was Thursday, the sixth day after they'd come hurtling out of nowhere into his aunt's garden, covered with mud, with Arianrod's voices ringing in their ears. Weirdly, he and Kate had found their bicycles safely put away in the garage.

''Yes,'' he said.

''It's because of all that,'' Kate said roughly, with certainty. ''It hasn't finished, has it? Anna's just as bad as she was before.'' She paused, watching Matt. ''I've seen *him,* too,'' she said.

Him. There was only one person Kate spoke of like that. Matt felt cold. ''You don't mean Kelly,'' he said, knowing she did. ''Where?''

Kate nodded towards the window. ''Out there,'' she said uncompromisingly. ''In the park, amongst the trees. He was looking up at our window last night.''

Matt rose and went across the room to the window. Outside there was the quiet road and the park, with trees and an open grassy space, and beyond it the main road. Cars were passing up and down it, normally, too far off to be heard. What sort of place was this, which looked so ordinary and everyday, and had witches in it at night?

"Isn't one of—Danu's Children supposed to be looking after us?" he said.

"Yes. Manannan," Kate said.

"Well, we'll be all right, then." Matt recognised one of the figures that came walking across the park towards the trees, long dark hair shining in the sun. "Here's Anna."

Kate got up and came across to the window. Matt sensed her relief as she saw Anna approaching.

"Maybe we shouldn't leave her on her own," he said, after a moment.

Kate glanced up at him, and frowned. "She's supposed to be old enough to look after herself! I don't see why it should be up to us to see nothing happens to her—she doesn't care about you, or me!"

Matt compressed his lips. "Yes, she does."

Kate shrugged irritably and looked back out the window. "She doesn't. She just wants *him* back."

"Oh, Kate, for God's sake—"

"Matt!"

Her hand closed on his arm like pincers, and he saw the colour leave her cheeks. He turned to look, blinking his sore eyes to focus.

He saw Kelly come out of the shadow of the chestnut tree, into Anna's path. She saw him and stopped short—then went straight into his arms and stayed there, as if she never wanted to move away. Her lips came up to his.

"Oh, Matt, he's back—he's got her again!" Kate cried wildly. She turned for the door. "Come on!"

Matt caught her arm. "Stay here, Kate! I'll go."

She shook him off, rushing outside. Matt went after her, and they tore across the road through the open park gate, into the shadow of the trees. Kelly's great clear eyes came up and met them.

"Hello, Matt; hello, Kate," he said as they stopped, panting, a few feet away from him. And smiled.

Matt felt that inward shudder again, weakening what

126

strength he had. This man scared him more than anything else. It was easy to call him evil, and wicked, but face to face with him words like these had no meaning, just as "magic" and "witch" meant nothing. Kelly was, and that was all.

"Let her go," he said hoarsely. "It's over. It's finished. She's not going to Cernunnos for you."

Anna didn't move, just stood there in his arms with eyes half closed. Kelly looked idly down at her, then back at Matt.

"Why, Matt, what's to stop her?" he said, softly; and the corners of his mouth turned upwards. "You?"

"We stopped you last time!" Kate shouted at him. Matt saw her willing herself to jump forward and catch hold of Anna, but just not able to. "The Children of Danu are on our side!" she shot out at him with sudden triumph, remembering.

Kelly's eyes flickered with real amusement, and he laughed soundlessly. "What, those dabs of light, Kate? I'm a scientist; I know too much to be afraid of will-o'-wisps or St. Elmo's fire. Don't yell, now. You're making the yokels stare."

Matt glanced round and saw some of the people in the park looking towards them, not affecting deafness as Londoners would.

"Not that I mind," Kelly added. "But they might tell Matt's aunt they'd seen you shouting at nothing, Kate."

"What do you mean, nothing?" Kate said huskily.

"I don't exist for them," Kelly said, and smiled. The drops of sunlight between the leaves rippled with a breath of wind, and the people and barking dogs seemed suddenly a long way off.

"Oh no—" Kate whispered, and her hand grasped at Matt's. "He's starting again, Matt—don't let him—"

Her voice broke off with a high, shaky note as the trees blurred away round them, the light withdrawing but for three pale haloes like candle flames. Matt heard the thread of Anna's voice.

"Oh, Ned—"

"You're safe, my heart." The words were whispered close to Anna, so soft that Matt wasn't sure he'd heard them right. Kate was clinging to him, eyes tight closed as if she couldn't bear it, while the shapes of the laboratory loomed towards him.

"No!" he said hoarsely, putting his arm round Kate. "Stop it—it's not real, we're not here—*we're standing in the park!*"

The shapes of the furnace, the cabinet, the charts in the wall, edged forward—then abruptly went back into the gloom, and Matt smelt trees again. Sunlight broke through, and the dappled grass and dogs and calling children were back. He took a deep breath, and heard Kate gasp with relief.

"Well, Matt, you're talented."

Matt looked up, and winced inwardly under the ironical gaze.

"Learning about dreams, are you?" Kelly said softly. "That's the way, Matt; but it's hard to tell the difference between truth and a dream; and the harder it gets, the thicker the dreams come, till you're no more than a dream yourself. The way to Lochlann has very few signposts; the way out has none at all."

"Be quiet!" Kate snapped. "Matt beat you, and that's all there is to it."

Again the soundless laugh. "Yes, Matt's full of surprises, Kate." But his eyes were as serene as ever—he let me win that one, Matt thought, he's just playing with us, like a cat with a mouse. The intent gaze came back, and he nerved himself to look up and meet it.

"Come on, Matt!" Kelly said. "Don't underrate yourself; that wasn't bad." He smiled, and the clear eyes lingered on Matt, speculatively. "You're a fighter, aren't you," he mused. "It's not many who can do for a Fomor Prince and come out of the Mound with a stolen cap still on their heads. Why d'you waste yourself, Matt? Go on fighting me and you won't last much longer, you know."

"It's not just me fighting you," Matt said thickly. "Kate is too—and Manannan."

"Ah," said Kelly. "Kate." His eyes moved on to her, and she pressed her lips tight together, stubbornly not dropping her gaze.

"Be careful, Kate," Kelly said softly. "The Dulachan was right to fear the Old Ones; you've been lucky once, but next time you may meet old Jack-in-the-Green, or the Horned One himself, and the whole tribe of Danu would be blasted into nowhere if they tried to help you then. White flowers can't stand up to much, you know—and when day dawns the morning star has to fade, hasn't it?" He laughed soundlessly as Kate's lips parted.

"Stop it!" she cried, and made a desperate lunge for Anna. Catching her arm, she dragged with all her strength. "Come on, Anna—he wants to kill you! For God's sake come *on!*"

Idly, Kelly took hold of Kate's wrist. She flinched with a sharp cry, and dropped Anna's arm as if it were red-hot. "Let her go!" Matt cried, starting forward.

"Back, Matt!" Kelly advised softly. But it was only the echo of Kate's cry that Matt heard—he caught hold of her, and his fist went punching at Kelly's chest.

It went straight through him, meeting nothing.

"Oh, don't!" Anna cried, as if it were her he'd hit. She turned in Kelly's arms and her warm, real hands came fending off Matt and Kate. Kelly dropped Kate's wrist casually as they fell back, and smiled at them again. Anna turned back and clung to him.

"Let them go, Ned. You don't want them," she whispered, so low they hardly heard.

"Not like you, sweetheart," Kelly said quietly, and put

both arms round her. His eyes went down to her like a caress. "Hush."

"Stop talking to her like that!" Kate cried passionately, unaware of a high sob in her voice. "You don't *care* about her—you just want her to die for you!"

Kelly's mouth gave not quite a smile. "What, you think just because I'm not human any more I can't love anyone?" he said idly. He looked up, and there was such a glow in the strange eyes that they seemed hardly his. "You're wrong there, Kate. I've cheated perdition for three hundred years, and twelve thousand innocents have died, just so that I can have these moments with Madinia. But perhaps that isn't your idea of love." He smiled and bent to touch Anna's hair with his lips. "Not women's magazine stuff, I agree," he murmured, seeming to laugh.

"Shut up!" Kate shot at him furiously. "Stop talking about love! You only want to send her to Cernunnos for you!"

"Kate," said Kelly softly, and the untroubled eyes glinted across at her: "you cannot always make everyone do just what you want. *Stop interfering*. . . . Listen, now, when I'm serious. You and Matt can turn and walk away from me now, and I swear—on your sister's life—that no harm'll come to you ever again. I can see to it. I'll make sure you have—more or less whatever you want, all through your lives. But go on opposing me—dragging in your pathetic brown boggarts and lights in the sky—and you're finished."

Matt felt sick. The quiet words went through his mind as if there was nothing there to stop them—*"whatever you want, all through your lives"*—and he seemed to know less and less about anything. Perhaps it wasn't impossible even for Kelly to have a preference for who lived and who died, but how could you tell, from those eyes?

"I don't believe you!" he said shakenly. "We've survived so far. I don't see why we should listen to you, anyway; you've made Anna think you're real, but you're not, you're like everything else—you're a ghost." He felt a spark of hate glow on that last word. "You're *dead*," he said.

"You're a fine one to talk," Kelly countered instantly. His gaze dwelt intently on Matt. "You shouldn't have worn that cap, you know. Even now you've one foot in Lochlann, haven't you—half of you planning what your next dream's going to be? I can stop that for you; just give me the word. Believe me, I don't want you to die. Or Kate."

"Don't worry about us," Matt said roughly. "Let Anna go and leave us alone."

"Well—" The suggestion of a shrug, and the clear smile. "I tried," said Kelly lightly, and took his hands away from Anna. "Go with your sister, darling."

Anna's eyes turned upwards, stricken. "Ned—" she said imploringly, and Kate trembled at the sound of that voice.

"Oh, not for ever!" Kelly said, and his eyes glowed again. He gathered Anna's hands in his own. "You don't want to leave me, do you?"

"No," said Anna desolately, in a whispering voice meant only for him, as if Kate and Matt didn't matter. "I'd do anything—you know." Her eyes seemed blind, able to see only him.

"You won't leave me," said Kelly softly. "You're my life, you know that."

"Yes. . . ."

"I'm always with you," Kelly said, and smiled. He released her hands. "Go now. You don't have to be afraid about anything. Neither do you, Matt, or you, Kate"—his eyes glinted—"so long as you keep out of the way. Otherwise, remember what happened to Anna's bicycle. I didn't particularly want to smash that, either, but these

131

things happen. Watch yourselves. Cheerio, now."

And he turned, pausing a moment to touch Anna's cheek with his fingers, then went easily away over the grass towards the park railings. There was a second when he seemed difficult to see, but before he reached the railings he was gone, out of the park, out of their world.

"Oh, Matt," Kate said on a sob.

"Come on," Matt said. "Come on, Anna."

She turned and looked at him, and her eyes were full of tears. "Has he really gone?" she said, chokily. "Oh, I thought this time. . . ."

Matt closed his eyes, but under the lids Kelly's face came as clearly as an image on a film screen. He opened them again, his head aching, and put out a hand to take Anna's. "Come on," he said again. "Let's go into the house, and have some lunch, or something."

"Yes," said Kate, and lifted her chin. "Your results have come, Anna. You've passed all your exams. I'll make the lunch." She moved out of Matt's arm and went firmly ahead to the gate; and Matt and Anna followed. Without glancing back Kate went into the house towards the kitchen.

"The postcard's in here somewhere," Matt said, leading Anna into the sitting-room. He saw the small white rectangle lying on the arm of the couch and picked it up. "Here."

She took it and looked down at it. After a moment he realised she couldn't read it, the tears in her eyes were blinding her.

"You've done really well," he said, stumblingly. "Grade A in English, French and history, grade B in geography and maths, I think. . . . Shall I read it?"

Anna bit her lip. "It's all right," she whispered, and brushed a tear away with her finger. "It doesn't seem to matter much, now. Have you got a hankie?"

Matt unearthed a crumpled paper one from his pocket

and gave it to her. She wiped her eyes, and he thought of how well she'd done; and yet she was right; amidst what was happening now it had no importance. If he himself passed English and art next year, he'd be lucky. He wasn't even down to take the maths. They didn't care for him much at school; "lazy" and "inattentive" figured on all his reports, as if the teachers couldn't be bothered to think up new adjectives from one term's end to another. . . . God, he was so tired, he couldn't even think straight.

There was a crash from the kitchen, and Anna shuddered.

"Oh, poor Kate," she said unsteadily.

"She's all right," Matt said. "Do you feel better?"

She looked up at him, brown eyes so raw and hurt that he bit his lip. "Matt," she said pleadingly. "I'm so sorry. . . ."

"It's all right—"

"I just can't let go of him." Her voice shook pitifully. "I see, now; he only came to—to *show* you and Kate that you *can't* separate us; no one could. I thought he came to be with me, for always . . . but I always do think that. He'll come again. And—you and Kate had better not try to stop him."

"But, Anna—"

"No, please, Matt!" Her voice almost broke, and the tears glittered treacherously. "Don't tell me. I know, but I can't bear to hear it—not just now. I don't want to be stopped. I couldn't go back to being like I was before, just drifting, not being anybody in particular. If you stop me, Matt, I'll hate you, I'll hate you and Kate for ever."

Matt opened his lips, then after a moment shut them again. What can I say, he wondered bleakly. I never even knew there could be anything like this. He didn't know what or how to think about it, or about anything else much, any more.

"Don't worry, Anna," he said at last, but his words felt

133

useless. "We'll—we'll look after you."

There was another crash from the kitchen, followed by two more. Matt looked at Anna helplessly, then went to the door. "Kate, are you okay?" he called down the passage.

Kate appeared in the kitchen doorway, arms tightly folded and her face looking pinched.

"The pans won't stay on the shelf," she said, and her voice wavered uncharacteristically.

"You've got to push them right back on it," Matt said.

"I said they won't stay on, Matt!" Kate exclaimed, dangerously.

Matt went down the passage into the kitchen. Salad was half made in a wooden bowl, tomatoes and cucumber on the table waiting to be sliced, and three pans lay about the floor.

Matt picked them up and pushed them firmly back on to the high shelf above the sink. "They're all right now," he said making sure they were steady.

"Are they?" demanded Kate. He turned to look at her, and the blue eyes looked back as if she hated him. "Just watch," said Kate, that tremor back in her voice.

Matt looked round, in time to see the frying-pan leap from its place so fast that it crashed against the opposite wall before clattering to the floor.

"Oh God," he said after a moment, hoarsely. Another pan jumped, banged the ceiling and came down on the table, scattering the tomatoes with a horrible look of mischief.

"It's him, isn't it!" Kate said, her voice ragged. "He's never going to leave us alone until he gets Anna!"

"Well, he can't have Anna, can he," Matt said wearily, and moved to the side of the room as another pan bounded merrily down.

"No, I know!" Kate shouted at him. "But how much are we supposed to put up with, Matt?"

Matt pressed a hand against his throbbing forehead. If only I could get some sleep, he thought, then maybe I could cope with all this—Otherworld, creeping inexorably into their own world at so many points. He moved to pick up the tomatoes.

"We can finish making the salad in the sitting-room," he said. The oven door opened and slammed, gleefully. Kate took the bowl, the knife and the chopping-board, and went quickly away down the passage. Matt followed with the vegetables, catching up a tin of corned beef from the top of the fridge. He closed the door behind him, and as he did so heard the crash of breaking crockery.

Going down to the sitting-room, he wondered how long it would take whatever it was to move out of the kitchen into the rest of the house.

9

JUST ONE SHADOW

1

"Well, it looks as if we've got poltergeists," said Aunt Phyllis with a touch of ruefulness, but nothing like the dismay Matt had feared. Home from work at twenty past seven, she stood in the kitchen doorway with Matt and Kate behind her, surveying the disorder.

The door of the crockery cupboard hung open, and cups and plates lay in fragments on the floor underneath. Tins of food rolled about the floor along with the pans and baking-tins, noisily, as if an invisible hand kept stirring them. The oven door swung zestfully to and fro, and one of the gas rings was flickering on and off.

"Poltergeists?" said Kate, blankly.

Matt glanced at her warningly. It was a totally new idea to her, so sure was she that Kelly had caused all this. But for heaven's sake keep quiet, Kate—do we really want to pour out this whole mad story to Aunt Phyllis?

However, Aunt Phyllis mistook Kate's tone for incomprehension. "Yes, it's nothing really to worry about," she said. "It isn't all that uncommon, I don't think. It's just some kind of upsurge of energy that we don't really understand. We'll have to put up with it for a while, but it'll pass, I'm sure." She glanced at Matt. "Is Anna around?" she said, with just a touch of constraint.

136

"Oh—yes, she's upstairs," Matt said awkwardly.

He knew Aunt Phyllis was worried about Anna. It was enough to worry anyone, the way she sat about in the evenings looking dreamily in front of her with a little smile coming and going, as if she was seeing something quite different from what was really there. And after what had happened this morning, it would probably get worse. He felt an unreasonable prick of self-reproach. Poor Aunt Phyllis, having to worry about two girls she hardly knew— and now poltergeists into the bargain.

"I'm sorry about the kitchen, Miss Cooper," Kate said. "We tried to tidy it, but it wasn't any good."

"Good heavens, it's not your fault," Aunt Phyllis said, with a gentleness Matt didn't quite understand. "Look, you two go along and watch television, and I'll get some supper together. You can't have had a very nice day, with this noise going on all the time."

"Oh, but you've been working," Matt said lamely. He didn't want to stay in the kitchen.

"Yes, but not awfully hard. It's been quite an easy day, really." Aunt Phyllis stepped carefully into the kitchen and opened the fridge door. Everything inside appeared to be intact, as if whatever it was had overlooked it. Perhaps they don't have fridges where it comes from, Matt thought, ridiculously; the thought of Kelly's medieval laboratory slipped into his mind, apparently unbidden. "There," said Aunt Phyllis cheerfully, "plenty of things here. Off you go, and I'll bring it through to the sitting-room. Perhaps you could call Anna."

"Yes, sure." After a moment, Matt followed Kate to the sitting-room. She went in and turned the television on.

It was just half past seven, and the portentous music introducing a current affairs programme rolled out.

"Do you want to watch that?" Matt asked.

"Yes. Why not?" Kate said. She took one of the arm-

137

chairs opposite the small screen.

Matt stood in the doorway, watching, as the well-known face of the programme's introducer appeared, with his usual purposeful frown. "This week—the unity of the Government is threatened over the proposed spending cuts," he said energetically, "and trade union leaders lash out at criticism of our nationalised industries. Abroad, the Athens hijackers continue their flight round the capitals of the Middle East; and International Red Cross observers give their estimate, in human terms, of the tragedy in Central Africa."

Matt came forward into the room, shutting the door behind him, and Kate sat very still in her chair. Matt looked at her helplessly. What could he do? Seeing these things on the news could only make it worse for her; her parents weren't going to come back and put everything right; but, the way things were, who could blame her for fastening on to any remote chance of hearing something, for sitting there *willing* those reporters to say what she needed to hear.

The camera drew back to show the studio with the introducer sitting at his desk. "Good evening," he rapped out grimly. "This week a junior minister resigned in protest over proposed cutbacks in the housing programme. . . ."

Kate said, without moving, "Listen in case Anna comes down."

Matt compressed his lips. If her parents were ever found, his father wouldn't leave them to learn it from the television news. Things like that were never broadcast before the next of kin had been told. Kate knew that. She knew it was pointless watching, but somehow it made no difference, just as it made no difference to the way he switched on his radio every hour to hear the news, and scanned the newspaper headlines every day.

"And now—the troubles in Africa," the introducer's

138

voice said, and Matt's attention jerked back to the screen. "Impartial observers from the International Red Cross have been studying the situation," the introducer informed him frowningly, "and today they made their report. They estimate that since the fighting began, just over a fortnight ago, there have been something like twelve thousand civilian casualties. Jeff Cooper reports."

The picture changed, and under a high blue sky Jeff Cooper looked at his son, as if at a stranger. There were khaki tents behind him, and a thorn tree, and black Africans sat in hunched, motionless little groups. It looked very still.

"These people have come from the north," Jeff Cooper said into the camera, quietly. "Altogether there are about eight hundred of them, and there are more arriving every day. They left their villages, most of them, when the soldiers came, and started the long trek south away from the war. When they got here, just outside the capital, they stopped."

The camera swung round to take a long shot over the neat rows of tents to some buildings in the distance. Modern tower blocks glittered above older yellow brick, and ramshackled huts spread out towards the camp. The camera returned to Jeff Cooper, and he looked into it, frowning as if the sun was in his eyes.

"Three days ago," he said, "Oxfam moved in. They brought these tents, they brought two doctors and some nurses, some medical supplies, blankets, and a little food. It isn't enough. These people have lost their homes, many have lost their families; they've walked a very long way, with very little food. Already the doctors and nurses are overworked, and already the camp is overcrowded. They've injected as many people as possible against typhoid and cholera, but they aren't hopeful."

He began to walk down between the rows of tents, the camera following him. Only the Africans' eyes moved, looking up slowly and without expression. Jeff Cooper's eyes looked intense, darker than usual.

"Despite all that," he said quietly, "these are the lucky ones. Everybody here can tell you about someone he knew who's dead. Their villages were captured first by one side and then by the other and, as the tide of war flowed backwards and forwards over them, they died. It didn't seem to matter very much whether they supported the Government or the guerrillas; the strategic value of their villages seemed to be more important than their opinions—or their lives. So the lucky ones escaped, and came south— those who didn't die of starvation or wounds on the road. It's impossible to tell exactly how many small settlements have been wiped out of existence by shelling, or exactly how many ordinary people have been caught in this exceptionally merciless cross-fire. The Red Cross estimate of twelve thousand is probably as accurate as any round figure can be. In the next weeks, unless something is done, this figure is likely to be swelled not only by the fighting but also by disease. For these reasons, the headquarters of the Red Cross in Geneva has sent out an urgent appeal to both sides to declare a ceasefire and get round the table together—"

Kate rose abruptly and switched off the set. "You don't mind, do you?" she said in a rough, unsteady voice, and went quickly to the window, turning her back on the room.

Matt put a hand up to his head. It was aching again, as if the hot, brilliant African blueness had come too close.

It was always strange to see his father impersonally on television, being Our Correspondent in Saigon, or Jerusalem, or Cairo; somehow it made him less his father— except that this time he hadn't been so impersonal. Behind the two-dimensional reporter's face and the skillful verbal delivery, his father had, unmistakably, been upset; and to see that jolted Matt. Was it just being in a refugee camp that had done it, or was there something more? Oh my God, he thought, resting his head in both hands, if only I could sleep. He dared not close his eyes, knowing that ranks of silent, starved black faces would immediately rise before him. And he was so tired it would take a big effort to banish them.

"Matt," said Kate's voice.

He looked up, and saw her leaning her back against the window, facing him, eyes as blue and intense as the shot of Africa. They seemed to be waiting for something.

"Yes?"

"What exactly are they fighting about?"

Matt grimaced, rubbing his forehead. "I dunno much about it," he said wearily. "I think it used to be a Belgian colony, and a lot of Belgian businessmen still own big estates there and run the banks and things. The guerrillas want to get them out and take over everything themselves. But I don't really understand it. I know the government doesn't want to lose all the Belgian investment, but not long ago the biggest Belgian companies agreed to gradually phase themselves out and let the Africans take over, or something. Everyone was surprised when the revolution suddenly started, because they thought everything had been settled."

There was a slight pause, then Kate said, "H'mm" rather expressively as if at someone showing off in a class at school. "How did you find all that out?" I know, Matt thought, I'm not supposed to be bright and know things you don't.

"Just from listening to the radio," he said. "And Dad talked about it a lot before he went."

"So did my Mum and Dad," Kate said, rather bleakly. "I didn't listen much, though. Well? Didn't you hear what they said about twelve thousand civilian casualties?"

"Yes. . . ."

The blue eyes looked at him, and Matt slowly saw the

brilliance of horror in them. "Well," Kate said roughly, "don't you remember what *he* said? About twelve thousand innocents dying?"

Matt stared, the sudden words knocking his headache into limbo—"*I've cheated perdition for three hundred years, and twelve thousand innocents have died.*"

"But—he was just *talking,*" he said stumblingly, remembering how Kelly used words to bewilder them.

Kate shook her head. "He never just talks! It always means something, if you can stay awake long enough to listen."

Matt struggled to follow her. "I—don't see what it could mean. All right, so he knows there's a war on, and people are dying. Why shouldn't he? He can probably see it in that mirror of his."

"It's more than that!" Kate said harshly. "He thinks the whole war happened just for him—so Mum and Dad could disappear out there, and he could get Anna!"

"But that's crazy!" Matt exclaimed. Kate said nothing, just looked at him, and his heart gave a lurch. "You don't believe him, do you?"

"I don't know," Kate said in a tight voice. "You remember how the Dulachan and Arianrod talked about a Shadow, and the Lord of Light being lost in it? Suppose it isn't just coincidence about the war. Suppose everything that's happening is part of just one shadow—the same one, everywhere."

Matt put his head back in his hands, and his mind reeled. This was his own world. Kelly and the Shadow belonged to Otherworld, where things happened crazily and without explanation—but in this world things made sense, they had reasons. There'd always been wars, you couldn't start ascribing them to witches and shadows.

Suppose she was right. Suppose the Shadow had crept into his world too, and was relying on disbelief like his to grow stronger, bigger, till it could eclipse all light—one

Shadow, Kelly just a particular face of it, able to say twenty thousand people had died simply to help him get his way. No! It couldn't be like that!

"Matt, for God's sake don't doze off now!" The appeal broke through in Kate's voice. He got up at once and came across the room to her, putting a hand on her arm.

"I don't believe it," he said hoarsely. "There are still lots of good things happening, everywhere. Kate, let's tell Aunt Phyllis about it. Let's see what she says."

"We can't," she said despairingly. "It wouldn't do any good—not now! Would you believe someone who told you they'd been back in time, and seen all those mad things? She's scared about Anna already. She'd just think all three of us had gone crazy!"

"Well, what then?" Matt asked.

"Oh, I don't know!" Kate's voice shook. "What's this Manannan guy supposed to be doing? I thought he was going to protect us?"

"Well, maybe he is," Matt said. "Nothing's actually happened to us yet, we're all still here—"

The door opened and Anna entered.

All traces of tears from this morning had gone. She came in as if not seeing them, the dark eyes rich and shining, head help up as if she could feel sunlight on her face. She stood there with her hand on the back of a chair, and Matt almost thought he heard her laughing with sheer joyfulness.

"*Anna—*" he said hoarsely, then stopped as he heard Aunt Phyllis coming up the passage, with what sounded like the supper tray. At the same time, the rattle of falling pans came from the kitchen, and he felt the almost familiar sense of hope dying within him.

2

The dreams tormented him again that night, and in the small sitting-room, despite the open windows, it was hot and close. By now he was so tired that he was losing control over them. Images seemed to come without his will, and for hour on hour sights of Africa rose before his closed eyes, intense and violent. Not wanting to, he found himself shaping pictures of those dead innocents, lying tossed like rubbish in the scrub or beside a dirt roadway; aching for sleep, even in the middle of a dream he felt himself rolling his head on his pillow, his lips shaping silent pleas to some unknown person to stop—stop—let him go to sleep—

Time always seemed to flow differently at night. Clocks pointing to two or three o'clock seemed to lack meaning, like signposts in nowhere. Matt didn't know when it was that he found himself lying on his back staring up at the cream ceiling of the sitting-room. He could see it quite clearly, and that struck him as strange, for the curtains were drawn to keep out the light of the street lamp outside. It was as if all the objects in the room had suddenly been charged with a kind of power, that made the darkness unable to mask them.

Oh, no, he thought, it's another dream. He felt on the edge of panic.

Go away, he told the room. *Be dark again.*

The uncanny visibility remained. Nothing actually moved, but everything he looked at—the armchairs, the coffee table, the blank television, even the patterns on the carpet—seemed alive and expectant.

Go away.

Nothing happened.

He tried to sit up, and did so with the dizzy lightness that seemed to prove he was dreaming. The room glimmered back at him. It didn't make sense. A dream in which everything just sat there, full of a mysterious immanence, and nothing happened? He wondered if he was becoming insane. Everyone knew lack of sleep could do that to you.

Then he heard something.

He listened, hard. It was coming from outside, just below the window; a soft, abrupt blundering, like something stumbling against the wall. It stopped.

Then it started again, as if not realising it could be heard. There were other noises too, reaching Matt's ears with preternatural distinctness—bumps on the concrete path round the bay window, crackles as if the rose bushes were being pushed about. He looked hard at the curtains.

The outline of the window frame was etched on them by the street lamp. But even as he looked at them, another shadow seemed to move—thin and chancy, like disappearing smoke. He strained his eyes, not sure whether to trust them or not. But the shadow never quite disappeared, and after a while there could no longer be any doubt. There was something out there. The noises went on, the brushing, the bumps.

Then the stairs creaked.

The third one from the bottom always creaked. Matt felt all his muscles knot—one in front of the window, one out there in the passage. Which way was he to go? This was a bad nightmare.

But the one thing he couldn't do was sit there and wait until they both came in. He must make a dash for it, whatever there was outside the door. His mouth feeling like sand, he eased himself cautiously off the couch, then leapt for the door, tore it open and hurled himself crashing out into the passage. He caught at the banister of the empty staircase to steady himself, but in the corner of his eye he saw something—something tall and white, by the front door—and the lock rattled softly.

The sense of dreaming fled. "Anna!" he shouted, and sprang to catch her and pull her away from that door, and the shadow that waited for her outside. In her pale nightdress, Anna resisted, silently, pulling against his arms as if they were inanimate things that could be pushed aside.

"Anna!" Matt said urgently, dropping his voice as he

145

remembered the thing outside. She turned towards him, as if wondering what sort of sound she had heard, and he saw her eyes—dark, drowned-looking, not knowing him.

His heart went up into his throat. It wasn't his dream. He was awake, wide awake; Anna was the one who was asleep; it was some dream of hers that had brought her down the stairs to fumble with the locked door, and was still making her strain against his arms to get outside.

And what was waiting there, outside?

"Come on, Anna," he said huskily, trying to lead her away from the door. You mustn't wake up sleepwalkers, the shock would be too much for them. No. He remembered. That was an old wives' tale. He must wake her, get her out of her dream, make her see what terrible danger she was really in. He shook her hard. "Anna! Anna, wake up!"

Her eyes creased a little, then seemed to open, suddenly widening, startled in the sight of him. Her lips parted. "Matt—" As she stared at him, memory slowly came, darkening the dark eyes like rain. Her gaze faltered; her head turned, casting a look of such longing over her shoulder that Matt almost lost his grip on her. "Anna!" he said, desperately.

"I've got to go, Matt!" she whispered, and the stricken dark eyes looked back at him. "It's Ned," she said, hardly on a breath. "He's waiting for me."

"No!" Matt looked away from those eyes. "It's not Ned," he said doggedly. "And even if it was, he's only waiting to kill you. For God's sake, come away from that door!" He dragged her roughly out of the passage into the sitting-room, shut the door and put his back against it.

Anna unconsciously put her hands up to her arms, where he had gripped her. She stood there in the strange luminescence, her hair falling darkly down her nightdress; and her eyes looked up desperately.

146

"Oh Matt, why don't you try to understand!" Her voice came low and aching.

Matt bit his lip. "I do," he said. Couldn't she see that he couldn't stand by and watch Kelly take her life from her?

"No." Anna shook her head. "Ned's given me everything. It's not like you and Kate."

Matt's wits were scattered momentarily. Kate? No, he couldn't bear to think about Kate, not now, not with that thing out there. Why hadn't he taken Anna upstairs, instead of in here, where only a sheet of glass separated them from it? The windows were open at the top, too. Kate at least was upstairs, still comparatively safe.

He saw the shadow move on the curtains.

"Look, Anna," he said, his mouth dry. "Look what it really is out there."

Anna turned her head, and in the strange light he saw the blood leave her face. The shadow was still there, still faint and blurred; but, slowly, they could make out broad shoulders, and a narrow questing head—and on the head, two wide spreading shapes. It was a beast with antlers.

They watched it shift to and fro before the window, quietly for so great a beast. It was as if it were puzzled, or not quite awake. Matt felt that in a moment he would choke.

"Oh, no—" Anna whispered, so low he could hardly hear—perhaps it had been "Oh Ned." He shut his eyes. Please, please, someone help. . . .

Strangely, no dreams started up under his eyelids. He could see only a vague brightness, as if a light was shining against his closed eyes. It grew there, spreading like the rays of a lamp, and oddly calming. After a moment, he opened his eyes again.

The room was light. The objects were not only visible but gleaming as light ran off them like pure, cold water.

147

He saw it come flowing round himself and Anna, and rise up over their heads, turning. Anna's fingers touched his, and sparks glimmered electrically round their linked hands. Now it was like standing in a castle of aerial, glass-like light; all his weariness was being washed away, all the cramped and knotted fears. He thought he could catch again the high disappearing music of Danu's Children. Spears of trailing light leapt out towards the window.

He saw the shadow of the horned beast go still, like an animal caught in a car's headlamps. As the light poured on to it it began to waver and lose shape like escaping smoke. It was as if the light were an argument it understood, sending it without struggle back to its own place. It thinned harmlessly away; and at last there was just the outline of the window frame, still and black against the curtains.

Matt looked up at the radiant cloud. They had come, after all—Danu's Children had not deserted them. He opened his lips. "Thank you," he said hoarsely. "Are you —Manannan?"

Both of them waited for the beautiful, crystalline voices, but the light was silent. It was ebbing fast too, as if now its work was done there was nothing to wait for, no words to say. A feeling of desolation came to Matt as it streamed away into nothingness, and the room rapidly darkened.

"Manannan?" he said again.

He thought the light hesitated; but then it was gone, leaving only the dim glow from the heavy blue curtains.

By his side he heard Anna sigh—low, but stabbing. He looked at her, unable to see her face properly now the light had gone. "Did you see what was there?" he said.

She gave a tiny nod. "Yes," she whispered.

"And you thought it was Kelly," Matt said. All at once he had to be cruel, he couldn't stop the words. "You thought it was him calling you, to be with him for always.

And instead it was—that. I know you think I can't under-stand, but can't *you?* He only wants you to die for him!"

Her hand left his. "I know," said Anna, her voice very alone in the dark. "It does hurt—a bit—that he tries to trick me. He knows he's only got to ask. . . ."

Matt's breath caught. Only to ask? Could she possibly realise what she was saying? "But *Anna,* what about Kate?" he said desperately. "What about your parents? What do you expect them to do—just let you die?"

She turned her head towards him, though he couldn't see her eyes. "Don't, Matt," she whispered entreatingly. "There just isn't anything else I can do."

"There is!" Matt said urgently, but the old feeling of despair was close. "You can tell him no!"

She shook her head, looking down at the floor. "It isn't any good," she whispered, throat sounding tight. "I *couldn't* do that, I might just as well kill myself. Oh, Matt"—she turned impetuously towards him—"don't you really understand? If it was Kate, wouldn't you do the same?"

Matt felt himself gasp. Him—die for Kate? His mind stuck at the notion, unable to take it in. "I—I don't know," he said stumblingly. "It's different. . . ."

He felt rather than heard a hopeless sigh as Anna looked back at the curtains where the horned shadow had appear-ed. Oh, Anna . . . he stood there helplessly, ashamed and knowing he'd never understand. All his feelings stopped where Anna's were just beginning.

"We might as well go back to bed," he said huskily, "if you're all right now."

She turned, one finger unconsciously brushing away a tear, and Matt bit his lip. All right? Unable to exist without that powerful double-dealing lover, waiting for death as he waited for the next morning—all right?

" 'Night, Matt," she said softly, and went past him out

149

of the room. He heard her go quietly up the stairs and into the bedroom, where Kate still, presumably, slept unmoving on the small camp-bed.

He went back to the couch and lay down, pulling the sheet over him. It wasn't until he closed his eyes that he remembered, with an involuntary wince, those dreams; but under the lids nothing came except a velvet darkness and, further back in his head, an elusive idea of light. He was still trying to catch this idea when he fell down and down into an unending chasm of sleep.

10

KELLY'S DREAM

When the telephone rang, Matt jumped as if that too was a poltergeist. They were very active this afternoon, and he could only be thankful that he had eight hours of solid sleep behind him. Now that he was properly awake, it was easier not to let them scare him.

The dreams were leaving him alone today, as well, or at least were staying far enough from the surface of his mind not to bother him. Perhaps Manannan's light of last night had had the power to drive away dreams as well as shadows.

He went into the hall to answer the phone.

"Hello, dear," came Aunt Phyllis's voice. "Oh, I'm glad I caught you in."

"It's a bit hot to go out," Matt said, wondering why she'd phoned. The air was very heavy both inside and outside the house. He sat down on the floor with the receiver. The small windowless hall was the most bearable place to be.

"Is it really?" Aunt Phyllis's voice came, surprised. "It's rather nice here in Manchester, for once. Hot, but fresh and breezy."

"It's like an oven here," Matt said. "Nothing's moving. Not even the birds."

Swallows built under the eaves of these houses, and were

usually darting about for insects most of the day, but this afternoon everything was still. Not a leaf flickered. The trees' summer foliage hung heavy and listless.

A milk bottle smashed.

"Oh, I heard that," Aunt Phyllis said, ruefulness entering the light, far-off voice. "Something's moving, at any rate. Are they bothering you awfully, dear?"

"They're a bit noisy," Matt said. But he didn't want to worry his aunt. "Kate and Anna are upstairs. You don't hear them so much there. It's okay, I've emptied the pedal-bin, so they can't throw the rubbish around any more."

"Oh, thank you, dear, that was thoughtful." There was a slight pause. "You're sure you're all right?" Aunt Phyllis asked, her voice carefully unworried.

Matt bit his lip. Poltergeists in the kitchen, Anna sleep-walking, a horned shadow on the sitting-room curtains. . . .

"Yes, we're okay," he said.

"The thing is," Aunt Phyllis said, tentatively, "I may not be able to get home tonight. Someone's got to have dinner with a prospective client, and the chap who was going to is in bed with summer flu or something, so I've been asked to take his place. It means hanging about till eleven or so, and drinking rather a lot, so I thought I'd book into a hotel for the night, rather than drive all the way back."

"Oh," said Matt, awkwardly. Alone with the poltergeists all night, alone with whatever else might come out of the summer darkness up to the windows. . . . "I see," he said, with a certain effort.

There was another pause. "I think, actually, I will come home," Aunt Phyllis said, as if making up her mind. "It's not really fair to leave you on your own with those wretched poltergeists."

Matt felt that prick of guilt again. It wasn't as if the poltergeists were Aunt Phyllis's fault. It must be exhausting enough doing a full-time job, without having to worry about three crazy kids and a haunting as well.

"We're all right, honestly," he said. "They usually stop after dark, anyway. We can manage."

"Look, dear," Aunt Phyllis said carefully, "are you absolutely sure? I can easily ask someone else to take over this dinner, and just come home as normal. I know you're not, well, children, but it isn't awfully pleasant to spend a night with poltergeists. In any case, we don't want Kate and Anna to be bothered by anything unnecessary. Do you think they might prefer me to come home?"

Matt hesitated. Having dinner with a prospective client sounded like quite a big responsibility; he knew it wasn't something she did regularly. It wouldn't look all that good for her to say sorry, I can't do it after all, my fifteen-year-old nephew and his two friends are frightened of poltergeists. Now he thought about it, he could hear that thought in her voice too, in the way she said "easily".

"No, honestly, we can manage," he said.

"Well," said Aunt Phyllis, "are you sure?"

"Yes, really," Matt said.

"All right then, dear," her voice came, still rather carefully. "But look, if anything does happen, do phone, won't you? The number's on the pad. I'll find out the restaurant's phone number and the hotel's, and leave them with the girl on the switchboard, so if you phone before five o'clock she can let you have them. Just in case anything happens this evening. Okay, dear?"

"Yes, fine," said Matt.

"I don't suppose anything will," Aunt Phyllis said. "But we might as well be prepared. So you won't forget to ring up for those other two numbers, will you?"

"No, I won't."

"All right, dear. Sorry to fuss. 'Bye, then."

"Have a good time," Matt said, rather awkwardly. " 'Bye."

He replaced the receiver. His hand was sweating where he'd held it, and he rubbed his palm on the leg of his trousers. The heat seemed to have grown more oppressive, so that even in the passage it was airless now.

There was a thud and the sound of things rolling. Matt's hand stopped still on his trousers; and he felt the hair prickle up on the back of his neck. The sound didn't come from the kitchen. It came from much nearer.

Between the sitting-room and the kitchen was the breakfast-room, which received the morning sun from the back of the house. One door opened into it from the passage, and one from the kitchen. Matt got up and pushed open the passage door, gingerly.

A bowl of fruit had fallen from the sideboard, and bananas, apples and oranges lay on the floor. Matt swallowed, then went in and began to pick the fruit up. As he did so, a brisk knocking started on the kitchen door, like someone asking to be let in.

The bowl couldn't have fallen off of its own accord. It was set in the middle of the sideboard, well back from the edge. As Matt put it back and deposited the fruit in it, he wondered, without wanting to, how long it would take the poltergeists to fling it all back on the floor. If they'd moved in here, not long.

The clock began chiming. One, two, three, four. . . . Matt glanced at his watch. Twenty past three. The clock, an antique in a carved mahogany case, did run slightly fast. But it went on to strike seven, stopped for the space of two chimes, then started again.

Matt began to tidy the place up hurriedly, removing everything breakable out to the hall table. If the poltergeists were coming in, they'd better find as little as possible to wreck.

The kitchen door burst open and the grill pan hurtled in like a cannon-ball. It missed Matt's head by millimetres and dived into the fireplace, knocking out a chip. Matt stood completely still for one moment, looking at that jagged place; then he turned and made for the passage door. As he closed it behind him, he looked up to see Kate coming down the stairs. Her eyes sharpened on his face, and she came down two at a time.

"What's happening? Are you all right?" she demanded. "You look *white*."

Matt moved his stiff lips. "I'm all right," he said hoarsely. "Don't go into the breakfast-room, though. The poltergeists are in there. I was trying to shift the stuff out so they wouldn't break it, and the grill-pan came whizzing at me. It didn't hit me, but it knocked a chunk out of the fireplace." Suddenly, he sat down on the bottom stair.

"Oh, God," Kate said in consternation.

"I'm all right," Matt said with difficulty. "It just surprised me, that's all. They've never actually tried to hurt us before."

"I'll make you a cup of tea," Kate said, turning towards the kitchen.

"Don't go in there!" Matt was on his feet, catching her arm.

Kate turned back, staring at him. The blue eyes grew scared. "We've got to eat, though, Matt. How are we going to manage if we don't go into the kitchen? All the food's in there."

"We can't," said Matt. 'We'll have to go out, get fish and chips or something." He swallowed. "Aunt Phyllis isn't coming back tonight."

"What?" Kate's eyes widened, looking really scared. "Why not?"

"She's got to go to dinner with someone."

Kate folded her arms rather tightly. "Matt, I don't
155

much fancy being on our own all night. I think your aunt being here has stopped anything really bad happening."

Matt looked away. You should have been down here last night, he thought, instead of upstairs, fast asleep. "I think I'll phone her and ask her not to go to this dinner," he said. "She said I could—"

The breakfast-room door clicked and opened. Catching at each other, Matt and Kate scrambled back up the stairs, Matt's heart in his mouth. Looking down, he saw nothing happening except for the door swinging gently.

Then a pot plant that he had brought out of the breakfast-room to the hall began to rock. It fell on to its side and rolled off the table. The floor was carpeted, and only a stem of the plant was broken, and some earth scattered.

"Oh, *no*," Kate whispered, her fingers tight on Matt's arm. "They're in here."

The telephone leapt from its place on the table, the receiver flung clattering from wall to wall. It wavered in the air as if a hand had got it, then gave a wrench and the wires came twanging out of the wall. The phone landed upside down on the floor, receiver trailing.

It was suddenly quiet. Matt looked down at the damage, and the meaning of it sank in. No phone. No ringing up Aunt Phyllis to say come home, never mind tonight, come home now.

He felt in his pocket. "Got any ten pences?" he said hoarsely.

Kate stared at him. "What for? Oh no, Matt!" she exclaimed. "You can't go *out* to phone! You'll never get to the door!"

"You want to stay here?" Matt said. He brought some change out of his pocket and examined it, wishing his hand wasn't trembling so obviously. Three tens. That should be enough to phone Manchester. If not, he could reverse the charge, maybe. "Stay in your bedroom," he said.

"I'm coming with you," Kate said decidedly.

Matt's lips tightened. "We can't leave Anna on her own! Look, Kate, they probably won't try to harm Anna—because it's her they want isn't it? Alive."

"Yes, but . . ."

"Well, you stay here then. I'll be as quick as I can." He let go of her, his mouth very dry. "*Don't* try to get out unless it looks absolutely safe. Okay? Look, someone's got to stay with Anna, Kate."

She bit her lip. "Oh, I suppose so," she said unhappily. "Go on, then. For God's sake be careful."

"Yes." Matt looked down into the hall. The telephone and pot plant lay still, looking harmless, but the air was thick with threats. He gritted his teeth and plunged down towards the front door.

He saw the phone shoot up into the air again, and flung an arm up to guard his head. The receiver swung down with a crack on his elbow, and he heard himself cry out as pain exploded up his arm. Coat-hangers flew from their hooks on the wall and came for him. Aunt Phyllis's umbrella hooked his ankle and heaved—he came down on one knee, hearing Kate scream his name while coat-hangers thudded into him. Somehow, he didn't know how, he got back to the stairs, leaving his coins scattered across the hall. Gasping, he sat down by Kate, nursing his throbbing arm.

"Matt, are you all right?" Kate cried, desperately.

He nodded, getting his breath. "Yes." He rubbed his elbow hard, and looked back into the hall. Coat-hangers everywhere, the dial of the phone cracked across, the plant broken with its pot in shards, earth all over the carpet, and a glass vase smashed.

"That vase nearly got your head," Kate said unsteadily. "Look at it. It's in smithereens. You're not trying that again, Matt."

"No," said Matt after a moment, feeling how shaken

he was. In Kelly's laboratory, lost in the Fomors' land, that was one thing; to be attacked here in his aunt's ordinary little house in ordinary Lancashire, by ordinary everyday bits of furniture—that was something else. He tried to pull himself together. "Come on, let's go to your bedroom," he said, getting to his feet. "They might not come in there."

They went up the stairs, to the sunny main bedroom that looked out on to the park. Kate shut the door firmly behind them.

Anna lay on the larger bed, dark hair fanning out over the pillow. She lay there as if asleep, but as Matt looked at her he saw her lips curve in that strange little smile.

"Anna," he said huskily, not knowing why he said it—unless it was to call her back from her dreams, make her realise again the present danger.

Kate came to stand beside him, looking down at her sister. "She won't answer you," she said bitterly. "She's dreaming about *him*, I suppose. I told you, she doesn't care what happens to anyone else!"

Matt nursed his still throbbing elbow. Poor Kate. No parents, hardly even a sister any more—could she be expected to understand Anna any better than he could? The thought seemed to mix with the pain of his arm.

"She does care," he said. Nothing would be worthwhile if he didn't believe that. "I know she does. . . ." He turned away, going to the window. "Look, Kate, let's think what we're going to do."

Kate followed him to the window. The lower sash was pushed up as far as it would go, and they leaned out side by side, arms on the sill.

Nothing moved. The park was empty, and the only cars were a few parked ones, their upholstery visibly sweltering. No dogs, no birds, not the stirring of a leaf, not the faintest breath of air. Matt could feel sweat gathering on his forehead again.

Kate leaned further out, looking at something in the garden. "What's that?" she said.

Matt followed her gaze. Directly below them was the roof of the bay window in the sitting-room. Round the bay ran a cement path, then there was the lawn, bordered on all four sides by flower-beds. Like the other gardens in the street, they were full of roses.

Kate was looking down at the flower-bed by the window. One of the rose bushes had been broken, a spray of buds hanging down on a splintered stem, and there were two large blurred marks in the soil by it, each roughly oval with a cleft.

Matt felt his teeth go into his lip. The dry soil hadn't kept a very good print, but he'd heard the noise last night, he'd seen the shadow on the sitting-room curtains, with its great, spreading antlers. There couldn't be any doubt. Two cloven hoofmarks, like the slots of a gigantic stag.

He turned away from the window, feeling as if he were choking in the airless heat, and sat down on the camp-bed. It was real. No shadow had broken that rose-bush and left those huge prints. And now they were trapped inside the house by poltergeists; Manannan had saved him and Anna last time, but would he be able to stave off a second attack? *"Next time you may meet the Horned One; and the whole tribe of Danu would be blasted into nowhere if they tried to help you then. . . ."*

"Matt," said Kate, unaware of what she'd pointed out to him. "I think I could climb out. I could easily get on to the roof of the bay from here, and then down the drain-pipe into the garden."

Matt cleared his throat. "It'd be too dangerous," he said, struggling to make his voice sound normal. "You'd fall."

"No, I wouldn't." Kate turned round from the window, and gave him a frowning look. "Are you sure you're all right?"

Matt tried to take a hold on himself. "Yes, I—"

There was a resounding bang as the sash slammed down, shaking the room. Kate gave a terrified gasp, freezing absolutely for a moment; then she flung herself at the window, heaving at the frame to get it open again.

Matt joined her, but before he set his hand to the sash he knew it was no good. The catch was undone, but the frame was stuck as fast as if it were nailed down. Alongside Kate he strained at it till his muscles cracked, but it wouldn't shift.

"We'll have to break it!" Kate said frantically.

Matt stepped back from the window, his arms and shoulders aching. "That's no good," he said dully. "Even if we smashed one pane, it'd be too small for any of us to get through. We'd have to break the whole window, frame was well, and unless you've got an axe. . . ."

Kate bit her lip. "Well, what are we going to do?" she flashed.

Matt sat down wearily on the camp-bed again. "We'll just have to wait. Maybe when it gets dark the poltergeists'll stop. Or Aunt Phyllis may try to phone, and when she can't get through she'll know there's something wrong." He looked up at Kate, and his mouth tightened wretchedly as he saw the trapped, terrified look on her face. He held out a hand to her. "We'll be all right, Kate."

She took his hand and slumped down next to him with a look of exhaustion. "It's not *fair*," she whispered, voice shaking. "Why does all this have to happen to us? The poltergeists and everything? I can't stand much more, Matt."

Matt put his other hand on hers, not knowing what to say. There was still a vague chance they might get out, they might be able to shout for help or something, or in the very last resort there was Manannan. . . . Hopelessly, Matt closed his eyes. What was the good of all this fighting?

160

What could three kids do against a man for whom wars started, and other worlds appeared?

Under his eyelids dark came, then a pallid, uncertain light mixing with the dark and not dispelling it. Shapes loomed in the corners of his eyes; as he realised what was happening, his stomach twisted with despair, revulsion— no! No! Not the dreams again! He made a panic-stricken effort to wrench open his eyes; but he was too late. He had entered the dream. He couldn't even feel Kate's hand between his own any more. . . .

Above the light of the candles, the charts could just be seen. There was the furnace, the pieces of the broken pelican lying on the floor beside it; there was the great cabinet with its hundred drawers, and the window, curtained. Matt saw the desk, two candles burning on it amidst the clutter; and Kelly sitting there with the black scrying-glass in his hand. He was half turned towards Matt, and as Matt looked, the clear gaze came sliding up from the mirror's surface and fastened on him.

"You're here," Kelly said, softly, as if by just saying so he could fix Matt there for ever. Shuddering inside, Matt tried to move his lips to say no, I'm not here, I'm at home in my aunt's house—but, as in many dreams, he couldn't speak.

Without taking his eyes off him, Kelly slid the mirror back into its case and laid it down on the desk. Then he leaned forward, hands clasped on knees; his eyes went on looking at Matt, and the silence rose in wave after wave, rose and swelled and broke in the dim laboratory. When at length Kelly spoke, it was softly and shiftily, so that Matt heard the roar of silence more than his words.

"Still fighting me, Matt? Yet you saw his shadow last night."

It wasn't the same as the other dreams; he couldn't control it; Kelly, sitting there, seemed to be deciding what should happen. Matt clenched his fists and tried to press

161

the nails into his palms to wake himself up. Dreamlike, his finger-ends seemed to slide away and disappear . . . he heard Kelly's voice going on, soft and sidelong. And the laboratory was still there. . . .

"He'll come again tonight. The way's been made wide open for him. Danu's daughter, thinking she was saving you, left a track for him up to your very door. He'll come, and lay his hand upon Madinia—no power on earth, or in the wide wastes of heaven, could stop him now. Least of all you, Matt, though you have the truest beginnings of power I've seen yet among mortals. But you and Kate would be the twigs snapping unnoticed under his feet. . . ."

Still Matt couldn't speak. Kelly's eyes dwelt on him, and for a second Matt saw something ugly and uneven jag their surface—it was smoothed over almost at once. "Look at you," said Kelly, "fighting me like a bull, as usual. Do you know I can see right through you to the wall?" The gaze permeated him. "Relax."

At once Matt felt the place come more into shape round him; he felt the stone floor under his feet, and the brooding, stuffy atmosphere around him. His nails pricked his palms. But he wasn't awake, he was deeper in the dream; and it wasn't his dream. It was Kelly's. He stood there in Kelly's world, a helpless visitant.

"See?" said Kelly, softly. "Easy."

Matt drew a breath. "What do you want?" he said huskily.

The corners of Kelly's lips turned up. "No, Matt—what do you want?" he murmured. "Still to die? You will, and little Kate too, unless you step aside. I told you; nothing can stop him now. Not even I, and my power is greater than any human being could conceive. Do you think I haven't searched every nook and cranny of my art for a way to stop him. . . ." An unrhythmic throb spoiled the flow of his voice; Kelly paused fractionally. "There is no way,"

162

he said, smooth and deliberate again, and smiled at Matt.

Matt's hair prickled on the back of his neck. He'd thought he knew what Kelly wanted, but every time the man turned out to be more than he remembered.

"But you want Anna to die," he said hoarsely. "You want him not to be stopped."

Kelly's gaze slowly turned away, and the shadows ran soft and wild round the room. "No," said Kelly, with a thickness in his voice that Matt had never thought to hear. "She's my saviour, Matt. I knew I'd find one—otherwise I'd never have been fool enough to drive bargains with the Horned One. Across all space and time I saw her. I cast her into darkness, so that she would turn to me." The serene eyes came back on to Matt and he shuddered inwardly. Kelly smiled. "Handy, that war, wasn't it? When you have power like mine, all the worlds fit in with you. I didn't really need twelve thousand peasants to die; but these things happen. Now, though"—the quick ugly glint, rapidly veiled—"now, I find I want her to go on living, Matt," Kelly murmured silkenly.

Matt began to feel sick, without knowing why. He wanted that, so did Kate, so did everyone else; but to hear Kelly say he wanted it too made Matt's spine crawl. Why?

"Well, stop him then," he said hoarsely.

"Haven't you been listening? I told you, no one, not even I, could stop him now." Kelly regarded him steadily. "Can't you understand the simplest thing, Matt?" he said softly. "I love her. I want her—for always."

The sickness churned in Matt. "You don't!" he shouted. "You couldn't love anybody!"

"That's just where you're wrong," Matt heard his breath rasp. Kelly rose, clasping his hands inside his furred sleeves, and paced slowly across the cluttered floor. Shadows leapt around him. "What do you know of love? A beardless boy like you? Is it strange that after three hundred years I should have grown tired of—being hated?"

He paced back and forth between the jumble of jars and instruments that glittered faintly in the uncertain light, and though Matt couldn't see, he felt that ugly glint coming and going in his eyes. "People have always made me an outcast. Years ago I came to John Dee's door, a crop-eared knave from Lancaster pillory, wearing a skull-cap to hide the damage—and he took me in. He wanted me enough then, wide-eyed as he was at my skills, promising me all manner of share in the wealth he meant to win. So I outstripped him; was that my fault? Oh, he was clever, I grant you, but a see-saw of a man, always hesitating, never making up his mind what he wanted. And now he hates me too. . . ." He paused, then said, very softly, "What is a man to do when he has nobody but enemies, Matt?"

Matt couldn't say anything. The laboratory felt worse, more stifling than ever; the candles made his signs on the charts dance in the corners of his eyes. Kelly had changed. He had never talked like this before. The thought came to Matt—he's mad.

"I'll tell you." Kelly turned and faced him, the strange eyes burning. "It's time for me to remake my universe. There'll be no more hate. John Dee won't be able to enter this new universe, as if he still lived upstairs like a rat in the thatch. . . . I'll shut him out. And Madinia will be with me, alongside me, for always. . . ." His words jolted. *"I must have her, Matt!"*

Under that awful brilliant stare, Matt prayed to wake up. He couldn't. Mad or sane, Kelly had the power to keep him in his unreal world. Hoarsely, he said, "What about Cernunnos?"

"Ah." The old serene, loathsome gaze returned. "That's where you come in, Matt," Kelly said. "I'll need your help. We can't stop Cernunnos taking her; but she won't die, I'm sure of that much. Dead things are no use to him." His eyes glimmered with a kind of delight. "Do

164

you see, Matt? Afterwards—when he thinks he is satisfied —we'll snatch Madinia back and leave him with *nothing!*''

Matt felt as if a hand was squeezing his throat.

"What do you mean, *we?*" he said chokily.

"I mean you and I." Kelly came a step nearer, gaze full on him. "To get Madinia back from him will be the greatest act of witchcraft ever performed. The Old Ones have had it their own way too long—dead gods, it's time they died! I'll outwit them; I, the greatest witch of all time. Why shouldn't I? They're not a very bright lot, after all. But I'll need power, more power than I've ever exerted, more even than I possess. . . .'' His gaze settled down on Matt, like a weight. "I'll need you to help me," Kelly murmured insinuatingly.

Matt could hardly breathe. His heart was pounding, and his lips parted for air. Oh please, please, let me wake up. . . .

Kelly came another pace nearer. "You're ripe for it now Matt," he murmured, while his gaze bore down. "Think how you overcame Elatha. Think how I always have to put in a bit extra when I want to make you do something—'' The quick uneven throb came, quickly suppressed. "Oh, you don't stop me," Kelly said softly. "Young and untaught, how could you? But think what you could do if you were taught, Matt. You've got power in you, deep and almost untouched, like a pool hidden in a forest. I know I've always poked fun at you—but I won't any more. I could tap that pool for you. You and me together, we could do almost anything. We could save Anna, for instance."

Horror came without warning out of the dark. Matt fought with it, trying frantically to think. To save Anna— surely he ought to agree, for that? But if she were saved only to spend an eternity with Kelly, inside Kelly's world

165

. . . . No, no, *I can't do it,* Matt thought with despair. Whatever it was for, I could never do it, not with him—not with Kelly!

"Come on, lad!" It was the old, soft bewildering voice. "Don't fight me so hard. I'm your friend, you know, I could make the whole world different for you; no more shyness, no more not knowing what to do—all you need is a little teaching, to release all that power."

The words wrapped round like a fog, and he couldn't think any more. He looked away from Kelly, round at the pieces of the pelican, wrestling for some kind of speech. "No," he said huskily.

Shadows chased over the room, so that he could hardly make out anything. "No," he said again, and had forgotten what he was refusing.

"I'll teach you, Matt," Kelly's voice came, soft and sublimal. "I'll withhold nothing—I promise. I'll show you how to gain whatever you want. Wealth, power, freedom from death, anything—oh, yes, even Kate. Yes, Matt, I'll show you how to bind a hundred Kates to you."

Kate. Matt fastened on to the word while the candles sent shadows reeling across his eyes, and Kelly's voice softly scattered his wits. He heard more promises weaving round him, and knew that in a few moments the spell would be complete, he would be changed into something different, something he could never recognise again.

"Kate!" he screamed, the only word he could think of. At once he saw Kelly's hands come out, pale and clawed in the candlelight; and then he was grasped and shaken, shaken until his mind went loose and his eyes came open.

Kate's blue eyes were in front of him, wide and scared. "Matt! Matt! Wake up!" she said insistently, and shook his shoulder again, hard. Matt drew a deep breath, and looked up at the small, sunny bedroom. Kelly and the laboratory had gone.

"It's okay," he said after a long while. "I'm awake."

Kate sat down on the camp-bed next to him. "You went out like a light," she said, the trace of a tremor in her voice. "And then you started muttering my name. What was the matter, were you having one of those dreams again?"

"No," said Matt. "It was Kelly's dream."

"What?" Kate cried, her voice shaking badly.

Matt clenched his hand. Wake up, you idiot. "It's all right," he said steadily. "It was just a dream. But—don't let me go to sleep again, Kate."

Kate looked at him, and bit her lip. In a lower voice she said, "Anna's awake now, too."

Matt looked up again, and saw Anna sitting up quite still on the larger bed, dark hair falling forward so that he couldn't see her face. Yes, Kelly had let her go, she who wanted him more than anything else in the world.

"Anna," he said.

She put a hand up to her face, and Matt got up, going over to her. "Anna," he said again, his voice taut.

She looked up at him, and he saw the slow tears go slipping down her cheeks. "He's got no one," she whispered. "No one'll be his friend. Oh Matt—he's so alone."

11

AN ISLAND OF THE WEST

At last the sun had dipped below the trees of the park; but, though the tiring glare was gone, the heat remained. Kate and Anna lay exhausted in the stifling room, but Matt sat grimly upright, keeping awake. It was about eight o'clock, and still the poltergeists wouldn't let them go downstairs.

Kate and Anna were lying side by side on the larger bed, Anna quite still, though not asleep. Kate stirred restlessly, sat up and looked out the window. After a moment she said, in an awed whisper, "Matt!"

"What?" Matt tensed, involuntarily.

Kate rose, going to the window. "Look at the sky! It's amazing!" She leaned on the sill, staring out.

Matt got up, feeling giddy for a moment from the lack of air, then went across the room to the window beside her.

The sun, visible through the trees, had turned red. The sky was a solid, staring gold, and everything the light touched had a petrified, lifeless look, like flies inside amber.

Matt touched the glass, and felt how warm it was. "There's going to be a storm," he said.

Kate gave a sigh. "I hope so," she said. "It's *too* hot."

Matt flicked an uneasy look at her. He hadn't told them

what Kelly had said in the dream, that Cernunnos would come again tonight to fetch Anna. How could he tell them such a thing? But with the sky looking like that something was obviously going to happen; it was as if the world had turned pale at the sight of something terrible approaching.

The coat-hangers downstairs started clattering, accompanied by further sounds of breaking—probably the china left on the hall table. Matt returned to the camp-bed, feeling drained.

Looking out of the window, Kate said abruptly, "Do you still think they'll stop when it gets dark?"

Matt tried to think of something encouraging to say, but the old sense of hopelessness was strong on him. The poltergeists might very well stop after dark, but if it was only to make way for Cernunnos what good was that? "I don't know," he said.

Kate gave no sign of being particularly distressed. She sat down on the bed again, sighing with the heat, but her mouth had a resolute and rather obstinate set to it. Matt recognised the look. Kate had had her time of being shaken and afraid, and had simply made up her mind, now, to stop it. Enviously, he wished he could do the same.

Outside the window, the sky slowly darkened, becoming dirty. All through the next hour, Matt watched a brassy gloom descend. At last he got up and tried the door that led out on to the landing. As he'd expected, it jammed. They were trapped in the one room.

Kate said, "Come over here, Matt. Get on the other side of Anna."

"No," said Matt. "You come over here—away from the window."

"All right," Kate got up, and Anna followed suit hesitantly.

"Matt—" The brown eyes gave him a pleading look. "Do you know what's going to happen?" Anna asked.

169

Matt hesitated. Kate sat down on one end of the camp-bed, took Anna's wrist and made her sit down in the middle. Neither of them is going to be as scared as I am, he thought; Anna expects it, and Kate's chucked being afraid. He said, "Cernunnos is going to come again."

Kate leaned forward. "What do you mean, *again?*" she said sharply. As she spoke, a rumble of thunder could just be heard.

"He almost came last night," Matt said. "Anna and I saw his shadow on the sitting-room curtains. But, this is the point, Kate—Manannan came. At least I think it was Manannan. The sitting-room got full of light, and the shadow went."

"H'm." Kate frowned. "He'd better come again. Looks like we're going to need all the help we can get."

The thunder sounded, nearer.

Anna said, her voice hardly louder than a breath, "If—if Manannan *doesn't* come . . . don't try to stop him taking me. Promise. Both of you."

"No—" said Matt.

"For God's sake, Anna!" Kate's voice drowned his. "Don't be stupid!"

"Oh, Kate, I mean it!" Anna whispered. "I'm not just pretending to be brave—you couldn't possibly stop him! You'd die; and suppose Mum and Dad came back, and neither of us was left . . ." She couldn't go on.

"Stop it!" Matt said hoarsely. "You don't have to worry, Anna. No one's going to die. Manannan'll come, you'll see."

The thunder muttered again, closer, with a menacing note. Cloud began to roll in from the west, thick, swift and black; after a brief struggle, the amber light died. It grew very dark. At length the first splash of rain hit the window, then blue lightning forked from the cloud, and thunder pealed fit to split the eardrums.

The trees all but disappeared behind racing sheets of

170

rain. Matt found himself on his feet. Kate and Anna up beside him. The lightning played blindingly over the sky, followed everywhere by crashing thunder. He screwed his eyes up against it, almost dazed by the noise and light. Freak winds lifted the rain and slammed it against the window, and trees were lurching in the park; the house shook around him, and he felt as if the world was weakening, beginning to break. Kate shouted something, at the pitch of her lungs, but he couldn't make it out; her hand went out, pointing, and he forced his tormented eyes to look into the flicker of violet light.

There was a hole in the storm. There in the sky he could see a round, dark opening, with the storm whirling off it in white lines of fire. First it was a pinprick, then wider, approaching steadily. Slowly, Matt made out what was there, silent and still in the eye of the storm.

He was very big. His head bore antlers, and he stood up like a man; but he was like no man or beast, only himself. He was borne closer and closer, as the centre of the storm came down towards them. Matt saw the long, narrow head, the fine curve of the nostrils, the shoulders of a man and the cloven hooves of a goat—he opened his lips to cry out, but didn't. Slowly, as his heart turned over and over, he began to lose himself, becoming just one human thing before the eldest thing of all; slowly the sight and the smell of Cernunnos slid deep into him, and men he had never heard of rose urgently up in him and called and reached out towards their god.

He was looking at them, with great luminous eyes that seemed opaque, not meant for seeing; and the hole in the storm closed softly around them like a mouth, cutting them off from the thunder and the stuffy little room. They were alone with him, in utter silence. And now there was no question of fighting; all they could do was stand there before that huge horned shape, in the dark place where two worlds met. Matt knew nothing any more but the climbing antlers and the look of those eyes.

At last Cernunnos moved, as a tree might move in the wind, and his hand came slanting down towards them from his vast height. It was a long hand, and Matt saw it in detail; terribly long and slender and pointed, with the nails shining like pearls. He felt an impulse to sink to his knees. Anna stepped forward. Neither he nor Kate lifted a finger to stop her.

Then, beside him, the light burst. It shot outward from a core brighter than the entire sky, and Matt gasped, feeling as if he were shaken back into himself. He tore his eyes from the horned thing, and before his gaze a shape reared out of the light, with flashing hooves and a mane. Behind it came a chariot, and standing in the chariot was pure light in the shape of a man. It was Manannan.

"Mount!" The single word cracked through the silence, damaging it. Leaping down, the man caught him and Kate and they were whirled into the chariot on a wave of light. "Anna!" Kate screamed, trying to get out again; but Matt caught her arms.

He saw the long, narrow head and the towering antlers turn; but his eyes were on those pointed fingers. They closed quietly round Anna's wrist.

Manannan stood before him, half his size, surrounded by glittering light. The horned head swayed, as if wondering and thoughtful; but Matt's heart shuddered and he waited for Manannan's light to fade before the great dark bulk of the Horned One.

Manannan raised a hand, and light came from it like spears on to the gleaming hide. Cernunnos moved a little, and Anna twisted in his grip with her mouth opening as if in a cry of pain. Manannan's lips parted.

Words came from them as no words had ever been, zooming and crashing amongst the utmost barriers of sound. The horse between the shafts of the chariot tossed its mane, and one hoof softly stamped. Cernunnos was still, as still as a tree in the depths of a forest where no wind could reach. And then Manannan's other hand came out, shining, and grasped Anna's shoulder.

Matt heard her scream, faint like an echo. Her eyes were shut, and she hung between the two, the dark and the light, as if only their hands were keeping her upright.

Manannan spoke again, massive crystals of words, and again the horned head began to sway, lowering like a beast about to charge. Manannan's lips shut, hard, and light ripped from him like a million shafts of glass, so thick that all Matt could see was the heaving antlers; Manannan tore Anna backwards into his arms and leapt into the chariot. The horse reared, sprang, and Matt caught at the rim of the chariot as it leapt upwards. Beside him Anna, clasped in Manannan's arms, hung lifeless with her face like paper; and Matt looked down and saw on her wrist, like a brand, the black marks of five clawed fingers and a thumb.

They broke through into the lightning. The storm was suddenly all around them, thunder crashing in their ears and the wind screaming. Matt caught a hand over blinded eyes. The wind buffeted him. It seemed never-ending, like an attack of very bad pain; but he felt the chariot still leaping upward, and heard again the crash of Manannan's voice. Then, just as suddenly, they were out of it. The noise died behind them and the chariot began to run free, the wind subsiding to a gentle touch of air. Matt kept his hand over his eyes. He felt exhausted in a way he had never felt before, utterly drained and finished up as if everything had gone out of him.

The chariot slowed, and he thought he heard the horse's hooves thud on grass, and the wheels rattle faintly. Then it was still. But he stayed where he was, his head still bowed in his hand; this weariness left him sick to his heart.

Gradually he became aware of sounds—a long gentle breaking of wave after wave on a shore close by, and the more distant murmur of open waters. He seemed to feel the sky stretch out above him, giving him room; the thought of that great space eased his mind a little, and after a while he opened his eyes.

He recognised nothing except an evening sky and the long wrinkles of a clear green sea. Manannan had gone, and so had Anna. The ground beside the chariot sloped down to a white beach where pebbles glinted wet and bright, and there the sea rolled and broke, empty to the horizon.

The chariot stood on grass, soft and uneven as if cows grazed there. Looking forward, Matt saw the horse peacefully cropping the grass; he turned away with a wince. The horse was too beautiful for him in his present frame of mind, its flanks and mane too generously shedding that dazzle of power and light.

Further back from the shore was a wood, green and gladed, without undergrowth, so that he could see the evening sun dappling the ground through the branches. He couldn't place the trees. They were long and trailing like willows, but bore golden catkins like hazels in early spring. Their bark was silver-brown, deep and grooved, and he could see berries amongst the leaves. Their long shadows came down towards him over the grass.

At his feet, Kate sat on the floor of the chariot with her head in her hands. The evening light lay gently on her yellow hair, and Matt looked down at her for a while. So she too felt that exhausted emptiness, that sense of being finished, done with.

At last he moved, sitting down at her side on the chariot's wooden floor. He put an arm round her shoulders.

He felt her tense. "Go away," her voice said, muffled. "Leave me alone."

The rebuff was familiar, coming like an expected guest. Matt took his arm away and, too weary to get up, leaned

174

his head against the side of the chariot. It was made of thin, light metal, wrought and polished outside, but inside smooth and cool.

Kate stirred, then raised her head, letting her hands fall anyhow into her lap. "I'm sorry, Matt," she said, after a moment, her voice thin but leaden. "I just feel so awful."

Matt looked at her. He had never seen those blue eyes look so dark and disheartened. "So do I," he said. "I feel as if I hate myself."

"We'd just have let Anna go, wouldn't we," Kate said jerkily. "Just have stood there and let—it—take her."

"Yes," said Matt.

She looked at him, lines round her eyes. "Wasn't it awful, Matt?" she whispered. "I was trying not to be scared, but it made all of me go to water. It was like having a nightmare come true."

Matt said, huskily, "Come on. Let's go and find Anna."

"Isn't she here?" The lines deepened harshly.

"She's probably somewhere in the trees," Matt rose, with an effort. "Come on, Kate."

With a sigh, Kate looked down at the ground. "We don't even know where we are, again," she said. "You go, Matt. Leave me alone for a bit. Please."

Matt hesitated. Then the horse snorted softly and shook its shining head; and Matt couldn't conceive of danger approaching while it was here.

"All right," he said. "Just call if you want me."

Kate nodded without looking up, and Matt turned and went up the slope towards the trees. As he entered the wood, a green whispering quiet closed round him, and he was glad of it.

He looked round for Anna and, seeing only trees, continued further in. There was no danger of getting lost, with the sun's rays slanting through the foliage straight into his face: he would only have to turn round and follow his shadow to get back to Kate.

The wood was quiet, seemingly without birds. The turf was soft and springy under his feet, and the trees moved only a little in the wind, with a soft meaningless murmur that soothed the ache inside him; there was a timeless peace that grew on him as he walked on, and whenever he paused to look round he seemed always to be in the middle of a glade, with the sun gold on the leaves and the air soft against his face.

I wonder where we are now, he thought, without any real urgency, glancing to and fro for Anna. The trees stretched away on every side with the sun brilliant through them; and he couldn't feel that Anna, if she was here, was in any danger.

If she was here. She has to be here, he thought; we can't have lost her now, not when Manannan came and we had to go through all—that. His mind flinched, skirting the thought of Cernunnos. He went on over the carpet of grass, through one glade into another.

He wasn't sure how long he'd been in the wood when the sunlight began to grow stronger, and he heard the murmur of the sea again. The thought came to him that this was an island. His step slowed, not wanting to leave the peace of the wood, but he thought of Anna, and tried to hurry.

The light beyond the trees was very bright, as if the sun was nearer than normal. He hesitated despite himself on the wood's edge, with a hand on one of the trunks; then he saw Anna.

The island ended in a cliff, breakers sounding far below. Anna lay in a hollow near the edge, as if asleep; and all the trouble had gone from her face. But Matt stayed where he was, not moving, for not a yard from her head Manannan stood, his face turned out over the sea towards the sun.

He stood in a man's shape, a cloak clasped on one

shoulder with a round brooch, and a sword at his side; his light hung visible about him, not deadened even by that big sun, so that his skin seemed silverish and his hair, rippling back to his shoulders, shot with blue. He was taller than a man, his profile straighter and stronger; and Matt found it hard to look at him, for, standing there so still, he seemed as high, far and remote as the sky. Again Matt felt that desolate pang, as when the light had come in his aunt's sitting-room, saved his and Anna's lives and then departed without a word. He thought, he's not like Arianrod; and for several moments he stood where he was, reluctant to leave the wood.

Not looking at him, Manannan said, "Come forward, mortal."

It was something like men's voices, but at once deeper and higher, like a chime of great bells rung all together so that their notes couldn't quite be distinguished. He seemed to speak quietly, yet the air was filled by the sound.

Nerving himself, Matt finally left the trees. He walked across the grass, feeling the cool air lift the hair away from his face; there was more wind here, on the higher part of the island.

"There is no danger," Manannan said, with his many voices. Arms folded, he still looked out to sea. "This is a safe place."

"Yes," said Matt after a moment, his own voice sounding thin and young after Manannan's. He had to narrow his eyes up against the sun. It was certainly bigger and brighter than he had ever seen it before.

Manannan turned and looked down at him. His eyes were not human, they had too much light, looking silver or gold; it was a pure, passionless light, without heat or human warmth. It seemed to go right into Matt's mind, turning and twisting into the most secret corners.

"You cannot stay here." The voices were softer, as if Manannan were controlling their crystalline ring. "It is not a place to live, out here in the far west. The setting sun is too close. You could not bear it for long."

"If we go back . . ." Matt stopped, and looked down; the light of those eyes was too much to look at for more than a few moments. "When we go back," he said, "will we be safe?"

There was a pause.

"I do not know." It was hard to tell if there was any compassion in his voices. "It is not a simple thing for the Horned One to come down into your world. His place is in the ancient forests, where life is young and violent, before the growth of reason. Long ago the Lord of Light bade him stay there, amidst their dense shadows; in the bare light of your world, he would weaken. But before all his strength lapsed, he would have done much—perhaps more than could ever be undone."

Matt tried not to think of the darkness, and the many men rising in him and calling out. "Will he come back again?" he said, not looking up.

"He may." The voices were without much human tone. "I have not conquered him, only thrown dust in his eyes. Where he has held, he does not easily let go. And he has laid his hand upon Madinia. She bears the marks yet."

Matt looked, without wanting to, at Anna. He saw on her left wrist the blackened marks of those fingers; even here, in the far west of the world, they made him shudder. Huskily, he said, "What's wrong with her? Can't you wake her?"

"She sleeps." The emotionless voices seemed untouched by the fears in his. Matt, looking down at the marks, felt momentarily lost and alone, with a sense of subtle knowledge beyond his reach.

"It is better so." Manannan seemed to soften his voices again. "She has been terribly torn. Look to her, when she wakes. She will need great tenderness."

"I know," Matt said. With an effort he looked up, back

178

at the glowing eyes. "But he mustn't come back again," he said, and heard a note of entreaty in his voice. "It's not just Anna—I couldn't bear it, and neither could Kate."

The light went into him, watching his mind; then, after a moment, Manannan turned his head and looked towards the wood. Matt followed his gaze and saw Kate standing there as he had stood, one hand on the grooved bark of a tree. Some of his worry went as he saw how the darkness had left her face; perhaps the wood had done its mysterious work on her too.

"Come, maiden," said Manannan. Hesitantly, Kate came out of the wood on to the windy cliff-top, and stopped close at Matt's side. "Your sister sleeps," said Manannan, his voices ringing clear and full. "And you also should be at peace. The first of your fathers worshipped Cernunnos and made him great; the seed of their worship is in all of you; it is no shame to feel it. The only shame would be to forget all you have made since, and worship him alone."

Kate said hesitantly, "He won't come again, will he? Not here?"

"No," said Manannan. "He could not cross this ocean."

"Where is this?" Kate asked, with a touch of timidity.

"It is an island of the west, beyond the sailing even of your ships." Manannan turned again, looking out over the sea to the big, close sun. The wind stirred his bluish hair, and light shimmered from it. "Over this horizon lies the world's end, where the tree of the sun grows with fruit that never falls. This is one of the heavens of Otherworld; there are many such, where the hunted and the scared may rest for a time. But now you must return."

"Back—home?" Kate's voice shook, despite herself, and Matt saw her cast a look over her shoulder at the quiet wood, so full of peace.

"Be courageous." Manannan turned back to look at

179

them. "I will not cease from watching. But one warning I give you. . . ."

The light of his eyes penetrated them, intent, seeming without pity.

"Do not seek death," the voices said, ringing low and high and loud. "Do not turn from all hope of life to death as escape or refuge, or as any means of safety. For then it would be beyond all my power to help you. Those who choose death go utterly alone. Remember."

Matt and Kate were silent; Matt felt uncertain, not knowing how he was meant to understand this warning, but something in the voices warned him not to question. He watched as Manannan walked to the nearest of the trees and, reaching up to the crook of a bough, took down a silver cup wrought with a pattern of curling leaves. He reached up again and plucked a cluster of berries.

"I have given Madinia berry-juice to drink," he said, turning back to them. "It will ease her pain and great grief. Now, you also will share a cup, and be strengthened. The worth of this fruit is great."

He squeezed the cluster of berries in his hand over the cup, and red juice ran bubbling down. The cup was filled, and Manannan held it out to Kate. "Drink, maiden, and leave half."

Matt felt Kate's hesitation. Then she walked over and, taking the cup, lifted it to her lips. She took a cautious sip, then another, and then a larger swallow.

"Enough," said Manannan, taking it back, and held it out to Matt. "Come."

"It's good, Matt," Kate said. Matt came, took the cup, and tasted the liquid with curiosity. It was rather like ripe cherries, but stronger and sharper with an elusive glow like wine. He finished it.

"Now lie down by Madinia," Manannan said, taking the cup back. His voices glittered, rough and beautiful.

"Lie down, and sleep without fear; wake strong and at peace."

Matt felt his eyes growing heavy. Sleep was coming, as if at the end of a long summer day in the open air. Kate gave a yawn and a stretch and lay down on the grass by Anna; Matt followed suit, and closed his eyes. The turf was soft. The weight slipped from his heart and he felt sleep come, with no dreams now to trouble him.

12

A MAN ALL IN GREEN

1

In was Tuesday, a few days later, when Matt, sitting on the front lawn and sketching the chestnut tree, looked round to see Kate come out of the house. She sat down on the grass beside him without saying anything, looked with heavy eyes at his drawing, then pulled moodily at the grass.

"How's Anna?" Matt said.

"Worse," Kate's voice was brittle. "Your aunt said she'd send for the doctor tonight if she isn't any better."

Matt put his sketch pad down. It was no good trying to distract himself, his heart wasn't in it. Anna was upstairs on her bed, fading away like some terrible Victorian heroine; perhaps Kelly had been right. Perhaps there was nothing Danu's Children could do.

Kate went on pulling at the grass. "I thought it was all going to be all right," she said, harshly. "That drink Manannan gave us made me feel fantastic when I woke up —as if nothing could harm us ever again. And now Anna's just—going. Every time I speak to her, there's less of her there to answer. What's Manannan *doing?* I thought he was supposed to protect us!"

"He is," Matt said. He hesitated. "I had another dream last night, Kate."

"What, one of your technicolor specials again?" Kate said uncaringly.

"No, not this time." Matt's lip tightened. Those dreams out of Lochlann were still haunting him, and he seemed powerless to escape from them; but last night, in the middle of a weary stream of visions that refused to end, a light had broken in and spread outwards through his mind so that all the dream-images were obliterated. Out of the light's core Manannan's face had looked.

"It was Manannan," he said, wondering if Kate was listening. "He said—Cernunnos is drawing her. But he's standing between them, he said, and stopping Cernunnos from actually getting her."

Kate didn't look up. "If he can stop him from getting her," she said, "I don't see why he can't stop him altogether."

"He can't," said Matt. "Cernunnos is too strong. He's much stronger than all of Danu's Children, because he belongs in this world and they don't. Unless Manannan's really careful, Anna'll just be destroyed, and Danu's Children along with her." He looked without seeing at the chestnut tree he'd been trying to sketch, and thought of Manannan's words—as cool and lucent as rushing water. . . .

"It is not right for him to have her. Kelly is his true prey, and the one called Dee; but it will take all my art to turn him back on to his right path. He is not controlled, at least not by such as us. . . . You and the young maiden must be careful, mortal. The Old Ones have a cunning beyond all reason; they may attack you next, to distract me. I must not be distracted. It would be the end of Madinia. Give them no opportunity. . . ."

There was a muffled thud inside the house, and Kate winced beside him. "Those *horrible* poltergeists!" Her knuckles whitened on a handful of grass.

Yes, they were still there, as full of malicious life as ever.

Their latest trick was overturning furniture—tables, armchairs, even heavy bookcases. Aunt Phyllis had wryly removed her breakables to a friend's house, trying to make a joke of it, and now they ate off paper plates and drank out of plastic cups. The friend, a doctor, was most intrigued; visiting to see for himself, he'd talked all through a chaotic dinner about scientific explanations.

Kate rose to her feet, a muddle of distress and anger in the blue eyes. "Matt, I can't *bear* sticking round here all of every day! It's driving me mad. I'm going for a bike ride."

Matt looked up, worry coming closer. "Oh . . ." He got up, leaving his sketch on the grass. "I'd better come with you."

"Oh, don't be stupid, somebody'll have to stay with Anna!" Kate's voice cracked. She turned away from Matt, fingers knotting together and the yellow hair swinging forward to hide her face.

"Oh, Kate," Matt said, not knowing what to say.

She didn't look round. After a moment she said unsteadily, "It's all so horrible. And I don't even know whether Mum and Dad are alive or not. Those poltergeists—nothing makes sense any more, Matt!"

"I know," said Matt. "But look, Kate, it'll be all right."

The hall table fell over with a crash, and Kate's fingers whitened against each other.

"I'm going!" she said huskily, and ran off towards the garage.

Matt stayed where he was, and presently heard the rattle of her bicycle as she got it out of the garage and rode away. Quietness edged back, broken only by the doves and a distant car.

He stood there for a moment, brow creasing irresolutely. Perhaps he shouldn't really have let Kate go off on her own like that, at least not without warning her to be careful. She hadn't been in any mood to listen to him, though.

And in any case, to face facts, it was obvious that the further you were from Anna the safer you were. Matt returned to his sketch. Aunt Phyllis would be home in about an hour, and Kate would probably come back then; it was easier to bear the poltergeists when Aunt Phyllis was there to pull a rueful face and smile as if they were only a nuisance.

The sketch wouldn't come right. Though the air was fresher as evening approached he began to feel too hot to bother any more. At last he put it down, and decided he ought to see if there was anything Anna wanted.

Since the night Cernunnos had come and grasped her, they'd all slipped into the way of treating her as if she was ill. She doesn't actually look ill, Matt thought, as he pushed open the bedroom door and went in; she lay on the counterpane, her hair as thick and lustrous as ever, with plenty of colour in her cheeks. Kate had lost weight and had blue shadows under her eyes; by comparison, Anna seemed to look the picture of health.

Then she opened her eyes and turned her head to look at him. Those great dark eyes with their lost and wandering depths, and the pitiful attempt to smile at him. . . . Matt swallowed. Without any physical wasting, Anna did really seem to be fading—thinning and melting away before them. The horrible thought came to him that already she was not so much in the room as haunting it.

"Do you want anything, Anna?" he said. It felt a useless question.

Anna managed to frame an answer, a mere breath of a word that looked like "No." No, Matt thought, there isn't anything I could get her that would make any difference. Her eyes gave him something of Kate's appealing look, as if Anna wanted to say she was sorry for not being able to talk properly—then they closed again.

Matt hesitated. There was nothing he could do, and yet it was hard just to go away and leave her.

She was wearing a long-sleeved shirt in spite of the heat, and the left-hand cuff was securely buttoned over her wrist. The marks must still be there, Matt thought; maybe Kate makes sure she puts on one of those shirts every morning, so that Aunt Phyllis won't see them. Oh, Anna. . . . Manannan, do something. Save her!

He closed the door quietly and went down the stairs, trying to ignore gleeful thumps from the breakfast-room as the poltergeists bounced the chairs up and down. Oh, stop it, he thought, with sudden weary contempt; do you think that's going to frighten me while Anna's disappearing upstairs? He went back outside and sat down by his unfinished sketch.

The evening air was stirring the trees slightly, and the sky was deep and clear and gentle. Swallows were flitting between the trees in the golden light. It didn't seem right for everything still to be so peaceful and lovely.

Presently he heard Aunt Phyllis's car going into the garage at the back, and then, after the engine was switched off and the garage door closed, her footsteps coming round the house. He looked round and she smiled, coming to sit beside him.

"Hullo, dear." She put her bag on the grass and leaned one arm on it, closing her eyes for a moment as if tired, then looking up at the sky. "What a glorious evening."

"I suppose so," said Matt after a moment, and pulled at the grass as Kate had done.

He felt her look at him.

"I'm sorry," she said, rather gently. "I know, dear. I'm afraid it's all a bit much, really, isn't it?"

Matt bit his lip. Aunt Phyllis didn't pry or fuss, that wasn't her way; but he couldn't help feeling she would gladly understand if he'd only give her the chance. He wished for a moment Kate would let him tell her everything, and just trust her not to think they were crazy.

"I wouldn't mind so much," he said, "if we could just *know* whether their parents are all right."

Aunt Phyllis nodded. "That would solve all our problems. Little Kate's bearing up wonderfully, but Anna's getting into rather a bad state. I was wondering about calling in the doctor. What do you think, dear?"

Matt hesitated. He wasn't accustomed to his opinion, being called for in such matters. "I—suppose it might help," he said, without much conviction. "If we could just get rid of the poltergeists, that might make things better. They're getting Kate down."

"Actually," Aunt Phyllis said, rather carefully, "I think the poltergeists may be part of the whole thing."

Matt felt himself stiffen. What did she mean? Did she guess? He looked up at her again, warily.

He saw her notice his start. "What I mean is," she said, gently, "that poltergeists don't usually happen except in a house where there's a—well, perhaps a rather disturbed young person. People say it's a kind of reflection of a young person's energies. Nobody really knows, of course. But I wonder if they might go, if we could just help Anna to straighten things out a bit."

Matt looked down again. "Anna's not disturbed," he said huskily. It hurt to think people could see her like that. "And Kate's just upset, that's all. It's not like that. Honestly it isn't." He wished he could explain, wished that when they came on the train up from London they hadn't brought all this trouble to worry his aunt with. It wasn't fair. It wasn't fair on anyone.

"Oh, Matt, love," Aunt Phyllis said, a touch of distress in her voice. "I don't mean to say anything awful about either of them. They're very sweet girls, Anna especially. Kate is too . . . though I wish sometimes that she'd be—well, a bit nicer to you, not so completely independent.

She reminds me of your mother, actually. You—like her a lot, don't you, Matt?"

Matt felt the colour come to his cheeks. People did notice, of course. His father knew, and so did Kate and Anna's parents; they didn't say anything, though they probably laughed about it when he wasn't there. But Kate wasn't really like his mother, was she, the mother who'd left him and his father?

"Yes," he said.

"All this is pretty awful for you, I know," said Aunt Phyllis, seeing his embarrassment and tactfully sheering away. "Particularly with your father thousands of miles off. And I don't help, being out all day. I wish I could be with you more—not breathing down your neck, you know, but sort of there. Matt, if it really does get on top of you, you will tell me, won't you? I promise I won't fuss. I'll just listen, and only do things if you want me to."

Matt felt self-reproach prick him again. It was awful for Aunt Phyllis too, half-knowing all that went on and feeling she oughtn't to probe, probably remembering how she'd hated adults to interfere when she was young. She wasn't used to kids. He could tell all the time that she wasn't sure how much to say to them. And she couldn't be there continuously, she had her job to do. But if only he could explain to her. . . .

"Do tell me to shut up if you want to, love," Aunt Phyllis said apologetically.

Shut up? It was years since he'd told anyone to shut up. "No," said Matt awkwardly. "It's not that. Thanks, Auntie."

"I talk too much," said Aunt Phyllis, with a hint of ruefulness. "Oh, Matt, is that your sketch there?"

"Yes." Matt picked it up, with a certain relief at the change of subject. "It's not all that good, though. I couldn't concentrate."

Aunt Phyllis looked down at it over his shoulder. "I see

what you mean," she said after a moment. "It's not quite as good as some you've done. But oh, Matt, it's got such lovely true lines. I wish some of our commercial artists could draw half as well."

Matt felt a slight glow at this praise, which, at least, sounded genuine. "Thanks," he said, with an upward glance.

Aunt Phyllis gave him a rueful smile. "I'm an awful bore, aren't I?" she said contritely. "You should have told me to shut up, dear. Well, let's go in and get some food, shall we? Is Kate about?"

"She went out on her bike," Matt said, getting up. Aunt Phyllis followed suit with rather an effort, looking tired, and again Matt felt guilty. After all, she was more or less responsible for all three of them. And she must be worried sick about Anna.

Aunt Phyllis glanced up the road. "Oh, here she comes now," she said; then the lines suddenly deepened round her eyes. "Oh—"

Matt looked round as the word was bitten off.

He saw Kate come weaving down the road on her bicycle as if she couldn't see where she was going. Her lips were parted, her face twisted and as white as paper. Matt tore the gate open and dashed outside, in time to catch her as she literally fell from the bike, and pull her clear as it crashed to the ground and lay there with its wheels spinning.

"Matt—" Kate hung on to him with all her weight, shaking as tears streamed down her face. "Matt—"

It wasn't a word, it was just a raw, throbbing cry, and she clung to him as if terrified he'd let go, her twisted face so unlike her that apart from the feel of her in his arms she might have been a stranger.

"Matt—"

It seemed to be all she could say. Was this the Kate who was supposed to be so like his mother, tough and decisive

189

and self-sufficient? It was as if two hands were laid on his heart, wringing.

"What is it, Kate? What's the matter?" he said desperately, trying to see her face. She hid it against his chest.

"Matt—" That raw, unrecognisable cry.

"Get her inside, Matt." His aunt was by his shoulder, face pale. "I'll bring the bike. Take her upstairs, if you can."

Matt tried to lead her into the garden. She seemed hardly able to walk, all her weight hanging on him. "Come on, Kate," he said, as calmly as he could, though his own voice was badly shaken. "It's all right. Come on."

Weakly, she came with him, still clutching him with both hands. Half-way up the path he stooped and lifted her up; it was easier. Arms tightly round his neck, she hid her face in his shoulders as he carried her inside and up the stairs. He managed to get her into the bedroom, and put her down on the camp-bed. He had to sit down beside her, for she still wouldn't let go of him.

He was just aware of Anna on the other bed, lying there with closed eyes and fainter, less substantial than before. . . . He gave her a quick look. It wasn't his imagination. She was paler.

He turned his eyes back down to Kate as she lay against him, yellow hair tangled round her face and sobs shaking her. Oh, no, he thought slowly, and all the brightness seemed to wither out of the world; he clasped his arms tightly round her. Oh, no. He bent his cheek down against her hair, feeling cold right to his lips.

"What is it, Kate?" he said huskily. "Tell me. What's happened?"

She only grasped him more desperately, the sobs thick and harsh. Matt closed his eyes for a moment, catching his lip between his teeth.

Oh no. Not Kate too.

He was in the front garden again when Dr. Anderson came downstairs, slowly, saying something to Aunt Phyllis but not clearly enough for Matt to hear.

He was Aunt Phyllis's friend, the one who'd stored all her china in his spare room and come to dinner to inspect the poltergeists. He was a cheerful sort of man, large and rumpled, with a northern accent; sometimes, during that dinner, a bit too large and cheerful. Matt didn't know why Aunt Phyllis had called him instead of her usual doctor, unless it was because he'd already seen something of the mess they were in.

They were standing talking in the hall, the doctor's rumble interspersed with Aunt Phyllis's lighter tone. The front door was open to let in the evening air, but they were talking too softly for Matt to make out the words. Trying not to listen, he pushed his hands into his pockets and studied the white rose-bush at the gate. Like the others, it had been badly broken in Friday's storm, and he and Aunt Phyllis had spent Saturday evening tying the stems up to bamboo poles. One bud of this bush had somehow escaped and was now opening, frail and pure with a glow of gold at the heart.

"Cheerio, then," he heard the doctor say, at a more normal level.

"Bye, David," Aunt Phyllis said, and the doctor's vigorous step came down the path.

Matt looked up reluctantly, not wanting to say much to him. In the midst of all this trouble, he was aware of a nagging uneasiness at having Kate and Anna inspected, like the poltergeists, by someone they barely knew. The whole thing seemed to be spreading, involving more and more people here in their own world; and that felt dangerous.

"Hullo, Matt," Anderson said bluffly, looking down at him from behind the thick lenses of his glasses. He leant a hand on the gate without opening it, his eyes giving Matt a quick automatic scan. "How are you, then?"

Matt swallowed. "I'm all right," he said. It took a pause and a slight effort before he could say, "What about Kate and Anna?"

"H'mm." Anderson frowned a little, and gave Matt a keen look from under his bushy eyebrows. "I'm not all that sure," he said, deliberately.

The blunt words accompanied by that sharp look sent a shiver through Matt. "How do you mean?" he said after a moment.

"Well," said Anderson, "I've been reasonably encouraging to your aunt, but I think I'm going to be straight with you, Matt. There's something very peculiar going on up there." He nodded his head towards the bedroom window above them.

Matt waited, seeming to feel a chill in the evening air.

"You see," said Anderson, more slowly than usual, as if it was difficult to express, "I'm a doctor. Now I know when something falls into my field—something I can cure, or at least recognise out of medical knowledge. And those two don't. At first sight they appear to be ill, but when I get down to looking at them, I can't tie their symptoms up to anything I could call an illness. I don't know what it is, but it's something quite different. Does that make sense to you?"

Matt looked away from the searching gaze. "I suppose so," he said at last, rather thickly.

Anderson said, bluntly, "Do you know what's going on, Matt?"

Matt gritted his teeth, feeling helpless. Witches, and horned spectres out of a storm, clouds of light that talked —Anderson could think he was crazy. All the same, he couldn't deny he did know.

He shook his head. "It doesn't make any sense," he said.

"Try me," said Anderson. "Those marks on the elder one's arm, for instance. How did she get those?"

Matt shook his head again. The impulse in them all, Kate especially, had been to keep this thing secret. He might want at times to tell Aunt Phyllis, but something always stopped him; much less could he pour it all out to a man he hardly knew.

He looked up and said, "I couldn't explain."

"H'mm." Anderson compressed his lips, then put a hand on the latch of the gate. "Well, if you don't want to talk to me, have a word with your aunt. But tell someone. It's important. I don't like the look of those two, and I'm speaking strictly as a human being, not a doctor. Okay?"

Matt nodded. "Yes," he said, bleakly.

"Okay." Anderson opened the gate. "If anything else happens, see your aunt calls me. The little one keeps asking for you, by the way. I've given her something to calm her down and make her sleep, but it might be a good idea to stand by. She obviously thinks you're the one to help her—not me."

Matt felt a hardness in his throat.

"Now, look after yourself, lad," Anderson said rather gently. Matt nodded, unable to answer, and the doctor went across the pavement to his car. He drove off round a corner and the noise of the car died away, leaving only the sleepy coo of the doves. Matt turned, taking a few steps aimlessly over the lawn, then stopped by the shattered wreck of what had been a bush full of red roses. His hands were clenched to fists inside his pockets.

Kate. It had all been bearable up to now, strange and terrible and full of fear—but bearable. I could face it if Anna dies, he thought, bleakly, and if their parents don't come back safe; it would be bad, but if I stood it when Mum went, I could stand that too.

But not Kate. Kate had always been there, with her yellow hair and live blue eyes, often getting impatient with him and calling him stupid—but always there, never shutting him out. Right now, it was his name she kept calling.

Without her nothing, not even his own life, would make sense any more; it would dissolve into a grey meaningless blur, without shape or colour or truth. Oh, Kate. He closed his eyes, and for a moment faces crowded there under the lids—Anna, Elatha, Arianrod, the Dulachan, even Kelly, all with the same piercing look of loss.

"Matt."

He heard his aunt's steps on the lawn, and a hint of anxiety in her voice. He turned and looked at her wearily.

"Yes."

Aunt Phyllis said, "Kate's asking for you again. She's quieter now, but she can't quite seem to get to sleep."

Matt looked down at the grass, an unbearable knot of pain tightening inside him. He had gone on so blindly from day to day, as if Kate would always be living next door to him—like someone deaf and blind and stupid, never thinking, never knowing.

Huskily he said, "Has she said anything—apart from my name? Did she say anything to the doctor?"

"No," said Aunt Phyllis, with an odd uncertainty. "Except . . ."

Matt looked up at the worry and confusion in her tired eyes.

"It was just once," Aunt Phyllis said. "David got a bit cross with her, and said she must tell him what had happened, straight away."

"What did she say?" Matt asked, his voice raw.

"Something about a man all in green. . . ."

13

ALL BLOWS MUST BE RETURNED

Kate and Anna were both in bed now, wearing the same white nightdresses. Anna lay with her eyes closed and her left hand under the sheets, very still. Kate looked up from her pillow, eyes puffy with tears, and Matt saw her lips move in the shape of his name. She reached out, and as he came her fingers fastened tightly on his hand.

He sat down on the bed, putting his other hand over hers. "Kate," he said as softly as he could. "What happened? Tell me."

She just continued to grip him. Her lips moved, weakly, but it was only in the shape of his name again. The blue eyes looked odd and far away, and Matt guessed it was the sleeping-stuff beginning to work.

"Kate," he said, still keeping his voice quiet, but more urgently, "for God's sake tell me! If you're just going to lie there saying nothing, I—I can't stand it!" He stopped himself, his voice beginning to shake.

She looked up at him, and Matt stared desperately into her eyes for something of the old Kate. Was it the stuff Anderson had given her that was making them look so blank? Then for an instant the blankness cracked, and a look of appeal so intense flashed out that it seemed to stab Matt to his heart.

"You've got to tell me," he said. "Come on, Kate, you've *got* to!"

Her lips moved, and Matt stooped to try and hear, hoping against hope that it wouldn't be just his name again.

"He—won't let me," came from Kate's lips, strained and distorted. "I can't—get away from him. He's too strong—and—I'm—all gone away and small inside myself. . . ." She broke off with a long gasp for breath then—"Help me!" she whispered raggedly.

"Who's he?" Matt demanded urgently. "The—man in green? Who is he, Kate? Not Kelly?"

She shook her head almost imperceptibly, breath coming hard and the strange blank look stiffening on her face again. Matt gripped her hand and felt her weakly trying to return his grip. The terrified look of appeal was hidden again.

The door was pushed open and Aunt Phyllis came in, looking more worn than Matt ever remembered seeing her.

"Perhaps we ought to let Kate go to sleep now, dear," she said quietly. "It's difficult to stay awake after taking those pills."

Matt said huskily, "Can I stay with her?"

"Till she goes to sleep? Yes, of course." Aunt Phyllis stooped to tuck in the sheet at the sides. "You'll feel better after a good night's sleep, Kate," she said gently.

Kate didn't move or answer.

Matt said, "I meant all night."

"Oh." Aunt Phyllis straightened, giving him a rather doubtful look. "Well, you ought to get some sleep as well, you know, dear."

"I just think I ought to be here," Matt said, "in case she wakes up."

Aunt Phyllis's gaze went down to their tightly-linked hands. "Perhaps you're right," she said after a pause. "Okay, I'll fetch in the armchair from my room, and if you put your feet up on one of the chairs you might be able to doze.''

"I'll get it," said Matt, beginning to rise. Kate's hand closed on his, and he saw distress flash across her face.

"Matt—"

"It's all right!" Matt sat down again, squeezing her hand. "I'm not going away." His voice was shaking.

Aunt Phyllis left the room and returned in a few moments with the light wooden armchair from her room. She put it down by the camp-bed and Kate, seeing it, allowed Matt to move from the edge of the bed and sit down in it. She kept his hand tightly between both of her own.

"Thanks, Auntie," Matt said.

Aunt Phyllis was watching Kate. Matt looked at her; she was lying huddled on her side, holding on to his hand as if it were a lifetime. Her blue eyes looked at him wretchedly, dulled from the sleeping pill, then wearily closed.

"I don't suppose you'll feel like sleeping yet, dear," Aunt Phyllis said quietly. "It's not quite nine. I'll bring you a cup of tea, shall I?"

They'd had no supper this evening; what with getting Kate to bed and calling the doctor, Aunt Phyllis had had no time to make anything. By now she was obviously too tired to, and in any case Matt didn't feel like eating. But a cup of tea would be welcome.

"Thanks," he said, in a low voice so as not to disturb Kate.

Aunt Phyllis said, "What about a book to read?"

Matt shook his head. He wasn't much of a reader at the best of times, and just now there was no possibility of concentrating on a page of print. "No, thanks," he whispered.

"The radio, then," Aunt Phyllis said softly. "You can use the earphone." Not giving him a chance to refuse that as well, she went quickly and quietly out of the room.

Kate was breathing slowly and deeply now, apparently asleep, though there was no slackening of her grip on Matt's hand. Matt was glad of the tea and the radio when they arrived; he listened to the nine o'clock news, using the earphone, but the only news of Africa was that the Secretary of State in Washington had proposed himself as mediator between the two sides. The head of another African state had immediately countered by proposing himself, and incidentally condemned the USA, Russia, Belgium and several other apparently inoffensive countries for fascist neo-imperialism. There was no report from Matt's father.

The time wore on, and Matt's arm grew stiff, but he didn't move for fear of waking Kate. Aunt Phyllis looked in on her way to bed, brought a chair from by the wall for him to put his feet up on, and tucked a cushion under his aching arm to make it easier. Telling him to call her at once if anything happened, she went to her own room, leaving both their doors open.

At last it grew dark, except for a pale crimsonish glow haunting the sky beyond the trees. Stars came, thick as daises on an uncut lawn, and one after another the radio stations closed down. In London there were plenty that went on through the night, but here all Matt could find in English was the World Service giving a talk on Sherlock Holmes. He switched it off and, not feeling very sleepy, closed his eyes.

The night was warm, and soon sleep began to come and go. Odd dreams drifted through his mind, at first dim and unexceptional—pictures of his father and mother, the house in London, his bicycle. . . . Then he saw someone riding his bicycle, and suddenly the dream was bright and sharp like a film in technicolor.

Just before he tried to stop it, he recognised the yellow

198

hair of the rider. Kate, on her own bike, not his, riding along one of the rough roads of the Moss. . . .

It was like starting awake, more than awake, as with all his energy he turned himself into the dream. He could hear the cawing of rooks over one of the fields, the swish of tyres and the tick of the wheels going round, see Kate's frown as she narrowed her eyes up against the sun.

She slowed, looking across the hills at something, and Matt knew what it was—the clump of trees that hid the ruined house. He wanted to call out to Kate, tell her to look away and ride on, but his voice couldn't make a sound.

She came to a stop, standing astride the machine and frowning across the fields at the trees. After a moment, decisively, she let the bike go down on the verge, stepped over it and went over the turf bridge into the fields.

Stop—stop—come back. . . . With all the force of his will Matt tried to turn her and get her back on to the road. It was no good. This dream was different again; he wasn't even in it this time, and he couldn't make that image of Kate do what he wanted. She went on over the field where the ripening barley rustled, over the next turf bridge into the field of grass, across that too, straight for the trees.

By the grove, she paused, looking across at the tumble-down house. The ruin seemed to change in Matt's dream, the thatch suddenly thick and new, the windows glassed and curtained and smoke curling out of the chimney as if the furnace in the laboratory was working. Then Kate turned away into the trees.

Matt seemed to feel the green coolness in there, out of the sun. Hands in pockets, Kate picked her way through the grass, tossing her hair back from her face. She paused thoughtfully by a stringy elm, then sat down in the grass at its roots, leaning back against the trunk and closing her eyes. Tired and hot, wanting a rest and the green murmuring peacefulness of trees. But these were not the catkinned willows of the far west, where Cerunnos could not come; Matt felt panic creep out of the trees at him, as if an enemy nearby were almost awake. There was a slow, deliberate rustle at the back of the elm, and out from behind it came the great Green Man.

Though the trees arched over him, he seemed to dwarf them—a giant, dressed all in green. Not the poison-green of the Fomors, but a rich, summer-leaf green—flowers and leaves and dragonflies glittered on his garments, looking too real to be embroidered. He stepped round to face Kate. His hair hung long and curling like tendrils of sweet peas, half-way down his back and mingling at the front with a flowering green beard.

Matt could smell him, the violent fragrance of heavy trees, warm grass and full-blossomed flowers, a rich rioting earth smell. The small trees seemed almost dead beside such gorgeous life. Then the giant stirred a little, and Matt saw that his skin too was as green as June grass; perhaps it was the trees filtering the light, but as his lips parted even his teeth looked green.

A sound came, like the murmuring of trees, or wind in tangled grass.

"I was sleeping lightly, maiden; I was dreaming of being awake; now you have wakened me."

Kate crouched flat against the elm, stared up at him with distended eyes. Her lips opened and moved, at first without sound; then—

"Go away!" Her voice cracked. *"Go away!"*

The giant's lip curved in a slow, meditative smile as he looked down at her. His skin was thick and smooth like evergreen leaves, not wrinkling.

"Would you be free of me?" he murmured.

The deep wild words were curiously accented, and held a kind of enjoyment, as if it was a long time since the giant had last spoken.

"Rise, then."

He stepped back, and Kate got up, her back still firmly pressed against the tree. Her face was rigid.

The Green Man drew something up from his side into his hands, each finger curling like a thick green stem. Matt saw with a sickening jolt that it was an axe. Its head was more than a yard long. The grip was roughened with hammered gold, and a pattern in green enamel wound along the haft; the head narrowed down to such a slender glittering edge that it looked as if a touch would be enough to draw blood.

The great green hands came out, offering the handle to Kate.

"Strike," said the voice. "But remember that all blows must be returned."

Kate stared at him, her face grey with pallor; then she looked down at the huge battle-axe, reached out her hands and took hold of the haft, well away from the thick green fingers.

The Green Man let go, and the axe-head swept down, burying itself in the ground. Kate struggled with its weight, lips parting as if to cry out.

"Come; strike if you would," the giant said, with a deep throb like laughter in his voice. He put his hands over Kate's and she flinched back; but he kept his grip, lifting the huge thing easily up and setting the haft over her shoulder, so that she stood breathing hard under its weight, the glinting edge turned towards him.

He put one hand up to his curling hair and drew it back to bare one side of his neck. It showed thick and green like the stem of a huge plant.

"Strike!" his voice boomed as he stooped and turned, presenting his bare neck to the blade. Kate heaved at the handle, face twisting; it came off her shoulder and the blade swung down in a flashing curve, cleaving his neck with a loud thudding *chunk*.

She dropped the axe as the head hit the ground, rolling with hair and beard streaming over the grass. Her hands went over her mouth, and she rammed herself back against the elm, shaking like a blade of grass.

For the giant's body didn't fall. No blood came from his neck; it was like a cut flower stem, as green as the rest of him.

He stayed where he was, still stooping. Then one hand moved, going out, feeling across the grass; he touched his own hair.

The thick green fingers closed on a lock of it. Then he swept upright, lifting the head up so that it swung by its hair; the eyes of it fixed on Kate, the green lips parted laughing.

Kate screamed with a high tearing sound, and hurled herself away from the tree, past the headless giant towards the field. He turned round, the swinging head looking after her.

"Remember!" his voice boomed from his mouth. "All blows must be returned!"

Matt saw Kate plunging away through the field, lips still open and screaming; and the dream dissolved in stars of light that hurt his head. He struggled with it, wondering if he was crying out, then the light waned to a pale flicker.

"You can stop it, Matt. Any time you want to."

Matt moaned softly, shifting in the chair. No. Not the laboratory. Not that soft insinuating murmur that tangled up all his thoughts. . . .

He felt Kelly's eyes on him, felt rather than saw, with the shudder they sent through him.

"Just say the word, Matt. You and me together, we can fix all this. You can have Kate, and I—well, you know what I want."

No, shouted Matt silently, no, no, no.

"Come on, Matt. Don't be a fool. You don't want old Jack-in-the-Green to come chopping Kate's pretty head off her shoulders, do you? Matt could see Kelly's face now, a little on one side, surveying him intently. "He will, you know. That's part of his game. She'll have to go back to the grove and let him return the blow. He'll get her, and Cernunnos'll get—Madinia." The clear eyes glinted with that quick furtive look, smoothed over almost at once. "Neither of us wants that. Where's the sense of it, Matt?" Kelly murmured, beguilingly.

Matt turned his head, feeling the cushion of the chair under it. Hardly knowing what he did, he called across void, across time—*Manannan! Manannan!*

Kelly was obliterated. Voice and face died away as the light came leaping cold and clear through the worlds to lodge itself in Matt. Its glow spread slowly outwards through his mind, pressing away the turmoil, clearing out the darkness.

"Why do you call me?"

Matt breathed slow, letting his mind stay for a moment on the sound of those voices. It was over. The frightening visions had gone.

He found himself looking into Manannan's silver eyes. Arms folded, he stood before Matt in a cloud of light, and Matt felt their gaze come sliding down into his mind. Once again, under that gaze, he began to feel small and alone.

"It's Kate," he said.

"Yes. Did I not warn you to take care, mortal?" The voices echoed, cold and pure. "If I look to her now, Madinia will be lost."

There was a moment's silence. Matt's throat tightened, as the light went into him without any comfort, and it seemed to him that what Manannan said must be true. Such light couldn't lie. But . . . if Anna was to escape Cernunnos, did it really mean that Kate had to be killed in this beheading game with another of the Old Ones?

"There is little time." The emotionless voices swept

aside his rising anguish. "This next night will see the end of it. If Cernunnos does not take her, Madinia will be free and I will have turned him back on to his right path. Take care of the young maiden. Next morning I will return and do what is needful."

A day, and a night. Still in the dream, Matt felt Kate's hands cold on his.

"Will she last that long?" he said, huskily.

"I do not know. You must use your own strength. Turn her heart away from death, and your own also. I have said that if you go willingly down to die, then I could not raise one finger to help you." The light streamed into him, bright and unpitying. "You are safer than Madinia, for once again she has been drawn into the Mound, and there are Fomors on every side; only her shadow remains in this world. I must return, or they will close in and cast her to Cernunnos."

Back in the Mound? Matt's heart faltered. Anna back in the Mound, Kate in the grip of the Green Man, and himself caught in a tangling web of dreams. . . . "But—Manannan—" he said, and his voice cracked. "If the dreams keep coming I *can't* look after Kate."

"They are your own dreams." The words seemed to come from far away, glittering and remote. "You have worn a Fomor's cap. That is the cause. Must you not bear your own acts, mortal?"

"Yes—but—" Matt stared up at him, feeling the bleakness of a being who was without warmth of human love. "Couldn't you help?" he said, huskily.

"I can do little to help." Manannan's light shivered a little, looking steadily on to him. "Your mind is too different from mine, mortal. These dreams are born of earth, but I am from the sky and must some day return there. I cannot care so for this world that it breaks my heart, as earthlings do. But the sky's blood runs in you also, though

204

you are mostly mortal. When the dreams come, look upward. It may be that the open sky will clear them."

His light was ebbing as he spoke, and the ring of his words receding. For a moment Matt tried to follow their echo upwards into a space where they seemed to resound. Suddenly he glimpsed a richness beyond words, of light laid upon light.

The feeling faded. After a while, he opened his eyes. He felt cold and stiff; but through the window he could see pinkness reflected in the west sky. The night was over. Light was coming again, with the strength to carry on. The swallows were up, with a sweet thin chirping under the eaves, and the grass of the park sparkled with dew.

14

RIGMAROLE

It was eight o'clock when Matt heard Aunt Phyllis come
out of her room and go downstairs. The sun was well up in
a cloudless sky, and it looked very warm again. Soon he
heard bacon sizzling and its cheerful smell drifted upstairs
mingled with that of toast and coffee. It was then that he
glanced at his watch and saw how late it was for Aunt
Phyllis to be getting up.

He rose, carefully sliding his hand out from between
Kate's. Her grip had loosened in her sleep, and she didn't
wake. She was sleeping as if exhausted, brow creased and
shadows still dark under her eyes. It didn't look as if she'd
wake very soon, and perhaps the longer she slept the better.

He glanced across at Anna. Her face was turned to the
wall and he could only see her hair on the pillow. It seemed to lie there so lightly, as if it would hardly be felt if
touched. Matt became aware of stiffness in his back and
shoulders, and particularly in his left arm. He stretched
automatically, hesitating a moment; but there wasn't anything he could do for them just now. He turned and went
out of the room towards the breakfast aroma.

"Hullo, dear." Aunt Phyllis looked up and smiled as he
entered the kitchen, but her eyes dwelt on him rather anxiously. "Is everything okay?"

Matt nodded. "They're both still sleeping."

"You sit down and have some breakfast then." Aunt Phyllis turned some rashers and a fried egg out on to a paper plate. "Help yourself to coffee and the rest."

"Thanks," Matt said. He sat down and picked up a knife and fork, and hesitated, not sure how to ask her what she was doing still at home. Usually she was gone before they even woke up.

"I'm not going to work today," Aunt Phyllis said quietly, putting some more rashers in the pan. "I'll go out and phone the office after breakfast. I can't very well leave you to cope with those two on your own all day."

Matt bit his lip. He felt that nag of guilt again at the worry they were causing her; now she was actually afraid to leave them on their own.

He took a hold on himself. There was one day to get through, and a night. After that Anna would be either freed, or lost to them for ever; but whichever happened, Manannan would then be able to come back and help Kate. They just had to survive the twenty-four hours.

"Try not to worry, dear," Aunt Phyllis said after a moment, coming to sit opposite him. She poured him a cup of coffee. "I looked in on you a couple of times during the night, but you were all sleeping. If Kate and Anna are both still in a bad way by this afternoon, I'll phone Dr. Anderson again. But I'm sure they won't be."

"No," said Matt, keeping his voice steady.

"I blame myself, really," Aunt Phyllis said ruefully. "I shouldn't have gone to that stupid dinner on Friday. You must have had an awful time in the storm. And the poltergeists had a field day too, didn't they?"

Yes. Poor Aunt Phyllis, driving home on Saturday morning to find her garden wrecked, two windows broken, and a house in chaos. It had taken almost the whole weekend to clear up. A local builder had come on Saturday afternoon to put new glass in the windows, but it could be days before the telephone was reconnected. When all this was over, if it ever was, he'd have to get his father to send her a cheque for the damage, and save up to pay him back. There would be more trouble there, explaining.

"The amazing thing is that the thunder didn't pass over anywhere else," Aunt Phyllis remarked. "It was a perfectly calm, ordinary night in Manchester, and everywhere else too, as far as I've heard. It must have been some kind of freak storm."

"I suppose so," said Matt.

There was a noise in the corner, and as Matt turned his head he saw the pedal-bin start rocking from side to side.

"Oh! Our friends are back," said Aunt Phyllis resignedly. "I suppose I shouldn't have mentioned them. It might be wise to move out into the garden, dear."

The poltergeists. Matt rose, reaching for a tray. The garden was the safest place to eat, for the poltergeists never went outside. But to sit down to a meal indoors was simply to invite the food to be tipped into your lap, or strewn gleefully across the floor.

Then his ears caught a creak from the landing above. There was a pause, then hurried, uneven steps went down the stairs. Matt put the tray down, and looked round, his eyes meeting Aunt Phyllis's.

"Go and see who it is, dear," she said quietly, reaching for the tray. She began to load their plates on it, and Matt made for the hall, quickly.

There was a rattle at the lock of the front door, and he saw Kate there, pulling it open. She was dressed, and her hand was shaking with haste.

"Kate!" Matt gasped, and lunged forward to grab her arm. She glanced over her shoulder at him with a blind look, then tried to shake his hand off, roughly.

"Let go. I've got to go." She turned her head away, her voice thick and blank. Matt's heart gave a lurch, and he caught her other arm, pulling her back from the open door and the sight of sunlight falling across vivid green trees. Kate struggled, hard, as if she had no idea who he was, and it was as much as he could do to hold her.

"Stop it, Kate! You mustn't go! *Kate!*" He dragged her back from the porch with all his strength.

"I've got to go . . ." the blurred, uncharacteristic voice muttered; she heaved against his hands as Anna had done that night when Cernunnos first came, as if he were something inanimate in her way. Matt got between her and the door, desperately.

"Kate, will you stop it? It's me—*Matt!*"

Suddenly she stopped, as if a current had been switch-off. The blue eyes came up to him. Kate's eyes, stricken and appalled, and all the strength went from her. Matt caught her in his arms before she sank to the floor.

"Matt—oh, Matt!" Her voice was her own too, high and shaking. She clung to him. "Matt, make him stop!"

Matt felt her terror. He held her close, fighting as if it were his own fear. "Come into the kitchen," he said. "Come on, it's all right. He—he's gone now."

Weakly, she allowed him to lead her down the passage to the kitchen. It was empty, except for the bouncing pedal-bin and cutlery rattling inside the drawers as if alive; Matt led her out through the back door into the sunny back garden with its high walls.

Aunt Phyllis was setting out two garden chairs, the breakfast tray on the grass. She looked up as Matt and Kate came out, and Matt saw worry return to her eyes.

"Oh, Kate, dear, are you up? Well, come and have your breakfast here with Matt."

"I'm—I'm sorry," Kate said in a trembling little voice. Matt took her to one of the chairs and she slipped down into it as if she had no strength left.

"There." Aunt Phyllis put her own plate of fried bacon

209

on Kate's lap, with a knife and fork. "I'll just go and have a look at Anna, Matt," she said, and went quickly back up the path into the house.

Matt knelt down by her chair, the hard pain knotting up again inside him. "What happened, Kate?" he said, trying to keep his voice steady. "Was it the Green Man—trying to make you go back to him?"

Kate nodded. "Yes," she managed.

Matt took her hand, feeling himself shiver. To see her like that, submerged in the power of someone else, unable to recognise him or speak with her own voice—that had been worse than anything.

"It's all right now," he said. "He's gone."

Lines creased under Kate's eyes. "He hasn't—he's still here. Oh, Matt!"

"What do you mean?" Matt gripped her hand in both of his. "Tell me, Kate. Please."

He saw her fighting for words, against the threat of returning blankness. "He's—here all the time," she whispered. "He's got me—like a hand closed round me. He was pulling—pulling me towards the door. He had an axe, Matt—and I—"

"I know," said Matt. "I know about that. Go on."

She looked at him, not understanding.

"I saw it all," Matt said. "In a kind of dream."

"Oh!" He saw her accept it, without comprehension; it was only one more crazy thing in a senseless world. "Well—I have to go to him again, Matt—and let him hit me back." Her eyes closed and she shuddered violently all over, so that the knife and fork almost slid off the plate.

"Well, you're not going!" Matt heard his voice harden. "Don't worry. You're not going back."

Kate's mouth twisted. "He'll make me," she whispered. "He's got me. He'll—start pulling again, Matt." She opened her eyes with a shuddering effort. "Can you stop him?" she whispered. "Please, Matt."

"I will stop him," Matt said roughly. "I won't let you go." He stopped, and took a breath. "Let's have breakfast," he said steadily. "Would you like some coffee?"

"I—I don't know," Kate whispered, and the sound harrowed Matt. Kate, so resolute, so mind-made-up, not even knowing whether she wanted a cup of coffee or not.

He poured some out, putting the sugar in for her. "Here," he said, and put it into her hand. While he watched her, she drank it; then he cut up the bacon for her and made her eat it, spread two pieces of toast with butter and marmalade and made her eat that too.

Aunt Phyllis came out after a while, with a small bottle of pills in her hand.

"How are you feeling, Kate?" she said gently, noting the empty plates and cup. "Better?"

Matt squeezed her hand, and Kate managed a nod. "Yes," she whispered.

"Well, have some more coffee and take one of these pills Dr. Anderson left you." Aunt Phyllis poured some more coffee into Kate's cup and gave it to her, then shook out a small yellow pill into her other hand. Kate put it into her mouth and swallowed it with the coffee.

"It might make you rather sleepy," Aunt Phyllis said. "Would you like to go back upstairs and lie down?"

Kate nodded dumbly, and Matt rose to help her up.

"What about your breakfast, Matt?" Aunt Phyllis asked. Matt glanced down at the plate of congealed bacon and the skinned-over coffee which he hadn't touched.

"Sorry," he said awkwardly. "I didn't get round to it."

Aunt Phyllis gave him a little smile. "All right, dear, I'll make some fresh and bring it up to you."

Upstairs, Anna was still in bed, eyes closed. She lay on her back and her left hand had crept up on to the pillow. Matt made himself look at it, as Kate lay down on the camp-bed—and he saw the finger-marks just as plainly as before. A shiver passed down his spine, and he stepped

211

over to the bed, took Anna's hand and tucked it back under the sheet. For a moment, he stood looking down at her.

Manannan had said that only her shadow was left in this world. Matt could see the truth of it; lying there, she looked substanceless, almost transparent. Her hand had been too light for a human hand. Now it was more like looking at an idea of Anna than at Anna herself.

"Matt—" Kate whispered. He turned and went back to the armchair by the camp-bed, taking Kate's hand in a firm grip.

The yellow pill seemed to take effect after a while. Kate lay there, not actually asleep, but not awake enough to do more than keep hold of his hand and murmur his name from time to time. Aunt Phyllis brought his breakfast up and he ate without noticing what it was.

Despite all the dreams of the night, he felt vividly and tensely awake. Now and again the bad dreams from Lochlann approached, but for the first time he was able to resist them; he had only to turn his head to the window and look out hard at the sky for his mind to clear at once. Manannan had been right. After a while they began to keep their distance, and Matt became aware of little else but Kate's pale face on the pillow. He noticed that the graze on her cheek had almost healed. Sitting there watching her, he hoped against hope.

The Green Man hadn't left her. He could feel his strong encircling grip as plainly as if it were round himself. Halfway through the morning, another struggle came, a sudden heave that forced Kate up on the bed. He got up quickly and pushed her back against the pillow, pinning her there by the shoulders.

"Fight him, Kate! Don't let him take you!" he whispered urgently, so that Aunt Phyllis wouldn't hear.

She struggled under his hands, her eyes wide and blank

212

and her face twisting. Then, as suddenly as before, the strength went out of her and he felt her go limp as a rag on the bed. He kept his hands on her shoulders, heart thudding with relief. His eyes closed momentarily.

"You can't have her!" he heard himself whisper.

Kate looked up at him, the blankness gone again. The dark smudges under her eyes were enormous, and she was as white as the pillow case; but it was Kate looking up at him out of those exhausted blue eyes.

"Matt." Her lips framed the word.

Matt let her go and sat down again in the chair. Her fingers linked slowly into his, and her head turned a fraction to look at him.

"So—tired." Her voice was a mere breath.

"It's the pill," Matt said softly. "It's all right, Katie. He's not going to get you. Try to go to sleep."

Her eyes flickered and closed. Matt went on sitting beside her, holding her hand; the hope inside him grew a little.

Those yellow pills, whatever they were, were supposed to calm Kate down and help her to sleep. If they carried on working this well, so that she just lay there in an unresponsive daze, the Green Man wouldn't be able to fetch her back to the grove. He can pull and heave all he likes, Matt thought grimly; she's too drugged to move.

The morning dragged on to midday, and Kate seemed to be asleep. Her fingers had lost their grip on his, and her breath was slow and light. Aunt Phyllis came up with some lunch which he didn't want, but he ate it, going on hoping. Only about eighteen hours left.

The poltergeists were lively downstairs, keeping up a continual din. The sun came round and began pouring into the bedroom.

Anna had still not woken. Matt looked at her from time to time, conscious of a peculiar wrench of the heart whenever he did so. She was so beyond anything he could do, trapped in the Fomors' Mound where only Manannan's light could guard her.

He wondered what the rest of Danu's Children were doing. Couldn't Arianrod, and all the others she'd talked about—Oengus, Eil Ton, Govannon—come and help too?

Maybe we're not the only ones, he thought, with a sudden coldness. Maybe there are hundreds of others like us, right now, all caught up in the Shadow. It was a bad thought, that picture of dark battling massively with light, and themselves only a small skirmish on the edge.

It can't be like that—surely! Maybe they just don't want to help. Why should they anyway? It's not their world.

He became aware, suddenly, that the noise downstairs had ceased. It wasn't just a pause between one crash and the next; the house had been quiet for some time. He looked at his watch. Twenty past three. Fifteen, may fifteen and a half hours to go. . . . Why had the poltergeists stopped? Was it a good sign?

He heard Aunt Phyllis's step on the stairs. She came into the room and glanced round.

"Hullo, dear. Hasn't Anna woken up yet?"

Matt shook his head. "No," he said quietly, so as not to wake up Kate.

Aunt Phyllis gave Anna a worried look. Matt wondered if she looked as light and insubstantial to his aunt as she did to him. Maybe not, he thought with a queer thump of the heart; maybe it's only because of the Fomor's cap that I can see it.

Aunt Phyllis came over to Kate. "I think they ought to wake up and eat something," she said. "Anna hasn't had anything since yesterday morning." She stooped and took Kate's shoulder, giving her a little shake. "Kate?"

Kate didn't wake. Her brows only creased a little, as if she was in pain, and suddenly Matt had a dizzying sense of danger. It passed quickly, leaving him confused and his heart hammering. What was the matter? What had come, to make him feel like that?

"She doesn't look terribly good, does she," Aunt Phyllis said doubtfully, and Matt looked at Kate's white face, the deep shadows under her closed eyes, the brows drawn with that look of pain. The coldness crept back.

He'd been a fool to be so sure. Just being in their own world didn't mean they were safe; Cernunnos had come here, to this very room. Otherworld didn't stay put, it broke right through into this world when it had to. And that meant that if Kate didn't go to the Green Man on her own legs he could come and fetch her, leaving her shadow behind to fool them as Kelly and the Fomors had done with Anna.

Aunt Phyllis took Kate's wrist. "Her pulse feels rather light to me," she said anxiously. "I don't know much about these things, though. Do you, Matt?"

"No," said Matt, huskily.

Aunt Phyllis straightened. "I think I'll go and give Dr. Anderson a ring. I expect they're both all right, really—but I'll feel easier in my mind." She looked at Matt and put her hand on his shoulder. "Don't worry, love, I'm just fussing," she said apologetically. "Sleep's probably the best thing for them. I just want to be absolutely sure."

Matt nodded. "Yes," he said.

"I won't be long. Will you be all right?"

"Yes," said Matt again, huskily.

Aunt Phyllis went out. He waited while she went down the stairs. He heard the front door open and close, her footsteps on the path outside, and the gate click.

"Kate!" he whispered, feeling so cold in the sunny room that he almost shivered. He took her by the shoulders and shook her gently. "Kate! Kate, wake up."

She was like a rag doll in his hands, limp and lifeless. He came out of the chair, shaking her with all his strength. "Kate!" he yelled, his voice hoarse and croaking.

Her head rolled about the pillow as he shook her, so like the green head that rolled in the grass that he stopped, trembling.

He seated himself on the bed, numbly. No. It couldn't be. She was alive, she was warm under his hands—no. She couldn't go from him like this.

Something seemed to crack inside him. There was no one to help; Manannan wouldn't come until the morning. And by then there would be no Kate left.

He couldn't bear it. The crack inside him gaped, letting in a chill emptiness. Then suddenly he found himself shouting into it as he'd shouted for Manannan, through a void between worlds—*"Kate! Kate! Kate!"*

He felt her jar abruptly and painfully under his hands. He shouted again, making no sound in the room, aware only of that white face.

She struggled up on the bed. He held on to her shoulders, but she shook him off, blue eyes wide and stricken; he caught her into his arms, and held on with all his might.

"Kate—wake up—it's me, Matt!" He could hear his voice, raw and shaking.

She fought him, with twice her normal strength; then again the struggle abruptly vanished and she sagged a dead weight in his arms. But he felt one hand touch his arm and grip faintly.

"Matt—" A thread of a voice. But it was Kate looking up at him from the great exhausted eyes.

Relief came, so massive that his sight swam for a moment. "Don't go to sleep again, Kate," he said huskily. "You mustn't. . . ."

"Matt—" Kate whispered, hardly audible. Her hand tried to grip harder, and couldn't. "He . . . had me. Till you called. Don't—let him—again . . . couldn't—bear it."

The relief slipped away from him. Her face was ghastly

216

white, but for the bruise-like shadows under her eyes. Matt held on to her, as the faint hold on his arm weakened and slipped away.

"Stay awake, Kate," he said, desperately. "Please. Stay here!"

Outside, the gate clicked, and he heard Aunt Phyllis hurrying in. The front door opened and closed, and she came up the stairs. He looked round as she entered the room, and saw her face tauten wretchedly as she looked at Kate.

"Oh, dear," she said under her breath, and came to the side of the bed. "Kate, love, is it getting worse?"

Kate never moved; it was only the wide blue eyes now that showed she was still just there. Aunt Phyllis sat down on the armchair beside them and looked at Matt, trying to hide the strain in her eyes.

"David can't come till six o'clock, Matt," she said. "He's had to take the afternoon surgery—one of the partners has been called away."

Matt tried to steady himself. "I don't think there's much he could do, anyway," he said hoarsely.

"No," said Aunt Phyllis. "He said that himself. But, Matt, he said something else, too."

Matt kept his arms around Kate. He hadn't cried since the age of six or seven, learning that tears were mostly despised in a boy; but now he felt as if inside himself he were crying, crying with a wordless anguish that would never end.

"What?" he said huskily.

Aunt Phyllis said gently. "He said he thought you might know something about all this, love. I—I don't want to pry. But it's got pretty serious now, hasn't it?"

Matt nodded dumbly.

"I think you ought to tell me, then." Her eyes searched his face anxiously. "I promise I won't pass it on to anyone —not unless I have to."

217

Matt put his cheek against Kate's hair, trying to choke down the inward crying. She was right. There was no room left now to worry about that any more, as Kate lay here in the grip of the Green Man.

"You really must tell me, love," Aunt Phyllis said, urgently.

Matt nodded again. "Yes," he said. "It sounds insane, though. It's crazy."

"Never mind. Just tell me."

Matt took a deep breath. Holding Kate close to him, he began to tell her; and a crazy enough tale it sounded, for the thought of Kate was so huge in his mind that he couldn't think straight. He stumbled through it somehow, telling her about Kelly and Cernunnos and Danu's Children, the Mound and the Fomors and the Dulachan, and finally how last night he'd seen the meeting of Kate and the Green Man in a dream. He couldn't bear to linger over this part and finished abruptly, not daring to look up, sure of meeting an appalled stare of incredulity if he did. There was a brief pause.

"Oh, Matt!" Aunt Phyllis's voice was shaken. "Why on earth didn't you tell me before?"

Matt did look up then, quickly. He saw horror on her face but no hint of disbelief. "You mean you—understand?" he said lamely.

"I don't think you're making it up, if that's what you mean," Aunt Phyllis said. "You wouldn't tell me a rigmarole like this if it wasn't true. Oh, dear, though." She looked helpless. "I just don't know what to do! David can't help, that's obvious. Who do I call? The *vicar?*"

"No," said Matt. He had met the vicar here a couple of years ago. He was a kindly man, but uneasy if talk turned towards the irrational. "There isn't time."

"No," said Aunt Phyllis, "I suppose not. Oh, Matt!" She put a hand over his for a moment, as he held Kate. "I do wish you'd told me before! How could you *bear* it, these awful things happening one after another?''

Matt compressed his lips. Muddled as the story had been, the telling of it had brought some sort of relief, and his head felt clearer again. "I don't know," he said. "We had to bear it, I suppose . . . and something always happened before it really got on top of us, like Arianrod or the island in the west."

"And Manannan?" asked Aunt Phyllis.

Matt hesitated. "I suppose so," he said, rather bleakly. "It isn't easy to talk to him, but after he's gone he leaves a sort of silver inside you." He remembered how Manannan had gone back to Anna, leaving him and Kate to survive as best they could, and tried again to stifle the crying inside him. "We just have to stop the Green Man getting her," he said roughly. "Manannan'll come tomorrow morning. We just have to keep her here till then."

"Matt, love—" Aunt Phyllis leaned forward, and he saw from her eyes that she knew how he was feeling. "I don't really understand all this," she said gently, over the strain in her voice. "I can't take it in. But if this Green Man can't force Kate actually to get up and go back to him —well, he'll take her here. That's what it looks like to me."

Matt closed his eyes for a moment, the anguish in him tightening to one unbearable knot. It seemed that all his life, up to now so vague, diffuse and day-to-day, had narrowed down to that one hard point—the necessity of Kate. It was all that mattered. And he knew now, quite clearly, that rather than have her die he would die himself, because without her there was no way to go on living.

"Yes," he said, not looking up at Aunt Phyllis. He knew what he had to do now. "I'll have to take her back to the grove."

Kate stirred feebly in his arms. "Matt," she whispered.

"Must go—making me."

"We're going." Matt got up, helping her gently to sit up on the bed.

"I'll come with you," Aunt Phyllis said hastily, rising.

Matt shook his head. His purpose was clear and hard inside him, the only thing left there. "Someone'll have to stay with Anna," he said. "You couldn't do anything, Auntie. It has to be me." He turned back to Kate. "We'll need the knife, Kate. Where is it?"

Kate shook her head, numbly.

"It'll be on your other jeans." Matt remembered how they had come back from the Fomors' land covered in mud. "In the laundry basket."

"I'll get it." Aunt Phyllis went out to where the laundry basket stood on the landing. Matt heard her sorting through it.

"Matt—" Kate whispered.

"It's going to be all right, Katie," Matt said. He squeezed her hand. "He's not going to use that axe on you. I promise."

"Is this it?" Aunt Phyllis came back into the room with the scout knife in her hand. Matt took it and fastened the sheath on to his belt.

"Matt—" said Aunt Phyllis.

Matt looked up and saw the fear she was trying to hide. Poor Aunt Phyllis. After all her worry, now to have this mad rigmarole sprung on her—she couldn't possibly understand, and yet he expected her to stay here doing nothing while he and Kate went off to meet some crazy demon all in green.

"I'm sorry, Auntie," he said.

"Matt, love, just be careful, for heaven's sake." She put her hands on his shoulders, her face taut with anxiety. "I can't not trust you, because—well, I think you know what you're doing. But do be careful. I'll stay with Anna, though goodness knows what I can do."

Anna. Even then Matt felt that small, different twist of pain. He looked across at where she lay, then let go of Kate and went to the side of her bed, putting his hand on hers over the sheet. He could hardly feel anything. It was like touching a shadow. I'll never see her again, he thought slowly, looking down at that transparent, insubstantial face. Oh, Anna . . . I understand now; but I was always too late for you. All I can do now is remember you, for as long as I last.

He closed his hand gently on the shadowy one under the sheet, and said inside himself: Goodbye, Anna. Then he came back to Kate, taking her hand. She got up, not needing as much of his aid as before.

"Goodbye, Auntie," he said.

"Be quick back," Aunt Phyllis said, very low. She put a hand on his shoulder momentarily. "Good luck."

Then, Kate's hand in his, they left the room and went downstairs towards the garage.

PART THREE

MANANNAN'S COUNTRY

15

THE WILD HUNT WILL WAKE

The sun was hot again, the west wind no more than a
breeze. Rooks crouched silent and black in the fields of the
Moss, instead of cawing across the sky. The only thing that
moved was the scanner of the radar station—that, and
themselves, speeding along the road. Kate was pedalling
so fast that Matt was getting breathless keeping up with
her.

The clump of trees drew nearer and nearer. Matt glanced at Kate and saw her crouched over her handlebars,
white-faced but for two hectic patches over her cheek-
bones. They reached the turf bridge and Kate let her bike
crash down anyhow in the road as she jumped off and
made for the field.

"Kate!" Matt shouted, pausing to drag both bikes on to
the verge. At the sound of his voice he saw her hesitate and
struggle, then she went on as fast as before. Matt raced
after her. He caught up with her half-way across the field
and managed to grab her by the arm. "Hold on!" he said
breathlessly.

She tried to pull away from him, but the blue eyes that
looked round at him were still Kate's eyes, wide and terrified. For a moment he felt her pulling both ways, towards
and away from him at the same time.

"Stay with me, Kate," he said. He put his other arm

round her, taking hold of her shoulder. "Listen—don't let him get you away from me. Do just what I say, not what he says. Kate?"

She shivered. "Yes," she whispered. "Come on, Matt. Please. It hurts."

"Okay." Keeping hold of her, Matt went on, quickly. He tried to keep to a walk, but soon they were running again, lurching against each other in their haste. Matt could feel them being pulled towards the grove. Suddenly they were in there, out of the sunlight.

Kate stood still, but Matt could feel her trembling all over. He kept one arm round her and drew the scout knife out of its sheath with his free hand. Sheffield steel. Instinct alone had made him bring this; no one had ever said the Old Ones, like the Fomors, feared iron. All the same, in his dream that axe-head had had a tawny gleam, not a grey one like iron.

They'd come right into the middle of the grove, and Matt felt something hard by his foot. Anna's bicycle. The grass was growing over it, and the dent on the tree-trunk nearby was no longer raw. The trees were repairing their wounds.

The back of his neck suddenly prickled, and a wind sent every leaf blanching. Matt whirled round, shoving Kate behind him, and the knife shot out in his hand. The grove dwindled and shrank as the face of the Green Man looked down at him.

"Ahhh. . . ." His head moved on his neck as if the axe had never cleaved it, a sound like a tree's groan coming from between his lips. He seemed greener than ever, as deep and huge as the forest in the Fomors' land, and Matt felt panic struggle in him. He forced his eyes away from the giant and fixed them on the small scratched blade of the scout knife.

"What do you do here, Iron Man?" The murmur was wild and heavy, like the threat of branches about to fall.

The flowers and flies on his clothes seemed to dance in the corners of Matt's eyes. "Go. My business is with the one who struck me, not with you."

"No," said Matt, his throat dry. The sight of the huge giant misted the edges of his mind, but nothing could fog the purpose inside him. "She's nothing to do with you any more. Let her go."

"She must bare her neck and receive my blow in return. She chose to strike me."

Kate's hands suddenly caught Matt's shoulders and gave such a heave that he almost staggered aside. But he had hold of her arm and he gripped with all his strength, forcing himself back against her. She struggled like a demon.

"Stop it, Kate! *Kate!*" he shouted, shifting against each heave she gave him so that he stayed between her and the Green Man. He heard her give a whimper of pain and abruptly the heaving stopped and she was leaning on him instead, her forehead against his shoulder.

"Ahhh. . . ." The Green Man's head turned on his neck again and out of the corner of his eye Matt saw the green lips grimace. "Great is the power of the Iron Man," the wild voice murmured. "But you are only man, for all your iron. Do you think you can stop us now? Once men bore me like a god through every village in the May-time; since that ended and the sleep came on us, I have had nothing to do but grow in strength. But now the Horned One has awakened. I have seen the mark of his hooves in my woods, and soon they will go down all your streets, and teach you the horror of forgetting him. Belisama will wake, and Epona of the horses. The fuaths will drag your ships down into the sea, and the oak and the mistletoe will wake and demand blood again. The sleep is over. You are only man, crawling out of the earth for a little while. You are mine. The lendings of Danu's Children will not last you long."

"We're not yours." The words formed themselves

227

almost free of Matt's will. "We're different now. We're sky as well as earth—all of us. And you can't have Kate."

"She has struck me. The blow must be returned." The green of his clothes flickered as if with its own sunshine. "If you were made all of iron, you could not cut through the bond I have laid on her. It is older than Govannon's swords. Stand aside, and let her bare her neck."

"No!" Matt gripped Kate's wrist hard behind him. She moved, but only feebly. Matt gritted his teeth—he was afraid, but not for himself, only for Kate. If he carried through his purpose she would be safe, and he would have gone where fear couldn't reach him. He mustn't falter. There was only the one thing left to do.

He said harshly, "You can't have her. You've got to take me instead."

There was silence in the grove. Then Kate gave a great gasp and her fingers ran into him. "No, Matt, no!" she screamed. "You mustn't, you mustn't! Remember what Manannan said! We've got to *fight!*"

"Shut up, Kate!" Matt said hoarsely. "Stay still."

She breathed deeply and shudderingly behind him, and hung on to him as if she'd never let go. Not lifting his eyes from the knife, Matt spoke again to the motionless giant.

"You've got to take me instead."

"Ahhh . . ." the Green Man murmured, and all at once the haze round Matt's mind lifted. He dared to look up into the smooth green face. The eyes were green and brown and changing, like sunlight through leaves. "The power of an unwed girl is great," murmured the green lips, "but greater than any is the power of a willing sacrifice. Yes—it would atone. Do you know, then, Iron Man, that not all the sky's iron could cut through this bond?"

Roughly, Matt said, "I know it's the only way."

"And would you stand unflinching with bared neck, waiting for the stroke of my axe?" The Green Man drew

228

the shining axe up from his side and let it lie in his hands.

Matt looked at that long razor edge. His mouth was like sand. But he had done it—he had said it, and there was no going back. And whatever he felt now, it was different from fear.

"Yes," he said.

"Aye. So you would," murmured the Green Man. His hands closed round the axe-handle, tightened—then slowly opened again. "But for all that, I will not strike, Iron Man; you have given yourself to more than me."

Matt stared up at him. Sunlight ran across the green face like laughter.

"Do you think you are master of your own fate?" That throb of enjoyment was back. "Do you think you can decide the time of your own death? I will not strike at your choosing. For this, the Wild Hunt will wake!"

Matt said hoarsely. "Let Kate go."

"Death will not come at anyone's bidding, Iron Man. I might have missed my stroke, and the maiden would have gone free. Even now, you may escape if you can outrun Gwyn ap Nudd, King of the Dead, and all his hounds. Run! Run, Iron Man!"

"Let Kate go," Matt said.

The green lips parted, smiling. "She is free."

Kate gave a gasping breath behind him, and he felt her move suddenly, with all her own strength coming back. He turned round to her and thrust the scout knife into her hand. "Get out of here, Kate!"

"Run, Iron Man! The hunt is up!"

"Matt!" Kate's eyes were alive again, huge and terrified. "You're mad! Manannan *said* we mustn't turn to—" Her voice twisted and broke.

Matt looked at her. A new wind had sprung up, and her yellow hair was tossing. He held the hand with the knife in it for a moment; it seemed that he had never seen her so

229

clearly before, or in just that way. The picture stamped itself on his mind, more real than all his previous thoughts of her; it was hard to let go of her hand.

"Oh, Matt—" Kate whispered.

"I've got a chance," Matt said softly. Words felt clumsy and difficult. "Go on, Kate. Please. Run. Be safe."

Her lips trembled. He saw her try to speak. But she couldn't, and he just saw a look from the blue eyes, then the yellow hair turning, and then the trees hid her from him.

The wind leapt up, buffeting the branches roughly. Matt heard a sound on the air—high, sharp and yelping.

"They have your scent." The green Man watched him, listening. Then he let the axe fall to the ground, with a loud slicing thud. "For your life, Iron Man!" He raised his great green hands to the sky, laughing.

Matt turned and raced out of the grove, away from those faint yelping sounds. In the heat of the sun he felt cold. Sunshine. Rooks. The ordinary green Moss. The sound— yes, the sound of a tractor in the distance. The radar station. Was he to be hunted to his death here—in this? A chance—a chance he might escape. The Green Man had said so. Was there—really—such a chance?

A ditch opened in front of him, too wide to jump. He'd come out into the grass-field, and over the ditch was the barley, then the road. He swerved right and ran towards a turf bridge—but he'd turned the wrong way, their bikes were at the other end of the field. Never mind. Get across, then run back along the road, grab the bike and cycle like mad for the town, and people.

What was happening? The sun—where was the sun? It wasn't evening, surely; it was afternoon! What was this dusk falling, then? And where was that bridge?

Be careful. Can't see so well. Don't want to fall into one of those ditches. Careful!

Matt paused, his lungs heaving. The air was thick round him, and for a moment he wondered if a black fog had drifted over from one of the industrial towns to the east. But the wind was in the wrong direction for that. And the air was still clear to breathe. No. This was nightfall!

He tried to look at his watch, but the dial wasn't luminous, and it was already too dark to see. It couldn't be more than six o'clock, but it was growing darker by the moment. And there were no street lights on the Moss.

He looked round at where he was. He must find that turf bridge and get over the field to the road. The bike would give him some sort of chance. But something was wrong—the stuff growing in the field was clumped and low down, like cabbages or lettuces.

He'd missed the bridge.

He turned back. It was no good running this way, it was just taking him further away from his bike.

The wind had changed, and swept in his face. With it came the sound—not so faint, deeper-mouthed, more like baying. It sent coldness right down to Matt's heart. They were coming on the wind, then; and his bike lay between him and them.

He turned back and ran on the same way, gasping for breath. Not all the will in the world could make him go back, towards that baying. He would have to trust his legs. People. Houses. There were houses to the south and west of the Moss. And which way was he running? There was no sun, and no stars in that thick black sky to tell him. Lungs burning as he ran, he tried to work out the map of the Moss in his mind. The sun, till it disappeared, had been over to his left. So that must be west. That meant he was running north.

And the hunt was coming up from the south, driving him north, away from houses and help. Matt slowed, his legs like cotton wool and his lungs heaving. He could see

231

no more than a few steps in front of him. If he went on at this speed he'd end up in one of the ditches, with a sprained ankle at least.

He must get out on to the road. There must be more of those turf bridges linking the fields; panting, he forced himself on, watching the line of the ditch beside him where it fell away into blackness. It was too dark now even to see across into the other field.

Suddenly he saw it—something less black curving away over the black ditch. He leapt for the bridge and forced himself into top speed again, sprinting over it into the field between him and the road. There was another ditch to his right, and the soil of this field was ploughed, slowing him down. Each breath was like a cry now, knifing his lungs as he struggled across the furrows. His foot struck turf again at last, and then he was falling in to the gritty surface of the road.

On the wind he heard the baying, as desolate as a lost soul. He felt colder than before. He struggled to his feet and ran on, gasping. A stitch came, and he bent low as he ran, one hand pressed against the pain.

He remembered he must bear west. This road met another one that travelled the right way; he'd have to watch out for it and take the left-hand turning; that would bring him to some houses. But it was a long road, long and weary even for a cyclist, and the baying sounded closer every time. Coming from the south, the hunt could cut across the fields and reach him easily. These ditches wouldn't bother hounds, not even ordinary ones; and these could probably see in the dark.

Suddenly, Matt heard a new sound straight ahead of him—a deep steady buzzing. He couldn't hear properly for his gasping lungs; he came to a lurching stop, took a great mouthful of air and forced himself not to breathe for one moment. The buzzing was quite loud and close. The radar station! The sound of the scanner going round! Surely there must be people there, to report on the movement of aircraft from the airport up the coast. And this road led straight up to it! Why hadn't he remembered? He hurled himself forward, lungs fairly screaming, and legs so weak he could hardly feel them. Come on—come on—faster!

The big wooden gates loomed up seconds before he crashed into them, their rough boards still warm from the day. Big solid brown gates, marked "Civil Aviation Authority" and "No Admittance" or something like that; it was too dark to see the notice. Matt pounded his fists against them.

"Help! Help!" His voice was more of a scream than a shout, torn with breathlessness. He beat with his fists on the door, then began to kick as well, with legs that felt like jelly. "Help! Help! *Help!*"

He took in a breath to shout again, and it came like a burning spear. His hands wouldn't clench properly, and his legs wouldn't hold him up. Doubling over the pain in his chest, Matt found himself on the ground, his head against the immovable gates. Above him, the shadowy mast swept steadily round with its loud hum.

No one had heard him. No one had come.

Perhaps he hadn't made enough noise. . . .

No, he thought, clasping his chest as it heaved for breath, and the desolate call of those hounds came on the wind. No. Either there was no one there or else no one could hear the sounds he made any more.

It was all over. The baying sounded again, and time went slower and slower. Hadn't he known this from the start? Hadn't he made up his mind, despite all Manannan's words . . . to die . . . so that Kate wouldn't? He had chosen. He didn't expect anyone's help. What did Manannan know of death—him, an immortal?

And then the Green Man had tortured him with talk of a chance to escape. That had fooled him. All the human fears and longings had leapt back, without his even noticing, forcing him to race like a madman through the dark and pound on these gates where no one could hear.

There was no chance. There never had been. But now he couldn't make his mind up to it the way he thought he had done before; now that Kate was freed and safe the whole pain and horror of dying without her rose up before him. There must be some help, somewhere. Manannan—Arianrod . . . Kelly . . .

His will revolted. Kelly could save him; he had only to call; but he couldn't, not if Kelly were the last man left on earth. A feeble anger with himself flickered up in Matt. If you're as squeamish as this you don't deserve to survive, he thought, and at the same time Kelly's musing voice echoed in his ears—*"a strange lad; so set on death. . . ."*

He gave up, the anger deserting him. The hounds cried again, nearer, and again hope froze in him. He was done for. No hope, no help. But there must be some help! I was a fool, I didn't mean it . . . oh, Kate. . . .

There was no one to see him cry. He leant his head against his knees, closing his eyes against tears and a long bright shaft of pain that wouldn't end. Thinking of Kate, he wasn't surprised to see her under his eyelids; she'd left her bike behind on the Moss and was running along a footpath that led straight across farmland to the town, her yellow hair tossing back with her haste. It was still day where she was. He couldn't bear it any more. Did he have to be the loser every time? Kate! Kate!

She whirled round, eyes wide. Her lips parted, and her eyes searched to and fro. He thought her mouth shaped his name. The pain swept round him like wind from another world and he called to her, now knowing what his words were—"Call Emrys! Fetch Emrys! Kate, Kate, help me—"

Colder than ice the hounds' cry came. The sight faded, and there was darkness all round him. Slowly, his hand felt for the gate, and he got up. A sky without clouds or stars stretched above him, and his mind thought for him, slowly and emptily as if it was no longer his own mind.

Go for the ditches. Hounds can't follow scent on water. Make your way through the ditches to the edge of the Moss.

He moved like a machine, hardly knowing which way he was going. He was two people now, one telling him he couldn't escape, the other dumbly forcing him on. The grass under his feet changed to pitted road, then back to grass again, and at last he saw the deeper blackness of a ditch. He put his hands on the edge and slithered down the steep slope. With scarcely a splash he slid up to his knees in water.

The banks stretched up on either side, leaving only the black sky above. He could just see the water, rocking gently round his legs but stretching away into complete darkness. He began wading, away from the bleak ringing bay that kept freezing the sky.

He couldn't go fast. The bottom was soft and muddy, and one shoe stuck in it. He left it where it was, and after a few more steps the other one slipped off as well. Then he came to a bridge that was solid earth with a round pipe stuck through it. The bank was too steep to climb, and he had to wriggle through the pipe head first, holding his breath because it was completely under water. It was only just wide enough for him. He came out on to an intersecting ditch, and chose the way he thought was west. It wasn't much more than a guess, but he had to keep going.

It was like walking in a tunnel that moved with him, a tunnel about ten feet long before and behind. Further than that it was too black to see. Wet through now, he was getting very cold, and again and again the hounds' bay echoed in the sky behind him. It worked its way into him along with the cold, so that his wading became slower and slower. The hunt was gaining on him.

Then something changed in the tunnel. At the very end, he thought he saw a low humped shape in the water. He stopped, straining his eyes to see. It wasn't there any more. Then it moved again, back. Something long and narrow, with a tail that ringed the water with ripples. Matt thought of otters, and knew that was impossible. The thing shifted, and he saw a ridge down its back, with ends trailing the water. A mane. . . .

He edged towards the steep slope of the bank, one hand clutching for a hold. The grass rustled under his hand, and the thing shifted its head towards him. He caught the gleam of eyes, and the trail of something like hair. A long arm came out and he saw, clearly, webs between the fingers.

He knew what it was. They had swarmed in the great wave that Eil Ton and Arianrod had saved them from—river-wraiths. Fuaths, the Dulachan had called them.

Matt hurled himself at the bank. Smooth and steep, grass unrooting as he seized it—he came crashing back into the water and a mob of them were on him, webby hands slipping slimily on his skin, a raw stink of mud and dead fish almost choking him, hair trailing him like weeds, and a face next to his with two holes instead of a nose. Matt struggled to keep his head above water, and one caught him around the throat, dragging his head back to force it under. The strip of sky tilted above him; the cry of the hounds pealed about his ears, and he saw the hunt racing down towards him on the wind.

The sky was alight around them. Behind the streaming hounds came riders, grim and pale on ghostly horses. There was no colour in any of them, except the hounds, and they were white with ears dark red like blood. Their cry came again, the long howl of the dead, killing hope off; he'd been a fool to think he could ever throw them off his scent. The cold hands of the fuaths were trembling, and he could hear a snuffling whimper from their noseless faces. Then the hounds were upon them, scattering them, and he could feel their icy breath and see their long pale teeth.

Parting the hounds, the riders came, swirling round him in a mist of cold so intense that he wanted to cry out. On the bank, in the ditch, horses wreathed round him, and he shrank down in the water. Then one rode down the bank straight at him, the hooves seeming to tread air rather than grass; he looked into the rider's face and recognised the leader of the hunt, the foremost rider, one with a crown of ice and eyes like glaring stones. The horse checked only for a moment as a hand came down, white as old bones, and took hold of Matt's shoulder.

The sky splintered before his eyes. The cold of that touch was worse than ice that had never melted since the world's beginning, worse than fire, worse than despair. Matt screamed soundlessly up at the empty night, and the cold sank into him like a spear.

Gwyn ap Nudd's hand gripped and lifted, and Matt was cast across his saddlebow.

16

THE CASTLE OF OETH AND ANOETH

1

There was such a dizzy upward swoop that Matt, eyes shut, almost thought he was fainting. But he could still feel the cold, and Gwyn's arm clasped across his chest. The swoop reached its zenith and paused, hovering; and he knew it was no use keeping his eyes closed any longer.

The light crackled about them. Matt looked down, and saw the earth far away below. There was the Moss, and to the south the town and the river—but they were changing. Every moment Matt saw more and more clearly. The trees were walking.

They were moving out over the Moss in a remorseless march of greenery. They grew and multiplied as they went. The cottage had already disappeared underneath them, and as Matt watched he saw the roof of the radar station crumple and fall, and the trees walk over it. They were altering the shape of the Moss; the drainage ditches broke, and the water flowed into new channels. Matt recognised the shape. Before his eyes, the Moss was turning into that ancient forested swamp where Fomors lived. . . . Otherworld was back.

To the south, the waters of the river parted and Belisama rose to the night, combing her hair with a golden comb. The town had vanished. Belisama's eyes looked up into his as she combed and combed, and waves rippled over the place where the houses had been. Matt saw, at the water's edge, the black hump of the Mound. Then the horse sprang on again, jolting him and the earth tilted away; he saw the sea instead below them. Gwyn's voice echoed out, colder than his hounds' cry.

"Ride! Ride! Ride! To the Castle of Oeth and Anoeth, built by Manannan the Wise!"

"Ride!" answered the dead voices behind him. "Ride!"

The land fell away behind them, and Matt watched it go As it dipped below the horizon, it seemed never to have existed at all; the cold was sinking into his marrow, and time meant less and less. Looking down, he could see only waves. He was so numb now that he himself seemed almost to have stopped existing; there was just the smoking light, the sea, and the hurtle of the Hunt through emptiness. He heard the name, Manannan, but it seemed only a word. All he wanted was to crawl into some hole and escape from the aching cold. His world had vanished beneath him. What more was there?

He saw something ahead. It was underneath the surface of the sea, but visible, white and humped and rippling as waves rolled over it. It looked like a huge beehive, or a mound, with a rough surface like coarse thatch. It was coming nearer. There was something round and black at the top, but it was difficult to see through the shifting waters. It looked like somewhere to hide.

The Hunt was curving down towards it. Gwyn's voice rang out, piercingly. "The Castle of Oeth and Anoeth! Hail to the Catcher of Souls!"

Castle? It didn't look like Matt's idea of a castle, that mysterious white rippling hump deep down in the sea. But there was nothing else in the whole dark hemisphere of the sky and sea—not a fish, a bird, or a single star. The Hunt circled above it in a rage of light and tossing spray, and

Matt's gaze settled on the dancing black hole at the top.

"Hail!" came Gwyn's voice. "Hail to the Lord of Oeth and Anoeth!"

"Hail!" echoed the riders. "Hail!"

The icy fingers bit into Matt's shoulder.

"Take your own, Lord!" Gwyn cried, and hurled him from the neck of the horse.

The light and flashing water swirled past him. The fall seemed to last a long time, and he thought he was crying out, but couldn't hear anything. The pale hooves of the Hunt vanished away above him, then suddenly all was green and silent, and he was lying on the spiky thatch. He was too cold to feel it, but he could see; it was made of long white bones.

The green currents of the sea played glintingly round the walls of the castle, melting away on all sides into darkness. He was too cold to feel anything, and too cold to think. He only knew that he couldn't be alive or awake here under the sea. The black hole was beside him, and he wanted to crawl down into it. Everything had gone, his world, Kate, everything; that was worse than the cold; the only thing left now was to be able to go too. He tried to move, and as he did so the waters began to glint with a different light.

"Enter my castle, mortal."

The old beautiful voices, crystals dropping through the green. Slowly, Matt looked up, and Manannan's subtle silver eyes went into him, unchanged.

"Manannan!" he whispered. "But—what about—Anna?"

Manannan stood on the bones of the castle by him, arms folded, his light turning the sea blue. The glowing gaze never flickered. "What have the dead to do with those who yet live, however weakly? All that is over for you, mortal."

The crackling words were difficult to understand. He

said he'd come, Matt thought; he said he'd come, in the morning. It'll be all right now.

"Is the night over?" he whispered.

"It is only just beginning."

Matt tried to move again, and couldn't.

"But you've—come to save me," he whispered painfully.

Steadily the silver gaze pierced into him. Manannan never moved, though his light rippled and ran with the water. His voices were harder than his shape, many-edged. "Can the Catcher of the Dead save those who come to him willingly?"

Matt felt time slowly come to a stop.

"This is the Castle of the Dead, at the bottom of the sea." The many voices shivered deep and high, without any human tones. "Always there have been those of your kind who sought death instead of life; their search was vain and terrible till I came. Long ages I watched till I comprehended it—I, alone of immortals. And I built Oeth and Anoeth for them. None who come here can be saved from what their hearts desire."

No, thought Matt, no. His heart was freezing inside him. "Manannan—please," he whispered, trying to find words. "You're our—protector—"

"No longer, mortal." The voices throbbed, almost too loud to bear. "Did I not warn you? This is my castle; to those who come here, I am a destroyer."

Matt's world, what was left of it, fell in fragments. He stared up at the shining, passionless face and could only think, stupidly, that nothing could ever return or be the same again. In the chaos, one last spark of hope glowed briefly.

"Emrys," he whispered. "I told Kate to call Emrys."

Something changed in Manannan's light. It grew whiter, hurting Matt's eyes. Manannan's own eyes left him, turning away as if suddenly blind. Amongst the silence a cry of unutterable grieving seemed to quiver through the ocean, beyond the reach of Matt's ears.

"Emrys. . . ." Manannan's lips moved, but the voices were brilliant, splintered, hard to understand. "There is no Emrys, mortal. He could not come to you."

The tiny spark of hope hesitated and went out. Cold pervaded the whole of his body. It was no good. It never had been. He managed to turn his head away from Manannan and that sudden intricate grief which he couldn't understand.

The black hole was before his eyes. Let it be over, then, he thought, with a feeling of break inside him. He couldn't bear any more. Dark and silence were the only good things left; life itself was only bitterness, betrayal.

He felt Manannan step nearer, and winced a little as the white light was shed over him. He could just feel a touch on his arm.

"Go, mortal!" The voices rang out, dazing his ears. "Enter my castle."

A lift, a turn, and the quiet black hole reached up to him. There was a moment, and then everything went black.

2

It was very still. There was no light, yet he could see; and, though he wasn't warm, the grinding cold had left him. There was a long funnel of darkness above him, with no end that he could see, and in front of him a narrow passage curved gently downwards.

At first he didn't want to move, but the dark funnel overhead fretted him. It led upwards, back to the world where everything was hopeless; so, slowly, he began to walk forwards down the passage.

It was only just big enough for him. Each shoulder brushed the wall, and the roof was barely an inch over his head. All the surfaces were evenly ribbed, feeling strange till he remembered the castle was made of bones. He ran a hand over the wall. Forwards, it just felt knobbly, but when he tried to move his palm back jagged ends of bones ran against it and stopped it. He took it away from the wall and went on.

The passage was a long gentle spiral going down and round, so that the same curve ran on ahead of him. It was good to have left the dark tunnel behind. As he went on, with slow monotonous steps each exactly like the one before, he seemed to leave more and more behind; first the ache of defeat left his heart, leaving a quiet nothingness in him; then the horror of the cold went sliding out of his body, till that too felt empty.

At first the emptiness seemed good, but after a moment, or a long time—he couldn't tell how time went in here, if it went at all—that seeming faded, and he knew he was afraid again. Just the long ridges of bones, with no light or darkness, warmth or cold—it wasn't a quick fear to send the blood pulsing through him, just a cruel nothingness without end. He hesitated for a moment and half turned, wondering whether to go back.

Even as he turned the spikes of bone pricked him—his arms, his shoulders, his legs and ankles, even the top of his head. Though it hardly hurt, there came with it, triggered like a gunshot, all the pain of his lost world. He flinched back with a cry worse than Manannan's soundless grieving; he couldn't hear his own cry either, and he turned and went on quicker than before, hurrying from the ghastly sense of loss.

He left more and more behind him. Pictures rose in his mind, one after another—a yellow haired girl, a man looking at him and speaking from a small square screen, a drawing of a chestnut tree—and each time the image slipped out of his mind as if through a hole in his pocket, and was left behind for good. The emptiness grew greater and crueller, but he was glad of it now. Behind him, there was no escape from anguish.

It began to be difficult to remember who he was. There was a blankness spreading inside him as more and more of his thoughts were left behind in the passage. He couldn't remember where he'd come from, either; it seemed that in all his life there'd been only the silence, and the passage of bones curving gently down in front of him. The blankness grew, white and merciful. Soon he stopped trying to remember.

He was tired. His steps were getting slower, and he thought longingly of rest, of not having to move or do anything any more.

The tunnel of bones gradually tightened its curve. He went on slower and slower, each step a greater effort than the last. Soon he would be utterly exhausted, and fall down in the passage without being able to get up again. Each step brought that moment nearer, as the spiralling passage grew tighter and tighter. One more step, then one more, then the last. The passage had petered out in the centre of the castle.

He was in a small square chamber of bones. Like the passage, it was neither light nor dark, warm nor cold. It was simply the end. There was a niche in one wall where a skull was set, empty-eyed and without terror. He looked up at it, ceasing to move, and after a while—there was no time in here—he felt that he had gone, leaving only that inanimate skull behind. He couldn't see his hands or the rest of his body now. He couldn't see. It was all over. He was just part of the castle now.

3

As there was no time, he couldn't tell how long it was before the quietness began to tremble. There was no sound at first; it was merely as if the silence jumped, became fidgety. And it was no longer quite possible to be nothing but a part of the castle.

He tried to blot out the disturbance, not wanting it to make any difference. But it grew more jumpy; unwillingly, he began to hear the shadow of a voice, searching. And then the passage outside flickered, making the crevices between the bones momentarily sharp and black as if real light had flashed. He could see again.

Low, like the sound of the sea, the castle began to mutter, bone against bone. The disturbance was nearer, breaking at seconds into sound; the voice was taking shape, becoming more and more insistent. The passage flickered again, and a frightening tongue of light licked into the chamber. He gasped; and the voice came, catching on to the hard shape of his shock.

"Matt! Come out!"

It was tiny, remote as something miles away, but to Matt in his nothingness it was louder than a crowd's roar. He was coming back. He could feel the edges of himself again; it was like watching a solution in a test-tube star into crystals. He struggled against it.

The light licked into the chamber again, transparent but golden, and caught him before falling back. It was warm. It hurt, like blood being forced back into frozen veins, and Matt moved with the pain. He was back; it was no good; he could even see himself; and the fear of the emptiness he'd longed for was back too. He wanted to scream.

"Matt! Come out!"

The distant voice was stronger, centred on him. The golden light darted again, blossoming in the room and laying warmth all over him, so that he felt himself to his fingers' ends. It hurt terribly. As the light fell back, the skull toppled from its niche and broke on the floor to powder that disappeared. With a cry, Matt hurled himself at the passage.

The bones ran into him. His head, arms, shoulders, legs —the sharp points stuck in and stopped him. There was no numbness now to save him from real pain. He screamed, hanging pinned on the jags of bone.

"Come out!" The wave of light swept over him.

"I can't! I can't!" He tried to move, and more points ran into him. He could feel the blood trickling.

"Come out!" There was gold in the voice, too strong to disobey, and the warm light entered his wounds like fire. He flung his arms over his face and forced himself on two steps, the bones raking him on each side and going into his feet like daggers. He crouched down, trying to shrink into as small a space as possible.

"Come! Come! The further you come, the more I can help you!" The light rolled down the passage in waves.

Matt pulled off his shirt and gripped it in pads under his hands. He began to crawl. His back and head were safe now, but the bones ripped along his sides; his feet were raw, his trousers in rags over his knees, his knees bloody. Each movement thrust him against more spikes, and they ran greedily into his flesh. He crawled on in a kind of madness, knowing only that if he were torn to pieces he could not disobey that voice or stay in that chamber like one more dead white bone. To think of that was sheer horror. How could he ever have let it happen to him? On—on—out!

The mutter of the bones was louder, as if the whole castle was moving. The golden light beat stronger and stronger round him, until he could feel the passage itself swaying and shifting apart. It was wider, not catching his sides any more—it was higher, high enough to stand in, to race up with long leaping steps that pierced his feet and sent the air gasping from his lungs. The bones were falling away all round him, the castle groaning; and at last with a rending roar it parted over his head, and two kinds of light fell in on him.

The cold pure light of Danu's Children glittered with sparks. "Back!" The crystal voices throbbed, without fear or passion. "Back to your place, mortal—back to your heart's desire!"

"Back, Manannan mac Lir!" The golden light roared in

on Matt, with a great wild voice. "Back, Sky-Born, and let my Earth be! Back, I say!"

Blindly, Matt reached out at the flooding gold that had saved him. Manannan's light was drowned in it; it swirled round Matt and, bleeding and panting with pain, he felt it bear him up.

17

A UNIVERSE OF YOUR OWN

Slowly the pain receded, and Matt felt himself swimming through confusion towards a smooth meditative quietness. The wild flood of gold had gone, leaving only a tingle on his skin. He could feel to the tip of every nerve. He seemed to be sitting in a chair, in a very ordinary kind of light. After a little while he opened his eyes.

He looked straight into Kate's blue gaze. She was kneeling beside the wooden chair, a hand on one of its arms; her eyes were enormous, and she seemed to be holding her breath.

A wave of feeling too strong to be called joy or relief pulsed through Matt. He had never before felt so alive; but it wasn't easy to throw off the horror of what he had seen at the bottom of the sea. He put out a hand and took a strand of yellow hair between finger and thumb. It felt smooth and soft and matter-of-fact.

"Are you—really real?" he said, in a low voice.

Kate let out her breath in a long gasp. She seized his hand and squeezed it hard. "Yes, you idiot. Oh, Matt, *why* did you—"

Kate's voice, rushing out with its old quickness, breaking off short. . . . Matt pressed her hand in return, not very strongly, but the life soared up in him. "You know why," he said, and smiled. Kate's face broke into a smile straight away. "Yes," she said, and kept hold of his hand.

Matt's gaze lingered on her, then he glanced round. "Where are we?" he said, beginning to be puzzled. The room was small and bare, with plaster walls and an oak beam supporting an attic ceiling; the door was oaken too, low and studded, with an iron ring for a handle, and the floorboards were bare. Matt's chair was by a small table set against the wall. The light fell over his shoulder, from a window opposite the door. And, though the room was completely strange, it was somehow impossible to be afraid.

All the same, anxiety entered Kate's eyes. "I'm not too sure," she said, in a low voice, and her eyes went past Matt's to something in the corner behind him. Matt turned his head to look, and Kate said quickly, as if to save him from a shock, "He brought Anna here, as well."

Matt's breath went in sharply as he saw the shape of Anna. It was scarcely more than that, lying on a straw palliasse in the corner; that peculiar pain stirred in him again as he looked at the transparent face and the thick brown hair lying too lightly on the rough mattress. He'd been sure he would never have seen her again . . . but was he really seeing anything of her now? If he touched her, surely his hand would go through her. And who was that, kneeling beside her?

Matt recognised the brown gown, like an artist's, the long milk-white beard, the eyes that, if opened, would be as blue as Kate's. The man knelt as still as as statue, head erect, his face grave almost to grimness, apparently quite unaware of them. Matt looked back at Kate.

"Doctor Dee?" he said, his voice very low.

There was a crease on Kate's brow. "I don't understand it any more than you do," she said, almost in a whisper. "I was going to get your aunt. I couldn't think of anything else to do, after the Green Man—you know." She bit her lip.

"Go on," said Matt, softly.

"Well, I was rushing back to the town as fast as I could, and then all at once I heard you calling me—as plain as anything. I thought you were coming after me, but I couldn't see you. I looked everywhere, but all I could see was the corn moving. Then I heard you again. It sounded like "Call Emrys; fetch Emrys," then your voice faded away. It was awful. I didn't know what had happened to you. Anyway, I stood there and screamed out 'Emrys, Emrys, Emrys' as if I was crazy. And things started to move. There was a sort of lightning, and footsteps over the grass; it was frightening, I suppose, but I just didn't care any more. Then all of a sudden I was here, and Doctor Dee was sitting in that chair staring at me as if he'd just woken up."

"Here?" said Matt uncomprehendingly.

Kate shook her hair back. "I told you, I don't understand it. I've given up trying. Anyway, I didn't wait for explanations, I poured everything out and said he'd got to help. He got up and started walking about, looking—I don't know—as if he'd been hit over the head or something. He started saying he didn't know what to do, and I said again he'd got to help. I think I was crying a bit. Anyway, he stopped walking about and looked at me, as if he'd seen me for the first time but recognising me as well in a weird kind of way; then he said very quietly that he'd try, and I was to stay here quite still and be quiet. So I shut up, and he went and knelt down over there."

Matt glanced over his shoulder again at the tall, motionless figure of Anna.

"He closed his eyes," Kate said, "and it was so silent, as if everything everywhere had stopped moving. Some kind of light started to come round him. I suppose I should

250

have been scared but—I don't know if you've noticed—it's hard to feel scared in here."

Matt nodded. "Yes."

"Well, he sort of went into the light and faded away. I was alone then, but I still didn't feel scared exactly; I was just wanting him tremendously to come back with you. I don't know how long that lasted. And then the door opened and he walked in, carrying you, and put you down in the chair. . . ." Kate's voice faltered a little, for the first time. "You looked awful," she said. "You still do. There's blood all over you, but you were as white as death then. Oh, Matt, you are really all right, aren't you?"

Matt looked down at himself. His feet were streaked with mud and blood, his trousers torn and his shirt in ribbons, and bloodstains were everywhere. "Yes, I'm all right," he said. "I'm not bleeding any more." He touched the dried blood on his arm, gingerly. The flesh was lacerated from shoulder to wrist, and his sides, knees and feet felt the same; but though there was a throbbing of pain he could bear it. It was the sort of pain that living people had.

"I put your shirt back on you," Kate said. "It was an awful job. You felt so cold." She studied him intently. "Your eyes look all right now," she said. She gave his hand a quick squeeze and went on, "Well, he went over there and knelt down again. I was getting you into your shirt, and when I looked at him again Anna was there on the bed. Well—sort of there. You can see more of her now."

Matt looked over his shoulder again. Yes, she lay there quite plain and visible, but as frail as a shadow. As he looked, he saw Dee move; the blue eyes opened, strangely dark, and scanned Anna's face. Then he bowed his head on his chest.

Kate squeezed his hand and whispered, "What—what happened to you, Matt?"

Matt didn't reply. There was a rustle of the long, brown gown as Dee rose from his knees, hands folded in front of him. He stood looking down at Anna for a moment longer, then turned, and Matt saw the stricken look in his eyes, as if he'd been clubbed.

"They took him to the Castle of Death, Kate," the man whispered, his voice a sudden deep music in the bare room. He came a step nearer, laying a hand on Matt's shoulder, hurting him. "Whatever possessed you, Matt? To try to drive a bargain with that—that incubus, that green devil . . . You knew the powers of death would come at his call!"

Matt looked up at the anguished face. He had never thought that help would come from this quarter, not since the day in the laboratory when Dee had turned away from them, ashamed and afraid. And yet he felt again what he'd felt then, that the man was somehow their friend.

"I had to," he said. "There was nothing else I could do."

Dee shook his head, and his voice throbbed. "That is how the Old Ones talk, as if there were no freedom or choice at all! They are wrong, and you were wrong to listen! Each of us can be master of his own fate. It is not easy—mastery must be fought for—but in the end it is one of the few real things!"

Matt's brow creased as he looked at him; he didn't quite understand this vehemence. But he heard a quick intake of breath from Kate; Dee's blue eyes shifted to hers, and something passed between them.

Matt said after a moment. "Were you that voice? And the golden light?"

Dee looked back, his eyes darkening again. "Yes; I called to you," he said quietly. "And you were strong enough to hear and heed. But to break open Oeth and Anoeth and let the dead fly free—it is shaking all the worlds! As we talk, time itself is breaking up." He closed his eyes momentarily, breathing in hard. "I hardly know what I have done. The power of Cernunnos is rising to its peak—I can feel it. Soon he will claim the lives owed to him, and if they are not given he will come down through the ruin of time to fetch them. . . ." He turned away, gripping his hands together as if he couldn't bear it. "Oh, Madinia!" he whispered, his voice throbbing like a harp.

Matt looked again at Anna, and seemed to feel a shadow of the Doctor's agony. "Will she be safe here?" he asked urgently.

"Where is here?" Kate asked.

Dee turned back, his face haggard. "This place is no-where," he said dully. "It is like the laboratory that Ned lured you to, outside your universe. Yes, it is safe, for you and me; nothing could ever cross this nothingness to me. . . ."

Matt saw Kate's eyes narrow at a tremor of self-pity just audible in these last words. Downrightly, she said, "You must have known this would happen when you—sold your soul!"

Dee's lips quivered as if he felt a blow. He shook his head, beginning to pace up and down the little room. "No. . . ." His voice rose on a burst of pain. "Never did I look to be as torn as this! Kate, I trusted Ned; the angel Uriel brought him to me; he was a friend in ten thousand. We seemed to be one mind, each able to perform what the other could not." He stopped by the window, plainly struggling to master himself. Matt saw Kate compress her lips impatiently, but Dee's voice went on again, whispering, as if he were alone and the past were the only real thing.

"We sought perfection . . . it seems childish now to look back on it! We sought to transmute base metal to gold, thinking that thereby our own base human nature would be transmuted. Always we failed. Always we seemed on the very edge of succeeding, only to fail again. And

253

then Ned showed me in a book the incantation to call up the Ancient One, in whose gift were all arcana. I would not—I had no faith in such drawing of circles and mumbling over herbs and holy water. Ned took the book away with him; and next morning he returned with looks so changed that I was half afraid. He held out a small glass jar to me, and showed me a reddish powder, and said it was the powder of projection.

"I disbelieved him; and he showed me. He took a warming-pan from the kitchen and held it before the fire, rubbing it with a few grains of the powder. Before my eyes it changed to pure gold.

"The secret of transmutation was his! And such a longing rose in me to possess that secret too, to be able to touch baseness with fire and render it into precious gold. . . . Such was my longing that he persuaded me. He prepared the magic circle for me, and the offerings, and then I spoke the incantation. . . ."

He broke off with a long shuddering breath, gripping his hands together. Matt glanced at Kate, uneasily; he wished Dee would stop this and get down to what was important, the saving of Anna from Cernunnos. Kate didn't return his glance. Her eyes were still narrowed, and rather hard.

"He came." The music of Dee's voice was suddenly harsh. "He stood, vast and dim and patient amidst our spells, content not to harm me; he stretched out his hand —that hand! with its long curving nails—and touched me. And I felt what I had asked for pass into me."

Kate's lips were tense now, but she was watching Dee steadily, and her eyes were difficult to read.

"Ned had asked him for power." Dee began to pace the room again, his voice once more hushed, but indescribably haunting. "I asked for wisdom. Yes, that was how our parting began. Neither was sure of the other's gift. Ned grew jealous for his own discoveries; I ceased to trust him; I left alchemy and magic; he felt scorned and turned his scorn on me. Oh, it is bitter to feel hate growing out of friendship! I could not have loved a brother more. But he caused unspeakable things through his folly as his power grew; power without wisdom is like fire, soon out of control. Famine, murder, black death, even war have sprung out of his whims—I know, I cannot help but know. There is an unbreakable bond between us, though now more like a hatred fetter between two captives; every motion of his I feel. When he called you three into his world the shock went through me like pain. Fear never leaves me"—his voice was sinking, low and desperate—"for if Cernunnos takes him, what will happen to me, bound as we are?"

Kate's lips hardened. Without troubling to hide her antagonism she said, "Look, it's all right for you! You've said it, you're safe here! But what about Anna? It's her we care about! And you never said she was safe!"

Dee seemed to flinch, and Matt wondered how the man could protect himself from Cernunnos and yet have so little defence against Kate's words. He turned away to the window, not looking at them, his hands twisting.

"She is not here, Kate!" The deep voice rose and fell, trembling. "I can shatter the Castle of the Dead and shake your world to its foundations—but I cannot wrest Madinia from the Mound!"

"*What?*" Kate's eyes dilated.

Dee turned from the window and paced the room, gown swishing, as if he couldn't bear to be still.

"Only her shadow is here." His voice throbbed with suppressed anguish. "I *cannot* approach the Mound to fetch her—Cernunnos is everywhere about it! Manannan mac Lir surrounds her with his light. It may be enough. It may be. . . ."

"Manannan!" Matt gasped, and all peace fell away from him. He pushed himself up from the chair, hardly noticing as his wounds tore at him. "But, Doctor Dee—

255

Manannan's the one who made me go into that castle! He's not our protector at all! He won't stop Anna from dying!"

"Matt!" Kate exclaimed.

"It's true!" Matt stared desperately at Dee's suffering face. "We can't leave her in there with him, Doctor! We've got to get her out!"

"Matt, Matt!" Dee whispered, and put a hand up to his forehead as if to hide from his and Kate's eyes. "Be still, I beg you! Manannan is your protector. He is also a Lord of Death. He tried to keep you from death, but you grasped at it, and so he would not stop you. That is his nature. Remember, he is born of light—he is not human."

"But—" Matt's voice shook and stopped. Dee never moved, except to turn away a little, and Matt felt all words desert him. What could he say to this man, who had saved his life and now wouldn't stir a step for Anna?

Kate got to her feet beside him. Brusquely she said, "What about you, Doctor? Are you human?"

Matt's brow creased. Dee's mouth looked suddenly drawn, and after a moment he took his hand away and looked at Kate, his eyes dark and somehow pleading.

"Kate—" he said, a roughness in his throat.

"Well, are you?" Kate said challengingly, coming forward. "I mean, look at this place." She stopped by the window, peering through the panes. "There's nothing out there. Absolutely nothing. I can't even see any outside to these walls." She turned and looked at Dee, then pointed at the door. "What's through there? Shall I go and see?"

"No!" Dee flung out a hand to stop her. Kate kept quite still, and Dee drew in a deep breath, then clasped his hands together again. "I do not know what you would see beyond that door," he said, his voice tight with control. "This room is not real. It is a memory of a room in the house that Ned and I once shared—you have seen that house, and the laboratory, where Ned worked. While he cast his spells down there, I meditated alone in this room.

256

But it is only a picture now—a dream. More of my dreams wait outside. In all of them the fear of the Horned One walks. Remember—this is my universe.''

''And how did you manage to get a universe of your own?'' Kate demanded. Her eyes narrowed as she stared at Dee; she pointed a finger again, this time at him. ''Why did I come here when I called Emrys?'' she shot out.

Dee stared at her. His blue eyes widened, and his clasped hands shook. ''Emrys?'' he whispered, and his voice fluttered like a shred of paper in the wind. He looked round at Matt, without seeing him, then back at Kate. ''Emrys?''

''Yes!'' said Kate, impatiently. ''I shouted out 'Emrys.' Matt told me to. And I ended up here. Why? What does Emrys mean?''

''I heard nothing.'' Dee put a hand up to his forehead again; the long fingers were shaking, and so was his voice. ''I felt only a pulling—a dragging—which it was not easy to resist. And then you appeared. I thought your fear for Matt must have given you strength to reach me. But— Emrys?''

Matt said hesitantly, ''It just came into my head, Doctor. Do you know what it means?''

''No.'' Dee gave a shake of his head, pressing his palms hard together. ''It is not a word, Matt, or a charm or incantation—it is a name, though whose I know not. And yet I do know . . . Emrys!'' His voice throbbed unbearably. ''I know you—Emrys—and cannot remember you. Surely he was close to me once, for that name stirs me till I hardly know myself. . . .'' He drew a deep breath and his suffering eyes looked at Kate. ''I am sorry, Kate,'' he whispered. ''So much is unclear. . . .''

Kate compressed her lips. ''Look, Doctor,'' she said, more quietly, almost pleadingly, ''are you going to help us?''

The knuckles whitened on Dee's hands. ''What can I

do, Kate?'' Fear and despair strove in his voice. ''If I approach the Mound, I will only die! Manannan . . .''

''Matt doesn't trust Manannan,'' said Kate, as if that was enough. ''You've got to help us. Don't you see that? You keep saying you're wise. . . .''

''Wise!'' The music of his voice harshened. ''Yes; I asked Cernunnos for wisdom, and I received it, or enough of it to know my own folly. I am wise enough to be safe—and to know what I have to face, in this eternity of safety before me.'' He looked round the room, his eyes sick. ''You will be safe here with me,'' he whispered, and turned aside.

''Doctor!'' Kate exclaimed, in a voice that couldn't be stopped. ''You can't just stay in here and let Anna die!''

His back to them, Dee shook his head a little. ''There is nothing else I can do,'' he whispered. ''I have saved Matt, and for that the worlds are tearing apart. Do not ask any more of me, Kate.''

''Listen!'' Kate went up close to him, catching his sleeve. Her voice trembled, not very like her for a moment. ''You—you said we're each master of our own fate. You *said* it. So how can you stay in here just as if it's a trap, as if you've no choice and there's nothing you can do?''

Matt heard Dee's quick intake of breath, saw him stiffen, then turn and look down into Kate's half-scared eyes. Kate bit her lip.

''Please,'' she whispered.

Dee looked away, into the corner where Anna's form lay. A sigh came from his lips. ''Ah, Kate,'' he murmured. ''You have spoken the only words which could save me —but must you kill me at the same time?'' Another long indrawn sigh. ''Well; let it be. Come, Madinia.'' He stooped and took Anna's hand.

She rose like a shadow from a flickering candle, and it was difficult to tell whether her eyes were closed or just cast down at the floor. Holding that transparent hand, Dee turned to them again; and in his other hand was a carved wooden staff.

"Do not touch Madinia," he said, quietly. "She could not bear it. Take hold of my sleeve again, Kate; and Matt, take Kate's hand. Good. Do not loose your grip until you must."

"Are we—going to the Mound?" said Kate, on a breath.

The blue eyes looked down at her, so like her own. "Aye," said Dee gently. "I cannot leave you here, for if I die it will go to nothing; and I do not think I will live. Courage. This will be the last trial, for all of us. Can you bear your wounds, Matt? I do not think I can spare the power to ease them."

"I'm all right," Matt said.

"Let us go, then." Dee lifted the staff, and a tongue of gold ran along it.

The room faded softly away from around them.

18

THE STAR'S GONE OUT

It was dark and a strong wind blew salt from the sea. Looking up, Matt saw clouds covering the stars. The only light was the glow from Dee's staff as he held it up before them, and it seemed a small light in the huge pile of darkness covering the forest.

They stood just clear of the trees, and before them was the Mound. The hair prickled on the back of Matt's neck as he breathed the violent mingled smell of earth and trees and salt water. He thought he recognised the mocking whisper of the seven young pines above, and there was a curious ache of fear in him as he remembered that the Dulachan couldn't come this time to rescue them.

As if hearing his thoughts, Kate whispered to him. "I've still got the knife."

"Hush." It was Dee's voice, low and tense. "Speak as little as you must. Madinia is very weak."

Kate closed her lips firmly, and Matt watched Dee. The man stood there, the staff in one hand and Anna's hand in the other, with the whites of his eyes clear in the dark. Matt began to be afraid that he was losing his nerve, and any second would break away from them, back to his own safe place; then the light on Kate's hair shifted as she turned her head and looked up at him. Something tightened in Dee's mouth and he lifted the staff higher, lips parting.

For a moment Matt expected to hear a spell come out, crashing words like those Manannan had uttered before Cernunnos. But Dee spoke only one word, whispered.

"Open!"

Golden light ran along the staff like levin. The Mound answered, with a tremor deepening to a groan. Matt felt Kate's fingers clench on his as the ground heaved under them; then the hillside roared and rolled apart.

Light blazed out on them, that baleful light more akin to darkness. There was a dagger-shaped cleft in the hillside, and Matt saw through it into the golden hall. It was as huge as he remembered, bigger than the outside of the Mound. He looked down all its length to the throne, and the pit of his stomach contracted. Elatha sat there, and the hall was full of Fomors. He saw Elatha start to his feet, and a crowd of bone-white faces turn to stare; then the mass of green writhed as every Fomor shrank away from the light than ran from Dee's staff. Matt's lips tightened as a soundless howl swelled inside his head.

"Aah! Myrddin Emrys! Aah! Aah!"

Dee stepped forward slowly, staff held high. The cry was redoubled, and Matt's eyes puckered with the pain of it. The cleft in the hillside arched over them as they stepped through from turf on to cold marble. The air inside the Mound struck chill, taking all the heart out of Matt. Dee took another step forward, then stopped.

"Hush!" His voice mounted above the silent clamour, urgently. "People of the dark, be still! I have not come to harm you!"

The howling wavered, then sank to a deadly murmur. The Fomors crowded in a solid mass across the hall, blocking the way forward. Their white faces twisted as Dee's light flickered over them, and every eye was fixed on him, murderous with hate. Dee took another step forward, and Anna, Kate and Matt went with him. The Fomors shrank from the light, but gave way no more than an inch.

"Back. Go, Myrddin Emrys."

Matt felt the hate beginning to weaken him. Beside him, Kate was frowning and peering, as if wondering where she was going; perhaps she can't see all this, he thought, perhaps I wouldn't see it either, if only I'd never worn that cap. . . . He found himself looking amongst the grotesque faces for Raudan's.

The Fomors were edging down the walls of the hall to surround them on three sides. Matt wondered if they were going to cut off the way back to the cleft. Dee stopped again as the hate flailed against them, and his face looked paler.

"Peace!" The music of his voice penetrated the raging silence, and a shudder ran through the crowd. "I swear I bring you no harm, Moundfolk! Only let me pass to the maiden!"

"Go back."

Dee took another step forward, and Matt felt the labour of it. Blood pounded in his temples; was Dee going to make it? The raw lacerations were hurting him again as the chill sank in.

There was a sudden break in the crowd, just before them; it parted, and Elatha came through.

The empty eyes were fixed on Dee, and the man came to a stop. Before him Elatha looked little and frail, but prouder than a king, and such pitch-black hate stared out from him that Matt felt an impulse to back away.

Dee stood quite still. His face looked drawn and pale, but not like the ghastly pallor of the Fomors; and the light from his staff flickered over him in living fire. It fell on Elatha's face too, and Matt saw the Fomor's mouth twist at its touch.

"Go back." The silence quivered with hate. *"Return to the rock under which Nimue hid you, when you were first besotted, Myrddin Emrys; or to whatever hole you have since found to hide in. Let us be!"*

The staff trembled in Dee's hand; and the blue eyes grew stricken once more.

"I do not understand your words," he whispered at last, with a tremor of despair. "Why do you call me Emrys, Prince Elatha? Who is Nimue, and what is the rock you speak of? Your words are like shadows, vanishing and impossible to hold."

Elatha's lips girned, ugly with pain as the live golden light darted over him. *"I know you better than you know yourself—emrys."* The word-shapes pulsed with hate. *"You have forgotten who you are. I tell you to go—before you remember!"*

"I cannot." Dee's voice was barely audible. "I beg you not to stand against me, Prince. Let me free the maiden, and make amends. . . ."

Elatha's face distorted again, baleful as a gargoyle's. *"Our master will come. He is coming. Can you not hear the trample of his hoofs?"*

"I have been hearing that trample all my life," Dee whispered. He lifted the staff higher and the light seemed to strip everything away from his face till it looked as undefended as a child's. "I do not think I can save myself any longer. But you—Prince—have mercy on your people! Lead them out of this dreadful Lochlann!"

"Where to, Myrddin Emrys?" Elatha's face went on girning at him like an animal's. *"Will you send us out to live under the sky?"*

Dee looked upwards. Matt followed his gaze over the heads of the Fomors, and noticed a high golden screen hiding one of the corners of the hall. Perhaps Anna was there. He didn't know if Dee noticed it or not; perhaps he only saw the dreary glare, and felt the deathly oppression of this place.

"How can you bear to live under the earth?" Dee whispered. His voice rose on a loud entreating throb. "It is said the Fomors came from the sea; return to it, Elatha—the sea is kinder than the land, and does not let the light through to burn!''

"And leave the earth to such as you?" The words boiled black with hate.

Matt felt himself shudder. Nothing could touch the void inside these dispossessed Fomors—no generosity, no compassion of any kind. He was afraid. Was Dee too appalled now to go on?

Silence lengthened between Dee and Elatha, and a mutter rose amongst the Fomors, increasing to a threatening rhythm inside Matt's head. *"Go—go—go—"* he saw Dee's eyes turn from Elatha, full of pain and indecision. He opened his mouth, but in desperation didn't know what to say; then the light on Kate's hair changed again as she turned her face to Dee and whispered, low as a breath, ''Hurry up, Doctor—please.''

Matt was sure she couldn't see or hear the Fomors. She was just standing there in the dark, keeping quiet as long as she could but desperate now to have the thing ended. Dee's eyes were luminous with fear, but at that his mouth tightened as much as it could.

He thrust the staff forward, almost clumsy in his haste to act before his nerve broke, and the light flowed all over Elatha.

''Stand aside, Prince!'' His voice shook.

Elatha's face twisted horribly in the rush of light. His hands climbed the air, clawed and skeletal, and his cry tore at Matt's brain as he sank writhing towards the ground. Matt caught a glimpse of Ruadan darting from the crowd to catch him, then Dee was plunging forward, drawing him and Kate through the sudden opening.

They fought their way forward. Dee held the staff high in front of him, and the Fomors seemed unable to bear that living light. They shrank away, white faces contorting, and soundless screams shot through Matt's head; holding on to Kate's hand, he followed Dee almost blindly. They reached the screen at the other end of the hall, and the Fomors fell back, their cries dying away into silence. Going round it, and seeing what was there, Matt saw why.

Anna lay before them, on a low couch. The dreary light of the hall didn't reach behind the screen, but she was plainly visible; about her, like a castle of glimmering glass, the light of Danu's Children stood.

Matt forgot the Fomors. He looked across Kate and Dee, a feeling of choking at his throat. For there too was Anna, her hand in Dee's and her eyes closed, or cast down. Kate's hand tightened and tightened on his, and when he looked at her he knew she could see this.

"So you have come."

The light quivered with a crystalline ring of voices, and Matt gritted his teeth. It was Manannan.

Dee stood looking up at the turning light. After a moment, Matt's gaze was drawn from Manannan towards Dee; and he thought the man had changed. Taller he seemed, and straighter, his eyes stronger and more sorrowful than ever before; and the golden levin was about him now, too, flickering from his hair and beard.

"Perhaps, Son of Lir," he said, in a voice like deep music.

"What of the mortals whose souls should be mine?" the voices asked, passionately. "What of the ruin of my castle? Do you know what you have done—Earthman? What of the mortal who stands by you, free?"

Dee shook his head, and an unutterable weariness showed on his face. His features seemed fined down to the bone.

"Let us speak of death when we have brought life back to Madinia," he said. He drew Anna forward so that she moved a slow step towards the couch; and Matt bit his lip as he saw, plainly, the two Annas.

"It is good." The light quivered softly round the other Anna. "My watching of her was disturbed, and weakened.

I do not think I could have kept the Horned One from her.''

"Make her rise, then. Hasten!" Dee's voice thrilled with sudden deep-throated urgency.

"Yes. He comes. Do you hear him?"

A river of sparks flowed round the form of the other Anna. She stirred; then, as if unwilling, she sat up. Her eyes too seemed closed or cast down, and she was crouching as if cold. Slowly, she slipped of the couch and stood up on the ground. She took a step, and so did the other Anna; they stood face to face, the real Anna and her ghost, and there was no telling which was which.

For a long moment Matt and Kate held their breath; then Dee held out his staff, so that the lambent gold scattered itself around the two foreheads.

"Anna," he whispered, and the air shook. Quietly the two forms moved towards each other—then met and glided into one, like two meeting waterdrops. Anna's brown eyes flew open and stared round, full of fright and hurt. Dee moved towards her, and in a moment she was in his arms with her face hidden against his chest.

Dee's eyes closed, then looked upwards with such pain that Matt felt a shiver go down his spine. "Alack, sweetheart!" he whispered. "I fear I have saved you only to lose you yet again. . . ."

"He comes, Myrddin. In great strength." The cool voices glittered.

Dee looked up at the cloud of light. "Go. Child of Danu!" he cried, with an unbearable throb of grief. "This strife is for the earth-born!"

"I will wait for you in the sky." The cloud rolled together and hid itself, and the gold of Dee's light was left alone, radiant as fire.

"Come," he whispered, turning, his arm still round Anna. Kate took hold of his sleeve again, blue eyes scared but not giving in.

"Where now, Doctor?" she whispered, and Matt knew that, like him, she was longing for the word home.

"Out of the Mound, Kate. I fear there will be no time for more. . . ." Dee's voice faltered as he looked down at her face. "Forgive me!" he whispered; without waiting for an answer he strode round the screen, his staff ablaze.

At the sight of him, the Fomors didn't even attempt to bar the way. They scrambled aside, girning with dismay, and again their torrent of howls rushed through Matt's head. Dee strode straight down the hall, staff held high, and it seemed to Matt that its fire beat back the glare of the hall and filled it with living tongues of flame. Then the black cleft loomed up; they stepped through and the salt wind blew darkness into their faces.

The night felt alive. There was the sound of animals in the forest, large ones, not just rabbits or foxes; and thunder muttered, not so very far away.

"Hadn't we better be quick?" Kate said, unable to repress the words.

Matt looked up at Dee. For the first time, the man was leaning on his staff like someone old, and all the time the levin danced brighter and brighter about him. He was looking up at the cloud-covered sky as if at something he had always feared. It was Anna who answered Kate.

"We can't escape." Her voice was a whisper, tremulous and weak. "He's almost here. Can't you hear him? I suppose he'll take us all now. . . ."

"Peace!" Dee's voice sounded old as well, low and anguished. "Hush, Anna! Yes, he comes. And I can barely lift my staff . . . alas the day I ever took it up!"

Kate's hand gripped Matt's hard. "Matt—I don't think I can stand it," she whispered.

Neither can I, Matt thought. He looked past her at the weird glory of Dee's face. "We've got to do something, Doctor," he said.

Without looking at him, Dee slowly shook his head. "I

cannot move from this spot," he whispered, with an old man's voice.

A trumpeting bellow came on the wind out of the forest, like a rutting stag. Kate froze; and then her hand crept on to Dee's arm.

"Doctor—"

At last Dee moved, looking down at her with blind eyes.

"I'm scared," said Kate bluntly.

Dee's face changed and he seemed gradually to see her. "Afraid, Kate?" he murmured sadly. "I am full of fear; it is ill you should feel it. Come"—he stretched his arms out wearily—"gather close around me. There is one trick left, though a prentice's one. It may serve."

They huddled round him, and the gold darted over them, tingling like a faint electric shock. Dee reached out with the point of his staff and drew five lines round them on the ground, without lifting the point from the earth. Light flowed off the staff, and Matt saw they were standing in the middle of a flickering five-point star.

"May Solomon's Seal protect you!" Dee whispered, and turned, leaning on his staff, to face the Mound. Kate peered past him, and her hand came grasping at Matt's.

"Look!"

Matt turned, and saw something amongst the trees on top of the Mound. It was too dark to see properly, but whatever it was stayed stock still, so that its shape grew steadily thicker and blacker and more solid.

"It's him," said Matt, under his breath. He could see the antlers above the trees, and as they grew easier and easier to see he thought the shape was growing. After a while he was sure of it. Cernunnos was small, and a shadow now, to what he would become.

He put his arm round Kate. She leaned towards him and whispered. "It's all right. I don't feel as scared as I thought I would."

"Don't you?" said Matt, low.

"I feel safe, inside this star thing. Don't you?"

Matt didn't answer. His lacerated limbs ached stiffly in the chill wind, and he wondered if he would ever feel safe again. Anna looked weak, and he put his other arm round her. She leaned against him passively, and he saw her eyes fixed on the top of the hill, empty of either fear or hope. She seemed only to be waiting until Cernunnos should step down from the Mound and put an end to everything.

The antlers went on growing against the sky.

Then Matt noticed that the blade-shaped glare from the Mound was failing. He looked down from the growing figure on the top. The light of Lochlann was weakening fast, and he could no longer see much of the golden hall inside; as he watched, it faded to complete blackness. Then he noticed a pale blotch gliding from it, and then another. The Fomors. They were stealing through the cleft, out of the Mound. . . . Matt looked round swiftly, and saw a ring of pallid faces behind them, on the edge of the forest. The Fomors were making a silent circle, all round them and the Mound.

He opened his mouth to say something, but neither Anna nor Kate seemed to have seen them, and Dee's gaze was fixed upwards as if he'd forgotten everything else. Matt hesitated. What could they do, anyway? Dared they move outside the star? A sound came.

It was a sudden harsh burst of singing, from many voices. There were no words in it that Matt could make out, and he thought it was inside his head until he saw by the widening of Kate's eyes that she could hear it too.

He looked round as it grew in volume. The mouths of the nearest faces were open—he could see them, and the glitter of their eyes. Had the Fomors at last found a voice? There was no tune in whatever they were singing; it was simply a menacing sequence of notes, all the same length, rising steadily and sending a shudder down his spine.

Looking back at the Mound, he saw that Cernunnos's

shadow was becoming thicker and richer. There was worship in this music. It climbed and loudened as Cernunnos grew; both seemed to draw on the night and its landscape, draining the virtue out of trees, water and clouds as they grew upwards. The singing wore at Matt, and he wished it would come to rest on a final note, but it went inexorably on as if it couldn't stop. Cernunnos had a shape now, and a sheen running over his antlers. Matt dragged his gaze away from him and looked at Dee; the man's face was fixed and ivory-pale. Matt tried to open his mouth and say something, but the dire music was too loud, too close; it would drown his voice; then Cernunnos moved, and lightning daggered the ground nearby.

For a moment Matt was dazzled, but he heard a scream rising through the Fomors' singing, where the bolt of lightening had struck there was a deeper darkness and the smell of burnt grass. Then Kelly came stumbling out of that blackness like a man pushed through a door, and his mouth was wide open in a yell that wouldn't stop.

He landed on the grass ten feet from the star. The succession of notes grew thicker and more raucous like a call for blood, and Kelly grovelled on the grass with his hands against his ears, yell after yell coming from his throat with hardly pause for breath. Matt caught a glimpse of his face and it was contorted to a caricature of Kelly, that look of serenity horribly transfigured.

Anna stirred. She turned her head away from him towards that figure on the grass, and Matt's arm tightened round her involuntarily; he heard a sound lower than a breath come from her—"Ned."

Kelly plunged towards them on all fours, eyes huge and brilliant with fear. "Anna! Madinia! *Save me!*" he yelled blubberingly, and his hand reached out at the golden star.

"*Back!*" Dee's gown swirled and his voice cut electrically across the Fomors' singing as his staff came out at Kelly. "*Do not break the pentagram!*"

Kelly blenched back, and Matt heard an echo of horror in Dee's voice. Kelly's great eyes shifted up to his drawn face, and something of Kelly came slowly back into those eyes, ugly and glinting. He moved a little in the light that glowed from Dee, cringingly.

"Let me in, John."

It was almost Kelly's old voice. Dee stared back, and Matt saw a sudden flood of anguish rise in him. It was as if he had to suffer then for all deeds of treachery that had ever happened; and Matt didn't think he could bear it, and the flood rose and rose.

"No, Ned," said Dee, and for once the music of his voice broke. The Fomors' singing hushed, and Matt looked involuntarily up at the top of the Mound.

Cernunnos stood above the trees, antlers high up in the middle of the sky. The world shrank small around him. Safe inside the star, Matt still couldn't look at him for very long; he felt the weakness, the emptying out of everything that was human, the inflow of ancient men who were different and terrible. He had the strength to look away, but before he did he saw the long hand with its glistening nails move and slowly point down from the top of the Mound at Kelly.

Kelly felt it; his eyes filmed over, opaquely. "Let me in, John!" he cried, the words blurring again. Dee stood like a rock, and the flickering staff went on pointing at Kelly, not letting him approach. Kelly's glassed eyes shifted wildly and fixed on Matt.

"Matt! Make him let me in, Matt!" He crouched there, rocking, his fists locked round clumps of grass. His words were shearing, losing their shape. "Matt, you know—I never meant to hurt Madinia—you know—you know I loved her, Matt!"

Matt's teeth went into his lip. Out of the corner of his eye he could see a group of Fomors creeping forward towards Kelly. It was hideous to watch the man rocking

271

there, throwing himself backwards and forwards like a stranded fish. And it was true. In his way, he had loved her.

"Matt!" It was a grotesque howl, and Anna shivered in Matt's arms, without looking away from Kelly. He thought he heard her echo Kelly's cry, in a half-breath, so yearningly that it made his heart turn over.

"Doctor," he said hoarsely.

Kate's hand closed on his aching arm, making his gasp. *"Don't listen,"* said Kate in a hard, abrupt little voice, and Matt saw Dee's sleeve go taut as she twisted her other hand into it. Tremors chased each other across the man's face, with nothing left to hide them.

"Matt! Make him! Matt!" Kelly's voice mounted, the words finally collapsing into each other to make a long-drawn howling without much human sound to it. Matt gritted his teeth; then he had to look away as any words in the howling grew quite indistinguishable, and Kelly began to beat his head against the ground.

Fomors slipped forward like shadows, keeping their distance from the golden fire of the star. They came on Kelly with a kind of gladness, catching him by the arms and legs and the folds of his gown and heaving him gloatingly off the ground.

It didn't look as if he struggled very much as the Fomors raced quickly up the side of the hill with him. The rest were singing still, so that any cries of his were drowned; the sound made Matt shudder, with its bitter, crashing chords rising to a crescendo of revenge. Amongst the pines, still a few yards from Cernunnos's hooves, the Fomors stopped; Matt couldn't see them properly because of the trees, but he saw the white patch of Kelly's face with a black screaming hole in it. They pushed, or threw him. He went staggering over the ground, and Cernunnos's hand reached down and caught him.

272

He hung in that grip for a long moment, his scream going high and bubbling through the air. Then Cernunnos's head was thrown back, antlers arching across the sky; he lifted his hand with Kelly dangling in it like a doll, and held him high up in the sky as if in triumph. Thunder broke loose, and sheet lightning unrolled over the forest. The Fomors were on their knees, and Matt couldn't see what had happened to the ones who had carried Kelly up there.

He saw Kate's hand still tight on Dee's sleeve. Dee himself stood motionless, his face turned up to the black bundle that hung far above in Cernunnos's hand. The lightning played blindingly, but Dee's eyes never blinked. His own light darted about him, and for a moment he seemed taller than he was, further away from them, monumental with grief.

"Ned!" he whispered, and the word was simple with despair.

"Doctor," Matt said hoarsely, thinking that now was the time, if ever, to go. Dee took no notice, and Anna felt frozen beside him; and Kate took no notice either.

"I cannot let it end like this." Dee seemed to have forgotten them, or else to be standing in a world of his own while thunder crashed and the Fomors cowered around them. "Ned! How often have I thought it would be easy to betray you! How often have I thought I only lacked the chance!"

Matt opened his mouth again, but knew it would be useless to speak, and Kate pinched his arm again roughly. He looked down at her, and the blue eyes gave him their scared, uncompromising look.

"He'll go. We can't stop him," Kate whispered. "Cernunnos won't go till he gets him."

Matt looked up, wondering how she knew. Even as he did so, he saw Cernunnos moving. Holding Kelly aloft, his

273

other hand slowly reached down from the sky towards Dee; and as Matt watched, he knew he had known this as well. He couldn't bear not to whisper "Doctor!"

It was lost in the thunder. Dee took a step forward, into a point of the star.

"I cannot let it end like this." His voice came clear through the thunder. "I should have known before that you are half myself, Ned!"

Kate's hand tightened on Matt's arm, and he could feel her holding her breath.

Dee's staff touched the point of the star; the racing fire parted, and he stepped through. It closed behind him. The thunder died, and the Fomors' singing stopped with a stabbing gasp.

"I am coming, Ned," Dee called, and his voice was a sudden loud glad music. He began to climb the hill with long firm strides, and the staff flamed in his hand. He looked all golden as he mounted the slope, so strong and sure that Matt, watching him go, felt a desolation hard to bear. At the top of the Mound Dee paused once, to look back without regret at the world. His face was so bright it was hardly recognisable. Then he drew the staff from him and reached up to grasp the great slender hand of Cernunnos.

There was an immense crash of thunder right overhead, and a tearing sound as a gale rushed down over the trees. Matt found himself on the ground with leaves, twigs, even branches hurtling past him; it was impossible to see or hear anything.

"Kate!" he shouted, and the wind whipped his words away. He reached out blindly, and somehow his fingers locked in hers. They crawled nearer together and held on to each other, crouching low as the wind screamed over their heads.

Kate was shouting something at him. He put his ear close to her lips to hear.

"The star's gone out!"

It was true. There was no golden fire left on the ground to protect them. That means Doctor Dee's dead, thought Matt with a sickening thud of the heart; he's dead, and there are no more safe places left.

There was a sudden shock of coldness flowing up his body, making him gasp. He put out his hand, and it came back to him gleaming wet.

Kate cried in his ear. "The river's flooding!"

Matt tried to look back into the teeth of the gale; his eyes streamed, but after a moment he could see through tears. He saw surf breaking round the trees, leaping and smashing itself against branches; he saw Fomors caught like leaves in the flood; he struggled to his feet, pulling Kate up with him as a foaming wave rushed down on them and broke round their waists. The undertow dragged them back towards the river.

"Where's Anna?" Kate screamed, hanging on to him.

It was chaos; there was no telling where anything was. Matt tried to look through the storm, eyes narrowed and hurting. Suddenly he saw something, but it wasn't Anna.

Waves in the sea and the estuary were leaping like waterspouts. Matt saw with sudden clarity, as if there were no wind or debris flying through the air; and then he saw the ivory and bronze of a greater shape. Belisama was there, playing at catch with tons of water; she turned her head, her green hair swirling across the sky.

For the third time Matt looked into those cool eyes. The storm hung still between them, spray veiling her like lace. He felt her look through it at him, half unaware of seeing him, half wondering what he was; her gaze went through him like a dye, till he felt he would never again be free of

275

her, or the rest of these immortals. Then it left him, and she raised her trident once more. The waves wheeled like horses and plunged towering down on him.

Kate was torn away from him as the sea came in over the land.

19

THE SINGING BRANCH

He was plunging down and down in a roaring darkness, sparks dancing before his eyes. Then he was coming up, to a mad gulp of breath and the sight of a black wave curling down—then down again, lungs bursting.

He struggled against the suck of the water, fighting to get back to the surface. It was too strong for him. But if he didn't breathe in a moment, he'd pass out; he jack-knifed upwards with all his strength, and colours exploded before his eyes. His head broke surface again.

He saw a wave leaning down over him. Third time under and you drown, he thought, dizzily; he watched it as it seemed to come very slowly down, and then everything was black and roaring again, but further away, dimmer, with no burning of the lungs, and a feeling that sleep was coming. . . .

He swallowed a gout of water as something tangled itself in his hair and yanked himself upwards. Suddenly air was forcing itself into his lungs again, and catching hold of something firm and hard he began coughing up the salt water, while a black and white sea surged indeterminately about him. There was an arm round him, holding him firmly against a huge broken branch that rode up and down over the surface of the waves with complete assurance. Matt hung on to it dizzily, his mind stuck in a queer helpless fog. He was just conscious of a sound by one of his ears, a bell-like sound with a hint of wildness.

"Look! Look! Few mortals have ever seen such a sight!"

Matt looked out weakly across the branch, water lapping his chin and his eyes going in and out of focus. Starlight ran across the waves, and moonlight so strong it was almost golden. He couldn't make out much at first, but then he realised in a confused way that the sea was alive with—with what?

They were swimming all round him, silvery-white fish leaping with the waves and throwing spray through the air like glittering loops of pearls. Matt stared uncomprehendingly, not knowing who he was or what was happening. They weren't fish. They were people. A white mermaid was dancing in the water in front of him, her hair flickering.

"We are freed! Freed!" said the wild clear voice in his ear, and then it rose, pealing. "Sing! Sing as we used to, my people!"

Matt's mind refused to come out of its fog, and half of him seemed still to be in that choking chaos underwater. But the voices soared up round him and he knew, dimly, that he had never heard music like that and surely never would again. It was wild, inhuman and piercingly sweet, and he didn't want it to stop. The salt water burned in his throat. The white girl looked over her shoulder, gathering a great shimmering bouquet of foam in her hands, and smiled as she sang. Her eyes were eager and liquid, like a seal's.

"Listen!" said the voice in his ear. "We are freed! Listen! Did you know there could ever be such singing?"

"No," said Matt, in a rough, formless croak. He still didn't understand what was happening; the moon and the stars shone and the singing soared up, all with an uncanny quality like a dream. He turned his head and looked at the wet gleaming face of the merman who held him safe on the branch.

The seal-like eyes smiled at him.

"You stopped me drowning," Matt said in that ungainly croak.

"It is fair; a life for a death. Do you not know me?"

Matt's mind jolted, and the fog lifted a little. He stared at the white face, not knowing—yet he did know—that wild slender face, those liquid eyes.

"Do you not know me, Iron Man?"

Matt gasped, and the fog lifted higher. Smiling, the merman turned his face, and there was a scar across his cheek. There was a cap on his head too, but it had changed to wet sealskin.

"Ruadan!" he croaked, the fog tumbling away.

"Aye, little mortal." Ruadan caught him in both arms and hugged him, and Matt could feel him trembling with laughter. "Did I not say we were freed? I had forgotten what it was like before we climbed out of the ocean to serve the Horned One; we were fools to do it, but he was strong then, and we had no gods in the sea. . . . But now Myrddin Emrys has forced him to free us, and we are returning home to the water!" With a cry, Ruadan let him go, and dived away through the spray.

"Ruadan!" Matt had remembered everything now, and his heart pounded painfully against his ribs. "Ruadan!" he croaked desperately. *"Where's Kate?"*

Ruadan turned, in a mass of flying waterdrops. "Nay, I know not." The liquid eyes looked at him consideringly over the waves. "You know better than I, dreamer of dreams. I have not seen her under the sea." He turned again, darting amongst the others.

"Ruadan!" Matt croaked, feeling suddenly desolate as the crowd of merfolk began to dive, and the singing thinned away. They seemed to be taking hope along with them as they dived, and he had an impulse to follow them.

"Do not fear!" It was the white girl, pausing on the top of a wave, her voice still half-singing. "That branch will keep you safe. You could not come with us down to our country Undersea."

Matt stared at her, unable to speak. She lingered, lifted up and down by the waves, and watched him with those sweet liquid eyes. Was she Ethlinn, Matt wondered, who had tried to tempt him in the orchard of Lochlann? But Ethlinn had been stiff and dead, and all these merfolk were so full of life.

Then another rose beside her like a seal, and shook back pearls of foam from his hair. "Come, Balor's daughter. Leave the mortal. Let his own care for him."

She gave Matt a last look, then bowed under a wave out of sight. The other rode the swell for a moment, looking at Matt steadily, and Matt saw a tiny circlet of gold glittering on his wet hair. Then he raised a narrow white hand.

"We will not forget you, Iron Man!" he cried in his unearthly voice, and then dived.

"Elatha!" Matt shouted. But it was no use. The sea was empty now but for the long rolling waves. It grew cold there on the surface, and the moon was setting.

The darkness that followed was one of the deepest Matt had ever known. It was hard to believe that he had seen the Fomors there, free, and heard them singing. A wind rose, rushing over the water with a cruel howl, and from its sound there was no land near to break it—no trees, no hills. He was alone on the open sea, with nothing but a branch. And what about Kate? Ruadan hadn't seen her under the sea, but how much did that mean? Perhaps she hadn't found a branch, perhaps she was already deep underneath those waves.

No. As Matt clutched the branch, the cold spray flying in his face, he suddenly knew with complete certainty that *he would see Kate again.* The knowledge collided with his fear, and his brain protested, shocked; how could he possibly be so sure? But he was. There was no denying it. He knew he was going to see Kate again as certainly as if it had already happened.

It grew colder. Unable to see anything in the dark, Matt wondered where the strong current of the sea was taking him. He knew he must be somewhere off the coast of the Fomors' land, and in a way that meant near home; for he was sure now that the Fomors' land was simply the Moss, centuries ago. He remembered how, up in the air on Gwyn ap Nudd's horse, he'd seen his Moss change into that never-to-be-forgotten watery forest. It was true that trees had once grown in a marsh there, before the land was cleared and drained for farming. Aunt Phyllis had once described how she'd seen a farmer, while ploughing, turn up a mass of bog oak.

It was strange how Otherworld mingled itself with his world. Which sea was he on now, the real or the Otherworldly one; and would it make any difference? You can drown in either, he thought. Remembering where the setting moon had been, he was fairly sure the current was carrying him westward; that meant away from the land. His hands were cramped and frozen on the branch, and there was a numbness creeping through his body. If he lost his grip on the branch, he wouldn't be able to swim. But—he couldn't drown. Not if he was going to see Kate again.

But the cold and the weariness grew. He tried to kick out every so often to fight the numbness, but it grew more and more of an effort. Gradually he was losing his sense of time, as he had done when flying through the air with Gwyn ap Nudd towards the castle of bones.

At last he realised he could see the waves around him. The white caps had gone, but he could distinguish between the long dim swell and the faint sky. He kicked out again, but knew he was growing weaker.

Then, without knowing how much time had passed, he

saw that the sea and sky were quite clear and separate. Both were grey and lifeless, the horizon a perfect circle without a trace of land. The wind seemed to have dropped. Then, after another queer gap, he saw the sky was in fact deep blue like evening, and the waves rippling under a crimsonish glow.

He heaved himself up on the branch, his limbs slow to move, and tried to look back over his shoulder. The branch bucked, and he slid clumsily back into the water, but the branch had turned under him, and he found himself looking into a sky streaked with colours—bird's-egg colours, green and blue, and faint yellow, between long gleaming clouds tinged with pink.

All the nerves in his body ached for the sun. Every moment the sky and sea glowed brighter; the rolling waves grew green, alive. Clouds bannered out over the sky as the pastel shades were chased away westward by rising flames of amber and rose. There was a moment when the horizon glowed gold, and then a dazzle darted down the sea into his eyes.

He blinked and felt his heart lift a little. It was hard not to feel something, while the great show of the sunrise played itself out before his single gaze. He looked at the east again, narrowing his eyes, and this time he saw a black shape between him and the sun.

It was a ship. He knew that instantly, though the sun's rays blurred it with light; but he could see the lift of wind in a sail, and the dancing swoop of the shape over the distant waves. His heart began to pump painfully, and sweat started out on his cold forehead. It was making for him, square sail head on.

Gradually the sun lifted clear of the horizon, and it was full day. Matt kept his eyes pinned to the boat. He wanted to shout or wave, but somehow, between the numbness and the pounding of his heart, he couldn't. The boat

shone. It was long and slender, with a high-curved prow
and stern: the sail was white, gleaming like silk, and the
timbers flashed like bronze. It had an insubstantial look as
it skimmed bird-like towards him, too light and shining to
be real. Matt felt stained and worn before it, like a frag-
ment of wreckage drifting.

He saw the water creaming under its bow as it came
near. Its figurehead was looked down at him, a small carved
dragon's head. He could hear the creak of its timbers
and see each plank and rope distinctly; but there was too
much light about it, not all accounted for by the sun. As if
at a word of command, the wind dropped to a dead calm,
and the boat came whispering alongside him and stayed
there, lifting gently up and down over the swell with her
sail hanging idle. She cast no shadow down on to the sea.
Matt looked up with the blood drumming in his ears, and
saw the helmsman.

Manannan stood, his hands on a single oar that went
through the hole in the stern and trailed in the water as a
rudder. This was where the light came from, white and
pure amongst the sun's rays; Manannan's silver eyes looked down at him, and Matt felt numbness close round his
heart, meeting the Lord of Death like this in an empty
ocean.

Manannan let go of the oar. He came to the side of the
boat and stepped over on to the water as if it were solid
ground. He walked two steps to where Matt clung to his
branch, and the sparking light rolled with him, dazzling
Matt so that he couldn't see any division between it and
the sunshine. He lowered his gaze, and saw wavelets washing over Manannan's gleaming feet. Then at last the many
beautiful voices broke the silence, echoing in the sky as if it
were a great glass bell.

"Give me your hand, mortal."

Matt looked up. He could hardly see Manannan for the

silver light, but he made out a hand held down to him, bigger than a man's. He felt battered and salt-stained, and very weak. He clung hard to the branch.

"No." His voice croaked, barely recognisable. "You— *can't*—take me back now."

The hand wasn't withdrawn. Manannan's voice crowded the air, almost visibly bright.

"No. I could not take you there, even with your will. Oeth and Anoeth is broken, and there is nowhere for the dead to go now."

Matt closed his eyes for a moment. They were sore, and stiff with salt. Manannan and the morning seemed to have come too suddenly out of the empty night, and he felt dazed by the ringing voices, not sure if he could understand.

"Come!" The voices throbbed, filling his ears. "That branch is mine; I sent it down the water to you, to bear you up. Loose it, and let me take it back."

Still dazed, Matt saw a hand of his unlock itself from the branch and reach stiffly up towards Manannan's. A flash of fear crossed his mind—was he trusting Manannan?— and at the same time he knew he had no choice.

Manannan's hand gripped him with a touch like heatless fire, and lifted. He came up out of the water as if he had no weight, up until the branch was bobbing in the waves at his feet; he was standing on the water, the sky arching away all round him.

Manannan stooped and picked up the branch. As it came up from the sea, his light rushed along it like fire, and Matt had to turn his eyes away from the brightness.

"Come!" Manannan held it above his head as he stepped towards the boat.

Matt stepped after him, hardly daring to breath. The water held under his feet like a skin of silk; then the smooth side of the boat was under his hands, and he had one knee over. The boat dipped under his weight, and then he forgot everything else as he saw a flash of yellow hair.

"Kate!" he croaked, scrambling down into the rocking boat.

She caught him by the hands, her lips framing his name but no sound coming out as she just looked at him, blue eyes brilliant, and squeezed his hands so hard that it hurt. She was standing in the bottom of the boat, and the sides were just high enough to have hidden her from him.

"Kate," said Matt again.

She let out a long sigh, gripping him less tightly. "Oh, thank *goodness!*" she cried fervently. "He picked us up ages ago—Anna first, then me. I was hardly in the water five minutes before it all went light and he was pulling me out. I wasn't really scared about you—he told us not to be —but all the same. . . ." She drew him over to the broad central thwart under the mast, and he sat down next to her. Then he turned his head, seeing Anna sitting on the other side of the mast.

Her brown eyes looked at him, and at once Matt didn't know what to do or say. Oh no, he thought, and all his gladness at seeing Kate again faltered before the look in Anna's eyes. She was whole, solid, no longer a shadow; but Matt had never seen such sadness in anyone's face. He shut his eyes, and leaned his forehead against the smooth, hard mast. The Fomors were free, but they three weren't. Kelly was dead, and Anna had loved him. And he and Kate were back together, but only as prisoners of a Lord of Death.

He opened his eyes again and looked towards the stern. Manannan stood there again in a cloud of light, his hand on the steering oar. The wind was back. Matt could hear it in the sail, and feel the swift rhythmic rise and dip of the boat over the waves.

"Manannan," he said huskily, "where are you taking us?"

Manannan turned his head, and Matt shivered a little inwardly, remembering how that look had rested on him at the bottom of the sea.

"There is no more need to fear me." The voices seemed less human than ever, full of echoes. "All my earthly power is being taken away. Can you not see how my shape is changing?"

Matt stared. His eyes narrowed against the beat of light; he saw it was more difficult to make out Manannan's figure through it. Even the silver eyes seemed different, now bigger, now further off, even brighter and more difficult to meet.

He tried, but hadn't the strength to wonder why. He felt worn out. I want ordinary things back, he thought with sudden longing—houses and gardens and cars in the road, and supper being cooked. "Please," he said, hoarse with weariness, "can't we go home?"

Manannan looked away from him, out across the sea. "Home," the voices repeated. "It is hard for me to remember now what that word means. It has no counterpart in my language. Be patient, mortal. This tale will work itself out in due time, and we will all be at rest."

A shiver went down Matt's spine as the voices echoed in the empty sky. There was a sadness in them that he hadn't heard before, and was still mostly beyond the range of his ears. It reminded him of Arianrod. Confused, he remembered how he'd once thought Manannan wasn't like her.

"Matt," said Kate, low. "I—think it really will be all right, this time."

Matt looked back at her, but the thought of Anna on the other side of the mast tugged at his heart. He shook his head, not wanting to speak. How could it ever be all right again for her? Cernunnos had been satisfied and maybe Manannan meant them no harm now, but she would never see Ned again and how could she bear it?

He saw Kate's eyes darken as if hearing his thoughts,

and he squeezed her hand a little. It was no good pretending that Anna hadn't been in love with Kelly, that she was only a kid, that she'd get over it; he and Kate had come too near the same thing not to know. Oh, Anna. . . . His wounds were throbbing anew from the salt that was drying in them.

"Take the branch again, mortal."

Manannan's voices seemed to scatter light over him. Matt looked up. Manannan stood with his hand on the steering oar, tall and bewilderingly bright; the subtle silver-gold eyes shone into him, looking steadily on to all his thoughts. The branch was in his other hand, changed.

Matt got up stiffly, staring at the branch. It was the same branch; though it could be held in one hand, it had the same look of hugeness. And yet it was wood no longer, but white silver, bearing fragile blossoms of crystals; it was as delicate as a harebell, with the same aerial strength.

Manannan held it out to him. Matt put out his hands, not knowing what to expect; as it touched his palms the crystal blossoms quivered and the silver itself felt alive and growing. He saw the flowers were veined with silver, perfect apple-blossom. He touched them, wonderingly.

They trembled under his fingers and a sound rose from them, a vibration of crystal and silver and air. It was the most beautiful sound he had ever heard. It was like the voices of Danu's Children that had been beyond the range of his ears, suddenly audible, whole, perfect beyond imagining. The weight lifted from his heart, and the soreness left his limbs, as if they too had suddenly become whole.

"Matt . . ." Kate breathed behind him as the sound died away. He heard her get to her feet. "Give it to Anna," her voice said hoarsely.

Matt turned in the rocking boat; Anna's eyes were on him, containing a sudden painful spring of life. Matt stooped and laid the branch on her lap.

"Touch it," he said.

The dark eyes looked down at the lovely thing. Sunlight threw a white aura round it. Slowly her hand moved towards the blossom and stroked it. The sound floated up again, and Matt saw that the marks of Cernunnos's fingers had faded completely from her wrist. He felt the warmth of the morning sun on his back, drying his wet clothes and hair. Perhaps Kate was right. Perhaps it was going to be all right now. At last, after all the fear and suffering, it was feeling good again to be alive.

Anna gave a little sigh and looked up. Matt seemed to feel the knot of grief inside her loosen, unravel, set her free. She was truly back with them at last, no longer separated either by magic or sorrow.

"It's lovely," she said softly. "Where does it come from, Manannan?"

"From my country." The voices were deeper, more like music. "From Emain of the Apple-Trees, at the world's end. If humankind could find their way thither, their griefs would be less."

"Less?" said Anna. "How, Manannan?"

"Because the sound of the trees brings sweet forgetfulness of every pain. Touch the branch again, maiden, and wish to be happy. In my country there is no more suffering."

Anna fingered the petals again, but shook her head. "No," she said, through the singing of the branch. "It doesn't make me forget—it just makes me able to bear it. It's better like that." Matt heard her sigh. "I couldn't forget," said Anna softly. "Ever."

Manannan looked at her, and Matt thought he saw a throb in the light, like a human heart pulsing.

"It is better to forget." The voices quivered high in the cloud. "I have loved like you, time and again; but now I could not recount to you any of their names."

Anna said nothing, just shook her head again. It's true, Matt thought, she'll always remember Kelly and never want to put it out of her mind how she loved him. It's the way she is.

"It is wondrous, the faithfulness of mortals!" Manannan's voices were fragmented, mostly beyond the range of their ears. "Danu's Children love and pass on without looking backwards. We cannot do otherwise. Our lives are too long to bear the burden of all our past; we must touch the singing branch and forget, or else our minds would break. It is you, who face death every moment, and cannot alter or forget at will anything that happens to you—it is you who are the stronger. . . ."

Matt looked, puzzled, at the troubled beat of light round that face which was now too bright to see properly. Again he thought of Arianrod, and how he'd once thought Manannan wasn't like her.

The sun had climbed high in the sky, and his clothes were almost dry. His wounds had stopped aching. He leaned his arms along the side of the boat, watching the glass-green sparkle of the waves running from horizon to horizon. He turned his head and smiled as Kate, with a backward glance at Anna, came beside him. The boat heeled over slightly, and Manannan shifted his weight to keep her on an even keel.

"I think it really is going to be all right," Kate murmured to him. Matt saw the glow in the blue eyes, the look of life, that had come back to her face as well as Anna's. He nodded. Since the apple bough had sung, it was impossible to feel anything that happened could be wrong.

"Look!" Kate wrinkled her eyes, staring out across the sea. "Look, Matt, dolphins!"

Matt watched the gleaming fish playing over the surface of the water. Sunlight glittered down their backs and flashed amongst the spray, and the sight mingled in his mind with the memory of the merfolk dancing. He had almost forgotten it in the cold of the night. But the Fomors were free now, free as the dolphins, singing in the sea. . . . For a long time the dolphins raced the boat, darting round and under them, then at last streamed away over the horizon to some other rendezvous; and the sun was westering, casting the sail's shadow back towards the stern.

Matt looked round at Manannan. Like them, he was watching the sea; and again Matt had the feeling, more strongly, that he was different. He looks more as if you could talk to him, he thought.

Manannan looked at him, the cloud of light shimmering as he turned his head. "The ocean is beautiful," he said. "Is it not?"

"Yes," said Matt.

"It's so big," said Kate beside him, still looking at the spaces of sea and sky. "And empty."

"Empty?" Manannan looked back at the waves. "It is not empty to me, maiden; to me it is a plain full of flowers. Riders pass by in shining chariots, though you cannot see them. There is a wood of fine acorns there under the prow of the boat, with leaves of gold and a scent like wine. The ocean is more than land to me, more than any world; and truly it has never seemed so rich. . . ."

Matt watched Manannan as he gazed at the invisible plain of delight all round him. He wondered at that ring of sorrow in his voices; of Danu's Children, only Eil Ton has seemed to know what it was to have a light heart, and he had only shown himself for a moment.

"Where are we going?" he asked again.

"To my country." Manannan looked westward, into the sun's light. "Look. It is there, above the waves."

Matt and Kate leaned over the side, making the boat heel again slightly, and round the edge of the sail they saw something floating between sea and sky like a long silver-green cloud. The sun was reaching down towards it, and the sky around was very bright.

The boat creaked, and Matt saw Anna stoop under the sail and go forward to the prow, the silver branch still in her hands. After a moment he and Kate followed, and all three of them stood there, not wanting to speak, watching Manannan's country draw nearer and nearer.

20

MY SWORD FREARGATHACH

"Where is it, do you think?" Kate said. "I mean, really."

Matt shook his head. The land was very close, and they were coming into a cove between two hills. A valley ran down to the strip of sand that edged the water, its floor covered by velvet lawns and towering graceful trees spaced out as if in a garden. Amongst them were apple-trees in blossom, and their fragrance wafted out to the boat on the breeze. Around the valley Matt saw a vista of hills threaded with silver waterfalls, and, furthest away, a mist of mountains. Everywhere there was a brightness that caught at the breath.

"I don't know," he said. "Somewhere in Otherworld."

"I don't think it has a where," Anna said softly, without taking her eyes from the shining land. "Not if the branch came from here."

The sail flapped, then hung idle as the boat came under the lee of one of the hills. The tide and her own way brought her gently in, and presently the keel crunched on sand.

Manannan came round the sail, his light seeming whiter and more than ever visible. He held out his hands without saying anything, and Anna put the branch back into them. Matt watched the brilliant face.

"Manannan," he said after a moment, "is something—wrong?"

Manannan slowly shook his head, but it was more like an unconscious gesture of sorrow than an answer to Matt's question. He stepped over the side of the boat on to the beach. Anna, Kate and Matt followed him, jumping down on to the clean white sand.

Manannan looked up amongst the hills; then back down at Matt.

"I called it my country." There was a long cadence like an elegy in the many voices. "Now I have lost it. A greater one than I in these worlds has claimed it; and truly I only held it in trust for him. Yet I did not believe he would return so soon. . . ."

The scent of the apple blossom drifted round them, and the light felt strong and warm. Matt wondered why peace seemed so far from Manannan, here of all places; with the sun so near and bright, it must be the western end of the world that he'd talked about, where the tree of the sun grew. . . . He looked at Manannan's face, and could hardly recognise it.

"Did I not say I could not break my heart caring for your world?" The words were whispering, as insubstantial as light. "Such talk is easy. Come. We must go to meet him."

"Who?" asked Matt. But Manannan turned and walked up the beach without answering, and Matt followed with Anna and Kate, content to be silent. Every last tension was melting away in the air of this place, and he supposed they would soon find out who Manannan meant.

It was like a holiday to walk the soft turf of the valley under those whispering trees, hearing the song of thrushes and blackbirds, and sniffing the scent of the apple-trees. Kate's eyes met his and she smiled without needing to speak. Looking ahead, Matt saw the apple-trees flooding in a white tide up the nearest hillside, right to the top; they grew like wild flowers, unordered. Manannan led them amongst their gnarled trunks, and soon they were climbing the hill with fallen petals round their feet. Glancing back, Matt couldn't see the cove any more, but he could still hear the long falling sound of the waves on the shore.

The crest of the hill was open to the sky. As they came out from amongst the trees they seemed to have stepped into the heart of this land's brightness. Standing there, Matt saw a figure turning to look at them.

He was as tall as Manannan, wearing a robe that trailed the ground and was either white or gold. It was hard to tell in the light. For a moment, Matt had to look down because of the sun-coloured radiance, and he wondered why the man didn't speak. But as his eyes grew more used to the light, and he looked up again at that glowing face, with its brillaint gold hair and beard, his own heart swelled; he saw it was gladness, overflowing, that kept the man from speech. He was simply looking at them, at Manannan, the trees and the light-filled sky, wordless with joy.

Manannan, standing under the tallest and oldest apple-tree, reached up with the silver branch in his hand. It took hold of the gnarled trunk a foot or so above his head and grew on there, and Matt thought he heard it sing faintly. Manannan let go of it and came forward in a smoke of light, white amongst the other's gold.

"Lord." The word crackled, alien and beautiful. "Welcome home, Myrddin Emrys—Lord of Light."

The golden man's hands came out, gripped Manannan's. He tossed back his head, with a laugh of pure happiness; then he turned to them, throwing out a hand.

"Kate! Anna! Matt!" His voice was a deep full music, alive with laughter. "Do you now know me?"

Matt's breath caught in his throat. That voice—he stared into the man's face.

"Doctor Dee!" Kate cried, and stopped short, uncertain.

Anna's lips framed the word "Ned"; but she closed them before any sound came out, with a little shake of the head.

Manannan spoke, his voices slow and remote, islanded in their own different light. "He is both. He is the Lord of Light, come again out of the grip of his Shadow; he is Myrddin Emrys, the Undying, the saviour of our land in old time; he is also Nimue, at whose hands he first fell into darkness; and since then he has had many names, in his long blind struggle towards morning."

"But . . ." said Kate uncomprehendingly, "*Cernunnos*—"

"Can only conquer fear, Kate!" The strong golden voice lifted their doubt away from them. "I went to him on my own will, and he had no more power over me. Indeed it is strange, and hard to understand; I went towards him, resolved to meet my death, and instead I found life, a thousandfold. Who could not marvel at these things?" He held out his hands to them. "Take hold of me! I am real!"

They hesitated, but only for a moment. Then Kate stepped forward and took hold of one hand. Anna took the other. Matt looked up at the glowing face, and had to let go of the last doubts; it was true. Dee and Kelly both looked out of it—there was Dee, clear and wise, but resolute now, with Kelly's tremendous strength. And there were more. For a moment, it was as if a crowd of faces looked at Matt, smiling; and in that moment, he seemed to know them all.

"So it was you I called," Kate said, low. "Emrys."

"Aye, Kate." Emrys's voice gentled, deep and tender. "Call me that always, for it is the best of my names. But in truth I am only a man." He let go of her hand, and stretched out to clasp Matt's shoulder, with a touch as solid

295

and living as it could be. "There! Is that any more than human?"

Matt shook his head. It felt like a man's hand; perhaps human beings were not after all the small, limited things he had once thought.

"Good." They seemed to feel the sun-like warmth flowing from Emrys, physically. "Stay here with me, then, for a little while. It will not hurt you, so long as you are within earshot of the sea; and we have farewells to make." He let go of them and turned to face Manannan.

There was a silence round Manannan, white and remote. His man's shape seemed almost to have melted away into the play of light; and when he spoke it was difficult to make out his words amongst the many crystalline echoes.

"Must my people go, Lord?"

Emrys looked at him for a long moment; Matt felt then, amongst the joy, a sudden knock of grief.

"Yes, Son of Lir." Emrys's voice was slower, with a touch of darkness in the gold. "This is not your world. I have destroyed your castle, for I tell you death is more mysterious than you could ever dream; I have taken back your country, to prepare it for mortal men again; and now I must send you from our world. It is time. See. They have all gathered on the mountain."

He pointed inland. Matt looked in the direction of his finger and saw beyond blossom-clad hills to the mountains rising blue and misty. Around the highest peak was the light he knew—pure, blue-white and turning. All at once he was thinking of swallows in the trees outside his aunt's house, at the turn of the year; how the loud air would be full of birds rising from their branches, darting a little way, then returning, and darting again, until at last the whole flock were in the air together, wheeling away on the long journey south.

Kate said, on a gasp, *"Leaving?* Danu's Children?"

Matt felt again that keening beyond the range of his ears; the hair prickled on his neck. Emrys was silent, and he looked at Manannan. He had to narrow his eyes against the white scintillations amongst which Manannan's shape was dissolving.

"Yes." Amongst sounds like breaking crystals, Manannan's words were hard to catch. "I know it; the time has come, too soon and swift, like snow in summer; but it is not a dream; the sun will not return; the winter is here. Lord! Grant me one wish, for I would not forget your world yet awhile."

Slowly, without looking at him, Emrys inclined his head.

There was a shimmer and a crackle of light, and Matt saw two hands holding something out to him.

"It is my sword, Freargathach." The words were high and brilliant, like stars. "Govannon forged him from the iron that falls in meteors from the heavens. Give me your knife, mortal, which overcame Elatha and the Man in Green; take this, and remember me!"

Matt's throat grew hot and hard. Manannan's sword and its silver scabbard shone almost too bright for his eyes; an exchange like this made no sense, a sword of celestial iron for a battered old knife—but, looking into that cloud of light, he could just see Manannan's face.

"Have you still got the knife, Kate?" he said hoarsely.

"Yes," Kate said. Looking down he saw it lying in her hand. She looked at him, the blue glint of her smile mingled with awe; then simply, as if there was no more to be said, held it out to Manannan.

One silver hand took it. The other held out the great sword. Kate hesitated.

"You take it," she murmured to Matt. "It's your knife."

Matt took it by the scabbard, just under the hilt. It seemed alive in his hands, light running through it like

297

blood. Manannan let it go, and his own light blazed up like a thousand moons.

"I come!" The wild crackling chimes hurt their ears. "Dagda! Govannon! Arianrod, my sister! I come!"

Matt shut his eyes, and wind rushed round him. When he opened them, a second later, there was only the warm golden light of Emrys on the hilltop, and white petals drifting round his feet; he looked inland, and saw a silver cloud of light fleeing towards that distant mountain. Kate, at his side, suddenly turned and went to a rocky place where the hillside fell sheer away; she stood there, looking down the slope with her back turned uncompromisingly on them.

Matt looked down at the sword he held in his hand. It took his breath away. The scabbard alone was a miracle, made of a white metal winking with enamel. Tiny leaves, beasts and birds were wrought on it. The hilt was plain, and sank into his grip as if his hand had been made for it; the crosspieces were smooth and plain too; but set into the pommel was a huge glowing amethyst, like a well of blood. He slid the sword a little way out of its sheath and saw the blade, a narrow sheet of light.

"*Matt!*"

It was Kate's voice, a sudden urgent gasp. He looked up and saw her standing very stiff as if she dared not move, one hand reaching out backwards to him. He went quickly to her; her hand found his arm and grasped it hard to make him keep still.

"Look." Her lips hardly moved, and her other hand pointed down the slope.

The hillside fell steeply down to a stream fringed with long grass and overhanging willow trees. Not seeing anything in particular, Matt looked at Kate again.

He'd almost thought something had happened to scare her; but now he saw in those blue eyes a dawning gladness as at something totally unexpected. "*There!*" Kate whispered, and pointed again. He looked, and this time saw.

A slim pale thing was in the water, white as new ivory. It weaved under the water like a fish, then slipped its head through the surface with hardly a ripple and tossed back a shower of shining waterdrops. Its hair had a frail golden gleam like buttercups. It seemed to lift its head and smile at the sun, and Matt saw its eyes—deep, happy, amber-coloured. Then it ducked under the water again and was gone.

"Did you see it?" Kate's eyes were sparkling, and her voice almost broke. "Oh, I'm so glad we saw that!"

"The Dulachan," said Matt slowly. He turned and saw Emrys watching them as if he knew what they'd seen and what it mean to them. But, even in this shining country, it was hard to believe. "Was it?" he said.

"He has come home." said Emrys.

Matt looked down at the stream, where not a ripple showed that anyone had been there. The thought in him was too loud not to be spoken. He looked up again, and saw Emrys still watching him.

"Does that mean," he said bluntly, "that—this is what happens after you die?"

There was a moment's pause. Matt felt Kate and Anna turn and look, but his eyes were fixed on Emrys.

"So," said Emrys at last, gently, but a shadow passed through his voice and across his face. "You must ask me that, you who have dwelt in Oeth and Anoeth; but it is a hard tale to tell. Death is as many things as life. And it is a hard knowledge too, one that it needs broad shoulders to bear; yet it cannot be refused to any who ask. Listen, then, and I will repeat to you what I know. . . ."

The words, going on, seemed to pierce Matt strangely; and then they were words no longer, but only a great grip on his soul, lifting him beyond words—beyond sight, beyond everything. He was never afterwards sure how to speak of what happened to him. But when at last he looked up and saw Emrys's face again, and the white trees, and heard the quiet sound of the sea far below, he knew he had been answered; from that great vantage, he had seen, and understood. A peace he had never dreamed of grew on him—but at the same time, immingled, a strange heaviness weighed on his heart, a sense of something forever at an end. . . .

"Be courageous," said Emrys softly, clear again amongst the golden light. "You see plain, Matt; you have the Sight, and it will not leave you, for you have worn a Fomor's cap. It can be a bitter thing, to know grief and disaster before they come. But darkness is needed, for the morning star to appear and lead in the light. Should I not know this better than any?" His gaze shifted, smiling, to Kate. "The Dulachan prophesied well, my white flower."

Kate shook her head. Matt looked at her, wondering if Emrys's words had told her the same things as him. "I couldn't have done anything without Matt," Kate said, with her most definite tone. "The Green Man would have got me."

"So," said Emrys. He came forward, and laid a hand on the crosspiece of the sword Matt held. "What could Matt have done without you? It is in my mind that the threads of your fate are bound close together. Share with him this gift of Lir's son; you have both fought light's battle."

Kate's fingers touched Matt's. He looked at her—Kate, who had called the Lord of Light back into his world. But then her gaze faltered a little, and he felt at once the same pang as, in the corner of his eye, he saw Anna standing there apart. He looked back at Emrys, lips tightening together. Yes, for him and Kate the battle was all won; but Anna . . .

The grave, deep eyes were resting on her, "Anna," Emrys said, low. He took her hands, and his voice altered, supple and changing as sunlight as he looked at her face. "It is hard for me to read your fate," he said, softly. "It seems to me that you will walk alone. But no . . . you will never truly be alone, Anna. . . ."

Anna's eyes looked into his for a long moment, and Matt had a feeling that they spoke to each other without words. He wondered what Anna had heard in that time when Emrys spoke, and everything had come clear to him. Then she looked past Emrys into the sky, her lips parted, and she said softly, "Look!"

They turned and looked; and Matt felt the heart come up in his throat. Cloud after cloud of light was streaming upwards from the mountain peak, joining it to the zenith of the sky with a long glimmering trail. They went so swiftly, without a second's faltering; and all around, echoing, flew fragments of their high departing music. In a moment the mountain was bare, and the sky above crowded with their light.

Kate's fingers had found their way to his hand. He returned her grip, and they strained their eyes into the sky after the fleeing light—so swift, so unlingering—until their eyes grew blurred and full of water, and the blue of the sky swam with vanishing glints. But it seemed to Matt that one last human look was cast down to them, bright-eyed like reflected stars, and two hands stretched toward him. "Arianrod!" he whispered, and his ears seemed full of her voices. But then even she was gone, lost in the sun's radiance, leaving only her silver wheel to roll through the night . . . And so, from the western end of the world, he, Kate and Anna saw the last of Danu's Children disappear back into the sky.

21

ALL KINDS OF COLOURS

1

They were back. Back in the ordinary, matter-of-fact park, with trees and a group of children calling through the evening air. Matt looked around at the gold-green grass and leaves, and the deep gentle sky. That feeling of heaviness, of loss, still weighed down his heart. If only they could have stayed there, at the world's end; this world seemed a poor exchange for all that glory.

He saw Kate and Anna's hand, with a regretful look round. There was no trace any more of the graze on her cheek, and he realised his wounds had disappeared as well. Anna turned her head towards them. She alone seemed free of that let-down feeling; though the dark eyes could never have their old untroubled look, now they were quiet, with some sort of peace.

Kate gave a sigh. "I suppose we had to come back."

"We couldn't have stayed there," Anna said, softly. "It'll be all right, Kate. I don't think Emrys is just in that country."

Kate gave a sober little nod, and Matt felt the blue eyes come and rest on him. "Matt?" she said, questioningly, as if sensing the oppression on his heart.

Matt looked down at the sword in his hands. Perhaps his were the first human hands that had ever touched it, that miracle of iron and light. Somehow it seemed more real to him than the park which he knew so well, more real than the road and the single car passing. And yet—it wasn't the memory of Emrys, Manannan and the world's end that was causing this sense of loss.

He looked up at Kate. "Something's wrong," he said, without quite knowing what to say. "It's nothing to be afraid of—it's wrong for me, not for you. . . ."

Kate gave a quick frown. "If it's wrong for you, it's wrong for me, too," she said decisively. She glanced across the road. "Come on, let's go. There's Doctor Anderson. He's seen us."

Matt looked up and saw Doctor Anderson coming down the path of Aunt Phyllis's house, staring at them as if he hardly believed his eyes.

"Come on," said Kate with a hint of a grin, beginning to lead the way towards the gate. "Before he explodes."

Matt and Anna followed her out of the park, across the road. Leaning on the gate, Anderson looked from one to another as if counting heads, eyes much bigger than normal behind the thick spectacles. He opened his mouth, closed it, lifted a hand as if to tell himself to shut up, then opened it again and said, firmly, "Are you all all right?"

"Yes," said Kate. "What day is it, Doctor?"

Anderson's jaw dropped a fraction. "What?" he ejaculated, then paused and visibly took a hold of himself. "It's Thursday. You and Matt went off on your bikes yesterday and haven't been heard of since. As for this young lady, she did a right disappearing trick last night—in her bed one minute, nowhere to be found the next." Question marks crowded his face.

"We're all okay now," Kate said reassuringly.

Anderson gave her an eloquent look. "All right," he said firmly, as if other words had to be resolutely swallowed. "Matt, you go in to your aunt, she's in the sitting-room. You two stay here, I've got something to tell you."

303

He opened the gate for Matt to come in, unable to suppress one unbelieving look at the sword. Matt entered the garden. Suddenly he wanted to stop; the weight on his heart was bearing down hard, and there was a line on Anderson's brow that made him want to pause and ask—he didn't know what. He made himself go on up the path and into the house. Putting the sword down carefully on the hall table, he went into the sitting-room.

Aunt Phyllis was sitting on the couch. She looked round at him; her face was pale, there were dark smudges under her eyes, and her mouth had the difficult, painful line of someone who had been crying for a long time.

She stretched out a hand to him. "Oh, Matt, love," she said, a tremor in her voice. "Are you really all right? You and the girls?"

"Yes. Yes, we're okay," Matt said. He came to her side and knelt down on the floor, taking her hand. He knew, without even needing to think about it, that it wasn't worry over himself, Kate and Anna that had brought that look to his aunt's face, or that tremor to her voice. The oppression at his heart seemed to be growing, opening out like a sombre flower. Yet still he somehow wasn't afraid. "What is it, Auntie?" he asked, low.

Her hand squeezed his. "Oh, Matt, love," she said again, her voice trembling, "it's your father. . . ."

Matt stayed quite still. His father. For a while, he couldn't speak.

He had known. That was what that weight over his heart had been, that oppression—the knowledge that he would never see his father again. Far away from him, in another country, another world, at some point during that night his father had died. Matt's heart opened to the truth of it, as it broke out through all his consciousness. Oh, Dad. . . .

But, slowly, a curious stillness rose. This was more than grieving; he seemed to hear in it that speaking of Emrys, that strong lift of the soul; and it was as if, returning to his

304

own world, he held all of his father within himself. He drew in a deep breath, in touch with something he couldn't name. It was not despair. . . . Though his father had died, it seemed, somehow, that they had never been so close. He shut his eyes for a moment, silent with the intensity of what he felt; then, presently, looked up.

"How did it happen?" he asked, very low.

Aunt Phyllis took his hand between both of hers. He saw tears in her eyes again. "There was a ceasefire declared last night," she said. "The guerrillas said they had Kate and Anna's parents prisoners, and that they'd release them as a sign of good will. Your father drove out to meet them, but the road he went on was mined. No one knows yet which side did it. He died straight away, love, it wouldn't have hurt him."

Matt looked at her tears, remembering that his father was the last of her family; her own parents had died long ago, and she had no other brothers or sisters.

"Are Kate and Anna's parents all right?" he asked.

"Yes. They're on a plane home."

Matt was silent for another moment. Things were turned upside down; the Marchants, for whom there'd been so much fear, were safe and on their way home—and his father, about whom no one had thought to worry very much, was dead. Oh, Dad. . . .

Aunt Phyllis took out a handkerchief and dried her eyes, making herself be calm. "Your mother sent a telegram," she said more steadily. "The TV people must have told her as well, because it hasn't been on the news yet. She's driving up from Cornwall. She should be here later on this evening."

Matt looked up, slowly. His mother? More than two years had passed since he'd last seen her; it was new and peculiar to think of, like unlocking a room that had seemed closed for good. But perhaps that room would be a good place to be now. . . . "Good," he said. Rather hesitantly, he pressed his aunt's hand. "Don't worry, Auntie. It'll be all right."

"Thank goodness you're here, anyway," Aunt Phyllis said, and gave a little smile. "It's been rather a grim time, first Anna disappearing and then those men turning up from the TV company to tell us. Poor chaps, they were awfully upset by it all. And I was rather worried about you." She returned the pressure of his hand. "Never mind, dear. You're right. It will be all right soon. The poltergeists have stopped, that's one thing." She glanced up at the window. "Oh, here comes Kate."

Matt looked round and saw Kate come running up the path. Anderson reached out an ineffectual hand to stop her, then followed, shaking his head. Anna came with him.

"Matt!" Kate rushed in impetuously; leaving the door to swing, and landed at his side with an arm round his neck as if she didn't care any more what anyone thought. "Oh, Matt, I am sorry," she said, her throat rough.

Her blue eyes were like stars, where joy and consternation struggled together. Matt couldn't grudge her the gladness of having her own parents back safe, alive. . . . "It's all right," he said again, gently, and put his arm round her.

Anna came into the room with Anderson. She said nothing, but reached down over the back of the couch and put a hand on Aunt Phyllis's shoulder. Aunt Phyllis looked up with a touch of surprise, then gave the deep brown eyes a grateful look.

"Well," said Anderson from the door, with a sort of subdued gentleness, "hadn't you girls better get tidied up? You've a train to catch."

The London train went at eight fifteen. Aunt Phyllis had already packed Kate and Anna's suitcase for them—it had given her something to do, she said with a rueful look, while she hadn't known where they were or what had hap-

306

pened to them. Nothing was said about the lost bicycles. Kate's might still be on the Moss, Matt thought, but there was no time now to go and look for it. Their train would get them to Euston by half past eleven, after two changes; people from the TV company would meet them there and take them to Heathrow to meet their parents' plane. Then pictures of the Marchant family being reunited would go out all over the country on tomorrow's six o'clock news.

"I wish we didn't have to go," Kate said impulsively, as they carried the luggage on to the platform of the small country halt, Anna and Aunt Phyllis some way behind. "I want to see Mum and Dad, but I hate leaving you now. I— kind of know how you're feeling."

Matt looked at her. Yes, she knew; she must have believed a hundred times in these past weeks that her own parents were dead. "It must have been worse for you," he said, "before Emrys talked to us."

The blue eyes looked up, serious and thoughtful. "Did he really tell you," said Kate, low, "about dying?"

"Yes," said Matt after a moment, putting down the case he carried. That speaking of Emrys was too large for him ever to be able to repeat in words; but he was aware of the knowledge in him, ready to be drawn upon—tremendous, precious, heartbreaking. "Didn't he you?"

"That came into it," Kate said, "But it was mostly about you—about living. It's hard to explain. He wasn't *talking*." She put a hand out and took his. "Matt, you will come back to London, for next term, won't you?"

"I—hope so," said Matt. Next term. School. It was hard to think of such ordinary things. "It depends on my mother, I suppose."

"Do come back," Kate said with all her old energy. "You must. Emrys said we were going to stick together, didn't he?"

"Yes," said Matt, after a pause, and felt something almost too intense to be understood. He had lost his father, and despite his new knowledge, the long dreariness of loss stretched out in front of him; but he had not lost Kate. His mother was coming back, too. . . . "We will, won't we?" he said.

" 'Course we will," said Kate with certainty, giving his hand a quick squeeze.

"Kate!" Aunt Phyllis called, coming on to the platform with Anna. "This bag of yours keeps coming undone. Can you do something with it?"

"Oh, that stupid old zip," said Kate, letting go of Matt and running back down the platform.

Anna came to put her suitcase down by the one Matt had carried, and Matt looked again at the changed brown eyes—changed, and yet somehow perhaps more beautiful. "Anna," he said after a moment, without quite knowing what he meant to say.

Anna looked at him, and smiled.

"What are you going to do now?" Matt asked after a moment, as Kate had asked him.

"I don't know," said Anna, pushing the long hair back behind her shoulders. "I haven't had time to think about it properly yet. Get a job, maybe; I don't think I could sit about in school any more. I'll have to talk to Mum and Dad about it."

"What about all your O levels?" Matt asked. She'd got eight, all good grades; that would normally mean A levels, and university.

Anna looked thoughtfully down the railway track, which curved away between lines of trees. "It's hard to mind much about them," she said after a pause, quietly. "They seem so far away, and—irrelevant, really. Things have changed so much. Everything used to be simple, and black and white, but now they're—all kinds of colours. I can't go on as if I just hadn't noticed the difference—if you see what I mean, Matt."

Matt followed her gaze down the track. Black and white

—light and dark. He remembered how he had longed for the safe, ordinary daylight of this world when Otherworld had seemed too dark and dangerous to bear. But it was in this world that his father had been killed, with a sort of random cruelty worse than anything in Otherworld; while in Otherworld there were the radiant islands of the west, and Emrys's country. It was impossible any more to disentwine the strands of colour making up the worlds. "Yes," he said, "I do."

The railway line rattled, and a train chugged into view. Matt and Anna picked up the cases again, and Aunt Phyllis hurried forward with Kate, breathlessly reminding them of the stations where they had to change. The train drew up at the platform, and they lifted in the cases. Kate climbed in, the bag with the unreliable zip clasped firmly under her arm, and Anna got in and closed the door.

"Goodbye, Miss Cooper," she said, leaning out through the window. Her changed face had a golden look in the evening sunshine. "Thank you for everything—you know. . . ." she smiled. " 'Bye, Matt."

The guard rang the bell from his van, and Kate took Anna's place. "Don't forget," she said swiftly to Matt, as the train began to move off, "term starts the twentieth of September. Don't be late!"

2

I will go back, Matt thought, later. It was about ten o'clock and he was in the park, alone. His mother had just arrived, wearing a yellow dress he'd never seen before, with her hair cut differently, and Aunt Phyllis had taken her inside to be revived with a glass of whisky after her long drive. She had looked quite different, but when she kissed him he remembered her perfume.

Aunt Phyllis had whispered to him to wait a few moments before he came in, perhaps wanting to brief his mother on what had happened to him and the two girls this summer. That was nice of her, for he didn't think he could do it himself, just yet; his mother seemed such a new person. So he had come into the park, Manannan's sword in his hands. The day was ending, and the branches of the trees were full of dusk. The span of grief and gladness inside him was still too wide to be dealt with like ordinary feelings, so he just stood there, watching the colours of the sky linger between day and night.

I'll go back to London, he thought slowly; Mum'll understand I have to do that. Perhaps she'll come with me. . . .

But it was difficult to think beyond the present just then. Matt looked down at the glimmering scabbard in his hands, took the hilt and drew the long blade out. It shone like a strong moonbeam in the twilight, a pledge that something else existed above the dark confused earth that was soon to be covered by night. Matt stood looking at it for a moment, then sheathed it again and turned back towards the house. He and his mother would talk a little before they went to bed, perhaps, just chat about ordinary things—they were both too tired for more. In the morning, they could start making plans for this new stage of their lives.

AFTERWORD

This story is a work of imagination, but some may be interested in the origins of the Otherworld figures, which come mainly from Celtic tradition.

The Celts inhabited most of Britain and Ireland in prehistoric times, but our knowledge about their mythology comes predominantly from tales written down by Irish and Welsh monks during the middle ages. Danu's Children were probably gods of the ancient Celts, but in the written tales they are depicted as wizardly people, skilled in magic and the arts, who descended to earth in a cloud. They overcame the Fomors at the Battle of Moytura, in Ireland, and drove them quite literally underground—into the mounds and barrows which since earliest times seem to have been considered as places of mystery in the British and Irish landscapes.

It is possible that this is one of the legendary battles which symbolise the triumph of a new technology—in this case, the working of iron into tools and weapons. The discovery of iron in prehistoric times was an advance comparable to the harnessing of nuclear power today, and users of this new metal were often deemed to be magicians. This seems to suit the character of Danu's Children. The iron itself was considered to have supernatural powers, and tradition has it that witches and fairies can be deterred by the sight or presence of it. I have ascribed a similar fear of iron to the Fomors.

Arianrod, whose name means "Silver Wheel," was probably a moon goddess. Manannan was originally a sea god, and was often encountered by sailors, travelling over the sea in his boat, Waves-weeper, or in his magic chariot. King Arthur is said to have been immured in his castle of bones for three days and three nights. The sea was another place of mystery to the Celts, which may be one reason why Manannan got the name for being a great magician.

The Fomors themselves are often described in the written tales as coming from over the sea, as well as from the mounds. Their king, Tethra, was certainly another sea-god. I have felt it right to return them to the sea in my story, and also to change their grotesque appearance for a more attractive one, since in the tales they alternate confusingly between monstrousness and remarkable beauty.

The Dulachan is a kind of hobgoblin who sometimes appears in Celtic myth, but seems to have an origin elsewhere. He may come from a foreign source, but I have made him the representative of an ancient people which died out after the arrival of the Celts in Britain. There was more than one such people, though almost nothing of their culture survives.

I have taken the story of the Green Man and his beheading game from the medieval peom *Sir Gawain and the Green Knight.* Here the poet combines the Arthurian motif with what are clearly old Celtic traditions.

The Horned God, Cernunnos, is frequently depicted in Celtic art, and must have been an important deity both in Britain and on the Continent. He seems to have been in sufficiently strong competition with early Christianity to be selected as the model for the Devil, complete with horns and hoofs; and perhaps for this reason, the Irish and Welsh monks included nothing of him in their tales. In fact, he may have been a beneficent fertility god, assuring increase of flocks for the herdsman and plenty of game for the hunter. But pagon gods were rather like the weather—sometimes good, sometimes bad, and either way profound in their effect on people. So I have chosen to show him as extremely dangerous if not propitiated.

John Dee and Ned Kelly come from sober history. They were sixteenth-century English alchemists whose dubious association was famous in its day; and as alchemy was a subject which in its less reputable form combined science with some questionable occult practices, legends were liable to spring up around it. So although Dee's and Kelly's lives are well-documented historical fact, a parallel folktale tradition claims them as magicians who had sold their souls to the Devil in return for supernatural powers. Hence, in my story, their bargain with Cernunnos. History tends to cite Kelly as the rogue and Dee as the tragically unsuspicious dupe; and Kelly certainly was both a fraud and a criminal (an excellent model for his later namesake, the nineteenth-century Australian bandit). But Dee was far too intelligent a man to mistake exploitation for partnership, and their association, which lasted several years, must have contained something of value to both. For those who are interested, the black scrying mirror can be seen in the British Museum along with other of Dee's personal effects, including a gold mandala engraved by Kelly.

Finally, a word about Celtic names. Some of the Otherworld figures have alternative Irish or Welsh names, and the only rule I have followed is my own preference. Where the names are extremely difficult, I have spelt them phonetically—for instance, Moytura instead of Mag Tuireadh.